T0113253

TOPPER
TAKES A TRIP

THORNE SMITH

TOPPER
TAKES A TRIP

Introduction by Carolyn See

THE MODERN LIBRARY

NEW YORK

2000 Modern Library Paperback Edition

Biographical note copyright © 1999 by Random House, Inc.
Introduction copyright © 1999 by Carolyn See

LIBRARY OF CONGRESS CATALOGING-IN-PUBLICATION DATA
Smith, Thorne, 1892–1934.
Topper takes a trip/Thorne Smith; introduction by Carolyn See.
—Modern Library pbk. ed.
p. cm.
Sequel to: Topper.
ISBN 978-0-375-75307-7
I. Title.
PS3573.M835T65   2000
813'.52—dc21   99-38788

Modern Library website address: www.modernlibrary.com

Printed in the United States of America

146855636

THORNE SMITH

Thorne Smith, the Jazz Age humorist best known for his charm-
ingly whimsical Topper novels in which he created the modern
American ghost, was born in 1892 at the U.S. Naval Academy in An-
napolis, Maryland. He was the son of Commodore James Thorne
Smith, who supervised the Port of New York during World War I.
Smith was educated at St. Luke's School in Wayne, Pennsylvania,
and later attended Dartmouth College. With the outbreak of World
War I, he left a job in advertising to enlist in the Navy.

Smith began his literary career writing comic stories about a sad-
sack sailor named Biltmore Oswald for the service paper *Broadside*.
Indeed, *Biltmore Oswald: The Diary of a Hapless Recruit* (1918) and *Out
o' Luck: Biltmore Oswald Very Much at Sea* (1919) soon proved enor-
mously popular with the public. After returning to civilian life, he
wrote *Haunts and By-Paths* (1919), a collection of poetry, and *Dream's
End*, an overtly somber novel panned by critics when it finally came
out in 1927.

The publication of *Topper* brought Smith immediate acclaim
when it appeared in 1926. A sophisticated spoof of middle-class
manners and morals, it chronicles the madcap adventures of
Cosmo Topper, a mild-mannered bank executive who is rescued

from his drab "summer of suburban Sundays" by fun-loving ghosts George and Marion Kerby. "There isn't a dull moment in the book," said *The New York Evening Post.* "Your eyes are filled with tears from laughter over its wild absurdities." A sequel, *Topper Takes a Trip* (1932), records the further ribald escapades of Topper and the Kerbys on the French Riviera. The improbable trio went on to inspire several movies, notably the 1937 film *Topper* starring Cary Grant and Constance Bennett, as well as a hit television series.

Following the success of *Topper,* Smith enhanced his reputation with a number of clever fantasies. *The Stray Lamb* (1929) features a Topper-like hero whose complacent life is upset when he is transformed into an assortment of animals. In *The Night Life of the Gods* (1931) Smith captivated readers with the nocturnal antics of an oddball inventor who cavorts around Manhattan with reincarnated Greek and Roman deities, and in *Turnabout* (1931) he offered up a screwball comedy about a jaded husband and wife who temporarily switch identities. *Rain in the Doorway* (1933) transports a harassed lawyer from the gloom of the Depression through a portal into a department store tinged with Marx Brothers lunacy, and *Skin and Bones* (1933) tells of a fashionable photographer who becomes a nearly invisible skeleton at the most inopportune moments.

Did She Fall?, Smith's one mystery, came out in 1930. "At times the book approaches something akin to literature," said Dashiell Hammett of this prankish who-done-it satirizing the amoral lifestyles of the rich. "If F. Scott Fitzgerald had written a detective novel, it might have resembled Thorne Smith's *Did She Fall?*" observed *The Armchair Detective* in 1993. "Like Fitzgerald, Smith truly evokes . . . the 1920s era of flappers and rebellious youth and liberated sexuality. . . . The murder mystery for Smith, it turns out, is merely a device [for revealing] the evils of 'high society,' much as Fitzgerald does in *The Great Gatsby.*" During this period Smith also wrote *Lazy Bear Lane* (1931), a children's novel, and *The Bishop's Jaegers* (1932), a metaphorical tale about chance-met passengers on a lost ferry boat who find unexpected sanctuary in a nudist colony.

The Glorious Pool (1934), in which a group of aging hedonists happen upon the fountain of youth, was the last fantasy Smith completed. While vacationing in Florida with his wife and two young daughters, Thorne Smith died suddenly of a heart attack on June 21, 1934. His unfinished novel, *The Passionate Witch*, was published posthumously in 1941 and adapted for the screen the following year by director René Clair as *I Married a Witch*, starring Veronica Lake and Fredric March. It later inspired the long-running television series *Bewitched* with Elizabeth Montgomery.

In assessing Smith's fiction in *The American Novel* (1940), critic Carl Van Doren wrote: "His novels were all farce and fantasy, perpetual gay adventures in a fluid universe. . . . Anything can happen, almost everything does. Thorne Smith's favorite hero is a man who, settled largely by chance in a dull life, discovers that he has a capacity for pleasure and at once finds opportunities swarming round him. Most of the courting in the stories is done by women, swift, witty, irrepressible daughters of nature who regard men as slow-going creatures that need to be civilized by laughter and love. The books have no problems and no penalties, since the plots are cheerfully irresponsible. They would be shocking if they were not so funny. Though the world Thorne Smith created is not in the least real, it is not remote in time or place. With an instinct for nonsense he took the smart life of his own day and let it run wild and free in his novels." As recently as 1997 *The New York Times* rated Thorne Smith "one of America's most significant humorous writers" and credited his mischievous ghosts with inspiring such movies as *The Ghost and Mrs. Muir, Heaven Can Wait, Beetlejuice, Ghost, Always,* and *A Life Less Ordinary.*

INTRODUCTION

by Carolyn See

He was the master of the pointless conversation, a wistful enthusiast of companionably naked women, a poet of hard liquor, proponent of public riot and mayhem. He loved to construct pages-long drunken bashes where folks hit each other with dead fish. He adored the idea of theft, but frowned on too much adultery; too much adultery, in his eyes, was almost as boring as marital monogamy, which was, in his eyes, unbearable. He loved nature, mountains, and oceans, or at least his fictional heroes did. More than anything else, Thorne Smith yearned after fun.

I first read *The Night Life of the Gods* in 1946, when I was twelve. I was spending the summer with my aunt and uncle in the Mohave Desert town of Victorville, California, where the average temperature during that season runs about 110 degrees. They put me up in a converted garage. I still have, somewhere in my mind's eye, an image: a foreground of the Thorne Smith paperback, a background of an ungainly scorpion on the cement floor elbowing past a huge dust ball. I hear myself laughing out loud. Thorne Smith, besides writing impassioned defenses of drinking, nudity, and wild parties, ministered to the broken-hearted all across the land.

His heroes are as lonely as the loneliest of only children. Cosmo

Topper, that most sedate of unhappily married bankers, is forced for company into the clutches of debauched ghosts. Hunter Hawk, depressed bachelor scientist, hero of *The Night Life of the Gods*, finds a lady leprechaun for company, and then a flock of pagan gods. Anything, Thorne Smith must have thought, to get out of going to church, or sitting down one more time to Sunday dinner, or entertaining stuffy guests without the possibility of a drink.

More than anything else, Thorne Smith was the literary patron saint of hard liquor. In 1920 the Volstead Act was passed in the United States and stayed in effect until 1933: The "noble experiment" of Prohibition gave organized crime a terrific boost and, on a personal level, managed to criminalize a large part of middle-class America. Almost everyone had his bootlegger, his supply of bathtub gin, his favorite speakeasy. My father's first job as a boy in Dallas, instead of running a character-building paper route, was pushing a baby carriage all around town with bottles of hootch tucked nicely under a handmade afghan.

It must have been so easy to rebel against puritan authority in those days. All you had to do was take a drink. And another one. And then begin to have "fun." No one subscribed to this theory more religiously than Thorne Smith. He saw himself as "writing for a world that has forgotten how to play." In tribute to his ideas of unabashed pleasure, which seem more lost to us in the nineties than ever, the Modern Library is reprinting three of his most endearing novels: *Topper, Topper Takes a Trip,* and *The Night Life of the Gods.* You might want to open these pages with a martini (or a whole shaker) by your side.

Topper was published in 1926, the year of Ernest Hemingway's *The Sun Also Rises,* the year Sinclair Lewis's *Arrowsmith* won the Pulitzer Prize. While Hemingway's Jake Barnes suffered tastefully in some of Europe's most scenic spots (and drank red wine from botas, without ever getting a drop on his chest), Cosmo Topper, a middle-aged married man, stayed home in New England with the tedious Mrs. Topper, dying for a drink, a joke, a friend—anything to take him out of the living death of daily life, those long and lonely Sunday afternoons.

Much has been written about Smith's creation of the "ghost" in American fiction. If Topper had not been threatened with one too many legs of lamb at one too many Sunday dinners, he might not have stormed out of the house and bought a used (and haunted) convertible. Its owners, George and Marion Kerby, had driven it into a tree, met their deaths, and come through on the other side as very "low-plane" spirits. Without the Kerbys and their thorough bedevilment of Topper we would have been deprived of countless literary and cinematic ghost jokes over the last seventy years. But to me it's not that the Kerbys are dead, it's that they're such good company. And that they drink so much.

Because they're dead they have time to loaf, to fool around. When Topper first falls in with the Kerbys, his glum position about life as we know it is this: "Fun fills the divorce courts and digs untimely graves." As a result of the Kerbys' attentions he's already had books follow him through the air; his hat has been yanked from his head and tipped at terrified passersby, alcohol has disappeared into *nothing* as his ghost comrades drink copiously to keep their spirits up. But the Kerbys are the answer to a lonely banker's prayers. George is a cheerful boor, randy as a tomcat. Marion is delicious, amoral, and madly in love with Topper. But she isn't a purring seductress; she's more of a human, a girl Topper can talk to. Soon Topper and the Kerbys run into Colonel and Mrs. Hart, two more low-plane, gregarious spirits, the colonel a cheerful thief, Mrs. Hart a happy lady with an outrageous appetite and even more outrageous thirst. They've got a great dog, too. Fourteen pages later the sad, shy Topper has thrown in his lot with this unsavory outfit. After he's had dozens of drinks—and before he's had dozens more—he says: "From now on, I cast decency to the winds. Let's strip ourselves naked and run around screaming." And, more or less, that's what they do.

Such simple wishes! Let's not go to the office. Let's go for a walk in the woods. Let's not make dinner. Let's do play some simple-minded tricks on somebody. And, by God, let's have about seventy thousand more drinks!

In 1932 *Topper Takes a Trip* finds Topper, deserted by Marion, reunited with his dyspeptic wife on an extended vacation in the south of France. The man is "lonely, excessively lonely," even with any amount of toothsome French maids and picturesque French *types* to amuse and distract him. Then, thank the god of low-plane spirits, the Kerbys once again turn up. George is soon distracted by an adulterous honey on a South American yacht, leaving Topper and the other three to raise hell in the same fictional hangout where F. Scott Fitzgerald would set *Tender is the Night* two years later. Fitzgerald took it all too seriously; Thorne Smith couldn't be bothered.

Smith loves to materialize and dematerialize his ghosts and their dog as they yank poor Topper through the air like a flying squirrel, demand new pairs of espadrilles and then parade in them, invisible and single file, past astonished Frenchmen and tourists. There's no point in attempting to summarize the plot because there is no plot. At one point, as Marion and Mrs. Hart—materialized and characteristically almost in the nude—scamper down a palm-lined boulevard of a French resort, Marion shrieks: "There go the briefs! . . . Hang on to yours, Clara. The godarme gendam—I mean the goddam gendarme got 'em." And we hear about the godarme gendam for several more pages, because there's no hurry in this novel. Nothing to do but get a tan, make love, play around with words. Have a drink.

Like *Topper, The Night Life of the Gods* begins in New England. Hunter Hawk is a bachelor, but his life is made a living hell by his bossy matron sister, and he soon falls in with a rowdy leprechaun. Hunter discovers early on the ability to turn humans into stone, and from then on they're in business, causing fracases, ending up in court, confusing the citizenry, getting naked, turning society parties into barbaric melees. Hunter gets the bright idea of waking up statues of pagan gods and heroes—Mercury, Bacchus, Neptune, Hebe, Apollo, Perseus, and Diana. When they wake up—unceremoniously jerked back from eternity into time—do any of them vouchsafe a profound remark? No. Mercury and Perseus get into an immediate spat about the respective merits of their snakes. Neptune demands dinner at a fish joint; Apollo starts flirting. And Bacchus—though he deplores the quality of Prohibition liquor—gets roaring drunk.

What kind of nation *were* we then, so starved for pure fun, so desperate to get away from middle-class morality, that we turned to evocations of Neptune, for instance, playing dead at the bottom of a hotel swimming pool, poking society matrons in their behinds with his trusty trident? We roared out loud when Thorne Smith turned a dog's paws—his paws only—to stone, so that he turned, in effect, into a tap-dancing dog. His silvery prose is gleeful, unrepentant, unregenerate. It laughs in the face of responsibility, clean living, and "family values."

In 1939 the *Big Book of Alcoholics Anonymous* changed all that. Things that Thorne Smith had never thought to write about began to come into the public consciousness. If you drank three quarts of rye after putting down a couple of bottles of champagne in any given evening, you were inevitably going to wake up with a crashing hangover. You were going to have a dry mouth and a pounding headache and your capacity for wacky repartee would be severely impaired. A wild party where people smacked each other with dead fish would seem depressing in the morning. Courthouse encounters with irate judges wouldn't be so funny. (Smith's one reference to the possible "evils" of drink turns those evils on their ear: "If the world kept itself staggering drunk for a couple of centuries," says Hunter Hawk's leprechaun companion, "there wouldn't be any wars. Armies would fall down and go to sleep before they could reach each other." Hawk agrees: "And when they woke up . . . the soldiers' hands would be so unsteady they wouldn't be able to do much damage.") But the Volstead Act had been repealed. Now, when you took a drink, you were a law-abiding citizen just like everybody else.

By the time Charles Jackson published *The Lost Weekend* in 1944, establishing for a new generation that there was absolutely nothing appealing in being a fall-about drunk, Smith had been dead for about ten years. It's a good thing in a way. The news would have broken his heart.

Judging from his books, all Thorne Smith wanted was a little fun—no, a lot of fun, more fun than might be possible on earth. That may be why he populated his tales with ghosts and animals and statues come to life. Maybe he realized that what he envisioned in the twenties and thirties just wasn't going to be possible. Nor would the hedonism that came to pass in the late sixties stay around more than six or seven years. It just doesn't work out that way in this country of ours.

My uncle and aunt had as much fun as they could. There weren't many laughs in that desert town, but they stubbornly held on to the Thorne Smith value system. They went to every party in the sure and certain hope that it would be the best time of all. They knew that life was *supposed* to be carefree, even if it wasn't. Because something in America cherishes the other stuff you can do on a Sunday afternoon. Stay away from the leg of lamb and go out on a picnic. Find a roadhouse and dance the twilight away. Stay up past your bedtime, so long that you watch the sun come up. Or, if you don't want to leave the house, pick up one of these novels. Thorne Smith would agree, and order more champagne.

CONTENTS

TOPPER
TAKES A TRIP

Morning Thoughts on a German Model

There was Topper. And there was the Mediterranean. A magnificent spectacle, that—Topper and the Mediterranean. Kindred
spirits well met, contemplating each other across an alluring girdle
of sand.

Not a large man, Topper—Cosmo Topper. Nor yet a small man.
Certainly not a small. A comfortable man, rather. Slightly plump, if
anything, and clad in a pair of blue silk pajamas. And there was the
Mediterranean just as it had been there for a considerable length of
time—much longer than Mr. Topper, for one thing. A vast expanse
of cool ocean as blue and virginal seeming as the garments adorning the figure then inspecting it from the *balcon* of a discouragingly
pale stucco villa set in a garden fairly bristling with grass of a repellent toughness—grass so hostilely tough that only a rhinoceros
could sit on it with any showing of dignity and aplomb. Unfortunately, as rhinoceroses are rarely if ever encountered in these drab
days sitting on Riviera grass in Riviera gardens, this observation
must of necessity remain merely one of those vast mental pictures
upon which to dwell during the interminable reaches of a family
reunion.

On this early morning, one which appeared about as willing to give as to receive of the good things of life, Mr. Topper had the Mediterranean very much to himself. In fact, he was quite alone with all that great quantity of water.

There was the man. And there was the ocean. Unique and distinct. One might even choose between them, if suddenly faced with such a disagreeable necessity. However, so splendidly did they go together, so well matched or mated were the two, that most persons of discrimination would have hesitated to separate them. They would have preferred to sidestep the issue and to retain both Topper and the Mediterranean intact. But, of course, there are some who might have wanted the ocean more than the man, or vice versa. Who can say?

We are fortunate in being able to have them both at their best, Topper on his *balcon*, and the Mediterranean in its bed.

Across the Mediterranean Mr. Topper cast an early morning look, and the Mediterranean graciously offered its full-bosomed amplitude to his inspection. And although it has been previously observed that both were of a virginal blueness, it should not be forgotten that either one of them was capable of pulling some powerfully rough stuff when the opportunity offered.

Topper, it is to be learned with some relief, was virginal more through circumstance than choice. This does not imply that his was a low and lecherous nature. Nor does it necessarily follow that he was epicurean in such matters. But he did like things nice that way. Most men do, when and if possible.

Topper had been a banker by profession. He still was a husband—an original error of judgment unrectified by time. Habit is a dreadful thing. Once he had commuted without realizing the error of his ways. Most men commute through necessity. Topper had done so ritualistically. In Glendale, U. S. A., the Toppers had been socially solid. All that had changed, but not through Mrs. Topper.

The fact is that rather late in the day Cosmo Topper had been subjected to the ultra violent rays of a series of amorous and disreputable adventures as incredible as they had been entertaining. These adventures had left his pulse still beating in perfect harmony with the more enjoyable if less laudable preoccupations of life.

They had not so much changed his character as ventilated it, given it a chance to breathe good, honest vulgar air vitalized by the fumes of grog. As a result, he had succeeded in washing his hands of work, but figuratively women still clung to them. There were times when those hands of Topper's fairly itched after women, which is the natural state of all healthy and enterprising masculine hands.

Even now, in the innocent face of this clean Riviera morning, the man was actually speculating as to the exact degree of nudity the German model would achieve on the beach a few hours hence. Yesterday, to his almost visible agitation, this lady of wolfish lines had reached what he had every reason to believe to be the absolute limit of anatomical candour. In spite of this awe-inspiring display, something told Topper that this German model, in her relentless quest of a coat of tan, still held a few more cubic inches in reserve which she would willingly sacrifice to the sun. Until she did this there was no peace of mind for any inquiring spirit on the beach. And when this greatly to be desired end had been attained, Topper both hoped and proposed to be stationed critically in the front ranks of a vast, admiring, and cosmopolitan multitude. He owed himself that much. Not that he lusted after the woman, but too long and too patiently had he attended in clinical expectancy to be, at the end, deprived of this point of vantage.

Once she had definitely and conclusively arrived at the climax of her revelations, Topper felt that he would be quite willing to call it a game. He had no desire to pursue his investigations further. All suspense would be at an end. The German model could go her way, while he would go his as if the incident had never occurred. Her crisply burned body would remain in his memory merely as a remarkable phenomenon, something to wonder about, like a landslide, subway rush, or Democratic Convention.

However, until that time Mr. Topper's interests were very much involved. True enough, so gradually had the German model progressed on her way to nudity that much of the shock had evaporated before fresh territory was opened up for inspection, but by the same token, the very deliberateness of the method employed lent to the business an atmosphere of terrific suspense. What the morrow would bring forth, or, rather, off, was the anxious speculation in scores of masculine minds. Women also wondered. Topper suspected several depraved frequenters of the Casino actually of betting on the results of the model's daily progress. For example, the fifth rib against the diaphragm, heavy odds against a complete torso.

Being bored abroad is one of America's favorite customs. And not without reason.

Mr. Topper held stoutly to the belief that within the short space of several weeks this German model had done more to establish friendly relations—to create a sort of *entente intime*, in fact—between her country and the Allied Powers than had been achieved by all the diplomatic gestures and disarmament conferences that had supplied the public with dull reading since the Armistice.

"And not a bad idea," he mused, yawning. "In fact, a splendid idea. Instead of holding a series of silly disarmament conferences at which everyone gets all hot and bothered and cables home to hurry up with more guns—instead of this, why not institute a set of disrobing conferences? Why not make a clean breast of it internationally? Let us strip ourselves of our all and face each other man to woman instead of man to man. No more beating about the bush or dangerous secret diplomacy. No more old men telling lies to other old men. At innumerable private conferences the idea has worked out not only successfully but entertainingly. Why not try it out on a large international scale?"

He considered his Mediterranean now as if in a trance. Topper was seeing in his mind's eye the American ambassador to England clad only in a pipe, looking at the German delegate trying to face the world in glasses. He saw a famous old French bargain hunter smilingly surveying the scene protected only by a blue *béret—très gentil.* And a gentleman from Italy clad only in a neat but shrunken black shirt—what a sight! Mahatma Ghandi taking everything quite naturally, together with a few grains of rice. Then there would be the ladies, supplied probably by an international theatrical committee: Miss America, Mlle France, Señorita Madrid, *et al.* Altogether a jolly party. A conference that would accomplish some results, at least, no matter what those results might be. Agreeable events would be sure to occur.

The Mediterranean invites the idle mind to do some very curious thinking, and Mr. Topper, it seems, had accepted the invitation. And all the while these and other equally unbecoming thoughts were corroding the mind of this erstwhile banker, within the pale villa, his wife was sleeping most unpicturesquely yet most thoroughly. In spite of the many sterling qualities of this really admirable lady, one could forgive without too great a struggle her husband for preferring to think of the German model.

There was so much of her worth thinking about and so many choice bits of that so much. And strange to relate, Topper had not the faintest conception of what she looked like—no idea at all of her face. Men are like that. Careless. Just grown-up boys with a few extra tricks tacked on.

He well remembered the day when she had first made her appearance on the beach. Like many successful men and women before her, she had made rather modest and cautious beginnings. Only a scant couple of yards of her were exposed to the avid caress of the sun that day. From that first casual view of her one never would have suspected that there was so very much more of the German model still left unseen. Yet as time went on and vaster expanses became exposed, one came to believe that perhaps this German model would never cease, but like the brook continue on forever. Now, most fortunately for everyone concerned, there was little left of the lady that remained unexposed. With characteristic Teutonic system and thoroughness she had succeeded in revolutionizing the color of her skin and at the same time hanging up a record for plain and fancy nudity on a beach where such a record was exceedingly hard to make.

She was a good influence, Mr. Topper decided, as he stood on his *balcon,* getting himself together for the day. She was the living symbol of one of the few interests that nations held in common. She drew men together, took their mind off grimmer if higher things. Furthermore, she didn't give a damn. Topper admired that. All his life he had given damns. Too many of them. For what she was, she deserved all the admiration and encouragement she received, although sweethearts and wives from Bronx Park to Brompton Road publicly denounced her while privately envying her proportions. So much for the German model, thought Topper as he turned to receive Scollops.

Scollops was Mr. Topper's personal cat. She wove herself out onto the *balcon* and, as her master had done before her, looked the Mediterranean up and down. Then she yawned at it. There was a tongue inside. It was curled like a red-hot spring. Topper, considering his cat's too knowing eyes, decided that she would go well with the German model. Both should lie in the sand together. They had much in common—everything male.

Mr. Topper gathered the cat in his arms and together they considered the day. He had brought this creature, this unregenerate cat, along with him at no little trouble and expense. At first Scollops had not been pleased. Travel had proved too confining, although there had been a moment or two on the ship—the captain's Tom. Why bring up the past? Why not, thought Scollops? Life was better now—ampler, lazier, sunnier. She found it to her liking, although she had noticed with a sense of alarm that there appeared to be a great many more French dogs than cats, and that these dogs seemed curiously volatile and distrait. It hardly mattered, though. One enterprising gentleman cat for every-day company and another just in case were all that Scollops demanded. She had speedily acquired both. Not bad, either. Scollops frankly liked her gentlemen cats ungentlemanly. It would be amusing to present Mr. Topper with a litter of Franco-American kittens, amusing but quite a bother.

Had the man holding this godless animal so carefully in his arms even suspected vaguely the nature of her thoughts he would have dropped her like a hot shot, little realizing that his own thoughts were, if anything, less edifying.

Some distance out on the blue a French destroyer went scuttling along to Nice. Probably out of Toulon. She knifed the waters spitefully, as if to remind them that men could hate and kill as well as love and live amiable lives. A subtle, deadly little craft. Neat. From the near-by training station three airplanes zoomed in formation through an inoffensive sky, then broke into a stuttering of dizzy spins and loops. Playful little devils buoyantly practising murder.

Topper raised his eyes to these man-created wasps, then lowered them to the sleek sides of his cat. Far, far better to consider the German model. No foolish ideas there about national prestige, the rights of invasion, or defense of honor. Catch as catch can was her way of looking at life. Live and let live, but preferably with some nice rich man.

Extending a brown hand, Topper gently touched a small pink rose that had crept up on the vine from the veranda below to take a look round. It was jolly up here. Better than looking all day long at that damn tough grass. The air brought to mind pine forests and hidden flowers, also, occasionally, fish. From the little cork factory down the street a fine red powder dusted the light breeze. Scollops sniffed delicately. An inspiriting figure of a French girl, mostly legs of the better sort, as was only right and proper, sped smoothly along a white road. With effortless grace she sent the bicycle ahead. She was singing "Ramona." All French girls were singing "Ramona." And almost all French men. Not singing it any too well, but singing it often and emotionally. Topper had hoped he had left that song far behind in America. Now, right here in France, the populace was breaking its collective heart over it all day long and late into the night. Idly he wondered if the French senate sang it. He grinned indulgently. Probably, if he were French, he too would be vocally breaking his heart over this Ramona trollop and her confounded Mission bells. Thoughtfully his eyes followed the provocative figure of the girl as she sped over the inlet bridge and lost herself in a little crooked street mostly made up at the moment of a donkey and his eternal cart. Whether the girl made it or not Topper never knew. He rather suspected she didn't, although the donkey remained unmoved.

"*Ma chatte*," he remarked, thinking to himself what a silly word it was, "my little cabbage, let us promenade ourselves." For a moment he looked back at the blue ocean. "Small wonder," he continued to his little cabbage, "that that strapping wench Venus, all set for seduction, sprang full blown from the foam of such a sea."

Leaving the Mediterranean to consider this at its leisure, Topper, bearing Scollops, quietly withdrew into his villa.

The fact was, the man was lonely, excessively lonely, but he refused to admit it even to himself.

MR. TOPPER SHAKES HANDS

Topper, still doing his best in spite of his blue-silk pajamas, emerged gloriously into his garden. Scollops also emerged under her own power. There did not appear to be much of it because she moved slowly on reluctant feet.

On his way downstairs Topper paused to look at his wife, then hastily followed this uninspiring inspection with a stiff bracer of cognac. As Mr. Topper understood it, this clever French distillation was to be considered more in the nature of a tonic than a tipple—when taken properly. Owing to the blessed fact that his wife was a late sleeper, Mr. Topper found himself at liberty to take it properly several times in the course of a morning. By rising early himself he could thus extend the length of his morning and accordingly increase the number of cognacs, all of which were taken properly. Husbands have their ways, God help them.

Topper, after looking at his wife, felt that the world owed him at least one drink of cognac properly taken. And he took it. Even in her sleep there had been about Mary Topper a certain grim rectitude which is especially depressing to those whose moral stature is only microscopically visible. Topper needed his cognac. He took his cognac. And although, as a result, his moral stature suffered a severe setback, he felt within himself much closer to God and man. His two favorites, Scollops and the Mediterranean, became even greater favorites.

Mention has been made of a series of adventures in connection with Mr. Topper. More should be said. Back in his suburban home Topper had met some exceedingly peculiar characters and enjoyed some equally peculiar adventures. From these adventures he emerged improved in every department. He was, perhaps, the only man of his day and generation who had actually and knowingly had familiar dealings with a spirit, or rather, with a person who, judged by all conventional standards, was entirely nonexistent. Topper knew better. However, because of this technical loophole perhaps no black marks can be recorded against him, in spite of the fact that he left behind him, in the course of his adventures, a clearly defined trail of chips from the Commandments he had shattered.

This morning, as Topper strolled along by his garden wall, he was thinking of his brief but lurid past. His thoughts made him restless, filled him with a poignant desire to live a little more amply and to associate again with those extraordinary companions of a vanished summer, especially with one of them, Marion Kerby. If he had her back again he felt that he could indefinitely dispense with the others. As a matter of fact, he would much prefer it. Colonel Scott and Mrs. Hart, those suave though disreputable affinities, would be far too expansive and uncontrollable along a coast offering as many opportunities for their failings as the Riviera. Even in the so-called dry States, they had seldom drawn a totally unalcoholic breath. And George Kerby—Topper felt that he could do very nicely without a great deal of George, Marion's quick-tempered, high-living husband, who was forever insisting that death did not them part, not by any manner of means. An engaging chap, George, and a delightful companion, if he would only give up claiming such dictatorial sway over the time and actions of Marion.

In his heart Topper knew that Marion was lost to him forever. She had told him herself that she was passing on to a higher plane, freeing herself at last from the carnal drag of the earth. The jovial

Colonel, the languishing yet ever hungry Mrs. Hart, and George Kerby would never pass out of the more pleasant influences of the earth. They had no ambitions to refine themselves. Topper felt sure of that. Those three liked themselves as they were, and Topper, thinking back, could hardly blame them. He, himself, had he been given the choice, would have preferred to remain a low-plane spirit, that is, assuming he was officially removed from this world. Then Topper's thoughts dallied with memories of Oscar, the Colonel's somewhat eccentric dog, that had only after the greatest patience on the part of his master learned to materialize in whole or in part, according to his mood and fancy. Oscar would have been an unusual companion for Scollops. He would have diverted the cat's thoughts from certain channels.

A bald head, fringed with a nicely starched ruff of gray, popping up alarmingly from the other side of the wall, brought Mr. Topper's own thoughts back into the present with a snap.

"*Bonjour, mon vieux!*" cried Monsieur Louis. "The times make fair, is it not?"

Mr. Topper's hand was suddenly snatched from him and twirled about in the most bewildering manner. In this operation the element of surprise meant all. Topper had no choice. He merely stood by watchfully to see that nothing that could not be mended happened to his hand.

"You carry yourself well today?" continued Monsieur Louis, suddenly forgetting all about Mr. Topper's hand and dropping it. "You promenade yourself a little? *Comment?*"

Mr. Topper hastened to assure Monsieur Louis that he, Topper, was exceedingly well pleased with everything in France, but especially with Monsieur Louis himself; that he, Topper, carried himself tremendously, and that he hoped Monsieur Louis was doing splendidly in the line of self-carrying; that the times had never made any fairer so far as he knew, and that owing to his blue-silk pajamas he was desolated that he could not please Monsieur Louis by projecting himself farther than a very little. And all the while Mr. Topper was saying these things he was wondering if Monsieur

Louis had actually called him common to his face. It sounded very much like it, that last word. These French could get away with murder if one failed to know their language.

"Me, also, I am well pleased," Monsieur Louis continued like God. "Now, behold, I work much. Tonight I play. *Tout à l'heure, mon ami, tout à l'heure.*"

And with this piece of gratuitous information of a rather personal nature Monsieur Louis ducked down behind the wall, leaving Mr. Topper on the other side vainly trying to get the meaning of his parting words.

"*Tout à l'heure,*" considered Mr. Topper. "What the deuce did he mean by that? Sounds silly to me—all at the hour. What hour? Can't help feeling a little embarrassed for these Frenchmen when they begin to talk. Seem to lose all control of themselves. He works much now, but tonight he plays, does he? Getting along in years for that sort of thing. And he brags about it, the immoral old devil. Wonder what his wife thinks of that?"

Topper decided that most likely Madame Louis did not mind at all. French husbands and wives were always so busy rushing in and out of the house on the way to and from assignations that they never had any spare time to check up on each other's movements.

This train of thought naturally brought him back to Marion Kerby. He recalled the day when he had purchased the Kerbys' car as a result of his exasperation at his wife's habitual attempts to thrust a leg of lamb down his jaded throat. George and Marion had been killed in that self-same car. A tree had objected to it. He remembered the day, the moment of awe and incredulity when they had first spoken to him out of vast spaces. How upset he had been. And he remembered, too, not without a slight shudder, how shockingly George Kerby had first materialized. What a dreadful sight that had been—a pair of golf knickers gradually taking form, and an inverted head dangling between their legs. At that moment Topper had wondered if George materialized were always going to be like that. Then Marion had made her presence seen as well as felt. He had first caught sight of her draped over a rafter in an old, abandoned inn. She had been about as abandoned as the inn itself. That night she had looked like an angel. There the resemblance had come to an abrupt end.

Once more Monsieur Louis's popping head shattered Mr. Topper's memories.

"In full truth," he warned Mr. Topper, seizing his hand as if to prevent it from striking. "Tonight I have of pleasure, but now, my friend, I cut. It is that I trim the garden. He is in disarray. Me, I shall introduce order and make all things fair. Regard! I clip, is it not?"

Inasmuch as Monsieur Louis extended in the air a pair of shears fairly dripping with vegetation, Mr. Topper saw no reason to start an argument.

"With them I work," continued the little Frenchman, philosophically regarding the shears, "but tonight it is a thing entirely different. *Au'voir, m'sieur.* I part."

With this Monsieur Louis flung back Mr. Topper's hand and collapsed behind the wall, from over which came the voice of a pair of agitated clippers.

"I wish he would stop doing that," Mr. Topper complained to himself. "It's more than disturbing. It's downright alarming, especially when done with clippers. Furthermore, I don't give a damn how much he plays, but if he doesn't stop popping up and down like that he won't be able to drag himself out of the house. Wonder where he goes to do all this playing?"

The whole thing had started from that night at the abandoned inn. What an excellent night that had been, dancing in the firelight with Marion and drinking Scotch with George.

Topper was not aware of the fact that an embryonic sigh escaped his lips.

And all the things that had happened after George had gone abroad. That interlude by the lake alone with Marion, that is, alone with her until Colonel Scott and Mrs. Hart, a pair of low-plane spirits with an equally low-plane dog, had appeared, casually drifting along in search of whatever pleasure the moment had to offer. They had made a party of it, the four of them, and he, Topper, had been the only one unable to disappear at will. It had been extremely inconvenient at times, and never more so than when George Kerby had unexpectedly returned to find Marion and himself together under highly compromising circumstances. They could hardly have been higher, those circumstances, nor more compromising. Then the weird duel which followed in which George insisted on his rights to remain invisible while Topper, unable to reduce his stature by one cubic inch, was forced to remain an exceedingly mortal target. Finally, the return to the inn, the farewell party, and the tree again. It had been a terrific smash-up. Topper had come back to consciousness in the hospital. Marion was gone, and so were the others. Even Oscar had withdrawn himself into a dimension unattainable to Mr. Topper. It was all over. Adventures end. Only Mrs. Topper remained, Mrs. Topper and his cat, Scollops.

Once out of the hospital, Topper had tried to make a go of it with his wife. An abortive attempt. As soon as she had got her husband back she speedily set about retrieving her dyspepsia and superior manner. In spite of her efforts to be human, she had gradually relapsed into her familiar rôle of conventional, self-satisfied, censorious matron with a social position to nurse. She had been grimly determined to make Topper comply. Now this is an impossible thing to do with a man who has once consorted on grounds of perfect equality with a set of low-plane spirits. To her intense chagrin, Mrs. Topper had found it so. She soon discovered that the once orthodox Topper had been utterly ruined for everyday suburban life. He missed trains, offended the neighbors, and cursed at things with a new and overpowering vigor. He refused to go to bed at the customary time, and was frequently seen in the company of low characters. Then, too, he suffered from occasional fits of abstraction in which the community of Glendale ceased to exist for him, and he would go wandering away by himself as if in search of something, the exact nature of which he had forgotten himself.

Once the man had attempted to tell his wife a little something about the less unedifying side of his adventures. He had felt the need to share, to recapture in the telling a little of the past. He did not get far. His wife, he could tell, was under the impression that his mind had been affected by his accident. It was all very discouraging.

In the end, Topper had made an attempt to furbish up his relations with his wife by taking her to Europe. No luck. In France Mrs. Topper was even more Glendale than before. Defensively and aloofly critical. Superior. Nonparticipating.

It was not Mary Topper's fault. No woman could be the way she was of her own free will. God had given her the type of mind she had, and her family had taught her to use it the way she did. She thought herself quite right. And that was just the trouble. She was quite right—a damn sight too quite for Topper. In this world people should probably live according to her standards, that is, those who wished to get along with the minimum amount of friction and the maximum of dull, numbing comfort. Her rightness had become such an obsession with her that she was never happy unless she was showing Mr. Topper how terribly, terribly wrong he was. Topper sometimes wondered how a man who was so consistently wrong as his wife made him out to be had ever escaped being hanged and had become, instead, a responsible officer in one of the world's largest banking institutions. As wrong as he was, however, he never made the mistake of asking his wife this question. It would have done terrible things to her dyspepsia, and God alone knew she needed little encouragement in that direction. Yet, somewhere deep down in his rather secretive heart, Topper nourished a genuine affection for this woman who had made such a sameness of his life. It was his fault, after all. Had he not permitted her to do it? And he had been much like her until a quartet of carousing characters who had left this world safer for domesticity by leaving it themselves, had taken him through some remarkably broadening paces.

Yes, Topper was fond of his wife, but being fond of one's wife and getting along with her were two and entirely different matters, as many a husband had found out before him. Perhaps it was not to be expected. Topper did not know. The problem had been too long with him. It was barnacle encrusted.

Monsieur Louis, or rather the head of that brave, saved him from attempting to solve it. Once more it popped up, and once more Topper's hand was captured and subjected to a friendly flinging.

"My friend," the little man announced, his wicked eyes sparkling with some hidden irony as only a Frenchman's eyes can sparkle, "this garden here is greatly encouraged. But why? There is nothing in it to grow. Alas, I reproach myself. In spite of which tonight I find my pleasure. *Alors!*"

Monsieur Louis was gone. Topper stood gazing vacantly at the spot where Monsieur Louis had been. So far as Topper knew Monsieur Louis had neither legs nor body. He had never seen these parts, though he imagined they were somewhere about. But on the witness stand he could not have taken an oath that there was any more to Monsieur Louis than one popping head, a quick little twisting neck, and a pair of agile arms. And the funny thing is that Topper never did know. That was all he ever saw of Monsieur Louis. Of course, had he taken the trouble he could have found out. Topper never took the trouble. What he knew of Monsieur Louis was quite enough. More of Monsieur Louis would have been too much.

"That little Frenchman certainly must be going to have a good time," he mused almost enviously. "He's so damned excited about it. Doesn't seem to be able to think of anything else. The French are funny that way. He and his pleasure. Wish he'd stop popping about it."

To protect his nerves from further incursions by Monsieur Louis and Monsieur Louis's head and arms, Topper moved away from the wall and walked down to the little gate that gave onto the white road separating the white villa from the beach. Here he was almost immediately joined by Monsieur Sylvestre, *patron* of the excellent Café Plage.

Monsieur Sylvestre, as if suddenly spying an especially desirable fish, pounced upon Mr. Topper's hand and did friendly things to it. Then he demanded of Mr. Topper how he *ported* himself this morning. Mr. Topper was once more *gentil* and admitted that he *ported* himself fairly *bien* and added that the times made fair. Monsieur Sylvestre, overwhelmed with both statements, again shook Mr. Topper's hand and asked him if it was that he would have to *boir un petit.* Mr. Topper thereupon shook Monsieur Sylvestre's hand and allowed that he would have of cognac to *boir.* Accordingly both shook hands for the fourth time and crossed the road, blue pajamas and all, to the little café squatting unpicturesquely on the sand. Here on the veranda they looked politely at several fishing boats and one tramp steamer from Denmark. They had to *boir* at the hands of Madame Sylvestre, who had first shaken one of Topper's. This sort of thing went on for about a quarter of an hour, until Mr. Topper felt his supply of amiability running low, upon which he withdrew, after cordially shaking hands with his hosts, who were desolated by his departure.

On his way across the road Mr. Topper was nearly knocked down by his *blanchisseuse*, who, compactly mounted on her *bicyclette*, had been on the point of delivering at the villa the beautiful results of her *blanchisseus*-ing. This slight contretemps brought down on Mr. Topper's head a deluge of polite lamentations. Things would have gone smoothly enough had they gone no further. The stricken lady insisted on tenderly shaking Mr. Topper's hand. There was still more. His blue-silk pajamas were brushed and examined with a thoroughness that would have given Mrs. Topper grounds for a separation back in Glendale. Mr. Topper himself became somewhat light-headed during these impassioned operations and clung to his pajamas like a little gentleman in order to keep from giving the diligent *blanchisseuse* fresh cause for apologies or congratulations. He then helped her to collect the scattered laundry, and clinging to his pajamas with one hand, falteringly carried the laundry back to the villa with the other.

Here he encountered the maid, Félice, whom he had certain reasons for suspecting of being much more than she pretended not to be. He deposited the laundry in a chair, took a hitch in his pajamas, and made a grab for the French girl's hand, thus making the morning a clean sweep of handshaking.

Félice evinced no surprise, although privately she was cast down that he stopped at her hand. She made no attempt to withdraw it and gazed back at the pajamaed gentleman with infinite understanding.

Sensing the reprehensible nature of the thoughts passing behind those melting eyes, he promptly dropped the hand and hurried upward to his bathroom. Here he stood looking thoughtfully at the tub. Had it suddenly remarked upon the weather and attempted to shake his hand he in turn would not have been in the least surprised.

"Funny people, these French," he soliloquized as he let his pajama trousers follow their natural inclination. "Polite to the point of danger. Can't make up my mind whether I like them or not. Some days, yes, and some days, no. That girl Félice, for example. A body isn't safe with her around."

Then he turned and regarded Vesuvius with profound skepticism. He could not quite make up his mind about this strange device, either.

III

Monsieur Grandon's Vesuvius

Vesuvius had given Topper some mighty bad moments in the course of their relations. Even now he was not sure just where he stood as regards to Vesuvius, and what was even worse, just where Vesuvius stood as regards to him.

Vesuvius existed in a metal box that did things about making cold water different. But Vesuvius had, Mr. Topper feared, potentialities of achieving other and more ambitious flights than that. It could, for instance, take its name seriously and emulate the volcano, exploding most horrifically. This might result in depositing Topper, still soapy but otherwise unadorned, in the bosom of a vociferous French family picnicking on the beach. This would not be *gentil,* neither would it be diverting, that is, not for Topper. He had no desire to compete with the German model.

Topper's first introduction to Vesuvius had been made through the medium of an extremely emotional Monsieur Grandon, one who claimed the distinction of being Mr. Topper's *propriétaire.*

"*Voila!*" Monsieur Grandon had exploded dramatically through his beard. "One has it!"

"What, Monsieur Grandon?" demanded Topper, slightly confused. "One has what, exactly?"

"In truth," explained *Monsieur le propriétaire*, running frantic hands over numerous pipes, taps, and levers darting dangerously from all sides of the box. "It is there—*l'appareil de chauffage.*"

Topper, none the wiser, read the name of the box and became restive.

"One pulls this one here and that one there," continued Monsieur Grandon, recklessly laying hands on various protruding bits of Vesuvius. "*Alors!* One pushes here, makes to turn there, then ignites this one here—but first," and here the Frenchman paused and darkly considered the blank face of Topper, "but first," he repeated with seeming reluctance, "one makes the water to run in the basin."

"What!" ejaculated Topper incredulously. "Is that quite necessary?"

"The one who would bathe," Monsieur Grandon explained with patience. "You, m'sieu, for example."

Mr. Topper was more astounded than shocked.

"I was merely thinking of my wife," he said coldly.

"Madame is your wife?" exclaimed Monsieur in a mixture of surprise and disappointment.

"But yes," replied Mr. Topper. "Is it that you believed her my mistress?"

Monsieur Grandon shrugged temporizingly.

"It is of an occurrence unique," he observed. "One expects more of an American when he visits our Riviera."

Topper turned on the tap as a gesture of possession.

"*Hein!*" cried Monsieur Grandon. "Now shall I cause him to march."

"Cause," replied Mr. Topper after a moment's hesitation. "But cause him to march with the utmost tranquillity. Cause him almost to amble."

"There is not of danger, m'sieu."

"But yes, my old," replied Topper. "Something tells me in a loud, clear voice that there is of danger—that there is even of stark peril. Upon the body of Vesuvius there are certain telltale marks that give me to believe he once went 'poof'!"

"Of a verity," admitted Monsieur Grandon. "It is a long time since that one there went 'poof'!"

"That, Monsieur Grandon, is most unfortunate," commented Mr. Topper, "because after his so great and profound tranquillity he may imagine it about the right time to go 'poof!' *encore.*"

"It is a thing not to think of," assured Monsieur Grandon.

"It is a thing I hate to think of," agreed Topper, "yet it is a thing from which I cannot tear my thoughts."

"Have of courage, m'sieu," urged the intrepid Frenchman. "His first 'poof!' was his last."

From what Monsieur Grandon allowed to remain unsaid he let it be delicately inferred that what had passed between himself and Vesuvius on the occasion of the first "proof!" had definitely settled matters for all time.

"But," observed Monsieur Grandon with an alarming reversal of form, "should it eventuate that he does go 'proof!' then it is that one makes water to run on a scale very grand."

"Have little fear on that point, m'sieu," Topper hastened to assure him. "If he ever takes it into his head to go 'proof!' in earnest, water will be made on a scale of the utmost grandeur and with startling promptitude."

"Is it not so?" murmured Monsieur Grandon abstractedly, as he did things to Vesuvius that made Mr. Topper shudder.

Thus it came about that Mr. Topper and Vesuvius, *l'appareil de chauffage*, met each other on terms of mutual suspicion which never quite wore off in spite of their daily contact. Those scars of a previous "poof!" were a constant reminder of an unreliable past. Familiarity had never bred contempt, although Topper was now able to pass through the ritual of ignition with his mind on other matters.

IV

Animated Discourse with a Foot

His mind was on other matters now as he made Vesuvius to march. He was still thinking of his other-world friends. As he watched the water flow into the tub, these vanished companions were all mixed up in his mind. He wondered if they had ever been or if he had dreamed them all in the hospital after the accident. There were times when he had almost convinced himself that they had been merely the puppets of his repressions. Most certainly George and Marion Kerby had been real enough once. Before they had come a cropper against that tree they had been a part of the social life of Glendale. Not an admirable part, to be sure, but, nevertheless, a tangible one. They had not been able then to appear and disappear at random, but had conducted themselves like ordinary human beings, only much worse, according to Glendale standards. Was it possible, he asked himself as he stepped into the tub—never a charming gesture—for a dog to be part dog one minute and no dog at all the next—merely a bark from another world? Yet these things had been, and Topper knew they had been. The old abandoned inn actually existed, and so did all of the other places he had visited with his companions in the course of those mad adventures which now seemed so distant and unreal.

"Seems an unreasonable waste of time and labor, this tub business," Topper reflected as he carefully lowered himself into the water. "With the whole wide Mediterranean knocking at one's front door, it is nothing less than a supine knuckling under to convention to drag a small part of it into the house and then to wallow in it." He groaned feebly and began to lather his body. The spirit of rebellion was in him, for customarily, Topper and his tub were boon companions. "A horrid thing, all this bathing. Mostly brought on by wives. They talk about you if you don't, and when you do they complain you're monopolizing the bathroom. No pleasing wives. People seldom keep up this morning tubbing or else one would hear of more old folks meeting their Maker in a bathtub. To bathe," he continued as he searched for the soap, "is to admit that one is not all that one should be. And that is not at all a fragrant admission. Yet in public a man will suddenly spring up and announce with an air of infinite virtue that it is his intention to bathe his body. The shame of the thing. A man should so live that a tub would be a novelty rather than a necessity. How much more dynamic it would be for a man to get up in public and announce that he had no intention of taking a bath for a long, long time; that he had taken a bath recently, and that he refused to make further concessions to public opinion, which was notoriously bovine and vacillating." Topper had found the soap and was warming to his theme. "Let him add," he continued, "that he really didn't need that bath, and that he was prevailed upon to take it only by the knowledge that his wife would go about saying to other wives, 'My dear, it's simply terrible. I can't do a thing with my husband. He absolutely refuses to bathe.' Some wives might try to hush it up, but the servants would be sure to talk. Somehow the thing would get out." Once more he fumbled for the soap, then thoughtfully considered his partially lathered foot. "Take that foot, for example," he went on critically. "It is neither better nor worse for its tub—worse, if anything. Unpleasantly shrunken by the water. Its full bloom is no longer with it."

Topper regarded the foot with sudden alarm. It seemed strangely changed. Somehow, it did not at all remind him of the foot he had associated with for so many years, shoe in and shoe out.

Then, even as he looked, out of the void shockingly came a voice, a disembodied voice, pitched in a note of warning. Topper jumped as if suddenly brought into contact with a furious electric eel.

"Listen," said the voice quite casually. "I'm perfectly willing to have you scrub my foot if you get any kick out of it—ha! ha!—but don't let it go any farther than that. I think that is fairly stated."

Topper quickly averted his dilated eyes from the foot he had been so critically considering. With a dreadful feeling he realized that in truth the horrid thing did not belong to him. Somehow or other an odd foot had managed to get itself into the tub, and he, Topper, had been industriously scrubbing this self-same foot. He had been performing the most demeaning of all labors—scrubbing someone else's foot. But whose? There was the foot as plain as the nose on his face. It was sticking up out of the water at a jaunty, un-compromising angle. Topper glanced again, then once more looked elsewhere. He could not stand the expression of that foot. It shat-tered him.

"Well," continued the voice rather impatiently, "since you've got it so nicely soaped you might as well go on with it. Scrub that foot, Topper."

"I have been scrubbing it," gasped Topper, addressing his words to the foot, "scrubbing it to my intense disgust. Damned if I'll scrub the crab-like object any longer."

"Oh, I say, Topper," said the voice, assuming an admonitory tone. "You greatly wrong that foot, I assure you. That is a typical Castil-ian foot, my dear fellow, worthy of the purest Castile soap. I jest, Topper. Smile."

"I am far from smiling, foot," replied Mr. Topper.

"Don't call me foot," snapped the voice. "Address me as sir or monsieur."

"To me you are merely a foot," remarked Topper, "and not a very good foot, at that. But what I want to know is: what is an odd foot doing in my tub, and where the deuce is your brother?"

"Don't be deliberately disagreeable, Topper," said the foot. "Your humor is in ill taste."

"Perhaps," admitted Topper, "but a foot, detached and talkative, is somewhat trying to the most rugged of bathers."

"Come, come, now, Topper," came the reproachful voice of the foot, "that's not at all neighborly."

"Can't see how I could be any more neighborly," rejoined Topper, "bathing as I am with your foot and God only knows what else."

"It is rather chummy, isn't it?" admitted the voice. "But if you must know, I really wasn't counting on your company. All I required of you was to draw my bath. You see, I don't understand that sinister-looking box up there. Vesuvius—a name hardly designed to inspire confidence."

"You should have made your wishes known," said Topper. "Had I known of your foot all the gendarmes in France couldn't have crammed me in this tub."

"This foot, Topper, seems to have got the better of you. What's wrong with the foot?"

"Practically everything," explained Topper. "But that's not the point. How would you like to take a bath with an odd foot?"

"I would take it without the slightest qualms," declared the voice. "In fact, I might use the odd foot to some advantage—scratch my back with it, for example. How's that for an idea?"

"Rotten," answered Topper. "Revolting. Almost unbearable. Would it upset you greatly if I called this bath off?"

"You wouldn't upset me," said the voice, "but I might jolly well upset you."

Topper sensed a hidden threat in the words. He remained silent and submerged. Pondering. The situation had passed far beyond him. He felt unable to deal with it. Experience had shown him that it was impossible to free oneself from the attentions of a low-plane spirit once it had set its mind on cultivating one's company. And although that same experience more or less familiarized him with the situation, he was far from being reconciled to it. One can very quickly get out of the habit of associating with partially material-ized spirits. To be sitting in a bathtub conversing with five toes still struck him as being somewhat unusual. He wondered who could be the owner of those five toes. Topper more than a little suspected the hidden presence of George Kerby. There was something vaguely reminiscent in the quality of the voice—a certain ironical inflection, a grim, almost ghastly playfulness. Now had it only been the foot of George's wife——Mr. Topper's meditations were rudely interrupted.

"Of what are you thinking, Topper of the unsavory mind?" inquired the voice. "Something nice and dirty?"

Mr. Topper started guiltily. He wondered if his disembodied companion had the power to peer into mortal minds. Topper fervently hoped not. If he had, his, Topper's, position would become most untenable. It would become appallingly dangerous. He attempted a disarming smile.

"My dear foot," he replied easily, "if such you insist on remaining, I was merely thinking how nice it would be if you would pop off and allow me to continue alone with my bath. No gentleman— no well mannered gentleman, that is—relishes scrubbing his body while sitting on the lap of an unseen bath mate. It is neither *gentil* nor *chic*, no matter how you look at it."

"I don't mind it in the least," remarked the voice indifferently.

"Only too well do I realize that," said Topper. "But consider the difference of our positions, if you will. To me you are nothing more nor less than a foot, five weird-looking toes protruding from the water. To you I am one complete body with all parts present and accounted for. In other words, all my cards are on the table."

"And there isn't an ace among them," commented the voice. "Furthermore, there are some parts of you I can't account for at all. Under any scheme of things. No matter how far I stretch my imagination."

"We won't go into that now," put in Topper hastily. "Anyway, I'd rather account for my own parts, if you don't mind. There is not one I would sacrifice with any degree of fortitude or comfort."

"How about that vast paunch?"

Mr. Topper leaned far over in an effort to conceal that object. This brought him face to face with the foot. From the water five long toes were wriggling up at him. Only a short time ago he had been soaping them with solicitude. The thought was decidedly disagreeable. Topper snapped back to his former position with alacrity. Why should he be ashamed of his stomach in the presence of such a foot?

"Merely a gentle declivity, my dear fellow," he replied with dignity. "A man must have some container in which to put his food."

"I don't," declared the voice proudly. "If I felt inclined I could eat my head off the while I snapped my fingers at my stomach."

"God grant you do not feel inclined," Topper retorted earnestly. "It's not a picture of charm. I think I should lose my reason if I had to watch you engaged in the doubly unpleasant operation of eating your head off while snapping your fingers at your stomach."

"Then you see what you're up against?"

"I suspect rather than see it," said Topper. "For all I know I might be up against Marcus Aurelius in the lighter vein."

"You don't know the half of it."

"Much less than that. Merely the beginning. Just a foot."

"If I made myself complete, one of us would have to leave this tub."

"That one would be me," said Mr. Topper. "I would go both gladly and promptly. Are you planning to be here long?"

"I'm ready to finish whenever you are," the voice answered agreeably. "We can let the rest of me go until some other time."

"We!" exclaimed Mr. Topper. "I hope to let the rest of you go forever."

"You can hardly do that, Topper, my fine fellow."

"This has been puzzling me," observed Topper. "If I let all the water out of this tub, what would become of the foot?"

"I could do one of two things," replied the voice in a considering tone. "I could shift it into a finger and let it slip down the drain or I could face you man to man."

"Try not to do either," urged Topper. "Can't you figure out something else?"

"Why, of course," continued the voice. "I could call the foot back into the fourth dimension, where the rest of me is at present."

"Good!" exclaimed Topper. "Why don't you do that? I can hardly leave an odd foot knocking about my bathroom, you know. It would upset the entire household. My cat might stray in and try to play with it—nibble its toes or something, although I'd hate to believe that Scollops would stoop so low."

"You put things rather gruesomely yourself," suggested the voice, "but I don't mind cats. Like 'em, in fact. Your cat can play with my toes and welcome to them. But no nibbling. Not that. I'm thinking about Mrs. Topper. What of her?"

"Yes," replied Topper blankly. "What of her. She would not appreciate an odd foot or any other odd part."

"Thank God she's yours," the voice declared. "You're welcome to her. But may I ask you, Topper, are you always so careful yourself of other men's wives?"

"Certainly," replied Mr. Topper, with a marked sense of uneasiness. "I always honor women."

"I like that," laughed the voice nastily, and Topper was sure now that he was in the presence of George Kerby's foot. "And I dare say crawling into bed with them is your idea of honoring them—the order of the Double Cross."

"I'm sure I don't know what you mean," hedged Mr. Topper.

"No?" continued the voice with increasing agitation. "You don't, eh? Innocent Topper. Chaste Topper. Bah! You bed presser." At this point the foot waved itself vindictively scarcely three inches from Mr. Topper's delicately quivering nostrils. "Well, mark me well, Topper," the voice continued. "If you don't keep your salacious old meat hooks away from my wife I'll drag you down into your grave before your time."

Mr. Topper was most unpleasantly impressed. He tried to bluff it out.

"Why, I didn't even know you had a wife," he managed to get out. "Mustn't be much company for her if you go around like that."

"I've a wife, all right," continued the voice, "or I did have a wife. Don't know where she is at the moment, but wherever she is it's ten to one she's raising particular hell. If I ever catch you two together—look!"

Topper looked and found himself confronted by two rows of

bared teeth. He had never seen teeth so shockingly displayed in all his life. Beside them the snarl of a tiger was amiability itself. It was by all odds Topper's most disconcerting moment. Those bared teeth grinning wickedly—a sight the most upsetting. Then suddenly they snapped with a click of horrid finality. Topper sprang from the tub. He could bear the situation no longer. Behind him the teeth clicked dangerously somewhere in the neighborhood of the nape of his neck.

"Remember!" gritted the pursuing teeth. "This is merely a friendly warning."

"Friendly," thought Topper frantically. "Oh, my good gracious God! What would it be like if he were furious? And all this on an empty stomach. It's too bad."

Throwing modesty to the winds, Topper dashed dripping from the bathroom, the blue-silk pajamas forgotten in his anxiety to seek the protection of his wife.

"Why, my dear!" exclaimed that lady, sitting up in bed. "I haven't seen you in such a state for years."

"You haven't seen me in such a state ever," replied Mr. Topper, snatching up his wife's bathrobe and tying its arms round his waist, giving to the garment a curious apron-like appearance, effective only when approached from the front.

At this moment a blood-curdling yell of defiance rang through the house. Mr. Topper spun around. His wife was unable to decide whether she was more shocked by what she saw than by what she heard. Both Topper and the yell were terrible. A moment later Félice, who had attempted to straighten up the bathroom, came tottering upon the scene.

"The towel," she announced tragically. "It agitates itself. It advances upon me and pushes out cries. Me, I am totally overthrown."

"So am I," agreed Mr. Topper, in his agitation turning his back upon the maid. "I *tombe* in ruins, myself."

For the first time Félice seemed to be aware of the presence of Mr. Topper. When she had thoroughly assimilated the rear view of the master of the villa she became even more vividly aware. For a moment it was difficult to tell whether she was going to fall in ruins or explode in mirth. Gradually an expression of pleased enlightenment overspread her face.

"A masque, perhaps?" she asked of Mrs. Topper.

"Does it look like a mask?" snarled Topper.

"But yes, m'sieu," said Félice.

Topper looked back and surveyed himself. Then he laughed bitterly.

"Perhaps you're right," he observed thoughtfully. "A tragic mask."

What Félice had seen of Topper, as fantastic as it was, served to keep her from losing her reason, for after one last inquiring, puzzled look, she demurely lowered her eyes and left the room with a coy flit of her own trim torso.

"What is it all about?" asked Mrs. Topper, trying not to look. "What are you doing that for, and who is being murdered in the hall?"

"I don't know," her husband replied distractedly. "It must have been an escaped parrot or some other wild Riviera bird."

V

ONE THING LEADS TO ANOTHER

The temps had started beau but had broken down on the way. An odd foot had thrown a monkey wrench into the workings of Mr. Topper's day. He was disgusted with the *temps*. Also he was disgusted with baths and bathtubs. He faithfully promised himself never to bathe again. He would never be sure any more of what he might find in that tub. Anything, any human part, was possible. Gloomily he sought the privacy of his own room. In his present attire this privacy was greatly to be desired by all concerned.

More through accident than design his sleeping quarters adjoined those of his wife. "The French would have it that way," he reflected as he passed through the door. "And a good idea, too, when given the right material."

He recalled the eloquent insinuations of Monsieur Grandon upon the occasion of his introducing them to the villa. The Frenchman had stood in the doorway between the two rooms, a hand extended invitingly toward each bed.

"*Regardez!*" he had exclaimed, a playful smile cracking the austerity of his blue-black beard. "*Monsieur est là et Madame est là.* What happiness!"

Mr. Topper, regarding the Frenchman, could almost see himself and his wife lying exhaustedly in their respective beds, yawning into the face of an uneventful night.

"It is of a simplicity desirable, is it not?" Monsieur Grandon had demanded. "One comes. One goes. At any given moment. It is accomplished."

Mr. Topper had refrained from pointing out to Monsieur Grandon that this constant dashing back and forth from bed to bed at any given moment might seriously overtax their failing strength.

"And the beds, m'sieu," here the *propriétaire* had raised his eyes to heaven in unholy ecstasy. "Of an *elasticité suprême—la, la!*"

This had been just a little too much for Mr. Topper. For some reason the world of meaning Monsieur Grandon managed to pack into that *"la, la!"* was unendurable.

"Let us not go further into the beds now," Topper had suggested a little primly.

"But no," the *propriétaire* had replied, somewhat shocked himself. "Later you shall both introduce yourselves into the beds, *et puis,* who knows?"

Topper had looked at Monsieur Grandon aghast, astounded.

"My God," he had thought, "is this little Frenchman bereft of all sense of delicacy, or is he merely trying to taunt me?"

Mrs. Topper had left the room.

While Topper was now radically rearranging his appearance, he was thoughtfully considering recent events, or as much of them as could be considered from the sketchy material at hand. This consisted of one detached and gesticulating foot, one pair of gnashing teeth, and one insufferably loquacious voice. Also one soul-splitting yell. All of these manifestations pointed to George Kerby. However, Mr. Topper was thinking more of what had not been seen, and which might at any moment be seen, than he was of what he had seen already—awful as that had been. Around him the air fairly tingled with currents of panic and calamity. He found himself wondering if Marion had drifted back to a low plane and had followed her husband to the Riviera. The possibility excited Topper. Life began to quicken. It retarded itself immediately at the thought of George and the Colonel and Mrs. Hart. What an open break that would be. Topper smiled in spite of himself. Almost any change would be agreeable to his present mode of existence.

His dressing completed, Topper, looking vastly more dignified, stepped into the presence of his wife.

"I hardly recognize you," she observed caustically. "You should go in for disguises and things."

"What do you mean by things?" he asked.

"Conduct that cannot be described," she answered quite comfortably. "All this has not been good for my dyspepsia."

She looked down and consulted the pages of a menu book. She became absorbed. This was one of Mary Topper's happier occupations. In its solemnity it was ritualistic. Each day before she arose it was her custom to take her dyspepsia out on a gastronomic hike along a path bristling with dangers. The very idea of what she might do to her dyspepsia if for a moment she relaxed her vigilance and yielded to some of the more alluring bypaths along the way or followed some of the seemingly innocent suggestions in her guide book, gave her much the same feeling as experienced by one cavorting dizzily through space on a hastily constructed but recklessly conceived scenic railway. She trembled pleasantly at the number of terrible things she could do to herself if she really let go her grip on the dietary rail; the effect of various spices, her reactions to a certain rich sauce, the hours of discomfort lurking in the depth of well seasoned gravy and the long, unrestful afternoons resulting from an overexposure to *pâté de foie, pâtisserie,* or *fromage.* And inevitably, after mentally passing through these hairbreadth escapes, Mrs. Topper, with unimaginative consistency and much to the disgust of her husband and Félice, would arise with some nice, wholesome, but perfectly spiritless menu firmly fixed in her mind. She had one so fixed this morning, and as Mr. Topper stood there looking at his wife, she glanced up and had the bad judgment to mention one of its principal items.

"How about a little *gigot* tonight?" she asked brightly.

Mr. Topper started and looked closely at his wife. The man had received a severe jolt. He was all at sea.

"How about a little what?" he asked uneasily.

"A little *gigot*," she answered almost coyly for her. "*Un petit gigot*, you know."

"I'm very much afraid I do know," replied Mr. Topper. "And just because you say it in French doesn't make it any nicer. I must confess, I'm surprised. As a matter of fact, I'm shocked."

"Oh, you never like anything," his wife complained petulantly.

"It's not a question of my likes or dislikes," he replied with dignity. "It's a matter of fitness. One does not propose such a thing at this hour of the morning. Suppose the servants should overhear?"

"Nonsense. They know all about it already. I tell them about it myself."

"You do!" exclaimed Mr. Topper, now thoroughly upset. "French servants don't need to be told. I had no idea you were so loose."

"What harm is there in a little *gigot*?" asked Mary Topper, looking penetratingly at her husband.

"Mary," he said, "I hate to appear in the light of a prude, especially before you. I'm not saying there's any harm in a little *gigot*. Many persons find it amusing. But it's not a thing to dwell on—to plan in cold blood."

"One can't very well make a secret of it," Mrs. Topper protested.

"Need one shout it from the housetops?"

"Nonsense!" snapped Mrs. Topper again. "Everybody knows about *gigot*."

"Undoubtedly," agreed Mr. Topper. "It is seldom out of people's minds, but nice people, especially ladies, don't make a practice of talking about it at the crack o' dawn, so to speak."

"Why not?" demanded his wife.

"If you can't see that for yourself, it would do no good for me to tell you." He paused a moment and scratched the back of his neck with a perplexed finger. Suddenly his expression cleared. "Will you kindly tell me just what in the world you mean by *gigot*?" he asked.

"You seemed to know all about it," said his wife.

"I thought I did," answered Topper. "I was afraid I did, but perhaps I was thinking of something else. Must have confused the word with *gigolo*. What does that queer sound you've been making mean, anyway?"

"Why, it simply means a leg of mutton," replied his wife. "One can't very well expect lamb in these peculiar French markets."

Topper's face was a study. The thing was much worse than he had expected.

"Did I travel at no little trouble and expense," he asked quietly, "did I uproot my life and manage some four thousand miles to leave Glendale and all its horrid works behind only to have a leg of mutton flaunted in my face? This is most discouraging. I thought we'd settled the lamb question a long time ago."

"I hoped all this travel might have made some difference," was the plaintive reply.

"So had I," said Topper. "I hoped it would make a vast difference in our daily diet. I hoped that over here you wouldn't be able to discover the old familiar things with which you have gradually beaten down my appetite for years. You can't change the nature of a chunk of meat merely by changing its name."

"But I only thought——" began Mrs. Topper.

"I know," he broke in on her. "You only thought. That's just the trouble. You thought out loud. If you'd said nothing about your damned *gigot,* I'd very likely eaten the beastly thing and been none the wiser. Suzanne and Félice, seasoning in relays, might have succeeded in disguising it. After all, Mary, as long we have to eat, we might as well bow to the inevitable and endeavor to make meals pleasant occasions—refreshing little interludes—rather than repetitious ordeals. We want to eat flesh, not to mortify it. Don't tell me about my food. Don't warn me about it—threaten me with it. I'd like to be surprised for a change. I have other things to think about than *gigots.*"

"What?" asked Mary flatly. "What on earth is there left for you to think about now that you've abandoned your banking? Surely not your past. I hope you're trying to forget that."

"What I think about, past, present, or future, is nobody's business," retorted Mr. Topper. "Because a man has stopped working it does not necessarily follow that he has stopped thinking. As a matter of fact, that's when he begins to think, when he begins to get a chance to think and look about him."

"I know what you look about at," said Mrs. Topper surprisingly, "that is, when you're on the beach."

"You do?" replied Mr. Topper, somewhat set down. "And what do I look at there, if I may ask?"

"More meat," replied Mrs. Topper with unexpected coarseness, "and it isn't a leg of lamb. I've seen that creature, too—almost all of her. You're getting senile. That's the trouble with you."

"I don't know what you're talking about, I'm sure," lied the good Topper.

"You know it so well you could draw it from memory," Mrs. Topper assured him.

"Draw what from memory?"

"It," said Mrs. Topper. "That disgraceful woman. Your naked friend."

"Mary," her husband replied accusingly, "I'm just beginning to learn that at heart you are an utterly coarse woman. I refuse to be drawn into any more of your vulgar discussions. Twice already this morning you have greatly shocked me."

"That's nothing to what you did to Félice when you so jauntily turned your back on her this morning."

"Fiddlesticks! Félice is used to it."

"What? You astound me."

"This is profitless," Topper broke out in an attempt to gain back a shred of his lost prestige. "If you ever mention a leg of lamb or mutton to me in any language I'll provide myself with a broadsword and hew the legs off of every sheep in France, and that goes for the pups, too. Failing that, I buy up all the rams and incarcerate them in a monastery so that the race will become extinct."

As her husband strode from the room Mary Topper did not appear at all impressed by the various things he was going to do. In fact, she was smiling slightly.

"And I believe I know what you thought *gigot* meant," she called after him.

"I don't give a hang if you do," he flung back. "You and your confounded *gigots*. Why don't you speak a language that has some sense to it?"

"That would have to be the sign language for you," his wife assured him.

"I don't hear you," he said. "What?"

"Oh, nothing. You wouldn't understand."

Topper, halfway down the stairs, paused and tried to think of some crushing and final retort. Failing abysmally in this, he continued downward in a state of high bad humor. That woman up there had the greatest knack of putting him in the wrong. It was uncanny. The morning was getting worse and worse. There was no telling where it would end. He hurried over to the buffet and poured himself a tot of cognac. While doing so he became aware of the presence of the maid Félice. He could feel her gaze resting on him. Worse than that. He could feel her gaze resting on a particular part of him. This was just too bad. He turned to meet her large, wondering eyes.

"M'sieu carries himself better now?" she inquired solicitously.

He very much feared he detected a smile lurking round the corners of her full red lips.

"I always carry myself well, Félice," he told her loftily. "It is not difficult."

"Quel homme!" breathed Félice admiringly as if to herself. *"Quel sang-froid! Merveilleux."*

"What's so *merveilleux?*" he demanded as he turned reluctantly to replace his empty glass. "What are you gaping at now?"

"Rien de tout," she replied with a shrug of her pretty shoulders. *"Une bagatelle, m'sieu."*

"Is that so!" said Topper, departing to the veranda. Then to himself, "These French trollops have more damned brass. It's their eyes. They're as eloquent as a couple of tongues."

He turned his own eyes to the little village stepping up the Esterels from the sea. Small white houses, occasionally a splash of color, red roofs and green, squatting cheerfully round the skirts of a great domed cathedral. On the shore the new Casino, its walls and its windows gleaming against the sun. Farther along the arc of the shore curved the more exclusive hotels—an expensive crescent studded with Americans and other rich. And far along the coast line lay the villas of the mighty dominated by the turrets of a château of much pleasure. Almost from Mr. Topper's feet the squalid, picturesque, gossiping little streets of the town casually meandered upward, paused for a breath in some white, quiet square where advertising posters and green shutters lent the only touch of color, then took up their way once more only to vanish entirely into farmlands and pine forests. Suddenly a burst of life. A high-powered motorboat looped out from the shore, then sped arrogantly along parallel with the beach, leaving noise and foam behind it. A few miles out, a scatter of sailing yachts, like white tents tugging in the wind, streamed through sun-washed waves. It was a quiet day. From far off came voices drifting. Planes droned in the sky. Topper's thoughts grew hazy. He had a pleasant feeling of nothingness, of remoteness and severed contacts. Yet also present was a vague sense of unease, an awareness of something waiting.

"*Déjeuner, m'sieu,*" came a soft voice behind him.

Topper turned slowly and followed the voice. He was wondering if he had taken his cognac altogether properly this morning. A few minutes later he had occasion to feel convinced that he had taken it most improperly as well as too lavishly. He did not regret this, for he felt the need of considerable extra courage and fortitude both of which were distilled deep in the heart of cognac—good cognac.

VI

UNSEEN AND UNINVITED GUESTS

Déjeuner, as cherished by the French, was a frightful misnomer for the orgy into which Cosmo Topper had plunged that customarily fragile and insipid repast. When he had first arrived in France he had for a while permitted this travesty of a breakfast to be placed before him. With growing but silent sedition he had observed inferior coffee being mixed on terms of equality with warm and dubious milk. With praiseworthy fortitude he had applied innumerable species of oversweetened *confiture* to toast that had died aborning. He had masticated with increasing gloom in the face of a smiling France, swallowed with obvious effort, then remained perfectly motionless as he wondered long and deeply. Then the little that had been before him being even less, if possible, he had arisen with a profound sensation of loss and bereavement. As he watched other people going through the same matutinal anticlimax with every visible evidence of enjoyment and animation he had the sensation of a man who alone out of a great multitude had missed the point of a joke, and who in an attempt to disguise this humiliating fact joins in the genuine laughter with false heartiness. To add verisimilitude to this craven deception, Topper would endeavor to leave his table with the air of a man replete with good things, of one saying to himself, "*Déjeuner* is a splendid institution. So quaintly French. For the life of me I can't figure out how I ever got along without it for all these years." But in his heart Mr. Topper knew quite well how he had been able to get along without it for all those years, and at last there came a day when he resolved to prolong that sacrifice indefinitely. To hell with what others thought and others ate. He was going to consume his breakfast instead of looking for it. After all, the French, as superficially amiable as they were, might be entirely wrong about this *déjeuner* business. Anyway, it was their breakfast and not his.

Accordingly, while still loving France either because of or in spite of its failings, Topper introduced into it an essentially American breakfast. To achieve this he completely revolutionized his manner and method of living. He took unto himself a villa, rented one—an operation, by the way, which has done more to promote premature grayness in France among friendly visitors and to change them to cynical and embittered critics than any other form of extortion, insult, and humiliation the supremely logical Latin mind has as yet conceived.

Emerging from this transaction spiritually disgruntled and financially bilked, Mr. Topper set about obtaining a supply of God-fearing coffee. This was eventually found after the exchange of innumerable francs. Eggs and bacon then entered into the scheme of things, new methods were introduced painfully to Suzanne, and eventually there came a day when, in solitary grandeur, Mr. Topper sat down to his own kind of breakfast beneath a roof that was temporarily his own. Both Félice, who served this sacrilege, and Suzanne, who had been forced to commit it, furtively watched Mr. Topper until assured that God was not going to slay him on their hands.

Mr. Topper had once labored under the mistaken impression that he disliked change, that he was a creature of fixed and inflexible habits and solidly set opinions. Then one day he discovered that all his life he had been terribly wrong and that his conduct up to date had been unnatural inasmuch as it had been based on a false assumption. Quite unexpectedly he discovered that he enjoyed change and reveled in disorder, that hitherto his opinions had not been opinions at all but the figments of a manacled imagination.

Marion Kerby had been instrumental in showing him the error of his ways. Topper changed, but in one thing he steadfastly refused to budge. Neither God nor man should for any considerable length of time interfere with either the composition or consumption of his breakfast. It had been ordained at the laying of the first egg conceived by hen and the first slice of bacon extracted from pig that the two should dwell in harmony together. And it was further ordained that their dwelling place should be a plate placed on a breakfast table for the nourishment and delight of man. Obviously this man could not have been of French extraction nor given a snap of his primeval phalanges for *petit déjeuner* or *café au lait.*

It was to such a breakfast that Mr. Topper anticipated sitting down. Things went no further than that for a time. The sitting section of the man was rudely arrested in its anticipatory and dignified descent and held grotesquely fixed in a position of suspended animation. Félice regarded the master of the villa with baffled eyes, then hurried from the room to tell Suzanne all about this, his latest prank. He was an *original,* that one, a veritable *type.*

"My dear chap," protested a voice through the small of Mr. Topper's back, "isn't this rather high-handed? Don't remain poised like that. Think of how it must be for me."

"Think of how it must be for me," gasped Topper, "to be rebuked by my own chair."

Nevertheless, he immediately reversed the operation of his internal jack and elevated himself with more celerity than grace. Hoping that there was, perhaps, something a little curious about that individual chair and that the others were normal, Topper selected another one and was about to occupy it when this time his descent was interrupted even more peremptorily.

"Hold hard, Topper," said a decided voice. "Take it away from me. Here I sit and here I stay. Scram."

As greatly as Mr. Topper objected to the use of the expression "scram," he felt that under the circumstances it eloquently conveyed an idea he very earnestly desired to put into practice. Accordingly he selected still a third chair into which he virtually plunged his body. A soft giggle greeted his arrival, his stomach was tenderly squeezed by two unseen arms—endearments which did more to speed his departure from that chair than had the other two harsher admonitions.

"Don't go," pleaded a woman's voice which he recognized as belonging to Mrs. Hart. "I liked you so much as you were."

"You wouldn't have liked me long," Topper assured her.

"Come! Come!" came the unmistakable voice of Colonel Scott. "None of that, Mrs. Hart, if you please. It's only breakfast yet, or, at least, it's supposed to be breakfast. I wonder if that is as far as we'll get. I've been sitting here all morning watching him swill down cognac."

"It's my cognac, isn't it?" Topper demanded.

"Rather let us say, it is *our* cognac," replied the Colonel. "One for all and all for one, Topper. How's that?"

"Not so good, Colonel," Topper answered. "You mean, all on one and one for all. That's the way it always was, wasn't it?"

"I will say, Topper, you were always a good provider. We expect no less now."

While this little exchange was in progress Mr. Topper was endeavoring to occupy the fourth and last chair at his own breakfast table. For his enterprise his ear was delicately nibbled and he received a slight pinch in an especially selected spot.

"Remove that, my old," said the well remembered voice of Marion Kerby.

A pair of coarse, cynical laughs which Topper would have preferred not to hear, came from across the table as Topper once more wearily raised his body. He was now in the position of a man unable to sit down at his own breakfast table. Marion's voice had thrilled him, but the situation was working him up to a pitch. He was in no mood for tender thoughts. His breakfast was involved, seriously endangered. For a moment he stood looking undecidedly at the table; then, his rugged New England ancestry overcoming his natural inclination to abandon the unequal struggle, he dragged a chair from the wall, placed it at the table well away from the others, and deposited himself in it with a defiant plop.

"Well, that's very much better, I should say," commented the Colonel. "Should have thought of it in the first place."

"Kindly step to hell," said Mr. Topper, wearily mopping his forehead. "That's all, just step to hell."

"Your language," admonished the voice of the foot in the tub, which could be none other than George Kerby's. "And your actions. What has come over you, man? First you invade my tub, then you sit on my lap. Great God, it's enough to drive a man crazy!"

"I wouldn't have minded either in the least," said the voice of the languid Mrs. Hart. "Especially the tub. Mr. Topper, I'll let you know the next time I'm making a tub of it."

"Let me advise you to do no such thing," came Marion Kerby's voice, cold, deliberate, and low with fury. "Keep your ectoplasm out of his tub, or I'll tear it to shreds."

"Here! Here!" put in George Kerby. "What's that man to you? What do you care about his tub and who goes in it? He's none of your business whatsoever. Understand that? And as for yourself, if I ever catch you even near his tub, I'll drag him down through the pipes."

Involuntarily Topper shuddered at the picture of himself being elongated through the pipes.

"I suppose it has not even occurred to you," he observed evenly, "that I might prefer to bathe entirely alone."

"That doesn't matter," said Marion Kerby. "Not one little bit. If we feel like it, all of us will bathe all over you whether you like it or not. And that goes for Oscar, too."

At this moment Félice entered bearing a tray laden with eggs, bacon, toast, and a large pot of coffee. Topper looked pleadingly from one to the other of the four apparently unoccupied chairs, but all to no avail. No sooner had the maid placed the tray on the table than its contents were literally whisked away from under Topper's slightly elevated nose. The coffee pot was snatched in one direction, while the bacon and eggs took another, but the latter changed direction several times, as if greedy hands were contending for possession, tugging the plate back and forth. Finally the eggs parted company together with the bacon and disappeared amazingly into the air, small portions of both dropping untidily to the tablecloth. The toast was acting oddly for plain ordinary toast—for any kind of toast, in fact. Four crisp pieces facing the four empty chairs were being snapped into nothingness. Mr. Topper, reaching for the fifth and last piece, experienced the unpleasant sensation of having it snatched from his fingers by an unseen hand.

All this was somewhat trying to observe, especially when the coffee pot became violently agitated in the air as if a determined dispute for its possession were silently in progress. Both Topper and Félice watched the antics of the coffee pot with fascinated eyes.

"There'll be quite enough coffee for all," said Topper under his breath. "Put the damn thing down. I'll get some cups."

He hastened to the buffet and returned with four extra cups, which he placed before the vacant chairs.

"Let me pour," he said beseechingly. "Just for the sake of appearances. You'll drive my maid mad."

"*M'sieu,*" babbled Felice, "*regardez là.* The breakfast, it eats himself."

Suzanne stood in the doorway with sheer horror deep in her eyes.

"Go away," said Mr. Topper wearily, "and eat yourselves. I'm too busy to explain, but everything is quite *tranquille.* Have no *peur.* And bring back all the bacon and eggs in the house—and toast."

"Plain bread will do," cried a ravenous voice.

"Rashers of bacon," shouted George Kerby, his voice choked with food.

"And make it snappy, my full-bodied wench," called the Colonel in his army voice. "*Bien vite,* or I'll haunt your sheets."

This last remark retarded rather than hastened the French girl's flight. She knew her essential English thoroughly. She had decorated more than one American villa. Pausing at the kitchen door she looked archly back at Topper, whom she held directly responsible for all these odd affairs. Had he not been acting strangely all morning?

"*Comment on est gentil, m'sieu,*" she murmured demurely. "*Est-elle une promesse?*"

"And while we're on the subject of keeping away from tubs and things," Mrs. Hart remarked lazily, "you, my good Colonel, had better keep away from that French trollop's sheets. We don't want any trouble at all, if trouble can be avoided."

Mr. Topper, in attempting to discover just how much remained of his breakfast, found to his disgust that there were no remains. Apart from a slight untidiness—a few crumbs—it was as if his breakfast had never been. Topper cast the chairs a look of supreme distaste. He was a hungry man, and he strongly objected to having his breakfast devoured before his very eyes.

"Well, at any rate," came the complacent voice of George Kerby, "I didn't do so badly on that grab." Here a few crumbs dropped to the table as if finger tips were being delicately brushed. "Are there no finger bowls in this establishment, Topper? After all, we are your guests, you know."

Topper laughed shortly.

"Even Einstein couldn't make that theory click," he said. "First you crowd yourself into my bathtub, then, not satisfied with that, you go shrieking through the house making nervous wrecks of everybody, including myself. After that gracious little display, you hurry downstairs and call in your gang. You take my breakfast table, and then you snatch my breakfast in the most revolting manner, and now, by God, you demand finger bowls. Listen, the sooner I see the last of you——"

"Pull in, my stout," interrupted the voice of Marion Kerby. "You haven't seen the first of us yet, nor the best. For instance, *regardez là.*"

The table was suddenly adorned by a pair of stunning legs which Topper also felt sure he recognized. These legs, drifting up to nothingness, executed a few clever tap movements, then slowly faded from view.

"And that's just for instance," continued the voice. "Have you seen enough, my gross?"

"Quite," her gross replied hypocritically because of George Kerby. "Let us have no more obscenities."

"Then you're easily satisfied," observed the voice of the Colonel cynically. "That's just where I begin."

"Why, Colonel!" exclaimed Mrs. Hart. "You petrify me."

"Marion," said George Kerby, and his voice was far from pleasant, "I would suggest that you lower your visibility considerably. You're not the mascot of the troupe, and your legs are not public property."

"No, they're strictly my private business," replied the voice of the legs.

"I'd like to twist them off," said George Kerby.

Mr. Topper closed his eyes on this picture. These spirits had evidently descended to even a lower plane. They were coarser than he had ever known them, and less restrained. Even the Colonel's invariable suavity had become somewhat roughened. Marion's next remark confirmed him in his opinion.

"Then why don't you materialize," she suggested unemotionally, "and cut your silly throat from ear to ear in the presence of us all. You deserve to die at least a couple of times, and we deserve to see you."

"I'm just waiting for you to materialize," her husband answered angrily, "and then I'm going to beat the hide off you."

"You'll get no hide off me," was the prompt retort.

"Please. Please," Mr. Topper protested feebly. "I hate to interfere, but, after all, this is my breakfast table. Don't make a brawl of it."

"Then wouldn't it be expedient to have something placed on the table?" suggested the Colonel.

"I could toy with a clutch of eggs myself," Mrs. Hart remarked in her casual voice. "My stomach, if you'll pardon me, is in a perfect frenzy."

"Why don't you all go away?" demanded George Kerby petulantly. "I found him first."

"You can have what's left of him when we're through," Marion remarked in a chilly voice. "Had quite enough of my legs, had he? Very well, we'll see all about that. I'll teach him how a gentleman should treat a lady."

Topper, with a feeling of keen apprehension, realized that Marion was in one of her mean, unreasonable moods than which there could be no meaner nor more unreasonable.

"Marion," he said politely, "I had no intention of suggesting that I had seen enough of your legs. I was merely trying to convey to you that the time was hardly propitious for their further contemplation."

It was a dangerous speech, and it had unpleasant results.

"What's that?" demanded George Kerby, hoarse with rage. "What do you mean by that? Are you trying to date my wife up on me right here before us all?"

"What did I tell you?" asked Topper hopelessly. "One has but to talk to you, and off he goes merrily on his way to murder. He almost accomplished it once."

"Now, listen here, Topper," cried the man's voice passionately. "Right here and now let's settle this situation. You want to keep well and healthy, don't you?"

"I hope you understand, George," his wife's voice cut in, "that if you do anything to Topper, anything serious, that is, anything definite and final, we will have him with us permanently. Would it not be wiser to let him live to an overripe and doddering old age beyond all possibility of competition? It seems to me that you should take very good care of Topper."

Mr. Topper listened to this conversation with a feeling of growing discomfort.

"I can make him suffer like hell in the meantime," said George's voice musingly. "I could cripple him."

"Yes," agreed Marion, "you might do that. You could tear off parts of him from time to time as a sort of warning."

Topper was profoundly moved.

"I could do worse than that," the man's voice replied with an unpleasant laugh. "Much."

"You mean worse for Topper?"

"Oh, very much worse for Topper," the voice continued gloatingly. "About the worst thing that could happen to a body to my way of thinking."

"No doubt it would also be to Topper's," said the woman's voice. "Both of you have rotten ways of thinking."

"You don't even know what I'm thinking about."

"I hope not. But look at Topper. He knows. See how pale he is."

She spoke the truth. Topper was pale indeed. More than that, he was sweating pale drops of perspiration. Like wan, lackluster jewels they crowned his forehead.

"Dear me," he protested weakly. "I wish you wouldn't discuss what you might do to me and mine as if I were not present. I find it most distressing."

"That's a good idea," spoke up the Colonel. "Let's think of all the things we could do to Topper without quite killing him, and the one who hits on the worst wins a bottle of his best wine."

"And I lose, whoever wins," Topper commented bitterly.

"I win the wine," declared George Kerby, "because I've already thought up the worst thing that could happen to Topper."

"Why don't you play another game?" Mr. Topper suggested. "Why don't you see who can keep quiet the longest or go away the farthest? I hope you all win."

"Now, Cosmo," came the mockingly pained voice of Marion Kerby. "You don't seem at all pleased to have us with you again, and I had thought it was going to be so different. Why, we've hardly done a thing to you yet in comparison with what we might do, or probably will do. I, for one, feel a bit depressed by this reception— saddened, I might almost say. Not having a handkerchief, I'll have to use part of this tablecloth. Pardon me, everybody, but I'm not made of stone exactly. I'm not a great slab of granite. I can't chip sledge hammers. I'm extremely thin skinned. Nobody——"

"Oh, for God's own sake," broke in Mr. Topper unfeelingly, as he watched one end of the tablecloth making delicate little dabs in the air. "Don't go on so. You're so thin skinned you're actually transparent. I can see clean through you."

"Go on, George!" cried Marion's voice. "Do what you said you were going to do. I don't care one little damn now. Tear the beggar asunder."

Topper caught a momentary flash of himself flying in all directions, of his various members decorating the Riviera. He closed his eyes on this, too. He found it difficult to decide whether Marion was more to be feared in one of her shockingly playful moods or when she was blindly ferocious. She played both to perfection.

"Let's all quiet down now," came the surprisingly amicable voice of George Kerby. "Let's pull ourselves compactly together and pray for food. We don't want to have any trouble here in Topper's own home."

"Speak for yourself," snapped Marion. "I want some trouble here. I want a lot of trouble."

"Here comes something much better," Mrs. Hart's voice cried out excitedly. "Clap eyes on that, Colonel. What a delicious looking tray! My mouth fairly slavers."

This time, upon the appearance of Félice bearing a fresh and more abundant supply of food, Mr. Topper made a better showing. He had made up his mind not to be caught napping again. If he had to fight like an animal for his food, he was fully prepared to do his best. He would claw and snatch to the last crumb. And that was almost literally what he had to do to salvage the modest scrap of breakfast he did. His guests were prepared to go even farther than himself in their eagerness to provide their apparently famished but unseen bodies with nourishment.

Félice, who loved a good frolic of almost any nature as well if not better than the next, was startled in spite of herself. She could not understand how Mr. Topper could be in so many places at once. The affrighted girl was rocked as if in the grip of a gale. Once or twice an indignant protest escaped her lips as if undue liberties were being taken with things other than Mr. Topper's breakfast.

Even when he returned to his chair with the spoils of conquest, Mr. Topper was not at all sure of his success. He distinctly heard someone breathing interestedly over his shoulder. It gave him an eerie sensation—the awareness of hidden eyes peering consideringly into the contents of his plate.

"That's a nice little bit," said the absorbed voice of Marion Kerby. "I think I'll take that one just to prove I've forgiven you."

Whereupon one of Topper's choicest pieces of bacon slid from his plate and halved itself in the air. Its ultimate disappearance was followed by a distinct click, as of teeth.

"How unnecessary," thought Mr. Topper.

It is surprising he did not think more about this weird breakfast and the strange things that had come to pass at it. The truth of the matter was that Mr. Topper had not been given much opportunity to do any thinking at all. He had been far too deeply involved himself. Astounding events occur with such a disarming air of naturalness that it makes one feel as if one had especially ordered them. One scarcely realizes their true nature until after they are over.

His friends had been changed but not improved. It was merely that the scope and effectiveness of their antisocial activities had been increased. One of these activities, although scarcely antisocial, was now in progress. An uninitiated observer would have gained the impression that Félice had been suddenly endowed with miraculous powers which she was using rather flightily. To the consternation of Mr. Topper she had elevated her fine French body about three feet above and parallel with the floor. There she remained for a moment alluringly poised on the wings of the fair Riviera morning.

"Leave her alone, Colonel," Mrs. Hart admonished. "If you don't put her down I'll walk out on you."

But the Colonel, having gorged himself, was now playful. Slowly but gracefully Félice was lowered to the matting, and her skirt, her inviolate *jupe*, was snatched from her waist. Félice, beside herself, was now only in step-ins and stockings. She looked greatly improved that way. The *jupe*, unoccupied, fluttered mysteriously in the air, then flopped down by the figure of its erstwhile tenant. Bereft of her skirt Félice was also bereft of her reason. That fine fortitude that had stood her in such good stead on other similar occasions forsook her now. To be unable to put up even a formal resistance seriously upset her ethics. Then again, when capitulating to a visible assailant one had something to go on, whereas with this one God alone knew what he looked like or what he was trying to prove. Whoever he was he seemed to have no definitely conceived purpose other than general low behavior. Félice tossed her fortitude into the discard along with her *jupe*. She began to scream in the most shockingly convincing manner. In the midst of this frightful noise she turned quite white and, so far as Mr. Topper could tell, died. The distracted man sprang from his chair and knelt down beside the stricken maid.

He was in this compromising position when Mrs. Topper appeared. The man glanced up at his wife and, finding no comfort there, glanced back at what seemed to him interminable leagues of step-ins and silk stockings. He was stunned by the amount of sheer leg that this woman had. The silence in the room was fraught with accusations. He was unable to let it continue.

"I just got here," he observed rather inanely.

"So did I," said Mrs. Topper. "It seems in the nick of time."

"What do you mean?" Topper demanded indignantly.

"Need we go into that?" asked Mrs. Topper, delicately arching her eyebrows.

"It's not that," explained Topper in a hopeless voice.

"Then if it isn't that," observed his wife, "you must have taken up murder, which is, if anything, a trifle worse. What is her skirt doing where it is instead of where it should be?"

"It flopped there," said Mr. Topper.

"A pretty picture," commented Mrs. Topper, considering the skirt. "It just happened to flop there. For all you cared, I fancy, it might just as well have been hanging from the chandelier. And, by the way, if you are interested in whether or not she is regaining consciousness I would suggest that you shift your eyes to her face instead."

This was a little too much for Topper, but there was still more to come. When he attempted to rise Félice, opening her eyes suddenly, flung her strong arms round his neck, and with a Gallic twist to the half-Nelson, tossed him easily onto his back. For a few moments Mr. Topper, stunned, lay down by his maid and stared up at the ceiling, upon which were many Riviera flies and a fine showing of mosquitoes recuperating from their night's revelry.

As if fearing another and more brutal attack, Mr. Topper sacrificed his dignity and rolled rapidly across the room. Then slowly he rose to his feet. Somewhere in the room a woman's voice was giggling, and it was not Mrs. Topper's. That good lady was watching the performance of her husband with detachment.

"Well, I must say," she admitted, "you move with surprising rapidity for a man of your age and bulk."

"What do you mean, my age and bulk?" he flung at her. "I'm as good a man as any along the Riviera, and I'll prove it quickly enough if you pull any more of those wisecracks."

"You almost did," was all Mrs. Topper said, but it was quite enough.

Topper, whose wits were still numb from the various shocks of the morning, could think of no reply to this. However, he could think of something to do. He gave the *jupe* of Félice an unreasonable kick and marched from the room.

"I shall expect an explanation," his wife called after him.

He laughed sardonically and collected his hat and stick.

"It would drive you mad," he said.

With a set face he departed in the direction of the village.

VII

A Self-tipping Hat

"And as for the rest of you," Topper shouted furiously but inadequately across the length of his garden, "I hope you choke."

"On what?" a voice at his shoulder promptly asked. "Man cannot choke on air alone."

"I wish to God you could, Kerby," Topper told the voice with the defiant inelegance of a baited man. He turned away.

Mrs. Topper, not understanding the reason for her husband's fervent hope, and thinking he was flinging insults at the servants, decided that the man had lost what little was left of his wits. Not so Monsieur Louis, who was still hot at it, encouraging his garden. Once more the redoubtable head popped up. With the deadly accuracy of an eagle's claw, a nervous hand seized Topper.

"Arrest you!" cried the Frenchman.

"For what?" demanded Topper, who by this time was surprised by no turn of fate.

"I near the end, *mon ami*," breathed Monsieur Louis.

At the moment Topper was not in the least sorry. The sooner Monsieur Louis came to a complete and definite end the better. However, he remained *gentil*.

"Not, I trust, before you have had your play," he remarked.

At the mention of play Monsieur Louis brightened shamelessly. "But yes, Monsieur Toppaire," he replied. "First I arrive at a finish, is it not? Then I begin to play."

"You're just like some friends of mine," commented Topper. "They arrived at a finish and then they began to play. They've been doing it ever since, at the expense of others. Monsieur Louis, I do not like these friends. No."

Monsieur Louis was at a loss concerning the true inwardness of Mr. Topper's remarks. He never had an opportunity to find out, for at that moment Mr. Topper appeared to spin round on his heels. From somewhere close at hand a woman's voice addressed him heatedly.

"You know that free-for-all Félice, don't you?" demanded the voice.

"I didn't know she was that," Topper got out.

"Never mind," the voice went on. "If you even so much as look cross-eyed at that jade I'll chase you clean out into the middle of that damn Mediterranean and then sink you. So help me God!"

"You, M'sieu, and Félice?" inquired the little Frenchman in a low voice, quivering with emotion. "She is good, that one—*voluptueuse.*"

"What do you know about it?" Topper demanded ill-temperedly, but did not stay to be told.

As he hastened down the road Monsieur Louis's bright eyes were darting from bush to bush in quest of one who could be none other than Madame Toppaire herself. So Félice was up to her old tricks, was she? It was of a convenience for the wealthy American visitor. He might prolong his stay to spend many good American dollars in their little French village. It was of a rightness. All the world would be well pleased save Madame Toppaire. She alone would not be elated. It was that Félice lacked discretion. That would come with the years. The little Frenchman thoughtfully shrugged his shoulders, then hurled himself at his garden, a complete picture of Félice at her best dwelling in his eyes.

In the meantime Topper was stepping diligently over yards and yards of drying fishing nets extending across his path. Innumerable dogs, attracted by memories of what the nets had once contained, did not speed his progress. To avoid a net and a dog at the same time required both quick decision and prompt action. Once he almost fell upon his fish-assailed nose. He had been pushed by an unseen companion whom he cursed passionately under his breath. The fact was, Mr. Topper was a very much haunted man. If anything, he was overhaunted. His steps were dogged by low-plane spirits. He realized this more and more as he took his way towards the center of the village, skirting sidewalk cafés already performing their convivial functions, and crossing streets wherein motor cars hooted French maledictions at every moving object, and the deeper tones of a passing machine gave notice of the American invasion.

When he turned into the main thoroughfare of the town in which were situated the *bureau de poste* and some of the more important shops and cafés that would never have been in existence had Columbus remained at home, the fact that he was not unaccompanied was most unpleasantly borne in on him. He was being given aid in a rather singular manner. His hat was tipping itself of its own accord, but with marked courtesy, at various passers-by. Perfect strangers, desirous of taking no chances, were returning his involuntary salutations with puzzled, back-thinking expressions in their eyes.

Mr. Topper began to feel exceedingly foolish, especially when he realized that people were turning and staring wonderingly after his dignified, well tailored back. This inclusive greeting meant little to the Frenchmen he met, for a Frenchman is by nature an enthusiast at the game and will flip a snappy béret upon the slightest provocation. A friendly smile will turn him temporarily into a hand-wringing symbol of welcome. Not so with others. Many persons not unreasonably object to being saluted by an individual unknown to them. This is especially true of certain gentlemen when accompanied by certain ladies. And because they realize that their escorts will become angry enough for two, women have trained themselves rigidly not to be offended when pleasantly accosted by strangers of the opposite sex. So well have they succeeded that it is yet to be recorded that a woman has been anything other than secretly pleased upon the reception of such friendly overtures.

Accordingly, Mr. Topper, in the course of his walk, was the recipient of numerous hostile as well as covertly appreciative glances.

One Southern gentleman had the bad taste to ask him who the hell he was taking his hat off to, and when Mr. Topper in his irritation answered, "I hope you don't suspect me of taking it off to what you have in tow," this same Southern gentleman made a chivalrous Southern pass at Mr. Topper's eye. But the blow never landed. Mr. Topper's companions might have been ill-advisedly helpful, but they had no intention of permitting others to take any liberties with his person. That was sacred to them. Mr. Topper had the satisfaction of seeing the Southern gentleman double up with a gasp of sharp anguish while his hands solicitously clutched at his Southern stomach. Synchronously with this involuntary but nevertheless grotesque action the assaulted gentleman's hat—a panama, especially purchased for the trip—was whisked from his head and tossed negligently to the street which had been traversed by horses as well as automobiles. This second misfortune, following so swiftly on the heels of the first, brought the Southern gentleman erect as if touched by a magic wand. That hat, that panama, meant much to him.

Now, it is an obvious conclusion that a man trying to decide whether to hit another man in the eye and then to rescue a new but slightly soiled panama from the street or to rescue the panama first and then come back and hit the other man in the eye is thwarted in both ambitions. While Mr. Topper slipped through his fingers, the Southern gentleman, standing in deep abstraction, watched with morbid eyes the completion of his hat's ruin as an automobile—an antiquated car at that—jounced blithely over it.

"Don't worry, Toppy, old scout," said George Kerby's voice in his ear. "We're not going to let anything happen to you."

"Thanks a lot," muttered Topper. "Your hearts, wherever they are, I'm sure are in the right place, but don't call me Toppy, and for the love of God keep your hands from my hat. The situation is most embarrassing."

Topper spoke through stiff lips. He feared that people would think he had taken up talking to himself in addition to his other eccentricities.

"Don't mind about your hat," whispered Marion. "We'll take care of that. We'll make it seem automatic. Only, of course, we don't know your friends from Adam. We'll just tip the damn thing at everyone, and that will make you popular."

"It will make me notorious," stiff-lipped Topper. "Why do you always insist on being so all-fired helpful?"

"We like you, Topper," came the Colonel's voice. "You're a real pal. And we feel for you because you're alone in a foreign land. From now on we're going to see that you get the best of the breaks."

"Even if we have to break your neck," added George.

Topper groaned. There was no escape. He continued down the street. This time he altered his tactics. Whenever he felt his hat preparing to leave his head he would reach up quickly in an endeavor either to hold it on or, at least, to give the appearance of tipping it himself. But his companions were too quick for him. When Topper's right hand shot up the hat would dart to the left. When he attempted to clutch it with his left hand the agitated object would cleverly dodge to the right. As a result of this, Topper gave the appearance of a man who for no apparent reason was diligently juggling his hat. Realizing the futility of his efforts he abandoned them and allowed the hat to have its way. There was nothing else to do about it.

"Be ready," he heard Marion whisper excitedly. "Here comes an important-looking person. Make this tip a good one."

As the important person passed by, Mr. Topper's hat flew off with a particularly graceful swoop, and the important person, in his anxiety to be equally courteous, nearly stabbed himself in the groin with his stiffly starched French beard. Greatly unnerved by this encounter, Mr. Topper paused in the cooling shade cast by the Byzantine mass of Notre Dame de la Victoire to catch a quiet breath and to consider ways and means. This sort of thing could not go on. He had lost his reputation already. He feared now that he might lose his liberty as well. But even here, in the shade of the great cathedral, his hat continued to bob up and down with industrious rapidity.

While this bobbing was in progress Mr. Topper noticed a tall, gloomy-looking individual watching him intently. The man had actually stopped and was standing with his gaze riveted on Mr. Topper's head. Every time the hat sprang to life the gentleman started visibly, then drew a little nearer, as if under a spell. Topper felt strongly inclined to take to his heels, but it was already too late. The gloomy man approached and addressed himself to Mr. Topper.

"I trust you will pardon me," he said, "but for the life of me I can't figure out how you do it."

"It's quite simple," replied Topper for lack of anything better to say.

"I dare say," responded the man. "The best things usually are. Would you mind doing it again?"

"Greatly," gasped the distracted Topper, but he had no choice in the matter.

Pleased by the attention their real pal was receiving, Mr. Topper's unseen companions treated the appreciative gentleman to a special display. This time the hat twirled rapidly round on its brim on the crown of Mr. Topper's head. Although the gloomy gentleman had been prepared for something he had not been prepared for as much of it as this. He stepped back a pace or two and regarded Mr. Topper with alarmed eyes.

"It's astounding," he said at last in a low voice. "Will you do it just once more?"

"Certainly not," replied Mr. Topper.

But the hat did do it once more, only this time it rose high in the air, then descended jauntily on Mr. Topper's head. This small-sized miracle was sufficient to cause several other persons to stop to observe. Soon Topper and the gloomy gentleman formed the center of an interested little group. Mr. Topper will never forget the embarrassment of standing there watching several dozen pairs of bewildered eyes moving slowly up and down as his hat rose and fell.

"Merveilleux!" a voice broke from the crowd.

"Un drôle de corps, ce type-là," observed another.

Mr. Topper flinched. Someone had referred to him as an odd fish. He objected to this, especially when he had no control over the circumstances that made him appear so in the eyes of this Frenchman.

"Is it your ears?" asked the gloomy gentleman.

Mr. Topper could not trust himself to speak. He merely shook his head.

"I could have sworn it was your ears," the man continued, his disappointment written large on his face. "Then you must have muscles in your scalp."

Mr. Topper was upset by this revolting suspicion.

"I am in no sense abnormal," he muttered.

"But, my dear sir, you must be," protested the gloomy gentleman. "You must be almost supernatural, or else you would not be able to accomplish such marvelous results."

"I'm glad they strike you as such," said Mr. Topper bitterly. "I think they are damned childish."

"Not at all," the man assured him. "You are far too modest. Is it possible you can flip your spine, perhaps?"

"How do you mean flip?" Mr. Topper got out as the hat crashed down on his head, completely covering his eyes. "Adjust the damn thing," he muttered aside. "I'm in total darkness."

"I don't know," continued the man, looking even gloomier. "It was merely a guess."

"Neither do I," said Mr. Topper. "Why do you ask so many ridiculous questions? Can't you see I'm busy? You should be satisfied just to watch."

"It's fine," admitted the man wistfully, "but I'd like to know. Used to be pretty good at that sort of thing myself."

"I wish you were doing it now instead of me," said Topper earnestly.

"I'd enjoy it," breathed the man.

"You would," remarked Topper disgustedly as his hat took to flight. "But I don't. It bores me."

"But aren't you doing it of your own free will?"

Topper laughed crazily.

"Do you think I would make an ass of myself for fun?" he demanded. "I'm not playful. This is being done very much against my will. If you'd like to know, I'm not doing it at all."

"Then what's doing it?"

"That hat is."

"What! The hat? How?"

"I don't know," answered Topper, feeling his grip slipping. "Can't you see I'm in trouble? Don't ask me any more questions. I can't answer and I won't answer. Let us say it's a disease—curvature of the hat, convulsions of the scalp, frenzy of the brain—anything!"

"I wish I could catch the hang of it," murmured the man, once more wistful. "It would make a great hit back home with the boys. Just think of walking down the street on Sundays with the kiddies and the little lady and surprising all the boys."

"You think of it," retorted Topper. "I don't like to. I'm busy surprising perfect strangers—persons I never saw before and who I hope never to see again."

For a moment Topper looked almost pityingly upon the gloomy gentleman. An overrich person from South America stepped from the crowd and slipped a fifty-franc note into the haunted man's hand. This was a shade too thick for Topper. In an excess of rage he reached up and, snatching the hat just before it left his head, dashed it to the ground.

"*Malheureux!*" muttered a voice in the crowd.

"*Quel dommage!*" exclaimed a second.

"*Ciel!*" shouted another. "*Regardez, bien vite! Il est vivant, ce chapeau.*"

The hat indeed was living, living to the utmost while it had the chance. No sooner had it struck the pavement than it bounded back and pounced upon Mr. Topper's head.

"Don't do that," said a rebuking voice in his ear. "Don't be childish."

Topper no longer gave a rap whether people thought he was talking to himself or not. He turned sharply and addressed space.

"Childish!" he exclaimed. "My God, I like that! You've made an old man of me. Could anything conceivably be more peurile, more inane, more off balance than what you've been doing to me?"

"Topper," said Marion Kerby, "you are God's gift to France. Through us you are amusing her children."

"I don't give a damn about that," he retorted. "I know you're making a blithering idiot of me. As it is I feel like falling down in the gutter and groveling like a—a———"

"Like a fish," suggested Marion.

"Fish don't grovel," objected George. "Worms do that."

"And cowards," added the Colonel.

"Listen," said Mr. Topper, "I don't care to discuss the matter. I'll grovel like an eel if I want to."

"How quaint," put in Mrs. Hart.

"Go right ahead," said George Kerby unfeelingly. "Do your groveling. I'd like to see you."

"No," declared the Colonel, "we must take steps. And promptly. Topper needs diversion. We all need diversion. All work and no play. Grab his other arm, George. Now, all together."

Before Topper had time to realize what was being done to him, he felt himself seized by either hand and dragged through the admiringly respectful crowd.

"He parts," said an awed voice, and Topper feared the man was literally correct.

"All is ended," quoth another, and Topper felt that he, too, had spoken the truth.

With the upper half of his body greatly in advance of the rest of him, a position which gave his legs a peculiar dangling appearance, Mr. Topper was dragged down the street. And if some people thought it an unusual way for a man to walk, Topper could not help it. It was not a matter of choice with him, although he did his best to lessen the oddness of his position by waving his legs frantically in an effort to get them as nearly as possible under his body. But he never succeeded in catching up with himself. The impression he gave was that of a racing bicycle rider, an impassioned bicycle rider, yet one who was deriving scant pleasure from his violent exertion.

"Listen," he said beseechingly. "Won't you please just throw me away anywhere—it doesn't matter where—and call it a day?"

"Topper," replied George Kerby, a trifle winded himself, "we're with you to the end."

"And that," panted Topper, "won't be long now."

VIII

Casual Conversation at the English Bar

"Phew!" exclaimed the Colonel after several blocks had been covered in the manner described. "This Topper party is no piece of fluff. What we need is a drink."

"For once, Colonel, you're right," agreed Mr. Kerby. "And I know the exact spot. Topper goes there often."

"But of my own accord," gasped Topper. "That makes all the difference. Don't drag me in there like this."

"Oh, we've got to hurry," said Marion. "Drag him along, George. Faster, if possible."

As a result of this callous adjuration Mr. Topper's body made an angle of forty-five degrees with the earth's surface. This, it must be admitted, is an arresting way for a body to perform. And it was in this manner and at this angle that a few minutes later Mr. Topper scooted through the door of the English Bar and curved up with what one might call a swan-like swoop in front of the bar itself.

"Good-morning, Peter," wheezed Mr. Topper, hoping to divert the bartender's mind from the singular manner of his entrance. "What's all this I hear about the Prince of Wales?"

Peter seemed neither to know nor to care what Mr. Topper had heard all about the Prince of Wales. He leaned far over the bar and looked for a long time intently at Mr. Topper's feet, then slowly his gaze moved upward until at last all of Mr. Topper had been carefully surveyed.

"People have staggered up to this bar in many queer and inexplicable contortions," he observed heavily. "Some have made it while others have fallen short. I had begun to believe that I knew every way a man could approach this bar under his own steam. I was mistaken, Mr. Topper." Here Peter shook his head sadly. "Never in all the years of my service has a customer, or anyone else, for that matter, arrived before me as you did just now. Might I be so bold as to ask you to do it again? Just once more, if you will, Mr. Topper?"

"Nonsense, Peter," replied Mr. Topper deprecatingly. "Don't go on so about it. That was merely an old, old trick of mine. I rarely if ever do it any more."

"Bravo, Topper!" cried several approving voices which Mr. Topper recognized as belonging to habitués of the place. "Do it again, old chap," and "Give us all a chance."

"Yes, please go on," implored another voice. "Do what you did again, or else I'll believe to my dying day that drink has touched my mind."

With a forced smile Mr. Topper shook his head. Suddenly, however, his forced smile became fixed, glazed over, and unnatural. He felt himself being unceremoniously yanked back to the door.

"All ready, Colonel?" muttered the voice of Kerby.

"Right," grunted the Colonel.

This time Topper was even better than before. He scooped through the room at an angle of thirty degrees. Like a fancy diver coming to the surface after describing a graceful arc beneath the water, he righted himself at the bar, his back slightly arched and his head well up. And like the diver he had so faithfully emulated, Mr. Topper, too, was breathless.

There was a general scraping of chairs as the occupants of the English Bar sat back and bent perplexed gazes upon the body and person of Mr. Topper.

"Damned if I see how he managed it," one gentleman at last admitted.

"No more do I," vouchsafed another. "Looked as if he were attached to wires or something, like an almost human puppet."

A tall, thin man who up to the sensational entrance of Mr. Topper had been sitting quite alone, his head held carefully between his hands, rose unsteadily to his feet and, clinging for support to the backs of chairs, made his way weakly to the door. Here he paused and gazed back long and reproachfully at Mr. Topper out of a pair of somber, miserable eyes. Then he made his way to his hotel, packed hastily, and returned without delay to London. The Riviera had been too much for him. Never again did he fully believe in its reality. He preferred not to be reminded of the place. He never mentioned it himself and when his friends returned from the South of France he requested them not to tell him where they had been. After the peculiar, inexplicable episode of the English Bar he realized that the only way for him to retain his reason was to drive it from his thoughts entirely. He refused to admit even to himself that the incident had ever occurred, that a man created loosely in the image of God had so casually, so ridiculously set aside His laws as well as a few of Mr. Newton's. In later years this man drank himself nearly to death and finally did die as a result of trying to repeat Mr. Topper's performance in a low-class pub. Thus, even at a distance and after the lapse of years, did the insidious Côte d'Azur claim another victim.

After the first ejaculations of astonishment occasioned by the repetition and intensification of Mr. Topper's odd entrance, the occupants of the English Bar once more sat back and considered the man as they would a god, their silent admiration not unmixed with a hint of alarm. Many were of the opinion that a man who had just done what he had done was capable of doing still more, was capable of doing practically anything, in fact—unheard of things. And he might not always be playful about it.

"Well," said an elderly gentleman wishing to propitiate the luckless Topper, "I am sure we have all been most handsomely entertained."

Mr. Blynn Nelson sold expensive motor boats entertainingly to the wives of the rich. It was suspected that his activities did not stop there. He now turned to Millie Coit, his neighbor, at a large, well filled table.

"In spite of which," he said in a low voice, "I thank my God people don't come in that way very often. The man must be double jointed."

At the bar Mr. Topper was not having a jolly time. No. He was not having anything nearly approaching a jolly time. Pressure had been brought to bear on him to the end that five champagne cocktails now stood on a row in front of him. The lifting of one of the cool, long-stemmed glasses to his lips was the signal for the others to follow. Topper gulped down his own cocktail, but the remaining four, after tilting themselves delicately, emptied their contents into the void. Topper, desperately moving from glass to glass in an effort to give the impression he was drinking them all, looked much like a circus seal snatching unearned rewards. Four distinct sighs of satisfaction followed the emptying of the glasses. A small but heartfelt groan escaped Mr. Topper's lips.

Peter had been privileged to witness all this. He now decided with his unerring sense of discrimination that it was high time to do a little line drawing.

"Mr. Topper," he suggested in a low voice, "you've done very nicely this morning. Amazingly well, I should say, but if you keep it up you will probably deprive a few of my borderline customers of their remaining shreds of sanity."

"I'll try to control myself, Peter," said Mr. Topper humbly.

"Would you mind telling me, sir, how you managed that last bit—those four separate and distinct sighs? To me that was most uncanny. I almost dropped my shaker. Had a feeling I was surrounded."

"I know how it is," replied Topper, laughing falsely as he drifted away from the bar. "Oh, I just did it somehow, Peter. Tossed them off, you know."

Peter did not know, and he looked it thoroughly.

Mr. Topper's friends made a place for him at their table and insisted on his sitting down. Everyone wanted to buy him a drink. A man who could do such things as Topper had already done should be received with a lavish hand.

As Topper was wearily seating himself, not at all sure whether or not the chair would be snatched from under him, Millie Coit turned to Hunt Davis.

"You were saying you lost your wrist watch?"

Hunt Davis was a writer of parts. Topper liked the man, but not so many others with the possible exception of Millie Coit. He now looked quite cast down about his wrist watch. Harold Gay inspected him with gloomy eyes.

"I know how you must feel, old boy," he remarked sympathetically.

"Did you ever lose a wrist watch?" asked Davis a little jealously.

"No," Harold Gay admitted. "I never wore a wrist watch."

"Then how can you possibly know how I feel?"

"Simply by putting myself in your place. It's not so difficult to put one's self in the place of a man who has had his wrist watch stolen."

"It may not be so hard to put yourself in the place of a man who has had his wrist watch stolen only once," admitted Davis, "but, by God, it's impossible to put yourself in the place of a man who has had his wrist watch stolen three times."

"It's harder," agreed Mr. Gay, "but it's not impossible. Not for me it isn't. I merely put myself in the place of that man three times. I triple my emotions, as it were."

"And how do you feel after you've put yourself in that man's place for the third time, may I ask?"

"Certainly," replied Gay. "I feel—I feel very much discouraged. I feel blue about it. Gloomy. I feel like giving up wearing wrist watches and asking other persons for the time."

"But that wasn't at all the way I felt," Hunt Davis objected.

"Would you mind telling me how in hell you did feel?"

"I don't recall feeling anything at all except no wrist watch. It was a most peculiar sensation."

"You mean feeling nothing was a peculiar sensation?"

"Not for some," said Hunt Davis. "Some people never feel anything and don't care a rap, but with me it's awful. I mean the way I felt when I was feeling nothing."

"But, my dear chap——"

"Oh, for God's own personal sake," protested Clyde Jones. "We don't care how you felt the first time you had a wrist watch stolen, much less the last. Frankly, I feel thirsty. One minute, Manley."

"Just the same it would be nice to know," pursued Harold Gay.

"I can't tell you," said Davis. "It was all too strange and awful."

"Will somebody change the subject?" asked Millie Coit. "All my words are too dirty."

"Like your subjects," observed Mrs. Willard.

"And the company they keep," said Millie brightly.

"Then tell us how it feels to lose one's virtue for the third time," suggested Mr. Nelson.

"Oh, I say," protested Commander Becket.

"It can't be done," was Millie's calm reply. "Virtue is a much overrated commodity that can be lost only once. In most cases it's tossed away."

"And that's my dish," said Mr. Topper surprisingly.

For this he received a sharp dig in the ribs.

"Hold your tongue," Marion Kerby whispered furiously in his ear. "Don't try to be smart and Riveraish. Here, I want that drink."

Obediently Topper held his glass over his left shoulder. Its contents were speedily drained.

"I hear the sound of lapping as of a cat," said Hunt Davis.

Topper quickly lowered his glass and relapsed into brooding silence.

Mr. Harold Gay, in spite of his comfortable size, was not a comfortable companion. He had a *penchant* for bringing up subjects which neither he himself nor anyone else knew anything about. And yet these subjects were of such a disturbing nature that they demanded some sort of definite settlement—even an erroneous one—before anyone could return to that comfortable state of mental torpor which is germane to man.

For some minutes now he had been fixedly watching a certain

spot on the floor, and while he watched he had been doing his best to persuade his intelligence that his eyes were all wrong. And yet what he saw was not in itself remarkable. In fact, it was nothing more nor less than a dog's tail, only in this instance—and this might be a trifle odd—this dog's tail was sometimes more and sometimes less. It was this that disturbed Mr. Harold Gay. And not without reason. A tail that can advance or retard itself according to the mood or necessity of the moment is enough to disturb the most hardened of characters. It is a tail to be reckoned with and not brushed aside. For Harold Gay it was a tail without precedent, a manifestation entirely outside the range of his experience.

This tail, this tail of a dog, was a hairy one—hairy to the point of artistic neglect. Bushy, it was. It was not an alluring tail. No. Not prepossessing. It was just a dog's sort of tail. It belonged to a dog of careless habits and indolent mind, to a dog either so high or so low in the social scale of dogs that further effort would avail nothing. It had either achieved all or had nothing left to lose. But here was the rub—the part that gave Mr. Gay to pause. The dog proper, which according to the laws of God should have rightfully belonged to this tail, had either misplaced its body or callously abandoned its tail. Strange as this may seem, the tail, in the absence of the directing head, appeared to be quite competent to carry on for itself. It had been draped across the matting, thrust out from under a table for a distance of from six to eighteen inches, roughly estimated. Mr. Gay later gave those measurements as being, in his considered opinion, the most nearly accurate. Manley was inclined to agree. On various occasions that morning in the course of his plying between tables, Manley had seen that tail. Quite naturally he had jumped to the conclusion that a dog was attached to it and that the dog was under the table, which, to Manley's way of thinking, was just like a dog. Harold Gay knew better. From where he was sitting he could see all. Not only could he see that there was no dog even loosely associated with this tail, but also that the tail itself possessed the remarkable virtuosity of being able to diminish and even to disappear entirely upon the approach of a threatening foot. Mr. Gay did not feel sufficiently confident of his own mental faculties to keep this tremendous knowledge to himself. He decided that he had to establish contact with other human minds. Accordingly, he made tentative advances.

"Will someone please bear me out in this?" he asked with due deliberation. "Is that thing, that hairy-looking object protruding from under that table, the tail of a dog?"

Everyone at the table concentrated his attention on the spot indicated. Mr. Topper, with mixed emotions, recognized Oscar's terminus, and as if the recognition were mutual the terminus wagged feebly across a modest arc of matting.

"It gives every indication of being the tail of a dog," Commander Becket declared after a thoughtful silence, "the tail of a dog animated by only the friendliest of feelings."

"So far so good," continued Harold Gay. "Now, am I right in presuming that that tail rates a body, or do tails no longer require bodies along the Riviera?"

"In my measured opinion," observed Sam Brooks, "there should be a body knocking about somewhere belonging to that tail—a doglike body of sorts."

"Perhaps," suggested Blynn Nelson without much hope, "some woman was wearing a summer fur and dropped that tail."

"So would I have done," observed Mrs. Willard critically. "If my summer fur had a tail like that I couldn't drop it too soon."

"Righto," agreed Nelson. "If that tail belongs to a summer fur, what must the fur look like? Shouldn't fancy the thing would be particularly nice to see."

Upon the reception of these unfavorable comments the tail sadly diminished in length. Topper felt sorry for its owner. He realized how humiliating it was to have one's tail so dispassionately discussed.

"Don't mind what they say, old boy," he called softly.

At the sound of Topper's voice the tail shot back to life. It wagged against the matting with frantic impetuosity. All at the table were startled, including Topper. The tail was regarded with respect if not with affection.

"Do you happen to be on speaking terms with that tail, Mr. Topper?" Commander Becket inquired.

"It strikes a responsive chord," said Mr. Topper evasively.

"Then will you ask it for me to go somewhere else and collect a body?" asked Millie Coit. "This sort of thing is getting on my nerves."

"It's not improving my condition," added an Englishman named Waddles.

"And what I am looking at," contributed Hunt Davis, "is actually doing me harm."

"What are you seeing?" inquired Mr. Gay.

"I am seeing—I'm afraid I'm seeing—a game of checkers playing itself very quietly, very orderly, but, nevertheless, playing itself without the assistance of human hands," replied Hunt Davis in a strained voice.

"I do hope I don't become hysterical," Mr. Topper muttered. "Let's all have another drink."

"Do you think it's possible that those we have already taken had a little something extra in them?" Millie asked in a low voice. "Something so subtle yet so powerful that our minds have all been affected alike?"

"Don't ask questions," replied Mr. Gay. "My thoughts are elsewhere."

"I'd swear there isn't a living soul sitting at that table," Clyde Jones mused aloud, "and yet it drinks champagne and plays checkers in the most accomplished manner. It passes human understanding."

"And under that table," said Millie Coit, "is a dogless tail. How queer does a thing have to be before it becomes a miracle? If the populace knew what was going on here they'd turn this barroom into a shrine."

"That relic is far from sacred," Commander Becket vouchsafed, pointing to the shaggy tail. "I'd call it an obscene manifestation of black magic."

During the course of this colloquy the disembodied game of checkers progressed with every indication of purpose and enjoyment. The red and black disks moved with dignity and deliberation. One of them would occasionally poise itself in the air as if in hesitation, then smoothly continue on its way. From time to time a glass filled with the finest champagne would elevate itself about lip high from the table, then return of its own accord daintily to its original point of departure.

"I've heard tell of fireless cookers," Harold Gay said at last, "but never of playerless checkers that drink wine in the presence of a tail bereft of dog."

"When you put it all together like that," remarked Millie Coit, "it does sound almost too much to bear. And I was just getting interested in the game. There seems to be a little sly cheating going forward, but so far the dishonors are equal."

"Look!" exclaimed Commander Becket. "As I live and breathe. That's not at all sporting. The reds are being snatched off the board every time that glass goes up."

The Commander, a stickler for fair play, rose and, walking determinedly over to the table, placed a restraining hand on one of the absconding reds. At the same moment he felt his wrist being sharply slapped. A growl issued from the tail, and the intrepid Commander received a stinging nip on the calf of his leg. This was more than confusing. It was both painful and dangerous. No game of checkers was worth it. Clinging to his dignity the Commander quickly returned to his chair and sat with his back to the checkerboard.

"I've been both invisibly slapped and bitten," he announced in a trembling voice. "Will someone, in God's name, tell me just what is going on?"

"I couldn't tell you in my own name, much less in God's," said Harold Gay.

"Were the teeth the teeth of dog?" asked Millie Coit.

"What the devil difference does that make?" demanded the retired officer. "I didn't stop to examine the teeth that bit me."

"Neither would I," replied Millie mollifyingly. "But if the choice were left entirely with me, I'd rather be bitten by the teeth of dog without any visible means of support than by the teeth of lion, for example, with nothing else but."

"I don't give a damn whose teeth they were," the Commander rapped out. "I jolly well object to being bitten by any set of teeth, whether fish, flesh, or fowl."

"Few fowls have teeth," said Harold Gay moodily.

"Name me one with a set of teeth," challenged Millie Coit. "One honest-to-God fowl."

"For heaven's sake, don't let's take that up now," Mrs. Willard protested. "Isn't there enough to talk about without dragging in birds?"

"I'm speechless," remarked Hunt Davis.

"Let us drink," suggested Topper.

"Well," admitted the Commander, thoughtfully prodding his calf, "the teeth might have been those of dog, as Millie insists on phrasing it, but the spirit behind those teeth was that of a snake in the grass. I'm not going to look at anything any more ever."

"Neither am I," said Mr. Topper. "That way madness lies. Let's none of us look at anything."

For several minutes everyone at the table concentrated his gaze on his glass. Then Manley approached and presented Mr. Topper with a bill.

"What's this?" asked Mr. Topper.

"The gentlemen playing checkers, sir, said it would be all right to give it to you," replied the impeccable Manley.

A strangled gasp escaped the Colonel.

"Did you see two men at that table?" he asked, his eyes growing wild.

"Only a moment ago," replied Manley. "There they are now, sir, just leaving."

The table gazed, fascinated. The backs of two nattily clad gentlemen, swaying slightly, were disappearing through the wicker doors. At their heels in a leisurely manner moved a tail. There was nothing more to it. Just that.

As the swinging doors closed upon those two swaying backs, fear appeared for the first time in the eyes of the watchers at the table. Their eyes were searching each other's faces, mutely pleading for enlightenment or denial—for any explanation that would rationalize even a little the things that had come to pass since the swanlike arrival of Mr. Topper at the bar.

"They must have been drinking a lot," said Mr. Topper at last, his eyes studying the slip of paper, the outward, visible sign of a couple of spiritual disgraces.

"Indeed they were, sir," agreed Manley. "Those two gentlemen knew how to drink."

"And what to drink," added Topper.

"And their dog knew how to bite," put in the Commander. "Do you mean to tell me that those two checker players were at that table all the time, Manley? Consider your words carefully, man."

"No, sir," answered Manley. "Sometimes they were and sometimes they weren't."

"Can you tell us where they were when they weren't?" asked Millie Coit. "That is, Manley, if mentioning such places does not overtax your admirable English reserve."

"Oh, they weren't there, madam, if that's where you mean," Manley replied.

"That's exactly where I did mean, Manley," continued Millie. "And if they weren't there, can you tell us where they were, those checker-playing wine bibbers?"

"I merely meant, madam," replied Manley with frigid dignity, "that I did not follow them there."

"Of course not, Manley," said Miss Coit. "Far be it from me to imply that you would ever do such a thing. However, the fact remains that you don't know whether they were there or not."

"Madam, I would not like to say," said Manley, looking almost noble.

"Of course. Of course," murmured Millie. "We don't want you to say anything that would hurt you. Well, I give up. We seem to be about where we started."

"I will admit," offered Manley, "they acted rather odd. Being there and not, so to speak. But you see, Miss Coit, I was quite busy myself, and I didn't rightly notice how they did."

"Clearly and convincingly stated," said Mr. Gay. "It strikes me that Mr. Topper, himself, is acting somewhat odd."

This was indeed the truth. He looked for all the world like a man who was being briskly bounced up and down on his chair.

"Is your seat uncomfortable?" asked the inquiring Millie Coit. "Hornets, perhaps?"

"It is nothing," chattered Mr. Topper, an expression of increasing embarrassment taking possession of his face as he desperately clung to the sides of his chair. "It will pass."

"My God, sir!" exclaimed the naval officer. "What do you mean it will pass? Are you having a fit in our midst?"

"I'm going to have," announced Mrs. Willard.

"Looks more like a bite to me," observed Millie Coit, thoughtfully studying the bouncing man.

"Perhaps he's squiffed and is playing horse," helpfully suggested Waddles.

"I should think it would be fatiguing keeping it up so long," remarked Harold Gay.

"Don't mind me," Mr. Topper shook out. "Go right ahead with your drinking."

He essayed a neighborly smile, but was forced to close his lips on his chattering teeth.

"You don't seem to get the idea, Mr. Topper," Commander Becket told him with some asperity. "We've got to mind you if you insist on conducting yourself in what I can only say is an extremely childish manner."

"I'm not doing it for fun," muttered Topper, his hair vibrating strangely on his head.

"Then what are you doing it for?" asked Mr. Gay. "Surely you can't be doing it for exercise."

"I'm not doing it at all," snapped Topper.

"Then we're all mad," said Commander Becket with dreadful conviction.

"Or perhaps Topper is possessed," offered Blynn Nelson.

"Do you hear grunting going on?" asked the Commander. "I distinctly heard two separate grunts detach themselves in the air."

"Could it be Topper, possibly?" asked Waddles. "I couldn't keep from grunting if I was doing all that bouncing."

This was too much for Topper. With a despairing look about him he released his hold on the chair and yielded himself to the forces that had been so industriously endeavoring to drag him from his seat. Like a cork released from a bottle he rose to the ceiling, gracefully skirted that obstruction and sailed out of the barroom through the open space above the doors. But even as he thus strangely departed Mr. Topper still retained the instincts of a gentleman. Twisting a strained face over his shoulder, he called back hurriedly, "Sorry I must tear myself away, everybody. Don't worry about that check, Manley. I'll be back."

"He doesn't have to hurry so far as I am concerned," said Commander Becket in a hoarse voice.

"This bar has seen me for the last time," put in a gentleman from Hollywood. "That man has more gags than a lotful of Harold Lloyds."

Slowly and without looking at one another the men and women at that table arose and took their separate ways. Before they left, however, it was tacitly agreed that nothing should be said of all that had occurred. As Mrs. Blake Willard expressed it, "Others would never understand, and they might think things. One is so easily suspected of mental disorders along the Riviera. You know how people are—unpleasant that way."

Mrs. Willard knew, for she, herself was one of such persons.

IX

"All God's Chillun Got Shoes"

It is difficult to say what the pedestrians on Rue Gounod thought of Mr. Topper's leaflike descent to the pavement after he had sailed from the English Bar. Fortunately there were few to observe, and they did not remain long. After one startled look at Topper they hastened to other and less disconcerting *rues*. Probably those who were privileged to witness his landing decided that he was either an acrobat casually practising a back flip or a slightly stout and unsober god arriving in haste from some well tailored Olympus.

What the pedestrians thought or did not think no longer concerned Mr. Topper. He was too deeply occupied thinking about himself, considering the state of his being and trying to adjust his body to his aërial mode of progress. At any moment he expected to be whisked from his feet and carried like a snapping flag down the main thoroughfare of the town. He might even find himself deposited on the dome of the cathedral of Notre Dame de la Victoire. Now that his companions had learned a new game he felt sure they would not abandon it until they had experimented with all its ramifications. For the moment he was vouchsafed a breathing space. He even entertained the extravagant hope that these same companions had departed in quest of other diversions and left him in peace. Methodically he felt his pockets for his possessions. His watch, passport, wallet, and cigar case had not been lost in his flight. Sheer centrifugal force had held them securely intact.

Then Topper saw something. It was not much, but it was sufficient to convince him he was not alone. Nor was he alone in what he saw. An elderly man holding a broom and sporting a green baize apron was standing in a doorway, also looking. There was a small pool of water lying in a hollow in the pavement. This pool at the most contained no more than a couple of cupfuls of water, but it was quite enough to be seen. As Topper and the man with the broom stood with their gaze fastened on the pool it gradually disappeared before their eyes. Those of the Frenchman's were filled with consternation. Mr. Topper's were merely disgusted. The diminishing of the water was accompanied by a peculiar lapping sound such as is made by the tongue of an extremely thirsty and not over-nice dog.

The man with the broom looked at Topper, who attempted to avoid his eyes.

"M'sieu," announced the man in an awed voice, "the little pool, he pants."

"I neither speak nor understand French," Topper almost truthfully informed the man.

"But, m'sieu, you can at least regard," insisted the man with the broom. "That little pool there is a pool no more. He is as dry as the palm of my hand."

Mr. Topper did not know how dry the palm of the man's hand was. The palms of his own hands were quite moist. He had to admit, however, that the man with the broom had spoken nothing less than the truth. The little pool was indeed quite dry. Oscar had polished it off, and following the polishing process came a satisfied grunt, the bestial emanation of a dog lying down heavily after a good drink. Topper could almost hear Oscar's unseen bones clumping against the pavement.

"M'sieu," said the Frenchman timidly, "it is unbelievable. The little pool, now he pushes grunts."

"Can I help it if your damn French pools insist on pushing grunts?" Topper demanded irritably.

The man did not understand, but he gathered from Topper's manner that he was being held responsible for the eccentric conduct of the little pool, or what had once been a little pool before Oscar had mopped it up. He leaned far out of the doorway and intently considered the spot where the pool had been.

"It is of a truth," he said, as if to himself. "The place of the little pool is now breathing in gusts. It is necessary that I part all at once."

Which he did, much to Mr. Topper's relief.

Subdued but animated voices attracted his attention. He listened with growing unease.

"It's ridiculous," he heard Marion protesting. "He is not at all suitably clad for the Riviera. In the first place, he needs sun glasses. He'll ruin his silly eyes. Then take a look at those feet. Altogether too formal. He must put beach shoes on them—*espadrilles,* they're called."

"Why don't you let the man alone?" George demanded. "You're not his wife."

"And you're not my husband."

"Don't let's go into that any more."

"Why do you think you're my husband? Tell me that."

"Because we both got smeared at the same time. Death did not us part."

"It didn't need to. Life had done that beforehand—life and your disgusting ways."

"Come, come," objected the voice of the Colonel. "This is a profitless wrangle."

"I'll make it a discordant brawl," declared Marion heatedly.

"But listen, Colonel," said George Kerby. "Just because a tree got in the way of our earthly activities it doesn't follow that the holy bonds of matrimony were severed, does it?"

"That is a highly technical question," replied the Colonel. "You see, in our present state there is no provision made for divorce nor any suggestion of marriage. Our relations, thank God, are informal."

"One can go visiting over week-ends," came the voice of Mrs. Hart, "without a Woolworth ring."

"Let's ask Topper," George Kerby suggested. "He might be one of us at any minute."

"Don't ask me," said Mr. Topper, speaking earnestly into space. "Don't draw me in. I've been drawn in and dragged out enough as it is already."

"Amusingly put," commented George Kerby. "Let's take the old boy shopping."

"That's what I said all the time," declared Marion. "Sun glasses first. His vision should be dulled."

"But I don't want sun glasses," Mr. Topper protested. "The lot of you make me look appalling enough as it is without decorating me with headlights."

"Oh, you must have glasses," Marion assured him. "We can't let you ruin your eyes for the sake of appearances. Grab his arms, my braves."

The braves grabbed Topper's arms with a will, and once more he was hustled off down the street.

"If I promise to get these damn glasses without making any trouble, will you let me walk like a human being instead of some anthropoid ape?" Mr. Topper asked breathlessly.

"How about it, Colonel?" said George.

"It's all right with me," replied the Colonel, "if he doesn't try any other sort of monkey business."

Whereupon Topper was released and allowed to walk in the manner to which he had been accustomed. Furthermore, his hat remained undisturbed upon his head. His friends had either forgotten about it or grown tired of the sport. Topper carefully refrained from reminding them.

"Turn in here," whispered Marion Kerby as they were passing a souvenir and jewelry shop. "It claims that one speaks English. Let's see if one does."

"One will be prattling baby talk by the time we're through," George muttered darkly.

"Can't we buy these glasses nicely?" asked Mr. Topper. "Why spread terror and confusion throughout France? This storekeeper may be a good sort, for all we know."

"Certainly, Mr. Topper," came the deep voice of the Colonel. "We're nice people. We know how to act."

Topper made no comment on this misconception of the Colonel. Fearing the worst, he obediently entered the shop.

The owner of the place was in no wise remarkable. He smelled pleasantly, smiled pleasantly, and spoke pleasantly. If anything, he was a little too pleasant. Topper felt that if the man even faintly suspected the true state of affairs, much of his pleasantness would evaporate. He said it was a good morning to Mr. Topper in English, then stood regarding him with an expectant eye.

"Have you any sun glasses?" asked Mr. Topper.

The man intimated promptly that he had one of the most exhaustive collections of sun glasses in all of France, if not the world. He proceeded to prove his point by heaping a counter with a varied assortment of these articles.

Mr. Topper selected a pair at random and diffidently placed them upon his nose. Immediately they were snatched off, but not by Topper. The Frenchman endeavored to conceal his surprise.

"Did they pinch, m'sieu, perhaps?" he asked.

"They almost bit me," muttered Mr. Topper, selecting another pair as unlike the first as he could find.

These, too, he placed on his nose and endeavored to hold them there. In the irritable struggle that followed the glasses snapped in two.

"No, no, no!" a woman's voice protested. "Most unbecoming."

"I'll pay for those," stammered Topper. "Must have slipped."

The owner of the store felt better, but still far from well. Mr. Topper looked at the man helplessly. He was afraid to select another pair of glasses. This, however, was unnecessary. The glasses were selected for him. A yellow-tinted pair deftly detached themselves from the group on the counter and moved upon Mr. Topper. In a desperate endeavor to make the best of a bad situation he thrust out his hands, met the glasses halfway, and helped to affix them to his nose. In spite of the fact that the owner keenly desired to make a sale, he had no desire at all to make it in this staccato manner. He turned from Mr. Topper and looked steadfastly through the window, his fingers drumming nervously on the counter. When his gaze returned to his customer it was immediately changed to a fixed stare. A pair of wearerless glasses were looking at him eye to eye. Mr. Topper was in another part of the shop apparently having a fight with a necklace which was jumping frantically in the air.

"You can't do such things," Topper was explaining to the necklace. "That's plain ordinary stealing."

The owner thought this was funny, but he had no time to think much about it. What was facing him was funnier still. He looked at the glasses that were intently peering at him, then moved cautiously behind his counter. Had a tidal wave deposited itself upon the lap of the town the store owner would have been dismayed, but not greatly surprised. Had wild beasts and reptiles suddenly invaded his shop he would have experienced a pang of regret, but by some stretch of logic would have been able to reconcile that occurrence with the less conventional hazards of life. These glasses came under a different category. It is difficult to maintain one's urbanity when being scrutinized quietly but fixedly by an uninhabited pair of glasses. One is prone to imagine things. One imagines unseen eyes looking consideringly through tinted glass—God knows what sort of eyes. The Frenchman tore his gaze away only to be met by another pair of glasses thoughtfully inspecting his neck. This inspection served to add embarrassment to alarm. For a moment the man did not know just where to look. He could hardly look at Mr. Topper, for what he was doing with that animated necklace, scolding it as he was, brought no comfort to the shopkeeper. Under the circumstances he did the only thing he could do. He closed his eyes and clung to the counter. The glasses were blotted out. When he felt himself rapped smartly upon the shoulder he started to crouch like a dog, but his legs were too paralyzed to obey this impulse. Mr. Topper was standing before him.

"M'sieu," asked the man in a voice that shook, "did you see the glasses unattended?"

"Are you mad?" replied Mr. Topper.

"Perhaps," admitted the man. "But they looked at me, m'sieu, those glasses. One pair even went so far as to inspect my neck. It was most suggestive."

"And most unnecessary, I hope," added Topper.

"But yes," replied the Frenchman proudly. "Were you not yourself undergoing a little difficulty with a necklace?"

"It got tangled up in my fingers," lied Mr. Topper, "and I became so unreasonably enraged that I began to talk to myself."

This seemed scarcely probable, although the Frenchman tried hard to believe it. A woman's laughter was heard without the woman.

"Things of a true incredibleness have taken place here," the shopkeeper observed with stubborn suspicion. "And they continue. There are now, for example, unseen voices."

"That is not of an incredibleness," retorted Mr. Topper.

"But yes, m'sieu," protested the Frenchman. "Where there are voices there should be bodies, or at the very least, some throats."

"I made those voices myself," again lied Mr. Topper.

"Then please make no more voices," said the owner. "Such admirable ability belongs to the stage. It is too much for personal relations. Conditions are sufficiently difficult. Do you really desire glasses, or are you merely amusing yourself?"

"I'll buy these glasses," Mr. Topper declared, seizing a pair that was even as he spoke wriggling impatiently on the counter. "And I'll pay for the broken pair as well as these two necklaces."

Feeling a little comforted, the jeweler expedited the transaction and accompanied Mr. Topper to the door. As he did so he experienced the final shock of seeing the necklaces emerge from the pocket of his disturbing customer.

"Here, take these," said a woman's voice, and two empty necklace boxes were thrust into the storekeeper's hand.

The necklaces themselves, one on either side of Mr. Topper, accompanied him down the street. Every time he tried to recapture them they jumped out of reach.

"I haven't had such a lovely present in a long time," murmured Marion Kerby. "Let's see yours, Clara."

"Mr. Topper knows how a lady likes to be treated," said Mrs. Hart as the necklaces changed places.

"I know how you should be treated," Mr. Topper replied in a low voice. "Those necklaces were bought to keep them from being stolen. That's all there is to it. And now you are making me conspicuous with them."

"Don't keep trying to snatch mine back," said Marion Kerby childishly. "I like to feel it in my hand. Did it cost much?"

"In mental anguish more than can be estimated," was Mr. Topper's answer.

That day the jewelry shop was closed. Souvenirs and sun glasses were probably bought, but not in that store. The moment Mr. Topper's back was flush with the jamb the door was closed upon it. Then the door was securely locked, and the owner, as if in fear of arousing his souvenirs to further outbreaks of ferocity, quietly tiptoed from the shop. He was at an end.

Some minutes later Mr. Topper, strongly if invisibly guarded on both sides, was making his wishes known to a suave gentleman who gave the appearance of one who devoted his life to bringing peace and happiness to the feet of others.

"I want a pair of beach shoes," said Mr. Topper brusquely.

"Les espadrilles!" exclaimed the gentleman, much gratified. "But yes, m'sieu. They are here."

He turned, and there they were—several boxes of them. Other boxes of shoes were being literally torn from their places by unseen hands. The clerk looked at the agitated boxes uncomprehendingly, then turned to regard Mr. Topper. That gentleman was frantically engaged in trying to help some panting unseen to drag a pair of beach shoes on his feet.

"Wasn't in the army for nothing," proclaimed a deep voice when the shoes were on. "I can tell the size of a foot at a glance."

"M'sieu," declared the vendor of shoes, "it is a thing disturbing, is it not? Those shoes, they have taken affairs into their hands."

"Yes, yes," agreed Topper distractedly. "I'll take these on my feet."

Without stopping to look at its denomination he crumpled a

note into the man's hand, then walked from the store. And as he walked there followed in his tracks at regular intervals four pairs of white canvas beach shoes proceeding according to size, the largest pair being first. As if stimulated by this singular demonstration Oscar succeeded in revivifying his tail and proudly brought up the rear. Down the crowded street of the town this quaint little procession made its way. Topper himself was happily unaware of his loyal following, until the amazed glances of pedestrians forced him to look back. When he did so he received the shock of his life. He felt like a man being followed by a large white cat and her three kittens with the isolated tail of a dog stalking the lot of them. When Topper stopped, the shoes stopped. Also the tail. In fact, Oscar seemed actually to lie down, for his tail drooped neglectedly to the pavement. Topper thought of his own white shoes. With them the line of march was composed of five units, not counting Oscar's ragged contribution. And to add to the situation the shoes seemed to bear themselves with a certain air of pride. Occasionally one would be raised from the pavement as if for a closer inspection. Now, even in a town as accustomed to beach shoes as this one was, a display of five new pairs, four of which gave every appearance of being unoccupied, walking Indian file down the street was easily enough to create a small sensation. These shoes did.

"Maybe he has them on a string," suggested an observer, "and is dragging them after him."

"But why should a full grown man behave in such a silly manner?" demanded the observer's wife. "Why couldn't he carry them home like a normal human being?"

"Perhaps it amuses him more this way," replied the husband. "A man who has to buy five pairs of shoes at once deserves some amusement. Keeping you in shoes is more than I can bear. Why not ask the man himself?"

"I wouldn't go near that man."

The fact that two rather flamboyant costume necklaces were accompanying two pairs of shoes did not greatly impress the populace. The human mind can only absorb a certain number of shocks in a given time. However, it was difficult for many witnesses to explain away the presence of that languid tail.

Mr. Topper was in a quandary. He did not know whether it was worse to stand still and regard those shoes together with the entire population of France, or to turn his back on them and to proceed on his way with the mortifying knowledge that they were methodically stalking his tracks. It was a delicate situation. He could not afford to stand there and collect another curious French crowd. His nerves would never bear up under the strain. He thanked God for the sun glasses. Perhaps he was not recognized. If he were, his reputation would begin to spread. He would be a marked man.

The largest pair of beach shoes began to shuffle impatiently. This decided Topper. He turned and hurried away. A soft, rhythmical pattering behind him made him horribly alive to the fact that the feet were following after. Topper knew of a square not so far off where taxicabs lived in happy discord. He hastened towards this square. Here he found an empty cab and sprang in only to be followed by three pairs of shoes. The fourth pair occupied the driver's seat, the driver at the moment being a picturesque part of a war memorial as he diligently perused his *journal.* The man did not even notice the abrupt departure of his property. What the citizens of the town were privileged to see was an apparently driverless cab—an open cab with a single occupant, Mr. Topper, in solitary splendor, with a dog's tail dangling untidily from his lap. They could not see the shoes in the car, nor could they hear the excited panting of the dog.

"Had no idea we were going for a ride," the Colonel commented complacently. "Topper is full of tricks."

"I dearly love these open cabs," said Mrs. Hart.

Topper felt an arm snuggle its way through his. He sensed the intimate nearness of Marion Kerby. He was filled with a desire to see her impudent face again. In spite of the situation, he found himself pleasantly alive.

"Topper, my brave," Marion whispered in his ear, "I could ride like this forever."

"I fear," her brave replied, "that this drive is going to be sadly curtailed. Do you realize we have stolen a cab?"

"Now, if Oscar would only stir his lazy ectoplasm and materialize," the Colonel interrupted, "Topper would look quite smart. Oscar is a dressy sort of dog."

"He's small comfort to me as he is," remarked Mr. Topper.

A few minutes later the cab turned into the lovely palm-lined boulevard that ran beside the sea. Here the sidewalk cafés were doing capacity business. Also, here stood a gendarme. Not a nice gendarme, but one of those gendarmes one can live quite happily all one's days without ever meeting. He had an acute eye, this one. As the taxicab curved gracefully round him he was electrified to discover that it had no driver. Never in his experience had such an offense been brought to his notice. The very magnitude of the thing momentarily stunned him. That moment was all George Kerby needed. By the time the gendarme had decided to take steps, the taxicab was well down the boulevard. A gentleman at one of the café tables paused with his glass at his lips.

"Am I a little bit that way," he inquired of the lady at his side, "or do I actually see a driverless taxicab?"

"You do," replied the lady, arresting her own glass, "and what is more you hear it. That taxicab is singing."

The cab was indeed singing. "I got shoes. You got shoes. All God's chillun got shoes," came shatteringly from it. At the same time three pairs of white shoes were proudly waved in the air. George Kerby even succeeded in placing one of his on the wheel.

"He must look awful," Topper thought with a shudder. "Thank God one can't see the rest of him."

The singing taxicab made a grand loop and returned down the boulevard. People were now standing up at their tables to get a better view of the driverless cab. They could distinctly hear the voices of men and women singing lustily about shoes, yet all they saw was a dignified gentleman of middle age sitting in the taxicab with his mouth grimly shut. Several observers, not knowing what else to do, cheered the speeding car.

"I got shoes. You got shoes. All God's chillun got shoes," chanted the Colonel in a deep bass voice.

Whistles were blowing along the boulevard. Gendarmes were appearing. Lots of them. There was an excited honking of horns. Yet above it all boomed the voice of the indomitable Colonel loudly informing France that all God's children were shod.

"We'll sing for you, Topper," cried George Kerby, "until you go down to defeat. You know how we are that way."

"Too well," replied Mr. Topper.

"I'm afraid Mr. Topper will have to be pulled in for the lot of us," the Colonel interrupted his singing to observe.

"It's a rotten shame," said Marion Kerby. "I'll go along with you, my old."

"Oh, don't do that," Topper hastily pleaded.

When a human wall composed of gendarmes and spectators made further progress inexpedient, Topper's companions, including Oscar, quietly melted away. God's chillun took their shoes elsewhere. Mr. Topper was asked to descend. Witnesses readily declared that they had carefully observed Mr. Topper and he had neither driven nor sung. How, then, had it all come to pass? the gendarmes insisted on knowing. Mr. Topper was cast down at not being able to be of help. He had stepped into the automobile in all good faith and innocence, then the machine had immediately started to march. Why the car insisted on singing he had no idea. He was not familiar with the habits of French taxicabs. Perhaps the car was happy. Did automobiles sing in France? The gendarme was baffled in several directions. Suddenly his face cleared. Obviously the automobile was the offender. Mr. Topper had been more sinned against than sinning. In the name of France the gendarme apologized. The automobile would be well arrested. Also its owner. That one would indubitably remain in jail all the years of his life. As for the automobile, that would be taken apart piece by piece and inspected with the utmost rigor. Mr. Topper was allowed to depart. The crowd regarded his back with admiring eyes.

For the first time it seemed in years Topper had the sensation of being alone. He hardly knew whether he liked it or not. He decided that for the time being he rather liked it. The other world had been too much with him.

Slowly he began to smile. By the time he reached his own house he was laughing unwillingly but well. It was a thing he seldom did. He was thinking of the sightless sun glasses scrutinizing the neck of the affronted jeweler.

Mrs. Topper, watching him approach and overhearing his laughter, decided he had been drinking. Topper was only too willing to let it go at that. His unexpected appearance in sun glasses and beach shoes confirmed her in this opinion. She had been given to understand that men who drank usually made some strange and ill-advised purchases.

The glasses, she decided, lent to her husband's customarily placid features a sinister appearance. They were violet in shade. There was about Mr. Topper the suggestion of a wild horse—one that laughed dangerously at its own evil thoughts.

Mrs. Topper was not at all satisfied in her own mind about the sanity of her husband. She suspected him of secret depths of depravity far too abysmal to be penetrated by ordinary mortals.

X

La Plage Tranquille

Topper owned a little book that went intimately into the climate, topography, diversions, and accommodations of the Côte d'Azur. He had paid four and a half francs for this little book, and had always found it to be at least fifty per cent accurate. It had instincts of veracity. The less agreeable features of the Riviera not mentioned were probably omitted with the knowledge that visitors would soon find them out for themselves. And because Topper found that this little book tended in the general direction of the truth he prized it highly and thumbed it assiduously. He knew innumerable bits about the Riviera that those who had been born and bred there never suspected—bits that would bring him neither pleasure nor profit. This little book had referred glowingly to the beach that he frequented as *la plage tranquille*. And indeed he had always found it tranquil enough until the arrival of the German model. Even then it had not become noisy. Merely alert.

The French are not loud people in the sense that Americans are. They are much more nosey than noisy. This does not hold for disputes, when animals of all species are prone to forget their manners. But the French can pack themselves by battalions into relatively small spaces and maintain a truly amazing degree of decorum—a sort of vivacious family monotone. However, they will regard. Their interest is quick to arouse and difficult to lull when once aroused. They will peer, scrutinize, and listen. What is even more disturbing to those unacquainted with the fine nuances of their language, they will comment with innocent frankness and abandon.

Mr. Topper was now on the beach. So was the German model. They were separated from each other by a scant six feet of sand. This afternoon the beach was crowded. There were large families present with baskets of lunch and bottles of wine. Some of these bottles had been thrust deep in the sand to cool. There were droves of children and a constant procession of couples that entertained nothing but the most agreeable ideas about one another. All was well. The *plage* was *tranquille*. Mr. Topper drew a deep breath and basked in the sun. After the excitement of the morning he felt at peace with France.

As he watched a well formed French girl shift dexterously from her dress to her bathing suit he idly wondered how she did it without revealing ever so much more of herself. Long practice, he decided. It was truly remarkable the way these French girls could dress and undress on the beach without in the least disturbing either its or their own tranquillity. Then he shifted his gaze to the trunks adorning some of the men. These always intrigued Mr. Topper. He wondered, in the first place, why they ever put them on, and in the second place, how they ever kept them on once they had been put. It was obvious that the average Frenchman gave little thought to his trunks. In his mind's eye he could see them emptying old chests of clothes in search of the drawers of their ancestors which thrifty hands could make suitable for the beach. A slash here and a tuck there, a casually affixed button and, lo, their loins were girded sportively for the sand.

Mr. Topper was not aware of the fact that all was not well on the beach until two of his fellow countrymen, who had evidently abused the indulgence of the beach café, drew his attention to what was to them a strange and absorbing phenomenon.

"Tell me, T. D.," said the longer of the two Americans, "has that dog dug its damn fool self down into the sand and allowed only its tail to remain exposed?"

"If it has, Joe," replied T. D., "it's the first dog I ever heard of acting in such a manner. Peculiar, I'd call it."

"I'd call it impossible," said Joe, "if it wasn't waving there before my very eyes. There's life in that tail."

Mr. Topper's eyes followed the direction of the Americans' gaze and saw no more nor less than he had expected. There was Oscar's tail waving negligently in the light breeze from the sea. However, Topper knew there was more to it than that—much more than met the eye. If Oscar's tail was present, then it followed that Oscar's companions were not far off. He cast a quick glance about him for unoccupied beach shoes. With a feeling of relief he was unable to discover any.

"Perhaps that dog's a sand hound," Joe suggested.

"Never even heard of any such dog," declared T. D.

"Might have any kind of dog in France, though," said the other. "Maybe he's looking for sand fleas."

"A dog with a tail like that doesn't have to look for fleas," wisely declared T. D. "He might be trying to get rid of some sand fleas."

"Well, I wish he would stop whatever he's doing," complained Joe. "I don't want to see his face, but I hate to think of him down there smothering himself to death. First thing you know that tail will collapse from lack of breath."

"For God's sake," breathed T. D., suddenly sitting up, "will you look at what he's doing now!"

The tail was slowly creeping across the sand in the direction of a large open lunch basket. Topper could picture to himself the stealthy movements of the rest of the dog.

"It's burrowing," said Joe, "like an—an—like a mole."

"But what speed," observed T. D. admiringly. "Do you think we drank too much and are seeing things?"

His question was never answered. Joe was too busy looking. The tail had achieved its objective. It was well under the lee of the basket now, and close to the sand. In another moment a sandwich emerged from the basket, quivered nervously in the air, then went out like a light. There was no more sandwich.

"Gord!" breathed Joe. "Can you match that?"

"Look," was all T. D. said.

This time the leg of a chicken made its mysterious appearance. Evidently the tail considered this piece of loot worthy of more serious consideration. Slowly the leg followed by the tail moved across the sand to the protection of a rotting rowboat. In the security of this object the leg was consumed at the leisure of the tail.

"*La jambe!*" exclaimed the mother of the brood attached to the basket. "*Elle n'est pas ici. Quel dommage!*"

Apprehending the nearest child, she administered a routine chastisement upon the scrap of cloth it was wearing. Joe looked at T. D., and T. D. looked at Joe. No word was spoken. Both rose from the sand and made their way to the café. As they passed Mr. Topper, Joe paused and asked him a question.

"Pardon me," said Joe, "but have you noticed anything peculiar going on—anything having to do with a tail?"

"No," replied Topper coldly. "I have seen nothing peculiar in that line, although I have seen some rather amusing as well as provocative examples."

"Let's hurry," said Joe to his companion. "He's harder to understand than the French themselves."

On this beach there was a huge push ball, the property of Monsieur Sylvestre. Mr. Topper was watching this push ball. So were a number of other bathers. It appeared to be pushing itself. Exclamations of alarm and surprise issued from the crowd. These were speedily augmented and intensified when the ball, suddenly tossing appearances to the wind, pushed itself over a family group inoffensively eating lunch on the sand. For a moment the family was blotted out; then it reappeared in a crumpled condition, its luncheon sadly attenuated. The father of the family picked himself up and in an impassioned speech demanded to be immediately informed who had made the *balle* to march not only over his lunch but also over his blood relations. As if it were an afterthought, the *balle* returned and smote the voluble Frenchman heavily upon his unguarded back.

This forcibly returned the man to his former place on the sand in the heart of his family. The ball passed on and made for the crowd. It seemed to have become infuriated about something. The crowd parted, and the ball sped down the beach, where it crashed against a tent, the two occupants of which would have preferred not to be seen. As if satisfied by this display of ferocity the ball came to rest.

By this time Monsieur Sylvestre was receiving a lot of complaints about his ball. He strode down the beach and confronted it with a severe eye. Immediately the ball set itself in motion. It began to march on Monsieur Sylvestre. This act of defiance enraged the good *patron*. He, in turn, defied the ball. He rushed to meet its advance. In this the Frenchman displayed more valor than discretion. There was no stopping that ball. It met Monsieur Sylvestre face to face, and it was the *patron's* face that yielded. When he dazedly arose he experienced the final humiliation of being chased back to the crowd by his own ball. The ball stopped short of the crowd and rested on its laurels. It was master of the field. None disputed its authority to go where it pleased. Monsieur Sylvestre had suffered a crushing defeat. He was stunned.

Throughout all this the German model alone had remained unmoved. She was gradually edging her bathing suit lower down on her body. A small towel served as supplementary protection. For once Topper was not interested. His eyes were on the springboard jutting out from the end of the bathing pier. Many eyes were centered on this spot.

Here he saw George Kerby, ludicrously clad in a flapping bathing suit which must once have been the property of a felon. George was poised on the extreme edge of the springboard. He was contorting his body in the most excruciating postures preparatory to diving. Suddenly he flung his striped form high in the air, scrambled himself there for a moment, then faded out. The bathing suit dropped to the water with a wistful splash. Before the astounded watchers had had time to recover from this shocking event, the tall form of the Colonel, clad like a patriarch in a flowing robe, appeared upon the lip of the springboard. The crowd was breathing heavily. One woman was actually praying, while several others were furtively crossing themselves. Even Mr. Topper was moved by the sight of the Colonel. Dressed as he was, it seemed likely that the priestly Colonel would, at least, ascend to heaven, instead of which he treated his audience to several dizzy flips, then landed in the water with a terrific flop. As far as the crowd could tell, the Colonel never came up, for his robe, too, drifted on the tide in company with the garment George Kerby had abandoned.

The bathers out on the float now began to experience difficulty in maintaining their footing. Topper watched them as one by one they appeared to hurl themselves into the sea. Only the ladies remained, and they looked as if remaining was the last thing in the world they wanted to do.

Mr. Topper decided that George Kerby and the Colonel must be very busy about having a good time. They seemed to be everywhere at once, causing disturbance.

When the men climbed back on the float they naturally wanted to know who was the dirty dog that had been so mentally warped as to push them overboard. This question was asked in several different languages, but in none pleasantly. This led to complications, for the answers were in all tongues an approximation of "go to hell." So enraged did one small man become that he struck a large man in the stomach. The large man in his fury literally threw the small man away. Not quite mollified by this rather drastic step, he turned and punched an inquiring stranger heavily upon the nose. The stricken man, realizing the futility of meeting the large man on his own ground, satisfied his exasperation by tearing the bathing suit off an elderly gentleman in spectacles. Not knowing what else to do, yet feeling called upon to do something, the elderly gentleman held the nearest head he could find under water. One show of ill temper speedily led to another. It was not long before the crowd on the beach was stricken mute with amazement by the condition of the float. Its occupants seemed to have gone in for murder. Half clad and totally nude they attacked one another like so many Neolithic warriors.

Blind unreason ruled the day. Blows rained, and imprecations rose. Murderous ambitions were frustrated by a splash. Whether all the occupants of the float ever returned to the beach or some drowned on the way was never satisfactorily settled. Topper remembered seeing one man, evidently unhinged by terror, swimming industriously out to sea. He assumed the man eventually returned. He could not have sworn to it. Topper did not care a great deal if none of them got back.

Exhaustion and salt water eventually put an end to the activities on the float. The crowd drew a deep breath and wondered what the admirable Monsieur Sylvestre was going to do about it all. That gentleman was moodily considering taking either one of two steps— putting his café, bath houses, and diversions up for sale, or sending for the gendarmes. His *plage tranquille* had suddenly changed to *la plage de la pandémonium*. He sank heavily down on the sand by Mr. Topper and asked him about it. Mr. Topper admitted that it was a little too much for him to explain. That push ball, for instance, could it have been in the clutch of a strong but self-contained wind? Monsieur Sylvestre stoutly declared that the conduct of the push ball would have been inexcusable in a hurricane. And as for those diving bodies that disappeared even as they dived, that was a thing inexplicable. No, of a truth *le bon Dieu* had turned His face against his, Monsieur Sylvestre's, beach. At this moment the distracted man caught sight of Oscar's self-propelling tail snaking its way across the sand in the general direction of another lunch basket. Monsieur Sylvestre's eyes started from his head. Several times he opened his mouth as if to speak, but no articulate sounds issued therefrom. Finally they came in awed accents.

"M'sieu," he said in a choked voice. "*Regardez!* Even now dogs have begun to forsake their tails. Soon the entire beach may be doing likewise. Who can tell where these things will end?"

Not waiting to see what disposition this forsaken tail was going to make of itself, Monsieur Sylvestre rose unsteadily to his feet and lurched off in the direction of his café and level-headed wife. Mr. Topper sighed deeply and turned to regard the bare reaches of the German model. Today she was barer than ever, there was no doubt about it. Too bad so much was going on elsewhere. She was not receiving the attention she deserved.

As Topper sat there contemplating the deeply tanned figure of the German model he received the uncanny impression that eyes were contemplating him. For a moment he fought against the desire to look about him; then his resistance broke down. Had he known beforehand that he was going to encounter the reproving gaze of a python, still he could not have refrained from looking. The gaze that he did encounter was almost as dangerous. If anything, it was more so for his peace of mind.

What he actually did see was Marion Kerby fully and perfectly materialized. It was the first time he had seen her since she had returned, and his startled glance told him that hers was by all odds the loveliest figure on the beach. Everything else was forgotten—the trying events of the morning and the excitement that had so recently been occupying his attention. The beach faded away, and he saw her sitting there with the blue of the ocean at her back. Her slim body had been poured into a small, black, and well worn bathing suit. Her skin was glowingly tanned. Curls clustered unreasonably round her back-tilted head. He remembered the delicate, almost childlike, features of her face, the small impertinent chin, and the arched lips with their roving smile. He recalled the mad, eloquent beauty of her eyes, and again he looked into them, then hastily looked away. They were regarding him with scornful malevolence. Those lips he knew so well were curved in a dangerous smile. Topper hated to think of it as a grin, but it was almost that—a nasty grin. Topper waited in dread. For a brief moment she let her baleful gaze rest on the unsuspecting German model, then she looked significantly at Mr. Topper, who, although avoiding her eyes, knew exactly what was going on.

"Nice Topper," she said in a low voice. "Animal man, Topper. I'll cook your goose and hers, too, you leaky old bucket."

Topper looked up at this odd appellation, but Marion Kerby was gone. A wild scream from the German model lifted him to his feet. She, also, was on hers, and now at last there was nothing left to prevent the sun from completing its task. The model was bereft of slightest pretense.

There were several things the lady could have done under the circumstances—several sensible, strategical moves she could have made. She could, for instance, have thrown herself to the beach and covered at least parts of her body with sand. Again, it would not have been unmannerly under the stress of the moment to snatch a towel from someone else and appropriate it for her own protection. She might even have used her hands and have run like hell for the bath houses, which were not far off. She could have done any one of these things or combined the best features of them all, but it just so happened that she chose to do none of them. Instead, she strode up to Mr. Topper, whom she mistakenly assumed to be the author of her predicament, and felled him with a single Teutonic blow. As the confounded man measured his length on the sand, the German model turned to find her bathing suit and towel dangling tauntingly before her eyes. The sight was to the lady as a red flag is to a bull. As the garments sped down the beach in the grip of an invisible force the German model sped after them. There was grim, implacable determination in the pumping of her legs. Her brown body with its narrow band of white was entirely forgotten in her pursuit of her stolen drapery. One arm was extended strainingly to reach what was rightfully hers, but her fingers, ever hopeful, never quite established contact. The towel and the bathing suit fluttered just beyond her grasp.

Thus passed the German model in impressive review. Spellbound, the beach regarded the spectacle, the climax of many mystifying events. At the end of the beach the flying articles turned sharply, and the German model followed after. When her ravished raiment came abreast of Mr. Topper, who had just risen, he received them full in the face. Once more he took the count.

"There!" came a voice in triumph. "I hope you got an eyeful as well as a faceful."

As the German model made for Topper he sprang to his feet and held out the bathing suit and towel. His eyes were modestly averted. This was not a wise move. The model snatched her property, then promptly knocked Topper down again. For the third time he measured his length on the sand of the tranquil beach. This time he remained measured. Until things quieted down he had no intention of getting up. It was a sheer waste of effort.

At this point Oscar intervened in behalf of his old friend, Topper. The tail suddenly got into action and pursued the model to her bath house. More than the tail must have been in action if the frightened cries of the fleeing woman meant even a little bit. Once in her bath house she screamed for Monsieur Sylvestre, who from one thing and another was almost at the end of his rope.

"There's a growl in my bath house," she called in perfect English.

"A towel?" inquired the *patron*. "Madame, but yes, I caused it to be placed there myself."

"Not this one, you didn't," cried the model, leaping unimproved from her bath house and frantically scratching at the door of another one.

The door flew open, and she stood confronting an elderly gentleman clad in spectacles only. This elderly gentleman had already received enough shocks on the float to scoot him through death's door. The formidable appearance of the model slammed the door behind him. He collapsed in a heap. The lady almost did the same. Also, Monsieur Sylvestre. The next bath house was empty. Into it the model plunged. Entering bath houses at random was, of course, child's play for Oscar. He was on the point of following the German model when he heard his master's voice.

"Oscar, you devil," called the Colonel. "Come here immediately and leave that lady alone."

The tail swung round and trotted off in the direction of its invisible master. There was a jaunty flip in its carriage. It was a tail of considerable achievement.

Monsieur Sylvestre had abandoned the model to her noise and her nudity and was addressing Mr. Topper.

"M'sieu," he was saying reproachfully, "at the proper time and in the proper place I am not saying that your conduct would have been other than quite correct, inevitable, in fact, but why did you undress the lady here on my once so tranquil beach?"

Mr. Topper raised his head wearily.

"I tell you, Monsieur Sylvestre," he said weakly, "I was not within six feet of the woman when the event occurred. I am not in the habit of undressing ladies either in public or private."

The *patron* elevated his eyebrows and gazed out to sea. He was thinking of how ungallant Mr. Topper was. So unlike a Frenchman, who was always willing to lend a helping hand.

There was only one thing left to do about it. Monsieur Sylvestre did that thing.

He shrugged.

XI

Interlude on the Rocks

Unseen wavelets slipping furtively over low-lying rocks. Night time now. Far out across the ocean the bald head of the moon is pushing up the darkness. Topper is on the rocks. Alone. He smells the night around him. Topper is almost dog-like about it. He has a yen for the fragrance of night. Mimosa blended with wet sea grass, and over all the heavy, sweet, compelling scent of tropical flowers swimming on the breeze from near-by estates. There are trees behind Topper. The sea lies in front. Under him and about are the rocks—dark, crouching, motionless. Somewhere close at hand lies a little sandy beach—a shallow scoop of sand about as large as a bathtub. This quiet secluded place Topper discovered for himself. He comes here when the mood is on him. He comes here and sits and looks and smells. Sometimes he thinks things. But what things he thinks would be difficult to say. Men like Topper, men whom life has given to believe that they are unoriginal, ordinary, humdrum creatures, have a habit of keeping their thoughts to themselves. Yet what thicker skinned poets glowingly put down on paper some of these stout and seemingly commonplace gentlemen have been nourishing in secret all their lives.

Topper is fascinated by this spot. Close to the surface of the water the rocks step far out from the shore. Occasionally a reef breaks through. When the sea is running strong and the wind blows flat across it he experiences a comforting sensation of isolation as the waves drive in around him. Even the sea gulls in this place seem to be of a different tribe—solitary, lost, and a little eerie.

"Not much pickings for them here," Topper had once thought. "Look sort of foolish, though, bringing a package along. Sea gulls don't eat crumbs. Great chunks at a gobble."

A little more than a week has passed since the episode of the beach, or, rather, the episodes on the beach. During all this time Topper has not been favored by the company of his unseen friends. He has been left with a sense of injury. Some explanation was due him, some slight form of apology. He himself had been forced to explain although he had failed lamentably. The story of the unveiling of the model had been told with extras to Mrs. Topper by her snooty English friends.

"What perverted impulse prompted you to snatch the bathing suit off that lewd woman?" Mrs. Topper had asked when the snooty friends had at last departed, their good works left behind them.

"I had nothing to do with her bathing suit," Topper wearily denied.

"You must have," went on his wife. "The woman actually knocked you down. Fancy that, being knocked down on a public beach by a naked woman."

"I don't like to fancy it," said Mr. Topper, closing his eyes on the horrid memory.

"I don't know what has come over you," Mrs. Topper hurried on. "Are you going to make your life just one attempted assault after another? First Félice, then this German model."

"No," replied Topper darkly. "I'm going to succeed the next time."

"Well, I hope you do," snapped his wife, "and get such ideas out of your mind for good and all."

"That German model was nearly naked, anyway," Mr. Topper observed.

"I know," Mary Topper replied, "but that nearly, as small as it was, meant everything."

"Yes," said Mr. Topper. "I readily admit that."

"It didn't seem to feaze her, though," Mrs. Topper observed, "the way she went rushing about in that shocking condition."

"I was a lot more injured than shocked," said Mr. Topper.

"I can well imagine that," replied his wife, "letting yourself be knocked down by a naked woman."

"But, my dear, if I had knocked the naked woman down," Topper protested, "people might have mistaken my intentions entirely."

"And they wouldn't have been far wrong," declared Mrs. Topper quite unreasonably. "What's going to become of you, I'd like to know? You can't go dashing about France pulling skirts off servant girls and bathing suits off German models."

Mr. Topper did not know what was going to become of him. He told Mrs. Topper that he did not care a damn. To proclaim his innocence any further would be, he knew, worse than useless. He collected his hat and stick and made for the door. His wife's voice followed after. It was her parting shot.

"And if you are seized with an impulse to claw the clothes off some woman you meet in the street," she told him, "I advise you to count up to twenty, no matter how much you feel like it."

Topper laughed mirthlessly.

"Thanks," he said. "I'm going to leave a trail of stripped bodies behind me."

"Well, don't drag them into the house," was all his wife replied.

Topper had been afraid to attempt the beach since the day he had been thrice knocked down upon it. He did not know what had become of the German model, but reports had it that she was back at her old stand. He wondered how she could do it. She was made of ruggeder stuff than he was, that was certain. What would she do to him if he appeared in her presence? Would she arise and knock him down—cause another scandal? Topper rather suspected she would. That German model seemed to thrive on public scandals. She was a public scandal herself.

Instead of frequenting the beach Topper took to the Esterel Mountains. Here in deep quiet valleys he considered many things at leisure, hardly realizing he was thinking at all. There was always some hustling little stream to keep him company, and the fantastic coloring of the great rocks rising high above him pleasantly occupied his eyes. It was quiet back here in the mountains. All the world seemed to have moved to the beach. It was a rare occasion when he met another human being. Even the bird life was of a desultory nature. Solitude was deep but not oppressive. When he caught the dark shadow of a fish moving in the clear waters of a stream he felt a sense of mystery and surprise. He was not entirely alone.

As a result of these long walks Topper was losing weight and toughening his muscles. He felt better physically as well as mentally. He no longer cared a rap what other people thought. And strange to say it was here in these solitudes that he discovered he loved France. His casual conversations with the back-country people he met from time to time in the course of his walks did much to dispel the impression made upon him by the franc-frantic denizens of the resort towns. Topper had a desire to return to these quiet places some day before he died. He scarcely realized how deep that desire was rooted in him.

He felt the same way about these rocks and the little beach he had discovered. This spot would dwell in his memory. He would harken back to it. The moon was up now. A silvery path ran from it to the rocks. Topper saw in fancy a figure drifting towards him down the moon path. Then, very quietly, a small hand nuzzled its way into his. He knew without turning his head that Marion Kerby was back. She would do a thing like that, taking his welcome for granted like a stray pup.

"Yes?" he said, still gazing out to sea.

"I feel like the incidental music for Amos and Andy," she murmured.

"It must be a terrible feeling," replied Topper.

"No, it isn't. It's nice for a change. I feel all holy and sunsetlike inside. Still, sort of, and very, very tender—like a good woman about to be bad."

"Your hair is blowing in my mouth," was Topper's reply to this. "Do something about it."

"Then bite it off," continued the low voice. "I'll grow some new hair."

Topper thought this remark far from holy and tender, but he made no reply.

"Oscar can do his hind legs now," offered the voice a little timidly. "And much of his upper rump."

"I don't care if he can do himself into a pack of bloodhounds," replied Mr. Topper. "Where have you been all this time? Answer me that."

"All right," said Marion in an injured voice. "Don't bite my head off. I don't mind about the hair. You can chew on that till the cows come home."

"I don't care to chew on that until the cows start out even," said Mr. Topper. "I'm not a hair chewer."

"I know you're not," Marion put in placatingly. "But I do think you might show some interest in Oscar's rump, especially his upper rump."

"Do you expect me to sit here on these rocks and go into ecstasies over the shaggy rump of a lunch-snatching dog?"

"Well, the Colonel is greatly encouraged, and we all feel sort of good about it. A fish did it."

"What! How could a fish possibly influence Oscar's upper rump?"

"Can't quite say," she replied. "But he saw a fish in a tank the other day, and from that moment he began to materialize his hind legs and upper rump." The voice trailed off for a moment, then resumed musingly, "I guess Oscar had never seen a fish before—not a real live fish, that is. Strange, isn't it, never having seen a fish!"

"And he probably thought," remarked Mr. Topper sarcastically, "that if a fish could get away with a funny tail like that, he himself had little of which to feel ashamed."

"Perhaps," Marion replied. "You may be right, but deep emotion has always affected Oscar's rump proper and upper rump."

"There's not a proper part in all of that dog's body," declared Mr. Topper.

"How about mine?" Marion asked demurely.

"Nor yours either," said Topper. "Are we to sit here all night discussing Oscar's rump? I've asked you where you have been for so long? And while we're on the subject of rumps, I'd like to take yours across my knee and give it a good sound drubbing."

"I'd quickly do away with mine," replied Marion. "On second thought, though, go right ahead. I don't mind brutality. I lived with a brute all my life."

"George treats you a damn sight too well. By the way, just where is he now?"

"I've given him the slip. He's drinking up all the francs he won by cheating at Monte Carlo. That's where we were—at Monte Carlo. We always go there when we feel the need of money. The Colonel thought it up."

"And the delicious Mrs. Hart put the idea in the Colonel's mind," said Mr. Topper.

"Wouldn't be a bit surprised," Marion agreed. "She's a rare trollop, that one, but a lovable old tear-sheet withal."

"And you're no lily, yourself," replied Mr. Topper.

"I am so," said Marion. "I'm a tiger lily. Feel my teeth."

Topper's neck was sharply bitten in a spot where the marks of teeth would be sure to attract unfavorable attention.

"You're branded now," continued Marion, laughing softly. "From now on you are my mustang. Go on and act wild."

"Marion," said Topper reprovingly. He hesitated a moment, then turned, and for the first time met the irresistible invitation of her eyes. "Oh, hell," he muttered, taking her in his arms. "You're the very soul of depravity, and yet, you're better than a sermon."

"Let's deprave," murmured Marion, snuggling her pliant body close to the man. "I'm not exactly off you, either, my old and rare."

Then Topper did act wild, wilder than he had ever acted in his life. Being thrice flattened against the sand was a small price to pay, he decided, for those moments of complete forgetfulness he spent with Marion by the little, hidden beach. The moon kept rising higher, and if it was at all disconcerted by what it saw, it did not bat an eye. The moon had been witnessing such meetings since the world was first made to shine on. At this late date it was shockproof.

"Saints preserve us," breathed Marion Kerby, her voice drifting back from the far end of time. "In the words of a lady you know, for a man of your age and girth———"

"None of that!" Topper broke in, blotting out her face with a large brown hand.

"Oh, all right," the girl spluttered. "But how will I ever get re-arranged?"

"It doesn't matter," said Topper. "Do you like this place?"

"It's excellent for the purpose," she answered. "Every prospect pleases. Don't let the others know a thing about it. By the way, what were your relations with that German model from Yonkers?"

"Not even close enough to be platonic," said Mr. Topper.

"Is that a lie?" asked Marion.

"That is not a lie," returned Topper. "My interest in her was purely academic."

"Academic, perhaps, but not purely."

"I won't stickle," said Topper.

"I wouldn't if I were you," she answered. "It sounds sort of bad. From now on I want you to keep your eyes off that wolf of a woman. If you value what little is left of your reputation, look somewhere else. Next time it will be your suit that gets snatched off."

"One can hardly keep from looking at so much bare flesh."

"I'll give you enough to look at," Marion replied grimly.

"Marion," said Topper rather primly, "you have sunk to the lowest of planes."

"I know it," the girl at his side admitted. "I've backslid terribly."

"How did it happen, Marion? I'm glad you did."

"You would be," she answered, smiling oddly in the darkness. "But it doesn't speak so well for me. I couldn't stand the upper strata. The atmosphere—too rarefied for me. Wasn't ready for it. I thought I was. I felt sure about it. Convinced. But this old earth exerts a powerful pull, my old. Especially with you on it—you all alone and puzzled about things."

"You don't mean that, Marion?" Topper's voice was low.

"I don't know," she answered slowly. "I guess I must mean it, or why do I let myself go like this? God knows it's not for your looks. I could improve on those with my hands tucked into boxing gloves."

"You like to make yourself clear, don't you?" Topper put in.

"I do," continued Marion. "And you're not admirable. In fact, there's nothing good about you—no redeeming feature, and yet, you're my sort of man."

"You're hardly a mother superior yourself," declared Topper.

"Oh, I just raise a lot of harmless hell. Take advantage of situations and all that. But I don't fall for any other guys. George has only you to worry about."

"Yes," allowed Mr. Topper. "He worries so much about me that I can't help worrying about him—a little."

"And that young buck tires to make every good-looking dame he lays eyes on," continued Marion. "I don't mind in the least. He was always that way. His parents had to give him a woman for his sixteenth birthday. They were extremely indulgent, his parents. And he exacted the same indulgence from me. Had I cared any I'd have made him a corpse quick as a wink, same as I'll make you if you pull any fast ones."

"I'm all right, lady," said Mr. Topper hastily. "You don't have to trouble your head about me."

"I won't," Marion assured him. "Your head will get all the trouble. I'll twist the dull thing off like this."

She illustrated this threat by a suggestive grinding of her two small fists. Mr. Topper could see his neck serving as the core for this painful operation. He looked away.

"Don't," he asked her. "Don't do that any more. I understand perfectly. Let's talk of something else."

"Sure," agreed Marion, "but that's about the way I'd do it."

"How did you get track of me over here?" asked Mr. Topper.

Marion rested her head on his shoulder and took up one of his hands much as she would a book.

"Well," she said, "when I backslid, the first person I called on was you. You weren't there. You weren't anywhere that I could find. So I just hung about the place until the letter carrier came and collected your readdressed mail from a servant. I snatched one of the letters out of his hand, read the address, then flung it back in his face."

"That was unnecessary," remarked Mr. Topper.

"Quite," agreed Marion. "He was greatly upset about it. Almost afraid to pick the letter up. I have fun that way. Not much, but a little. I was feeling good about finding out where you were. After that it was all quite simple. I collected the rest of them and induced them to take the trip. George is always game for any kind of diversion."

"Including torture and murder," added Mr. Topper. "He found me first, did George, in a most embarrassing situation."

"Oh, no, he didn't. I was there all the time."

"Good God!" exclaimed Mr. Topper. "While I was taking a bath?"

"While both of you were taking a bath," said Marion, nodding contentedly. "Behind that wicker laundry basket of yours. I tried to get in it, but the damn thing was full."

Mr. Topper was profoundly shocked. He rose to his feet and helped Marion to hers.

"That was not at all nice of you," he said.

"No," replied Marion complacently, "but it was highly amusing. If George hadn't been there I'd have bathed with you myself, perhaps. Who knows?"

"Come," said Mr. Topper. "We had better take a walk."

"Will you buy me a drink?" Marion asked him.

"I'll buy you a swarm of drinks," Topper assured her.

"Not too many tonight," said Marion. "I must look up George to see if the coast is clear."

"Just what are you planning on doing?"

"Oh, nothing much," she replied evasively. "Just scouting about. After we've had our drink I'll take you home."

And that is what Marion did. Rather wistfully she left Topper at his gate.

"Where are you going to sleep tonight?" he asked her.

"We have unoccupied rooms at the best hotels," Marion told him. "The maids can't understand why the beds are mussed up every morning. I might sleep in one of those bath houses, though, just to be nearer you."

"Don't do that," said Topper. "Go to your hotel and get a good night's sleep. And think of me. I have to go in there now and listen to a lot of drip from my wife's unendurable friends—England's worst exhibits on the Riviera."

"Tell 'em to go to hell," murmured Marion, kissing him as she faded out. "I'll see you soon, my old and rare."

Topper stood at his gate. He was alone now. The night spoke of his solitude—intensified it.

"Marion," he called softly. "Marion, where are you?"

Silence. Waves against the beach.

Topper turned and walked thoughtfully towards his villa, pallid in the moonlight. In the next villa—not Monsieur Louis's—a woman's figure was outlined against a window. She was standing there watching—always watching. She seldom left her window, that old, mean-minded French hag.

"Like to shy a rock through the pane," Topper mused darkly as he stepped onto his veranda. "It would damn well serve her right. Hiding her own wickedness behind a curtain while looking for the worst in others."

XII

THE ECCENTRIC BEHAVIOR
OF SCOLLOPS

When Mr. Topper stepped into his villa he was on the verge. Exactly what he was on the verge of he could not have said with any degree of certainty. But he knew he was on the verge of something. He felt like it all over. It might have been the mumps, or, again, it might have been murder. So far he had never committed either. And when he entered his sitting room to be confronted by a stack of four Sutton-Trevors and one Mary Topper he knew that the verge of whatever it was had been left far behind. He was over it and plunging headlong into all kinds of trouble—folly, indiscretions, and even better, Marion Kerby.

Accordingly, when Mrs. Sutton-Trevor looked up at Mr. Topper with more interest than approval and said, *"Bonsoir, Monsieur Topper. J'espère que vous vous portez bien. Comment?"* Mr. Topper looked back at her disgustedly and replied, "Must you make those alien noises?"

It was one of those insulting remarks that people pretend either not to have heard or not to have understood. Mrs. Sutton-Trevor laughed unnaturally. Mr. Topper thought of a lake of seamed, rubberlike ice suddenly splitting open, then closing up again. Topper looked closely at the lady in an attempt to discover if he had heard aright. Her face gave no indication of ever having departed from its set grimness. Nothing lingered there. Mr. Topper blinked rapidly several times.

Mr. Keith Sutton-Trevor then took up tennis with Topper. Keith Sutton-Trevor was still considered an only child, although he was easily Mr. Topper's age. He was a man with teeth and the face of a hard-bitten ridge. Mr. Topper leered at the ridge and declared he hated the game, which was a lie. Mr. Topper loved tennis and played it atrociously. Keith's mother protested violently in English. She endeavored to give the impression of having become so accustomed to speaking French that she found her native tongue tough sledding. She groped spasmodically for the right word and made herself look altogether horrid. Mr. Topper informed her brutally that he still detested tennis, that he had come to France merely to drink and indulge a couple of other low whims of his, and that he approved of Soviet Russia.

"Liars, thieves, and murderers," muttered the elder Mr. Sutton-Trevor who up to this moment had been quite satisfied in listening to the sound he made by breathing heavily through his nose.

"But, my dear Mr. Topper," interposed the wife of Keith Sutton-Trevor, who in a past incarnation had been an ill-favored horse and who had not been improved by the change, "there's not a gentleman in the government."

"How about your own?" asked Mr. Topper.

"You mean our Labor element? Ah, Mr. Topper, its members are rapidly becoming gentlemen. England always does that to its radical politicians; then they become statesmen and can't afford to be radical any longer."

"Political eunuchs," snapped Mr. Topper.

"Why, Cosmo!" exclaimed his wife.

"Pretty strong—pretty strong," objected the elder Mr. Sutton-Trevor. "I say, Topper, there are ladies present. Yes, by gad, there are."

"You surprise me," said Mr. Topper. "How does it feel?"

Mrs. Topper's dyspepsia was increasing by leaps and bounds.

"My husband jests," she gulped unhappily.

"While you indijest," retorted Topper. "How's that, Trevor-

Suttons?" he demanded, deliberately reversing their names. "Think it's worth a cognac? I do. It's very funny."

"Sutton-Trevor, Mr. Topper, *if you please*," objected the wife of the breather with steadily mounting emphasis.

"Suttinly," replied Mr. Topper from the buffet, at which he was taking a double portion of cognac most improperly. "That's very funny, too. And I'm not even half trying."

"You don't need to try at all," commented Mrs. Topper, "so far as we're concerned. Mr. and Mrs. Sutton-Trevor have asked me to motor to Paris with them, and I'm thinking of accepting."

"It would be the last thing in the world I'd think of doing," said Mr. Topper quite inoffensively. "It's your dish at a gulp, though. I can see that. Let nothing stop you. Keith and myself will stay at home and play tennis morning, noon, and night. How about it, Keith?"

"My husband is an exceptionally fine player," put in Mrs. Keith.

"You mean, for a man of his age," Mr. Topper replied with ready sympathy. "I fancy he can pull some sneaky ones. Well, I'm a pretty stealthy player myself. It will be sneak meeting sneak. Don't trouble to acknowledge that one. It came too easy."

Topper loudly smacked his lips, polished them on the sleeve of his coat, and sat down, reiterating that he dearly loved to drink. He was deliberately trying to start a row.

There was really very little left that Mrs. Topper and the Sutton-Trevors could talk about in the uncouth presence of the drink-loving Topper. A brooding constraint fell upon them, and into this walked Scollops in a manner with which nobody present was even remotely familiar, including Scollops, herself.

Casually and without haste Mr. Topper's personal cat sauntered across the sitting room with her back legs dangling thoughtlessly in the air. It was an effortless performance in which Scollops seemed to be taking no part. Topper realized full well that Scollops was not responsible for the ridiculous figure she cut. He suspected the Colonel and Oscar of experimenting with his pet. What did surprise him was the complete lack of interest Scollops displayed in what was being done to her. Few cats permitted such liberties to be taken with their persons. Dogs, yes. Dogs were natural born clowns.

Not so cats. Those creatures of habit were conservative to a fault. Topper reflected that the Colonel had a way with animals. Inexhaustible patience. He took one look at his cat, then rose and returned to the cognac. The inverted Scollops followed him. Topper felt somewhat like a ring master in a circus.

"Is this one of your stupid tricks?" his wife demanded.

"It appears to be Scollops' idea entirely," remarked Mr. Topper. "I claim no credit at all. Give the little lady a big hand."

"I mean, have you strung her up on a wire or something?" Mary Topper persisted.

"I'm not so anxious to amuse you as all that," her husband retorted.

"You're not amusing me in the least," interposed Mrs. Sutton-Trevor. "I refuse even to look at such an unnatural and undignified animal."

"That cat is far from amusing," wheezed old Mr. Sutton-Trevor. "The Lord God of hosts never created a cat to walk in that fashion."

"I think I could bear it a little better if she would only reverse her position," said the old gentleman's daughter-in-law, "and walk on her back legs instead."

At this remark the back legs referred to began to pump busily in the air as if the cat were riding a bicycle upside down. Mr. Topper himself was a little upset by this uncalled for demonstration. Even Scollops contrived to look back and up at her speeding legs as if surprised by their sudden activity.

"Perhaps the cat has something in her foot and is trying to shake it out," suggested Mr. Keith Sutton-Trevor.

"Nonsense," said his mother impatiently. "That would be a silly way to go about getting it out."

"No," agreed Mrs. Topper. "If I had something in my foot I'm sure I wouldn't stand on my hands and shake my legs in the air."

"Don't!" said Mr. Topper hastily. "Even the thought unmans me."

"Well, she's your cat," continued Mrs. Topper, ignoring her husband's remark. "I wish you'd make her stop whatever she thinks she's doing."

At this moment Félice entered to collect the coffee cups and liqueur glasses. After one look at Scallops she forgot the object of her quest.

"The cat," she murmured, "she is foolish. She claws at the air in reverse."

Snatching up several cups she hurried from the room. Topper had a bright idea. He hoped the Colonel, or whoever was manipulating Scallops, would play up to it.

" 'Bout face!" he ordered.

Immediately the cat described a neat flip, landed lightly on her hind legs and stood at attention with her forepaws elevated. Topper laughed inordinately.

"That's one of the funniest things I ever saw," he said. "Damn my eyes!"

"I wish you'd go somewhere else and look at that cat alone," Mrs. Topper told him feelingly. "She's upsetting my guests."

"Also herself," added Topper. "Carry on, Scollops."

At this command Scollops did a strange and unladylike thing. She resumed the position of a normal cat, walked deliberately over to Mrs. Sutton-Trevor and spat at that good lady. Mrs. Sutton-Trevor started violently in her chair.

"My word!" exclaimed her son. "Do you think the beast is mad? Will it attack us, perhaps?"

Scollops, as if understanding these questions, turned and looked long at the Englishman. Then, crouching close to the floor, she emitted a fearful scream and sprang, claws distended, into the horror-riven face of Mr. Keith Sutton-Trevor. There must have been more weight behind Scollops than mere cat, because the assaulted man, with a scream rivaling hers in fearfulness, rolled out across the matting as the back of his chair hit the floor.

"I'm dreadfully sorry," said Mrs. Topper, bending solicitously over the sprawling gentleman. "It will never occur again."

"Once was too often," the Englishman's mother replied for him. "An incident like that should never occur at all. Your husband's cat will have no opportunity to insult me and assault mine a second time."

"Nonsense," said Mr. Topper, seizing the fallen man by the arm and dragging him ruthlessly over the matting in an abortive effort to help him to his feet. "What should a tennis shark like your son care about a little cat? He plays with their guts."

"What!" ejaculated Mr. Sutton-Trevor, growing purple in the face. "This is too much—too low to be tolerated."

"Your husband is less endurable than his cat," the younger Mrs. Sutton-Trevor told Mrs. Topper. "What a disgusting thing to say about poor Keith."

"Not at all," grunted Mr. Topper, pulling the arm with all his might. "If you had any sense at all you'd know that tennis rackets are strung with catgut."

"I wish they were strung with yours," grated the elder Mr. Sutton-Trevor with a complete reversal of manners.

"Oh, what a horrid wish!" said Mr. Topper, pausing for a moment in his pulling. "Did you hear what he said, everybody? I merely stated a general fact. He's getting personal about my interior."

"If you would kindly stop trying to pull my arm off," interposed Mr. Keith Sutton-Trevor bitterly, "I might be able to get up off the floor for a while."

"Sorry, old chap," replied Mr. Topper. "Wasn't thinking of what I was doing. Hope it isn't spoiled for your tennis."

"I couldn't even play ping-pong with it, the way it is now," the man replied ruefully as he painfully endeavored to wriggle the injured member back into position. "May I ask what you wanted to do with my arm?"

"I don't want to do a thing with any part of your malformed body," Mr. Topper assured him. "Between the bunch of you you've broken my cat's heart. Look at the poor creature."

Scollops, when last seen, had been crawling under the chair of the elder Mr. Sutton-Trevor. That gentleman, looking down, was distressed to see a long shaggy tail lying between his feet.

"That is a strange cat," he observed, "but she can't be so strange as to grow a tail like that all at once."

Gingerly he moved his feet apart and leaned down closer to the tail in question.

"Is there a dog in the house?" he asked.

"No," said Mr. Topper. "Do you want one?"

"There are enough low animals present as it is," replied the old man significantly. "Whatever that queer object belongs to, it can't stay where it is. I don't like the looks of the thing."

With this old Mr. Sutton-Trevor reached down and laid violent hands on the tail, giving it a rude tug as he did so. The tail snapped out from under the chair and was immediately followed by a deep growl.

"My God," said the old gentleman, turning white, "I've pulled the beast's tail off, and it merely growls. What manner of an animal is it?"

At this moment the tail began to wiggle excitedly in his hand. With a yell of fear Mr. Sutton-Trevor dropped it and drew his feet up off the floor. Like a thing of life the tail sped round the room. Scollops suddenly appeared from under the table and lengthened out in hot pursuit of the tail. The tail left the floor and landed on Mrs. Sutton-Trevor's lap. Scollops did likewise, and it was there that the battle was joined. While this admirable English gentlewoman made noises like an American Indian on the warpath, Oscar, unseen but vocal, and Scollops, a flash of screeching fur, fought to a draw without budging an inch from their original point of contact, i. e., Mrs. Sutton-Trevor's agitated lap. As a result of this trying experience, the good lady, as soon as the cat and the tail had removed themselves from the field of battle, had to be assisted from the room.

"There's something decidedly peculiar about this villa," she announced upon returning to the sitting room. "And I'm not referring altogether to Mr. Topper either."

"That's good of you," put in Mr. Topper with a malicious grin.

"It was unintentional, I assure you," the lady resumed, "but when undogged tails begin to bark and bite and dash about the house, and when cats start to walk like acrobats and fight like distracted demons in my lap, it's time to draw the line. I draw it now. Mrs. Topper, I'm exceedingly sorry, but I can't let my family remain beneath your husband's roof. It's altogether too dangerous. At any moment my husband might have a stroke or my son might lose his mind."

"Well, I draw the line at that," Mr. Topper retorted, "although, for the life of me, I can't make out how either one of them would be greatly changed. The old chap's been the grave digger's darling for years, and as for your slightly faded son, he can hardly lose what he hasn't."

"Oh!" gasped Mrs. Sutton-Trevor. "Strike him, Keith. We have never been so insulted."

"England expects every man to duck his duty," said Mr. Topper nastily.

This was too much for Keith Sutton-Trevor. He stepped up to Mr. Topper and raised his hand. It was immediately filled with cat. How Scollops managed it no one will ever know. Mr. Topper suspected the Colonel of having dropped her there. At the same time not only the tail but also the complete rump of a dog came charging across the room at the trembling legs of the outraged Englishman. It was more than human flesh could bear. Even gods would have been disconcerted. Mr. Keith Sutton-Trevor had in his composition no strain remotely godlike. He dropped the cat, side-stepped the rushing rump, and fled from the house.

"Where's he gone?" demanded his father.

"To look for the rest of that dog," Mr. Topper suggested cheerfully.

"And where is she going to?" continued the old man as Keith's wife dashed after him.

"To look for what's left of him," replied Mr. Topper. "He's hardly worth the trouble."

"If I were a day younger, sir, I'd thrash you within an inch of your life."

"And if you were a day older there wouldn't be an inch of your life left to thrash."

"Oh!" cried the old gentleman. "This bounder is insufferable. Take me away."

Topper was drinking cognac.

"Yes, Mrs. Sutton-Trevor," he said, "hurry up and draw that line. Drag him out with it."

This lady chose to ignore Mr. Topper.

"My dear," she said to his wife, "I advise you to come with us tomorrow on that trip. This is no place for a woman of refinement."

"I'd like to start right now," was Mrs. Topper's reply as she followed her guests to the veranda. "I will let you know in the morning. Ever since his accident there has been something queer about him. Especially of late."

When she returned to the sitting room she glanced at her husband and decided she had stated the case with admirable fairness and restraint. There was most assuredly something queer about him. He was slouched down in a chair and he was holding a glass of cognac in his right hand. On one knee Scollops was sitting contentedly while on the other lay either the start or finish of a dog consisting principally of a shaggy tail. In the presence of that irreconcilable manifestation Mary Topper did not linger long. There was little to be gained and much might be lost. Averting her eyes from her peculiar husband and his even more peculiar pets she hurried upstairs, an uneasy sensation creeping the length of her spine.

Topper sipped his cognac and looked meditatively down at the tail. Those hyphenated snobs had got what was coming to them. Too long had they desecrated his Riviera for him, smearing entire chunks of starlit evenings. Had he come to Europe to meet Glendale with an English accent? No, he had not come to Europe to do that. Glendale was too much with him as it was. He was comforted to know that the Sutton-Trevors had been roundly insulted and injured.

"Now where the devil has the Colonel gone?" he wondered. "This dog here is left on my hands. Can't turn a dog in his condition away from my door."

It did not matter. If his debauched master had wandered off in search of other diversions, what little there was of Oscar could bunch itself up in a chair and sleep right here. He could entertain Scollops—keep her at home at night, for a change.

XIII

A LADY'S LEG BETRAYS

Topper drained his glass and deposited his burdens in the chair. After life's fitful fever they slept well, their former antagonism forgotten in their mutual defense of the man. Scollops opened her eyes drowsily and contemplated the neatly arranged but nevertheless dogless rump. Then she closed them, and a slight shiver ran through her graceful body. This was an entirely new make of dog to Scollops. She would probably grow hardened to it. A cat had to get used to many disagreeable facts in life. Previously she had always been able to consider the faces of her sleeping companions. No matter. A friendly rump in the chill hours of the night was better than no rump at all. What there was of Oscar was warm and shaggy. Scollops appreciated this. She would make the most of the little the gods had granted. The sound of a dog yawning immoderately completely filled her left ear. Once more the cat opened her eyes. This time she looked with fastidious disapproval at the spot whence the yawn had issued. If this rump intended to yawn like that occasionally throughout the night the situation would indeed be most trying. Scollops could get used to the rump, but not to its yawns. The sharp, gasping yelps with which they terminated were especially difficult on the ears. The cat glanced up at Mr. Topper inquiringly, as if to ascertain what he thought about it, then returned her gaze to the rump. With a philosophical shrug of her sleek shoulders she closed her eyes once more and attempted to make the best of an unparalleled juxtaposition.

Topper moved restlessly about the room, glancing from time to time at the bottle of cognac standing on the buffet. Let it stand. No sense in waking up in the morning with a dull head. The cognac could wait. He walked out on the veranda and scanned the face of the moon. Automatically the woman in the villa at his right planted herself at her window.

"The evil-minded old hag," he muttered, looking belligerently up at the shadowy form. "Some day you'll get that rock if you don't mind your own damn business."

The watching woman had put a curse on the night for Mr. Topper. He turned his back on her and sought the privacy of his villa. Closing the long shutters on the sea he stood by them, listening to the foaming of waves on the beach, then slowly mounted the stairs with a backward look at the peculiar group in the chair. Mary should be in bed by now. He heartily hoped she was. To indulge in any further conversation with that lady tonight would be far from expedient.

In the course of a single evening Topper had touched romance and roundly defeated his enemies. Also, he had indulged in more cognac than was his wont. He was willing to call it a day, and not such a bad day at that.

Quietly he passed through his wife's room and on into his own, leaving the door ajar in accordance with well established tradition, the reason for which he could not understand unless it was to encourage a fair and friendly exchange of Riviera insects. Mrs. Topper and her dyspepsia were sleeping confidingly together. They were self-sufficient. Not so Mr. Topper. Moonlight lying on water was not good for his peace of mind. It disquieted him. Had he been a dog he would have bayed soulfully at the moon. Deprived of this emotional outlet he undressed slowly without troubling to turn on the light, donned a regal pair of pajamas, and maneuvered himself into his bed of an *elasticité suprême*.

"How nice!" breathed a soft voice in his ear. "I love silk things."

Topper gasped as his pajama trousers were tugged violently and inquisitively felt by some unseen companion who loved silk things.

"Don't!" he whispered in the moon-filtered darkness. "You'll yank the damn things off me."

This impassioned plea was met by an unholy giggle.

"Nothing ventured nothing gained," said the voice at his side.

He turned his head and found himself looking into Marion Kerby's moon-touched eyes. In the half-light of the room her face looked small and pale and impish. Her defiant nose was hardly six inches from his. Her lips were dangerously near.

"Go on back to your bath house," said Mr. Topper, "and keep your hands off my pajamas."

"I won't," she snapped back at him. "I'm quite comfortable where I am, and I do like your pajamas. I'll tear 'em to shreds if I feel like it."

"Don't feel like it," said Mr. Topper. "Stop feeling altogether."

"You should never deck your body out in silk when I'm about," whispered Marion. "I can't keep my hands off it."

Topper considered her closely.

"What have you decked yours in?" he asked suspiciously.

"Merely the top of a pair of yours. I can hardly find myself in them. Want to try?"

"Don't talk like that. It's not right."

"What should we both do—say our prayers and then go to sleep?"

"It would be far, far wiser. You've backslid terribly."

"And I'm going to drag you with me."

"Do you realize that you've got yourself uninvited into bed with a married man, and that you have a husband of your own somewhere close at hand—too close at hand?"

"Yes," quietly. "I realize that."

"Has it ever occurred to you that it is a wrong thing to climb into bed with men?"

"With how many men?"

"With any number of men."

"I don't know about it's being wrong," came the voice. "I know it would be unwise."

Mr. Topper was stumped.

"Have you no moral values at all?" he asked at length.

"I haven't a thing for sale, if that's what you mean."

"That's what I don't mean."

"Then you'd better stick to simple sentences. A slight misunderstanding might make a whale of a difference."

Topper found himself unable to continue looking into Marion's glowing eyes. He turned his own way.

"Why don't you go back to your hotel?" he asked.

"Nobody there. The gang's out. George has gone away in a motor boat with a dame calling herself Mrs. Blake Willard."

"I know her," replied Topper. "A charming woman."

"Did you ever go away with her?"

"No," said Mr. Topper. "Myself and Mr. Blake Willard are the only two men on the Riviera who have not availed themselves of that pleasure."

"Then she's that sort of woman?"

"Very much so."

"What a joke on George!"

"He is merely following the conventional precedent, that's all."

"Of course, he was greatly boiled," Marion observed with a scrap of loyalty. "Usually he's a choosy sort of person."

"Mrs. Blake Willard is not a matter of choice. She's a matter of routine."

Silence, then a small voice, softly:

"Do you like me, Topper?"

"What has that got to do with your crawling in bed with me?"

"I didn't crawl, to begin with, and isn't it right for people who like one another to see as much of each other as possible?"

"Certainly not," Mr. Topper objected. "Such inquisitiveness would lead to all sorts of complications."

"I don't understand," said Marion.

"Listen," Mr. Topper explained patiently, "if every couple that like each other crawled——"

"I wish you wouldn't say crawl," the low voice interrupted.

"All right," said Mr. Topper. "If every couple that took a fancy to each other got themselves into a bed there wouldn't be enough to go round."

"Enough what—beds or couples?"

"Beds, of course."

"Then why beds? Let 'em think up places. I could."

Once more Topper was stumped. It was like talking to a savage.

"Do you realize this," he asked presently, "that my wife is asleep on one side of me and that on the other your space-devouring husband, fed up with Mrs. Blake Willard, may most horribly appear at any moment?"

Marion chuckled.

"It would be amusing if they appeared at the same time."

"It would be just too bad," said Mr. Topper. "He would literally tear me up and toss me away, and she would tell the pieces exactly what she thought of them."

"I wish you'd think more about me and a great deal less about George and your wife. If you're not more entertaining, I'll crawl into bed with her, as you so graphically put it."

"That would be friendly, especially in the top part of my pajamas."

"Then choose between us."

"I'd rather take a walk," hedged Mr. Topper. "Let's."

"If you try to leave this bed I'll have her in here in no time."

"If I don't leave this bed I'm afraid she'll be in here anyway. Can't I even close the door?"

"It would be advisable," replied Marion. "Things are looking up."

"Don't be bold."

"One has to be a damn sight more than bold with you. A body has to be downright overbearing."

When he returned to the bed Marion was snuggled down in his place. One slim bare leg was tucked outside the coverings. Grumbling about the nerve of some women, Topper lay down where she had been.

"I can't sleep on this side," he complained.

Marion laughed unpleasantly.

"What makes you think you're going to sleep?" she asked. "Where are your manners?"

Topper looked at her with startled eyes.

"Aren't we going to sleep?" he demanded.

"No, we're not going to sleep," she mimicked, sticking out the tip of her tongue at him. "You great big cow."

"For God's sake," said Topper. "I've had a tough day. What are you planning on doing at this time of night?"

"Well," replied Marion consideringly, "we can't play polo, and we can't run races, and it would bring in a flock of mosquitoes if we lit the light and broke out a deck of cards. We might play twenty questions, though."

"I need only one," said Mr. Topper. "Are you going to get out of this bed and go home?"

"All right," answered Marion, "but you'll be sorry."

She slipped from the bed and walked over to the window, where she stood in the drifting moonlight, an odd-looking little figure.

"I say!" whispered Mr. Topper. "You can't go like that."

"I can go like that," she whispered back furiously. "I can go in less than that. Here! Take your damn circus tent."

With this remark she tore off his pajama jacket and flung it to the floor. Then, quite unexpectedly, she hid her face in her hands and began to cry softly but effectively. Topper could not stand this. He looked at the gleaming figure, then blinked stupidly at the world in general.

"Marion," he whispered uneasily, "don't go on like that."

"Naked I came into this world," she said brokenly, "and mother naked I'll leave the damn thing. You don't care."

Topper heaved himself out of bed and went over to the window.

"Don't touch me," said Marion, leaning heavily against him. "Don't come a step nearer."

"It wouldn't be physically possible," observed Topper.

Was she laughing now or crying? Topper was unable to tell. He felt two smooth arms creeping up to his neck and a small wet face pressed against his. He knew when he was licked, and he liked it.

"My old and rare," she murmured, holding onto his ears and dragging his head down to her lips.

There was nothing for Topper to do but to carry her back to the bed.

"I knew you understood all the time how a gentleman should treat a lady," she murmured. "Now, if you'll be so kind——"

Topper dropped her suddenly, and her sentence ended in a gasp.

"Now, for God's sake, be ready to dematerialize at a moment's notice," said Mr. Topper a few hours later. "Don't fall asleep and forget yourself."

"I won't," murmured Marion drowsily. "There's been enough of that already. I'll fade at the crack o' danger, Mr. Topper."

The room became quiet save for the sound of deep and regular breathing and the dream-spun cadence of the surf.

Mary Topper awoke early the next morning. This was due to the fact that she had arrived at a definite decision. She would leave that morning for Paris with the Sutton-Trevors in their motor. The conduct of her husband on the previous evening had been inexcusable. Furthermore, unnatural and sinister things were going on in the house—dogs' tails and all that. She did not care to think about them. Her husband could take care of himself. She experienced a passing qualm when she thought of the fair Félice. Then she shrugged her shoulders. If a man intended to be a man there was no way of stopping him.

She got out of bed and slipped on her dressing gown. She must inform her husband at once of her decision. It was odd that he still remained in his room. Then, for the first time, she noticed that the door between the two rooms was closed. This was even odder. Worse than that. It was actually insulting. She faced the door grimly, then flung it open.

The first object that greeted Mrs. Topper's gaze was altogether delightful, although, it must be confessed, the good lady did not look on it with any apparent appreciation. What she saw was a slim bare and brown leg—an exquisite example of feminine decoration—lying innocently exposed on the covering of the bed. Where the continuation of the leg was Mrs. Topper was not sure, but she naturally imagined it to be farther up, huddled in the bedclothing. Of one thing she was sure, that leg did not belong to her husband. It was far too slim and shapely. She hated to admit this galling fact. Himself, the perfidious male, was lying comfortably in bed with the possessor of that leg—had been so lying all night long. And he was not in his accustomed place. He had even broken a habit of years— a thing he had never done for her—and slept on the left side.

Mrs. Topper's blood boiled. For the first time in her life she became an elemental, militant woman. Yes, she would leave the house, but she would leave it in ruins first—the house and everyone in it, especially these two.

With a stealth gathered from her primitive ancestors still lurking in spirit in the shadow of the cave, she crept up to the bed and seized the leg by the foot. Mr. Topper was rudely awakened by a smothered ejaculation almost in his ear.

"Damn!" said Marion Kerby. "My right leg's asleep, and I can't do a thing with it."

"Why do anything with it at all?" Mr. Topper asked lazily, endeavoring to open his eyes.

"Simply because your wife's got a-hold of it," said Marion with convincing earnestness.

"What!" exclaimed Mr. Topper, his eyes wide and staring.

He took one look at his wife's set face, then covered his own with the bedclothes. Mary and the leg could fight their own battles. This was one of those situations in which a man should keep himself to himself. There was no occasion for him to barge in and make matters worse.

"Coward!" panted Marion Kerby. "Do something about all this. Rub my leg and make it wake up."

To rub his companion's leg at that moment was the farthest thought from Mr. Topper's mind. Far be it from him to add fuel to the fire.

"Some other time," he muttered. "I'm busy."

"There won't be any other time, if you don't pry this woman loose."

Exactly what Mrs. Topper intended to do with the leg once she had succeeded in getting it is difficult to conjecture. It is doubtful if Mrs. Topper knew herself. Probably she had some vague idea of dragging it, together with the body, through the streets of the village, after which she would return for Topper. It is certain she had no intention of dragging the leg from its body. Not that such a feat would not have given her a great deal of well merited satisfaction. She merely doubted her ability to perform the act.

With one despairing grunt the leg yielded to Mrs. Topper's tugging and parted company with the bed. So sudden had been the capitulation that Mary Topper sat down heavily with the leg resting lightly across her lap, its small pink toes wiggling protestingly.

"My God, what a wife you have," came Marion's voice feebly. "I'm mere putty in her hands."

Topper could not restrain his curiosity. One of his eyes morbidly took in the novel scene.

"Isn't that thing awake yet?" he asked in a depressed voice.

"It seems to be in the grip of a terrible awakening," replied Marion. "I don't know what's wrong with it. Either it has ideas of its own, or she's paralyzed the poor thing. Scared it stiff, so to speak."

While this strange conversation between her husband and the leg was in progress Mary Topper had been gathering her forces. At first she had looked down slightly dazed at the prize she had so ruthlessly drawn, being particularly repelled by its gesticulating toes. Then the loquacity of the leg was not exactly calculated to soothe her nerves. With increasing irritation she listened to the leg address her husband as if it had some claim on him. It had even asked to be rubbed. The thought of this highly improper request stung Mrs. Topper to action. She sprang to her feet and began to wave the leg wildly about the room. Topper, peering over the edge of the sheet, took one look and shivered. Then he hid the scene from view.

"For the love of Pete," called Marion, "will you tell your wife to quit flinging my leg about like an old piece of rope? What the hell does she think she is anyway—a cowboy? Say there, Mrs. Will

Rogers, will you lay off that leg? I'm getting dizzy, honest to God, lady."

"I don't know who you are nor where you are, and I don't care what you are," cried Mary Topper, in a wild, unladylike tone of voice. "I've got this leg and I'm going to keep it. I'm going to bite it with my own bare teeth."

"It would be hard to bite that leg with somebody else's teeth," said the rapidly revolving object, "but I must admit you can think up some pretty mean little tricks. That settles it, Topper, old boy. You simply must get up and take my leg away from your wife. I don't want the sweet young thing to be bitten by a woman."

"Oh!" cried Mrs. Topper, increasing the speed of her twirling. "Your words are driving me mad."

Topper sprang from the bed and was immediately floored by coming into violent contact with the leg. Mrs. Topper laughed harrowingly.

"Take that, you dog!" she cried.

"Ouch!" exclaimed the leg. "That hurt like hell."

"It didn't improve me any," said Topper from the floor.

"Shouldn't mind a lady's leg," replied Marion. "Why doesn't she throw me away and pick on you instead? Look out! Here I come."

Topper ducked in the nick of time, and the leg swished harmlessly over his head.

"I'll batter his brains out," panted Mrs. Topper.

"He doesn't seem to have any," observed the leg.

"What business of yours is that?" Mrs. Topper demanded.

"None at all," hastily disclaimed the leg. "I was merely twirling and thinking—that's all, I assure you."

"I feel like chucking you through the window," said Mrs. Topper.

"Good! Why don't you?" replied the leg. "Any change would be better than this. Better still, why not set me down in a corner until you've got your breath?"

At this moment Mr. Topper made a desperate lunge at the leg, only to fall ingloriously upon his stomach. The leg had disappeared.

"Sorry, old boy," came the voice of Marion Kerby, "but I am not at all responsible for the caprices of this leg of mine. It snapped out of its dope of its own free will. Just in time, too. I'm all twirled out."

Mary Topper, deprived of the leg, looked thoughtfully down at her prostrate husband. There was only one thing left worth doing to him, and she could not bring herself to do that. She refused to soil her hands with the murder of a creature so low and depraved. Impotent with anger unappeased, she looked about the room. Then she conceived one of those distractedly ridiculous ideas that occur to persons only at moments of consummate rage. On Mr. Topper's bureau was a bottle containing a particularly obnoxious fluid used for the whitening of shoes. Seizing this, she emptied its contents on the back of Mr. Topper's head and neck.

"There!" she muttered. "Take that."

"I've taken it," said Mr. Topper from the floor. "All."

Without indulging in another hostile demonstration she turned from the strange-looking object at her feet and left the room, slamming the door behind her. From her own room came the sounds of furious packing.

Mr. Topper, still dazed by the terrific activity of the last few moments, rose and did futile things to his head and neck with a towel. With his voluminous and colorful silk pajamas and his face oddly smeared with whitening where the liquid had spread, Mr. Topper made a tragically festive appearance. In make-up, at least, he was fitted for the rôle of Pagliacci. He made no attempt to sing, however, satisfying his vocal inclinations with deep-seated oaths.

"I say, old dear," came the cautiously pitched voice of Marion, "do you think after all we've been through you could arrange for a little cognac?"

From the veranda below came the sounds of industrious sweeping. Mr. Topper stepped out on his *balcon* and made queer motions at Félice. The motions were entirely unnecessary. His face alone was sufficient to attract her closest attention. Félice gave it one astounded look, then dropped her broom. She was afraid to run into the house because Monsieur might run down to meet her. To rush out into the public highways would not be seemly. She temporized by staying where she was. She would humor this mad Monsieur.

"Félice," he called in a low voice. "It is that I have need of a bottle of cognac. *Voilà!*"

Topper tossed down to the maid a rope which Monsieur Grandon, in his anxiety to provide his tenants with some means of escape from Vesuvius, had seen fit to attach to the railing of his *balcon*.

"The bottle, Félice," continued Mr. Topper, "attach it thus."

Here the man wrung his hands so gruesomely in an attempt to make his meaning clear that much of the color departed from the cheeks of Félice.

"But yes, m'sieu," she faltered, nodding her head rapidly. *"Tout de suite."*

Perhaps if she complied with Monsieur's strange request he would remain drunk all day in his room, which was an occurrence highly to be desired by all concerned.

When Topper returned to the room Marion Kerby, clad in a silk pajama jacket, was sitting on the edge of the bed. She looked oddly frail and subdued.

"Do we get it?" she asked in a small voice.

"The affair is in motion," he told her.

Both of them were suddenly electrified by the sound of an infuriated voice fiercely denouncing Félice, whose own voice was raised in protest.

"She's up there!" cried the voice. "I know she's up there. First I'll slit his throat, and then I'll beat her."

"I get more than you do," observed Mr. Topper with the resignation of a man ruined beyond all hope of recovery.

"It's George!" exclaimed Marion.

"In the flesh," replied Topper.

He looked through another window and beheld an unnerving scene. George Kerby was confronting Félice on the veranda. In one hand he held a carving knife which had been snatched up from the buffet. As Topper watched he saw the enraged husband place the knife between his teeth and seize the rope with both hands. Then he paused, removed the knife from his mouth, and, taking the bottle of cognac from Félice, placed it to his lips.

"Thanks," Mr. Topper heard him say as he passed the bottle back to the maid, returned the knife to his mouth, and sprang at the rope. "I'll go up this damn thing like greased lightning."

Topper turned to Marion.

"Your husband is climbing up that rope like greased lightning," he informed her, "and he is holding most horribly between his teeth a carving knife with a blade sufficiently long to slit the throats of the entire community."

"I go," replied Marion, "with speed the most terrific."

There was a twinkling of bare brown legs as Marion flappingly dashed into Mrs. Topper's room. That lady, her packing completed, was standing before her mirror clad only in a dressing gown. This garment Marion neatly slipped from the other woman's shoulders.

"I'll take this," said Marion, and disappeared on a dead run through the door on her way downstairs.

Mrs. Topper looked nakedly after her, vaguely wondering how many women her husband had managed to secrete in his room overnight. In the meantime, Topper, from the depths of a clothes closet, had the single pleasure of seeing George Kerby's head appear piratically over the railing of the *balcon*. To Topper the man seemed to be composed entirely of knife. Springing into the room, he looked wildly about him.

"Where are they?" he shouted. "Topper, your time is up—I mean, come."

In the clothes closet Mr. Topper's face became even whiter than its whitening. He saw himself in ribbons. For a moment George Kerby prowled about the room like a tiger on the hunt, then, suddenly spying the door to Mrs. Topper's room, he dashed through it, brandishing the knife and awesomely shouting, "Show me a throat and I'll slit it."

It just so happened that Mrs. Topper, because of the absence of her dressing robe, was in a position to show George Kerby much more than her throat. It was an encounter not easily to be forgotten. The infuriated man's anger was dissipated through sheer shock.

Mrs. Topper, in seeking protection behind a wardrobe trunk, forgot everything herself in the exigencies of the moment.

"Madam, I beg your pardon," said Mr. Kerby. "Had I only known——"

"Well, now that you not only know but also see," Mary Topper interrupted coldly, "will you take both yourself and your knife out of my room?"

"But, madam——" began George Kerby, feeling that he had not half sufficiently apologized for the enormity of his offense.

"Write me a letter about it," cut in Mrs. Topper. "That door leads to the lower floor. Go out of it and keep going."

Kerby hastened to obey the lady's instructions.

While this brief encounter was taking place, Topper had just enough time to gratify the watching woman in the villa next door by sliding down the rope George had so swiftly mounted. Topper, too, was like greased lightning. If anything, he was even greasier, because, unlike George, he was descending to earth. Arrived there he rushed into the dining room and collapsed in a chair.

"My God," he thought wearily, "no motion-picture camera could have followed the activities of this morning!"

"M'sieu," whispered Félice, gazing at Mr. Topper with admiringly sympathetic eyes, "the little Mademoiselle, she is on the beach. Ah, m'sieu, *très-chic.*"

Because of the stultifying fact that the lady's husband was looking at him from the door, Mr. Topper did not trouble to tell Félice that the little Mademoiselle was in full truth a Madam of no little experience. On George's face were the marks of his recent encounter—lines of shock and bafflement.

"God Almighty," he muttered, "is everything abnormal in this house? What's the matter with your face?"

"Hello, George," said Topper briefly. "Sunburn. Have you had breakfast?"

"Have you seen my wife?" asked George.

"Why, no," replied Topper innocently, "but Oscar's knocking about somewhere. That is, part of him is knocking about."

"Well, I've seen yours," said Kerby in a low voice.

"Oh, did you, now?" answered Topper in an interested voice. "What did you think of the lady?"

"She was a sight for sore eyes," replied Kerby with unnecessary frankness. "I'm sorry, Topper, but your wife was unclad."

Topper was prompted to reply that George had nothing on him, but he tactfully restrained the impulse.

"That was too bad of you, George," he said mildly, "but it's a good thing I'm not an unreasonably jealous man. I trust you—er—let matters rest at that."

"Oh, quite," put in George hastily. "I assure you you need have no fear for the honor of Mrs. Topper."

"You seem to be well satisfied on that score," said Mr. Topper, with a slight smile. "However, I feel that way about her honor myself. Will you cognac yourself with me?"

Topper rose and walked over to the buffet. George followed him suspiciously.

"Are you sure you haven't seen my wife?" he demanded.

"I think you're hardly in a position to ask me such a question," Topper replied, looking steadily at George. "And I do wish, old chap, you'd put that decidedly ugly-looking knife down. It gives me the creeps."

"Well, what was that rope doing hanging down from your balcony?" George continued, abandoning the knife, much to Mr. Topper's relief.

"Ah, that," said Mr. Topper with a depreciative laugh. "We are not all blessed with sympathetic and convivial wives, George. That rope is the means to cognac when other sources of supply are cut off."

George Kerby's face cleared. The idea amused him. Old Topper and his rope. How could he ever have suspected the man? He drank deeply with his host, and drank again. Then he sat down and ate a hearty breakfast. Neither gentleman was aware of the happy fact that Mrs. Topper, bag and baggage, had made her exit from the scene by way of the back door.

"Will you help me find Marion?" George asked when he had consumed the last morsel of food. "I want to beat her."

"Certainly," replied Topper quite unmoved. "I'll even help you beat her. By the way, what's the name of your hotel? I'll meet you there after I've washed up a bit and dressed."

"The Splendide," replied George Kerby.

"Aren't they all?" said Mr. Topper.

XIV

At the Hôtel Splendide

Mr. Topper was as good as his word. He met George Kerby at his hotel, the Splendide. He did even better than that. He actually took up his temporary abode at that luxurious establishment. This radical alteration in his manner of living was made for rather than by Mr. Topper. He had no choice in the matter. Marion Kerby, in the course of a stolen conversation, had made it clear that she would not consider his occupying the villa alone with that good-looking French trollop whose amorous nature was as easy to arouse as it was difficult to curb. Consequently, soon after Mrs. Topper's abrupt departure through the back door, the master of the villa requested Félice to carry on like a good and beautiful young thing for a while and in patience to await his return. Félice, in turn, had assured him that he could find her alone in the villa at any hour of the day or night. This, Topper frankly doubted. Nature had never created Félice for the impalpable arms of solitude.

"And if you attempt to sneak back to that place alone," Marion had assured him with every indication of sincerity, "I'll burn it down to the ground and quench your spluttering cinders in the sewer."

Topper was not at all particular about what Marion did with his spluttering cinders once he had arrived at that unfortunate stage, but he did most definitely object to the cinder-producing process itself. Moreover, he presumed that the excellent Monsieur Grandon, the owner of the villa, would prefer to retain it intact for the comfort and entertainment of future generations of American visitors. Mr. Topper had discovered to his sorrow that French property owners had strongly fixed ideas about such matters, the cracking of an already chipped teacup being sufficient to cause them to send their eyes rolling in consternation to heaven in search of their thrifty God.

For the past fortnight now Mr. Topper had been a modest, self-effacing part of the social life of the Hôtel Splendide. During all of that time he had unrelentingly sought the company of George Kerby. So assiduously had Topper dogged the footsteps of George that George had become quite fed up with Topper. Marion's jealous young husband had become convinced that if he never saw Cosmo Topper again on any plane whatever, still he would have seen too much of him. He even began to feel sorry for his wife when he saw her listening, with an expression of hopeless dejection, to one of old Topper's interminable disquisitions on the theory and practice of banking or the dangers of an overabundant gold reserve. No danger there for Marion, Kerby further decided. He had greatly overestimated Topper. The man was merely a rich, good-natured bore, getting well along in years. George little realized that in the person of Cosmo Topper the stage had lost an actor of considerable tenacity, if not ability.

To Topper alone was due the honor and the glory of eventually relieving the situation by ridding the party of the disturbing presence of Mr. Kerby. George literally flung himself into the arms of a rich South American widow and begged her to take him away from Topper for an indefinite stay on her palatial yacht, a request the South American widow was not at all backward in granting. Topper had the deep satisfaction of seeing them off on their cruise. He even tossed in a casual reference to the beauties of the west coast of Africa, of which he knew nothing, and the thrills of big-game hunting, of which he knew even less. The idea of knocking a lion for a loop strongly appealed to the volatile nature of George Kerby if not to his companion, who, nevertheless, insisted that lions were an old South American dish.

Immediately upon the departure of George, the Colonel and Mrs. Hart began to do some pretty tight moral eye-closing, a feat which they found not at all difficult to perform. In fact, they became morally blind, always having had a tendency in that direction. This gentle failing made possible certain desirable rearrangements of sleeping quarters, which made things more convenient for all hands. Soon Topper and Marion Kerby were living together under circumstances of the most cheerful licentiousness, while the Colonel and Mrs. Hart, according to a long-established custom, occupied adjoining rooms. In other words, the four of them merely adapted themselves to conform with the charming convention of the Riviera. And as for the dog, Oscar, he slept wherever he found a safe anchorage for his rump.

The little party was now seated comfortably on the lawn of the Hôtel Splendide. In four brown hands sparkled four tall glasses of equally brown ale shot with the golden glow of the dropping sun. Topper had been playing tennis at the club with no less a person than Mr. Keith Sutton-Trevor, whom he had roundly defeated. In the past two weeks Topper had roundly defeated the best players the club could send to the front. Topper's success at the sport had become a sensation that threatened to develop into a scandal. The members of the club had never before seen such peculiar tennis played. This semi-stout American, unheralded and unsung, had virtually revolutionized the game. His racket appeared to be all over the court—frequently not even in his hand at all. His opponents to a man complained that something interfered with their rackets whenever they needed a point, and that not infrequently in decisive rallies they were pushed, tripped, slapped, and subjected to even more humiliating indignities. However, as none of these so-called indignities were visible to the eyes of the judges, these gentlemen were reluctantly forced to ascribe the objections of the defeated players to bad sportsmanship.

Marion greatly delighted in gently flipping a player's racket whenever he attempted to serve. This inevitably led to the player's serving doubles and thus presenting Topper with a point. On the other hand, Mrs. Hart found it more amusing violently to push a player whenever he was off balance, a piece of ruthlessness which resulted in numerous painful falls. The Colonel had a habit of seizing the ball in the player's court as it rebounded from Topper's service and putting it through the most baffling twists and dodges. To the spectators it frequently looked as if Mr. Topper had nothing at all to do with many of his best passing shots and returns. He could even turn his back on his opponent and still win. There were times when the onlookers received the distinct impression that the tennis ball was being personally conducted from Mr. Topper's court and deposited in some unattainable spot in that of his adversary's. On several occasions a ball from Topper's racket had been seen to poise itself alluringly—some said, tauntingly—before a player, and to remain suspended there until the infuriated man was driven to smash at it, only to discover that the ball had cleverly dodged round him and was continuing merrily on down the sideline for a well earned point in Mr. Topper's favor. It was the consensus of opinion that this mild-mannered American player could do things with a tennis racket and ball that had never before been accomplished or even attempted by man. His habit of maintaining a low-pitched, scolding conversation with himself was considered slightly odd, but then his whole game was slightly odd. Had the spectators known it, Mr. Topper was merely protesting against being slapped encouragingly on the back and in other ways fondled by Marion Kerby and her friends. After one of these one-sided matches Topper's three companions were invariably as weary and thirsty as he himself.

As the Colonel sat delicately sampling his ale he was thinking of how best to turn Mr. Topper's remarkable ability to his own financial advantage. Thoughts like this were frequently in this enterprising gentleman's mind. There had never been enough francs printed to satisfy the Colonel's requirements. The overhead, or, rather, down the throat, upkeep of Mrs. Hart was terrific. That dear lady was so extravagant that, although stockings were noticeably absent along the Riviera, she wore holes in hers, nevertheless, in the privacy of her room. It outraged her ideas of a woman's rights to keep the same stockings in her bureau drawer for more than a week. What were a pair of legs coming to if men get to taking them for granted? Mrs. Hart had no intention of letting the Colonel forget hers. Therefore, it was quite pardonable for the Colonel to gaze unseeingly at the cool blue reaches of the Mediterranean and to evolve plans for making money from Mr. Topper's tennis, which, in full truth, belonged to them all. His game was a joint effort, Topper being merely the play instead of the lay figure.

"Topper," he began with tentative indifference, as was his wont when approaching delicate matters, "the three of us could make you the champion tennis player of the Riviera—of the world, for the matter of that—if you'd let us."

"God, no!" exclaimed Topper. "You've done too well already. May I ask what was the idea in dragging the trousers of Sutton-Trevor down round his ankles this afternoon? That isn't a tennis stroke."

"A mistake," said Marion briefly, pulling off her béret and shaking out her curls until she looked nice and wild and untidy. "My hand slipped. I was trying to yank him over backwards."

"To begin with," admonished Topper in a gentle, reasonable voice, "you shouldn't yank gentlemen over backwards, and in the second place, it isn't quite nice to pull their trousers down."

"Shut up, or I'll pull yours clean off," Marion told him, then added thoughtfully, "drawers and all."

Realizing that Marion could be even better than her word when the mood was on her, Topper remained silent. He had no desire to appear with the wrong half of him unclad before the guests of the Hôtel Splendide now assembled on the lawn.

"Of course," continued the Colonel, not to be deflected from his subject, "if we took up the idea seriously, the ladies would have to restrain their natural inclinations."

"Whattayoumean?" demanded Mrs. Hart in a lazily hard-boiled voice.

"I mean, my dear," replied the Colonel, completely immune to her tone, "that you and Marion would have to abandon your practice of endeavoring to undress the players. If we can make our opponents give the appearance of being slightly—er—fuddled, it would be to our advantage, of course."

"Fuddled," said Marion sarcastically. "I'll make the beggars look frantic."

"And we should always remember our audiences," resumed the Colonel, bending a dignified eyebrow in Marion's direction. "We must endeavor to keep them diverted."

"At my expense, Colonel?" Mr. Topper suggested easily.

"Certainly not," replied the Colonel. "By no means, my dear sir. At the expense of your competitors."

"Am I going to play more than one at a time?" asked Mr. Topper, not quite so easily.

"You might," said the Colonel thoughtfully. "It's an idea. With our help you could play ten men at the same time and win in straight sets."

"Sure," agreed Mrs. Hart, "but we'd be busier than a rabbit at a dog show."

"Not so busy at that," observed Marion. "We could trample half of them under foot and get the others fighting among themselves."

"I realize that," said Mr. Topper. "The trouble is, you all make me do things that are humanly impossible. That little idea of having the ball sail out of bounds, then suddenly duck back when my opponent isn't looking is simply more than the public can bear. It's silly. I even feel silly myself. Besides, it's a dirty trick."

"Oh, dear me, Mr. Topper," drawled Mrs. Hart, "we don't mind that in the least. A super-player like yourself cannot afford to be too finicky."

"Well, I'm not going to play one man," retorted Mr. Topper, "let alone ten."

"Then," said the Colonel, as if it did not really matter, "there's the financial aspect of the thing. On side bets alone we could clean up enough money to endow an orphan asylum."

"Occupied exclusively by the products of your own folly," dryly observed Mrs. Hart. "In all sizes, shapes, and shades."

"Mrs. Hart!" objected the Colonel, bending two dignified eyebrows upon that lady. "If you please."

Mrs. Hart whispered something to Marion, after which both of them glanced at the Colonel and giggled.

"Most annoying," complained the Colonel to Mr. Topper. "And most unjustified."

"Oh, quite," replied Mr. Topper. "I cannot imagine you in connection with any slight irregularity of conduct, Colonel."

"That feeling is entirely reciprocated, I assure you," returned the Colonel heavily.

"They think they're a couple of other guys," Marion informed Mrs. Hart.

"I don't know about Topper," declared Mrs. Hart, "but that alcoholic ward of mine can convince himself at times that the bloom is still on the rose."

"Oh, I say!" expostulated the Colonel. "You are actually overstepping the bounds of decency."

"Overstepping 'em," said Mrs. Hart jeeringly. "We looped-the-loop over those bounds years and years ago."

"That's neither here nor there," resumed the Colonel impatiently. "I wish you would refrain from introducing purely irrelevant subjects at this particular moment. Where were we, Mr. Topper? Oh, yes—the financial aspect." The Colonel paused and drew thoughtfully on his cigar. "Topper," he continued abruptly, "man to man, I want to tell you it irks me to be short of funds. I am much too great hearted to be without money."

"You mean, Clara Harted," put in Marion.

"How clever you are," that lady murmured.

"Ignore them, Topper," continued the Colonel. "They are as savages or children. To resume. Although I have the greatest reliance on your generosity, still it is not meet and fitting for me to depend entirely on it."

"Oh, no," agreed Mrs. Hart. "Mr. Topper might die or lose his mind or fancy another pretty face."

"If he takes a fancy to another pretty face," Marion Kerby said with painful distinctness, "he'll both lose his mind and die."

"I'm trying to listen, Colonel," put in Topper. "Go on. Let's waive those last two remarks of the gentle ladies."

"Well," said the Colonel, importantly clearing his throat. "Because of the various little services we have been able to render to you in the past—small but invaluable attentions——"

"Such as?" suggested Topper.

"We won't go into that now," said the Colonel hastily, "but because of one thing and another, I feel—and I believe my companions will back me up in this—that it would sit ill on you not to become the tennis champion of the Riviera."

"Is that your case?" asked Mr. Topper.

"In a nutshell," replied the Colonel.

"Then," said Mr. Topper, "you can take your case, place it in your little nutshell, and do whatever you think most definitely negative with it."

"I could offer a suggestion here," interrupted Marion.

"Don't," replied Mr. Topper. "My fortune is at your disposal, Colonel, but I'll be damned if I came to the Riviera to live on a tennis court, as you suggest. If you have a yen for making money, why not try Monte Carlo, Nice, or Cannes? I'll stake you to a stack."

"I have a grand idea," spluttered Marion, exhuming an ale-flecked nose from her glass. "The races are on tomorrow. We could do well with horses, Colonel."

Colonel Scott gazed thoughtfully at Marion for a full minute. Then he nodded his massive head three times.

"My dear child," he observed benignly, "we could do more with horses than even the people who ride them. Shall we discuss this little matter later? There is no need to bother Mr. Topper with our plans."

"Don't," said Mr. Topper. "I prefer to retain my peace of mind. And if the races become a riot, you can't blame me. I am not a party to any funny business."

"But you will join us?" inquired the Colonel.

"I'll do better than that," replied Topper, who in spite of himself was fascinated by the idea. "I'll charter a car and drive you there myself."

"Magnificent man," murmured Mrs. Hart.

"Pure cane sugar," commented Marion. "A trifle too refined."

"Looks more like beet than cane," the other lady observed.

"That's the ale," said Marion.

"We'll need plenty of ready money," the Colonel dropped suggestively. "It's a commodity that seems to be growing increasingly more unfamiliar to my touch."

"For this unholy enterprise," said Mr. Topper, "you can depend on me for financial backing."

"Good man!" exclaimed the Colonel.

"Positively lordly, say I," from Mrs. Hart.

"What a lover!" put in Marion. "Mine, all mine."

"I am doing this," continued Mr. Topper, choosing to ignore these unnecessary remarks, "for two reasons. I know very well you would steal all my money if I didn't give it to you willingly; then again, I have every confidence in the ability of Colonel Scott to make the crookedest track turn in his direction. Anyway, I feel that it would be an act of divine justice to get a few francs back from the French for a change—honestly, of course."

"That last bit goes without saying," piously observed the Colonel.

"Also without believing," Mr. Topper added. "For the moment I'm going to tear myself away from your depressingly strait-laced company. Perfect all necessary arrangements, then look for me in the bar."

As Topper walked away, the three of them followed him with expressions of respect and admiration.

"He would go far as a low plane," Colonel Scott observed.

"That's an idea, too," said Marion in an odd voice. "He has no human contacts to keep him officially alive. His cat—she's almost human—is about the strongest tie he has. One can always do things to Scollops."

"Who can always do things to Scollops, and how?" asked Mrs. Hart.

"Well," replied Marion reflectively, "we could settle for all time that controversy about the nine lives."

"Giving us three whacks at the beast apiece," observed the Colonel.

"Let's wait till the weather gets a little cooler," suggested Mrs. Hart.

"Of course," agreed Marion. "I didn't mean for us to dash off at the minute and fall upon the poor cat. It was merely a passing fancy."

The Colonel and Mrs. Hart looked thoughtfully at their companion. Marion, her small chin resting lightly on the rim of her empty glass, was gazing enigmatically out to sea. As the Colonel considered the determined line of the girl's firm jaw he privately decided that if he were a life insurance agent he would stay clear of Cosmo Topper and his cat. Both were bad risks.

At dinner that night nothing untoward occurred, that is, nothing especially so. The Colonel's mind was still engaged with matters of high finance.

"Do you know what the trouble is with Americans on the Riviera?" he inquired.

"You tell us, Colonel," answered Marion. "I'm weary of the subject. The only trouble I can find with them is merely that they are on the Riviera. And that holds for nationals of all countries."

"Yes," agreed Mr. Topper, relieved that everything was going so nicely. "The greatest trouble with Americans on the Riviera is to be found in books about Americans on the Riviera. I once knew a dog who sucked one egg—just one egg—and to his dying day that dog was known far and wide as an egg-sucking dog. As a matter of fact, he was nothing of the kind. He merely tried one egg and found he didn't like them that way. Scrambled, yes."

Marion was regarding the speaker pityingly.

"Your Hoosier philosophy appalls me," she said. "Why don't you take up whittling sticks and sitting on fence rails? We'll build a fence for you, if you have any special preference; then we can knock you off when you get too awful."

"Don't mind her, Mr. Topper," put in Mrs. Hart, placing an affectionate hand on his. "I understand perfectly what you meant about that poor dear dog and the one egg he unfortunately sucked.

You are trying to tell us nicely that all Americans on the Riviera are suckers, and you nearly succeeded."

"I wasn't trying to do anything of the sort," Mr. Topper retorted uncomfortably as he noticed Marion's glittering eyes fastened on the hand that was holding his. "I was simply stating a fact—drawing a parallel."

"I used to draw the sweetest flowers when I was a girl," said Mrs. Hart moistly. "All wild. Ah, youth, youth, and the patter of bare feet."

"Whose bare feet?" asked Marion. "I'll bet they weren't your husband's."

"I was speaking symbolically," murmured Mrs. Hart. "My first husband always wore slippers—the cutest things—plush. We could never hear him coming."

"Who's 'we'?" demanded the Colonel.

"None of your business," replied Mrs. Hart. "Those slippers cost me a comfortable home. Ask the waiter to pour."

"Isn't this terrible?" the Colonel inquired of Mr. Topper.

"No, Colonel," Topper replied, smiling sympathetically. "I find it rather sad. Mrs. Hart had a hard life."

"You mean, she led a hard life," declared Marion. "She was a trull before she could toddle."

"Oh, Marion," Mrs. Hart protested. "What will poor Mr. Topper ever think of me? I was never really a trull, dear. Merely a practical amateur."

"Ladies," broke in the Colonel, "let us return to my original question."

"I didn't find it original," commented Marion.

"But my answer is," replied the Colonel. "The trouble with Americans on the Riviera is that there are no speakeasies. They can't accustom themselves to getting drunk lawfully."

"But they can with the 'l' left off," remarked Marion.

"Very clever, my dear," said the Colonel, looking as if each word hurt him. "Now my idea is——"

"Isn't he gay!" broke in Mrs. Hart. "He wants us all to get awfully drunk."

"That is not my idea at all," objected the Colonel. "You're that way already. Now, my idea is——"

"Oh, I know!" cried Marion. "He wants to get a law passed. Isn't that it, Colonel?"

The Colonel looked at Marion for fully half a minute, during which time his heavy eyebrows struggled furiously to establish contact with his even heavier mustache.

"Oh, Colonel," the girl murmured admiringly. "They almost meet."

"Bah!" exploded that gentleman. "This is too much, Mr. Topper, my idea in a nutshell is——"

"Remember what happened to that last nutshell," said Mrs. Hart warningly. "Why not put this idea in something else?"

"A safe, for instance," suggested Marion. "Or put it out of your mind."

"Or in moth balls," added Mrs. Hart.

"I was thinking," began the Colonel, "of opening——"

"Pardon me, Colonel," said Mr. Topper politely. "I must have a word with the waiter."

While Mr. Topper held a protracted debate with the waiter regarding the low state of coffee in France, a debate, by the way, in which he came out second best, the Colonel looked wearily round the dining room, his fingers drumming patiently on the table. He could not bring himself to look on the faces of the two ladies. To do so would have released the terrific pressure he was placing on his emotions.

"Now, Colonel," continued Mr. Topper affably, "why are you so hesitant about giving us your idea? Let's have it, man. No need to beat about the bush, you know."

Colonel Scott gasped.

"Beat about the bush," he got out. "These women have erected a soundproof wall between themselves and intelligent conversation. Anyway, my idea doesn't seem so good to me now. Much of its freshness has worn off. In fact, I'm sick of the damn thing."

"I'll bet he wants to open up a chain of speakeasies along the Riviera—basement rooms and grilled doors and the inevitable Tony," broke in Marion. "Wasn't that it, Colonel?"

The Colonel turned away, his face filled with pain. Speechlessly he nodded.

"In a nutshell," he said at last in a faint voice.

"Why this frantic scramble for money?" Mrs. Hart inquired. "Do you want to buy France? I understand that lots of these Continental countries are going for a song—the Bankers' Blues, they call it."

"Would you like to be barkeep, Topper," asked Marion, "or would you rather play Tony and peer through the grille?"

"I'd rather play the part of an unlawful drinker," Mr. Topper replied.

"If you would be courteous enough to allow me to explain," the Colonel essayed.

He was never allowed.

The manager approached the table. In the background lurked a gendarme.

"There is a formality in progress," the manager apologized suavely. "It is necessary to borrow the passports of all guests but recently arrived. There are certain cards—you understand?"

"Certainly," replied the Colonel courteously. "Is that distinguished-looking gentleman back of you the Mayor of New York, or is he a prominent gambler?"

Even as the manager turned, the Colonel began to fade. Soon he was entirely gone.

"That gentleman——" began the manager, turning back, then hesitated, a look of blank amazement overspreading his face. "But the Monsieur is gone," he explained to Mr. Topper. "Yet how could he have gone?"

Mr. Topper laughed unnaturally.

"Ha! Ha!" were the sounds that Topper made. "How could he have gone? He mustn't have been here at all. That's all there is to it. Frankly, I was wondering to whom you were talking."

"But the plate!" exclaimed the manager. "There has been a fourth present."

"Oh, that," replied Mr. Topper, fighting for time. "That plate. Who can that person be?"

Once more the old dodge worked. As the manager turned to look behind him, Marion, at a signal from Topper, whisked the plate from the table and hid it in her lap. Mrs. Hart deftly tidied up the place where but a few moments ago the cowardly Colonel had sat. When the manager turned back, Mr. Topper pointed to the empty space.

"Are you jesting with us?" he asked the manager. "There has been no fourth—merely these two ladies and myself. We are three."

At this moment the plate slipped from Marion's lap and crashed to the floor. There was the clatter of knives and forks. The manager was more than surprised. He was startled. He hesitated; then, sacrificing dignity to wonder, he stooped down and peered under the table. When he arose, the table was empty save for a considerably disturbed Mr. Topper. The manager had time to catch a glimpse of two plates bearing eating tackle hurrying down an aisle in the direction of a tray. Several waiters also witnessed the progress of the plates. The entire dining room heard the shattering sound they made as they dashed into the tray.

"Now why did they go to all that trouble," Mr. Topper wondered, despite his preoccupation with other things, "only to break the damn plates at the end? Perhaps they became nervous or tried to make a race of it. I'm nervous as hell myself, and I'd certainly like to make a race of it."

When the manager had mastered the emotions caused by the self-removing plates he turned back once more to Mr. Topper.

"You have seen?" inquired the manager.

"Nothing," replied Mr. Topper coldly, "except your rather unusual conduct, m'sieu. You come to my table and demand a fourth. You start. You peer. You—you—er—fidget. In short, you spoil my dinner. You call me a recent arrival when I have been your guest for days——"

"But your friends?" the manager craftily interrupted.

"I have no friends," replied Mr. Topper, not to be outcrafted.

"Furthermore, you have already seen my passport. I shall expect some explanation."

He rose from the table.

"It shall be forthcoming, m'sieu," replied the manager, "if any explanation can be found, a development which to me seems exceedingly unlikely."

In the lounge of the Splendide, Mr. Topper was joined by the ladies. Taking him by either arm they led him rapidly up to a large screen through which they apparently passed, leaving him standing with his nose practically pressed against it.

"God bless my soul and body!" exclaimed a gentleman with white hair and a red face. "I've just seen the most peculiar thing. But, tell me first, is that man actually smelling the screen? And where are the two ladies who were with him only a moment ago?"

"I don't know about the two ladies," a large woman at his side replied, "but if I ever saw a man smelling a screen—which I don't think I ever have—that person is certainly smelling that screen. Actually sniffing it."

Several persons were regarding both the screen and Mr. Topper attentively. One man went so far as to walk across the room and look behind the screen. Then he reappeared and stood looking at Mr. Topper. Mr. Topper felt the man's eyes curiously studying his face. He resorted to a weak subterfuge.

"Near-sighted," he muttered as if to himself yet loud enough for the man to hear. "So damn near-sighted. Lost my glasses. I'd love to examine this screen. Looks interesting."

To make good the deception Mr. Topper fumbled between the chairs as he hoped a near-sighted man might fumble, and slowly made his way from the room.

"Poor chap," thought the man. "He must be nearly blind, or else I'm seeing too well."

On the lawn Topper was once more joined by the ladies.

"I want to talk to both of you," he began.

"So do we," said Marion, hanging affectionately on his left arm. "We want to know if you'll buy us a couple of little drinks."

"Count me in on that," said a deep voice from nowhere.

"But——" protested Mr. Topper.

The ladies hustled him through the pleasant evening while the Colonel did helpful things in the rear.

"All right," said Topper. "Don't push, and quit tugging. I'll buy the drinks if you'll only not tear me to pieces."

"Do you hear?" said Marion happily. "He likes to be with us."

"Now about that chain of speakeasies," began the Colonel, returning in person to life.

Several strollers stopped to listen to Mr. Topper. He was hurling horrid words at someone who must have been standing far away on the unseen African shore.

XV

Six Well Fixed Races

At the races the next day Mr. Topper found himself very much alone. From the alacrity with which his companions left him to his own devices Topper suspected the worst. He parked the car in front of the Casino with the quiet observation that in case of any slight misunderstanding giving rise to hot words and violence all hands were to rally round this spot with no loss of time. After locking the car he carefully secreted the keys in an inside pocket as a provision against possible doublecrossing. Topper had no desire to be left alone with an infuriated race track. With promises that before the day was done the entire party would be self-supporting, the Colonel, with Oscar and the ladies, departed to make arrangements, the exact nature of which Topper decided he would be more comfortable to remain in ignorance. However, he could not keep from wondering why they went to such elaborate trouble to acquire wealth when they could so easily loot a bank, pick well lined pockets, or pillage the villas of the rich. Too tame, he decided. The Colonel enjoyed casting a thin veil of honesty over his nefarious transactions. The man was so tortuously crooked that he took pleasure in burlesquing honesty.

Some time later Mr. Topper came face to face with the group of acquaintances that had witnessed his peculiar conduct at the English Bar. It was not an easy meeting on either side. Vividly recalling his meteoric departure from the place on the last occasion, these charming people were far from indifferent to the complications inherent in this present encounter. For all they could tell, this retired American banker might take it into his head to go swooping round the race track in hot pursuit of the horses. Or he might be seized by a violent attack of bouncing brought on by the excitement of the races. However, their fear of the strange potentialities of the man prompted them to mask their true emotions. He was cordially absorbed into the party and presently borne away to the clubhouse, from the veranda of which he later saw not all, but nearly all, of what there was to be seen.

Owing to the undefinable nature of their activities it would be a far better thing to deal as briefly as possible with the Colonel and his companions rather than to enter into the details of how they set about eliminating the element of risk from six races. Suffice it to say that their plans had been carefully laid and most eventualities anticipated.

The ladies, gowned exquisitely and provided with all necessary credentials by a thorough and thoughtful Topper, by making promises of a most lurid character, succeeded in enticing a well established bookmaker into a private room of the clubhouse. Here the disillusioned man met with a reception far different from the one he had been given every reason to expect. In other words, he was the one to be disrobed, but first he was knocked both down and out. The Colonel thereupon appeared, and with his deft assistance the unfortunate gambler was stripped of his sportive outer garments, disclosing under ones of an even more sportive hue. After this he was bound, gagged, and dragged out of harm's way. The ladies then abandoned their own garments while making a concession to modesty by disappearing themselves. On the other hand, the Colonel, now suitably attired in the ravished outfit of the unconscious gambler, returned to the location frequented by that person, and thereupon began to lure, provoke, and browbeat large chunks of francs from members of the general public. All of the Colonel's betting arrangements, with a few exceptions, were strictly cash transactions, but as he quoted unusually favorable odds, that is, apparently favorable odds, and because of his impressive voice and eloquent gestures, he was soon virtually pauperizing a steady string of clients no less avaricious than himself but far more trustful. The fact that his trousers were a trifle short and his coat a shade over-styled slightly disturbed the fastidious sensibilities of this ex-army exquisite. Otherwise he was in his element. He even wondered regretfully why the idea had not occurred to him before.

Mr. Topper, in the course of a short stroll, inadvertently came across the Colonel in full cry. Topper was considerably impressed and no little alarmed by the tremendous business the Colonel was doing.

"God help all the favorites," he murmured as he turned away from the brilliant scene, speculating idly on the possible activities of Marion, Mrs. Hart, and Oscar.

Had he been aware of the true nature of their activities his prayer would have been even more fervent. His heart would have gone out not only to the favorite for the first race, but also to entry number seven, contemptuously referred to by the French populace as an "ootsaidaire," a term which Mr. Topper later discovered simply meant an outsider—a horse far removed from the money.

Amalek, the favorite for the first race, and the horse upon which the hopes of many of the Colonel's victims were centered, was speedily found in his stall by the unobtrusively investigating ladies. According to the Colonel's instructions they began to work on this horse after first having concealed Oscar's rump beneath a pile of straw, a situation from which the curious creature seemed to derive some faint amusement, especially when he was able to make his colleagues scramble frantically with the straw when he thrust his tail through. A queer dog, Oscar, taking him all in all, which was difficult to do because he was seldom that way.

Marion and Mrs. Hart then proceeded to disturb, dumbfound and infuriate Amalek—upon whose evenness of temper much money depended—into a condition bordering on homicidal irresponsibility. This was not difficult to accomplish. Such a trick as suddenly pulling out the horse's tongue and blowing on it immediately changed the animal's mental outlook. The unexpected repetition of this indignity just when the horse was beginning to believe that that was over, at any rate, served only to heighten his bitter resentment. It is bad enough to have one's tongue pulled out and blown on under the most favorable circumstances, but to have it pulled out by unseen hands and blown on by unseen lips is very much more disagreeable. At least, Amalek seemed to figure it out that way. The horse hated it. He was not only embarrassed but also alarmed. No one can say positively exactly what thoughts passed through his mind while his tongue was being pulled out, but it is probable he feared he was being attacked by some rare equine disease such as seizure of the tongue, or the latter half of that foot and mouth trouble he had heard so much about. Other arts and dodges were practised on Amalek, things that made him forget entirely about racing and think only of revenge. When Marion suddenly chattered in his ear like a demented squirrel Amalek was fit to be tied. For the safety of France he should have been tied. Amalek should have been securely tied to the post instead of started from it. A thumb tack gently tucked under his saddle completed the business of unseating the creature's reason. He broke into a cold sweat while still endeavoring to conceal his murderous purpose behind his wicked eyes. That thousands of francs had been wagered on his winning this race meant little or nothing to Amalek. If anything, the knowledge gave him a certain ironical satisfaction. The more fools his backers. Amalek intended to show the world that a race horse in good standing could not be subjected to the indignities he had suffered without swift and terrible retaliation. His hand was turned against man and beast alike. He would do things and go places.

With growing amazement Mr. Topper's friends followed from the clubhouse veranda the impassioned reprisals of the horse. Topper was unamazed. Had he seen Amalek dragged bodily from the track and hurled into the bushes he would not have been amazed. He knew from past experiences how ruthless his absent companions could be once their interests had become involved.

But when Amalek left the track he did so of his own free will. Before his departure, however, he threw consternation into the ranks of the competing horses. Every living thing within reach he attacked with his teeth and heels. The only horse to escape his wrath was already so far behind in the race as to escape the attention of the general public. This was the Colonel's horse—his hand-picked favorite, number seven, lucky number seven, ironically known as *Le Plongeur*, or in a reasonable language, the Diver.

Topper had been mysteriously advised to bet his francs on this tattered shred of horseflesh. He had done so. And because of the weird proclivities his friends attributed to him they also had wagered heavily on the seemingly impossible success of this ruined "ootsaidaire."

Upon the shoulders of Marion and Mrs. Hart and the rump of Oscar devolved the responsibility of seeing to it that Amalek and the Diver reversed the logical order of march. It was a heavy responsibility and one that involved no little activity. In fact, all hands were exceedingly busy.

While Amalek employed himself in the line of unseating jockeys with his teeth, deflecting honest horses from their courses with his feet and making a menace of himself in general, Marion, with the rear end of Oscar, hurried to the same end of the shambling Diver and incited the dog to attack. At the first sharp nip at his fetlocks *Le Plongeur*, or lucky number seven, stopped effortlessly in his tracks and looked back to see what new affliction his God had seen fit to punish him with for not having run faster in the days of his youth. Marion, standing well out of the way of the horse's hoofs, eyed his reactions with professional interest. She figured out that even the slowest horse, if bitten by the rump of a dog, would feel inclined to move a trifle faster. She was right. *Le Plongeur* blinked several times very rapidly as if to clear his eyes of the familiar dust of other horses, then he bent his gaze more intently upon the semi-detached rump of Oscar. Once more the Diver blinked, this time to clear them of a vision far more disturbing than dust. As realization slowly dawned upon the dim mind behind the eyes, an expression of horror overspread the poor animal's face and continued on until his entire body was held in the clutch of fear. Here was an object to be avoided at all costs. Here at last was a cause that justified real honest-to-God leg work. It was then that the Diver started into a run such as neither he nor any other horse had ever run before. The inspired speed of his mount was even more of a surprise to the jockey than it was to the horse itself. Gamely he stuck to various sections of the flying beast and hoped that his luck would last. Even had Amalek not involved his fellow horses together with their riders in a hand-to-hand combat for survival itself, the Colonel's choice would have won by several convulsive lengths.

"Will someone more familiar than I with the finer nuances of racing kindly explain to me what the hell Amalek thinks he's doing with himself and all these other horses?" Millie Coit inquired in a hushed voice.

"That seems fairly obvious," Blynn Nelson replied. "After having either murdered or mutilated all other competitors in the race save one he is now trying to climb the fence in order to attack the judges' stand in the rear."

"I can count at least four jockeys struggling in agony on the track," vouchsafed Harold Gay. "And just a moment ago I fancied I caught a glimpse of a dog that was not all there. Of course, I must be wrong." Mr. Gay removed his field glasses from his eyes and looked suggestively at Mr. Topper. "What little I saw of the dog," the speaker added slowly, "looked startlingly familiar. Would you care to look, Mr. Topper?"

"Heaven forbid," replied Mr. Topper hastily. "I'm seeing too much as it is with my naked eyes."

Oscar, having seen the Diver off to a good start, concealed his invaluable rump in a flower bed and awaited further demands upon his peculiar talents. By this time the stands were quite naturally in an uproar. The judges were trying to throw their hands away while discharging streams of inquiries and objections in the general direction of God. The once proud owner of Amalek was sneaking down a side street and seriously entertaining ideas of assuming a disguise. His horse, his magnificent Amalek, he now considered an unclean reptile. Little did that matter to the reptile himself. Having tossed his jockey to the winds, he had succeeded in putting the fence between himself and the track. Here, in the center of the field, he was now defying man, beast, and God to get together and try to do something about all the horrid things he had done. While the other demoralized horses were casting about for their jockeys, the Diver, with stark terror in his eyes, tore along the track in an earnest effort to remove himself as far as possible from the thing he refused even to think about. It was a neat display of concentrated space-eating speed. In spite of the fact that the Diver's success would be their loss, the spectators began to cheer.

Hunt Davis, who had been born and bred in blue-grass regions, rubbed his eyes in bewilderment.

"Damn me," he observed in an admiring voice, "if I ever saw a horse run any faster than that in all my born days. Looks like he's downright scared about something. Maybe he'll kill his fool self."

"Not before he wins, I hope," said Millie Coit. "That's our own little private favorite, that rocket out there. After he's made it a race he can die a thousand deaths, and may God rest his soul each time."

"Then Topper was right about betting on him," advanced Waddles. "I wonder how he knew?"

"One wonders no end of things about dear Mr. Topper," observed Mrs. Blake Willard insinuatingly. "For example, how does the man contrive to play such an astonishing game of tennis?"

"Isn't there enough to wonder about?" Mr. Topper mildly interposed. "Both Amalek and our Diver there are more astonishing than I am."

"So long as he makes me a rich woman," Millie Coit declared, "I don't give a rap how he goes about it."

While this casual discussion was going on, so was the Diver. Lucky number seven was going on and on and on. Even now it is not definitely known whether he ever stopped. When he found himself face to face with the finishing line he was seen to hesitate for the first time in the course of his mad progress. Now the Diver knew nothing at all about finishing lines. He may have heard of such things, but the crowd had never waited long enough to let him complete a race. Before the tragic eyes of the judges and in the presence of the hooting multitude the horse felt out of place and alone.

Should he go on with this new venture? He looked back fearfully, then the memory of that terrible nipping rump bounding so jauntily about the track overcame the horse's embarrassment. Emulating his name he plunged past the post. If he did not win the race he might lose his life. This was no time to stand on ceremony. As fresh as if the race had just begun, the Diver kept on going.

"We'll have to send a wireless to that horse's jockey to let the beggar know he won," Commander Becket remarked in a disgusted voice. "I've seen horses run in all parts of the world, but this is about the raggedest race in my recollection."

However, the retired naval officer was destined to witness even raggeder races than this one before the day was done. From the first race to the last, things went from bad to worse. Horses grew more restive and jockeys less sure of their seats—less sure of anything, for that matter. The concerted efforts of Marion, Mrs. Hart, and Oscar succeeded so well in unnerving the horses for the second and third races that only a few of them were able to appear in public, the heavy-money horses invariably losing to the most unexpected entries. Apparently the goddess of chance was at last taking pity on physical wrecks in the line of horseflesh.

The fourth race was perhaps the most ridiculously futile of all. It was won by a deaf horse. And the deaf horse won this race solely because she was a deaf horse and consequently unable to hear the disconcerting and objectionable sounds Marion Kerby and Mrs. Hart cleverly created the impression the other horses were making. No brain other than that of a woman could have conceived a device so embarrassing both to the horses and to their jockeys. Even the starter was involved in the misunderstanding arising from what the poor chap had every reason to believe to be a group of talking, cursing, and vulgarly offensive horses. The only horse that appeared to retain both her poise and her self-respect was named La Sorcière. And La Sorcière was deaf. Stone deaf.

As the already nervous animals were busily engaged in lining up at the starting barrier, Marion Kerby, placing herself close to the mouth of one of them, suddenly smote the air with a wild, unnatural scream. The horse, greatly upset, strove to give the impression that such a desperate, unhorselike sound could not have issued from him. He turned his head and looked accusingly at his neighbor, who in turn looked severely at the horse next to him. And this kept up until finally all the horses were looking frowningly at each other. To see a number of horses suspiciously inspecting each other's faces is an unusual thing. Very. At any rate, the starter seemed to think so. He, too, looked suspiciously at all the horses, his scrutiny including their jockeys. When Mrs. Hart contrived to place a truly dreadful sound in the mouth of still another horse the starter started himself. He was moved to words.

"Gentlemen," he said, addressing the jockeys of the two offending horses, "is it that your mounts are in pain? Such noises sound far from well. They are, truly, altogether new to me, those sounds."

The two accused jockeys stoutly denied the imputation that their horses were anything other than the healthiest and most well bred of beasts. Monsieur the starter must be thinking of a couple of other horses.

A burst of ironical and defiant jeers interrupted these protestations. La Sorcière alone, of all the horses, retained her poise.

"A thousand thunders!" exclaimed the starter. "You must do something about all this. Your horses, they are unbecomingly boisterous. Quiet them, if you please."

"One thousand and one thunders!" shouted a horse in a reckless voice. "No more nor no less."

The starter looked pained at being out-thundered by a mere horse. He looked even more so when an especially offensive noise issued from a horse standing in the center of the group. Even the horse's jockey looked a trifle dismayed. It was such a sound as crude persons employ when giving another person the raspberry in almost any language. The starter had his own ideas about being given the raspberry in French. He looked angrily at the jockey.

"Your horse," he demanded, "did you make him to push that distressing noise?"

"M'sieu," protested the jockey, "is it that you fancy I would encourage my little cabbage to give issue to a sound so unrefined as that?"

The starter had his doubts about this. The jockey's reputation was none too savory. His mount had a mean eye—far from one of refinement. The starter intimated as much. Marion tugged the horse over to the starter and by a series of irritating pinches made the frightened and bewildered creature endeavor to deposit his front feet heavily upon the starter's chest. The starter climbed up on the fence and disqualified both horse and rider. High-pitched neighs of derision now became general among the horses. Marion and Mrs. Hart were in full tongue. Surprisingly effeminate shrieks and catcalls fell from the lips of the perturbed jockeys. In the midst of this hubbub one jockey was distinctly heard to allude suspiciously to the sex of another jockey. The upshot of this was an exchange of blows and several new disqualifications. By this time it was a toss-up between the horses and the starter as to which would be disqualified first. It was obvious that the horses were as unfit to start as the official was to start them. He was brought to a full realization of his ridiculous position when he heard La Sorcière announce in a bored but ladylike voice:

"Monsieur the starter, one grows fatigued on one's feet. Me, I am prepared to march."

This public rebuke by the least favored of animals on four legs was just a little too much for Monsieur the starter. He released the few remaining qualified horses and departed in search of a substitute to take his place. Under the circumstances the horses ran as well as could be expected, but it was plain to see that their thoughts were on other matters. They could not be disturbed by mere racing. La Sorcière, anxious to retire from the public eye to the comfort and seclusion of her stall, hurried right along. As a result of the indifference of her competitors the Colonel had the satisfaction of seeing still another of his favorites jounce home a winner. It is doubtful if La Sorcière even realized she had actually won a race, and as no one could tell her about it she probably never found out.

For the fifth race the Colonel radically altered his method of procedure. Instead of picking a favorite, his instructions were merely that at all costs John Bull and Coquette should be prevented from placing.

"How will we do that?" Mrs. Hart inquired. "Do you expect us to wrestle with a couple of infuriated horses?"

The Colonel shrugged indifferently.

"That's your end of the game," he replied. "Don't bother me. Why not hang onto the beggars' tails?"

"That's our end of the game," said Mrs. Hart.

"Not a bad end either," replied Marion. "We need a little diversion."

Accordingly, when the fifth race started, Marion and Mrs. Hart, clinging gamely to the tails of John Bull and Coquette respectively, found themselves being hurtled through space amid a great clattering of hoofs.

"Gord!" gasped Mrs. Hart. "I might be invisible to the eye, but I still retain some feelings."

"These fool horses aren't giving us a tumble," complained Marion. "Might just as well not be here at all."

"Do you find the motion soothing?" asked Mrs. Hart.

"A little hard to breathe," admitted Marion.

"Hang on for the first turn!" cried Mrs. Hart.

"Oh, why did we ever take up racing?" asked Marion. "This is no place for a lady."

"Not even for a kite," said Mrs. Hart. "Port your helm."

After they had weathered the perils of the first turn the conversation was resumed.

"I'm a grand old flag and I'm tied to a nag," Marion sang out.

"I'd like to give Coquette a piece of my mind," said Mrs. Hart. "The old girl has a wicked wobble."

It was only to be expected that this steady flow of conversation between the two ladies should arouse some interest on the part of the jockeys. The need to know just who was doing all this talking right behind their backs became so urgent that both of them turned round in their saddles in an attempt to discover its source. This maneuver caused them to sacrifice much valuable ground.

"At whom are you looking, my old?" Marion asked nastily in French.

"What a repulsive face mine has," observed Mrs. Hart.

"From where I am I'm not getting a noble view of horseflesh," Marion announced.

"Far from it," replied Mrs. Hart. "In fact, I'm getting a very low opinion of horses in general."

"If John looks as bad in front as he does behind," commented Marion, "I'd hate to meet him face to face."

"It couldn't be worse than the face of my jockey," declared Mrs. Hart in plain but painful French.

The jockeys were getting mad. They were burning up. The intensely personal remarks of the ladies had deeply wounded their impressionable French natures. No man likes to have such insinuations made about his face. The insulted jockeys found themselves unable to concentrate on the important business at hand. Their mounts began to lag farther and farther behind. They were growing weary of the pace.

Meanwhile the two ladies were considering what next to try to discourage John Bull and Coquette and to humiliate their jockeys. The last turn lay close ahead. The animals might be holding back for the home stretch.

"I'm going to twist this devil's tail," announced Marion.

"I'll try it on mine, too," said Mrs. Hart. "Clean off."

Upon the putting of this crude suggestion to the test it was the horses that looked back this time. With large, inquiring eyes they inspected their twisted tails. What was going on back there, they wondered. Why should anyone want to do that to them? There was something sinister about all this. The interest of the horses in their tails was fatal to their heads. Speeding blindly as they were in a semicircular position, they suddenly became entangled and fell in a large, untidy heap from which their jockeys, more indignant than injured, presently emerged with a couple of stories to tell that no one ever believed. Once more the Colonel's will had been done.

"That makes us all the richer," said Mrs. Hart as the two ladies returned to the starter's barrier in search of Oscar, whose services would be needed in the last race.

"In experience as well as francs," remarked Marion. "No more horsefly tactics for me."

"I felt like a sneeze in an earthquake," Mrs. Hart declared.

"Neatly turned," said Marion.

For the sixth race the Colonel had perversely set his heart on a veteran of many decades, Voiturette, a name which at the time of the animal's christening had meant little carriage because in those remote days motors were still unknown in the provinces. In all of France there was not a follower of the track who expected this horse to do anything other than to occupy her customary position to the rear. In this the Colonel, Mr. Topper, and his friends were the lucky exceptions, Topper having been previously advised to place all his winnings on her success. Voiturette had been playing anchor horse for so many years that she had become a well loved national institution.

In the bushes near the starting barrier Marion and Mrs. Hart were having a desperate time with Oscar. For the sake of original-ity they had set their hearts on making the dog utilize his head in order to gain their ends. Oscar could not understand.

"Oscar," Marion was pleading, "this is a serious matter. Won't you forget your rump for a moment and be just a head—a terrible head with lots of teeth and a leer, perhaps?"

"Yes," chimed in Mrs. Hart sweetly. "Show all the bad horses your pretty teeth, old kid. Snap from a tail to a head."

"Come on, Oscar," urged Marion. "It's heads we win, tails we lose. How about it?"

Oscar's rump was quivering nervously. He seemed to realize that something good—something extra special—was expected of him. And although he did not know exactly what this was he was trying his best to please. Crouched down in the bushes he concentrated on the business until the sweat dripped from his almost invisible body. Part after part of himself he materialized in the hope that one of his offerings would give satisfaction. Because he was using his head so furiously he completely forgot to display it.

"He doesn't seem to know he has a head," Mrs. Hart complained in a low voice. "All those parts he's been showing us might do—God knows they're awful enough—but for the last race of the day they don't seem sufficiently spectacular."

"We haven't much time left," muttered Marion. "If Oscar doesn't do a head soon we'll lose our pants. Don't be a duffer, Oscar, old dear. Make a nice head for the ladies—a nice, awful head."

This odd entreaty gave inspiration to Mrs. Hart.

"Be a mad dog, Oscar," she suddenly commanded.

In Oscar's confused mind these words struck sparks of intelligence. Certainly he would be a mad dog for the ladies. He knew all about playing mad dog. It was one of his favorite games. Why hadn't they asked him the first time? Suddenly and grippingly Oscar's rump gave place to a head. Both ladies instinctively edged away. Even when one expected the worst of Oscar it was no laughing matter to get used to him. His mouth was flecked with foam, his eyes rolled insanely, he did revolting things with his tongue, and his dripping fangs could not be long endured by human eyes, much less by those of a high-strung horse.

"For the love of God," breathed Marion, "he's about the maddest damned mad dog I ever did see."

"He's cute," said Mrs. Hart a little nervously. "But the Colonel should do things like this. After all, Oscar's his dog. I hope the beast doesn't take this business too seriously. One sight of him will kill most of those poor horses."

"Yes," reflected Marion. "It would take years and years of the closest intimacy for any horse to get used to that head. Nevertheless, better a few dead horses than a financially crippled Colonel. Guess we ought to congratulate the poor idiot."

"Isn't he cunning?" exclaimed Mrs. Hart in a false voice, gazing with difficulty upon the horrible head. "Don't bite me, mad dog— ugh, you're just too awful for words!"

Pleased by this tribute, Oscar made a few playful practice snaps in the general direction of the ladies, who huddled together in space.

"I don't think he's ever been quite so mad as all that," murmured Mrs. Hart. "Do you think he's really just playing?"

"Well," replied Marion with conviction, "I'm not going to show a scrap of my body to find out."

"If he isn't in earnest," said Mrs. Hart, "he certainly has a slapstick sense of humor."

"He's all right," answered Marion. "After all, slapstick humor is merely the laughter its critics wish they could have created themselves. It's close to the hearts of the gods. The pie has not yet been thrown that I can't laugh at."

"It's mighty hard to get a laugh out of Oscar," Mrs. Hart observed. "He's the most frightful display of ectoplasm I've ever had the unhappiness to meet."

"We've got to snap to it," said Marion as the horses began to arrive at the barrier. "Take that around to the first turn where there aren't any close observers. When the main body of horses come along, turn it loose about fifteen yards in front of them and tell him to go plumb crazy. I'll hold Little Carriage well in the rear until that dog has had his day."

With her enthusiastically mad dog, Mrs. Hart departed through the bushes that luckily hid him from view. Marion drifted over to the head of Little Carriage and unobtrusively placed her hand on the grand old mud hen's bridle. All was now in readiness for the final race of the day.

"Good!" exclaimed Commander Becket as the horses broke evenly from the barrier. "Looks as if we were going to have a real race this time."

"They're off to a good start, at least," agreed Millie Coit. "All except our horse. There's only one way I can't stand being ruined, and that is financially."

"Be calm, my dear," said Mr. Topper knowingly. "Voiturette can't lose this race. They've been saving her for years."

"Looks mighty like she's still being saved," remarked Harold Gay.

"Indeed it does," put in Blynn Nelson. "If they don't begin to draw a little interest soon I'll have to sell a fleet of motorboats to break even with my obscure little wine dealer."

Running low and well in a flying wedge the horses were nearing the first turn. Proceeding leisurely from the barrier came Little

Carriage, nervously trying to free her bridle from the disturbing grasp of an unseen hand. Little Carriage did not mind trotting slowly through a race, but she did not exactly fancy walking through one. In a few years, perhaps, but——

Then Oscar, suddenly pushed by Mrs. Hart, made his cataclysmic appearance. His immediate vicinity seemed to be composed entirely of jaws and teeth, both working with a will. The day was done for the horses so far as racing was concerned. If a horse breathed that was so anxious to win a race as to pass that head, he or she could have all three places for the asking. The flying wedge put on the emergency and skidded. For a moment it looked at Oscar's working face, then wheeled about and sped back in the direction whence it had come.

"What's this?" demanded the Commander indignantly. "It's a rout, by God, not a race. A shameful retreat. I'd rather lose all my money than all my wits."

The majority of the spectators seemed to be of the same opinion. A great clamor arose. This last race was just a little too steep for the best natured of crowds.

As the horses passed Voiturette plodding along in the opposite direction no greetings were exchanged. The poor creature looked wistfully after her friends as they rushed by on either side. Reluctantly she yielded to the unseen but not unheard tugging at her bridle. Marion was cursing steadily. An unpremeditated glimpse of Oscar's head peering drippingly through the bushes caused Little Carriage to sit down with a gasp of dismay. This is perhaps the first time on record that a body of racing enthusiasts has ever been treated to the spectacle of a solitary horse sitting in the middle of a race track while the main body of competitors were doing their best to get themselves off it as speedily as possible. Philosophically the jockey belonging to Voiturette clung to the grotesquely squatting horse and contented himself with hoping that the animal would not lie down entirely and die so far from home and friends.

It was at this point that Marion lost her temper. She not only took the bit but also the teeth of the sitting horse, and endeavored to pull them out of her head. Failing this, she rushed to the rear of the horse and kicked her vigorously. And all the while she maintained a steady stream of indecent language. The jockey who could only understand English when it was cursed understood a lot of it now. Finally her efforts were rewarded. Voiturette, growing weary of being kicked, rose and plodded off down the track, Marion tugging her furiously by the bridle.

"That animal gives me the impression that someone is pulling it along," said Clyde Jones. "See how its neck stretches out and jerks back sort of protestingly."

"Looks as if our horse is going to win in a walk," observed Commander Becket. "First time I ever saw a race won in a walk."

"You'll see this one won in a creep," replied Millie.

As Little Carriage came into the home stretch the demonstration swelled to a terrific outburst. Voiturette's squatting act had restored the crowd to good-humor. What with kicking, swearing, and pulling, Marion Kerby was nearly winded. Entering into the spirit of the occasion the jockey bowed ironically in the direction of the stands. Slowly and painfully the old horse approached both her own and the race's finish. Step by step her stiff joints cut down the few remaining yards. From the crowd in the paddock boomed the deep voice of the Colonel.

"Speed, Little Motor!" he shouted.

"Mind your own damn business," came back the bitter voice of an unseen woman. "Keep your stolen shirt on. I'm practically carrying her as it is."

Far off on the brow of a gently rising hill the brave steeds that had so gallantly started the race were ingloriously tearing up turf in their anxiety to obliterate for all time the memory of the horror their eyes had looked on that day. Unseated and disgruntled jockeys were limpingly returning from all points of the compass. When Voiturette dragged her exhausted body across the finishing line the amazed and delighted French multitude—for once forgetting its love of francs—tore loose and gave the old girl a new thrill. Within the space of her own length from the line she let go her legs and hit the track with a grunt. From that spot she refused either to budge or to be budged. Little Carriage was through. She had won her first and last race.

Marion brushed the palms of her hands together and drew a deep breath. It had been a tough race for her, and she felt tough.

"If I ever see another horse again during the remainder of my supernatural days," she muttered, "I'll choke its blooming tongue out."

Snatching a hip flask from the pocket of the nearest bystander, she hurried across the field, guzzling as she went. When she picked up Oscar and Mrs. Hart she was feeling decidedly better.

XVI

The Ascension of
Colonel Scott

No bookmaker—honest or otherwise—who accepted money as freely as had the Colonel, could expect to retain it all. It was hardly possible for some of his many clients not to win occasionally. However, the Colonel was a gentleman whose expectations surpassed all laws of logic. They were seldom if ever disappointed, and never discouraged. He could expect the most prodigious things and realize them with surprising ease if not the strictest honesty.

Even had he paid his fortunate clients the winnings that were rightfully theirs, he would not have been much out of pocket. His own vast, ill-gotten gains would have hardly noticed the difference. But on this occasion greed had overcome whatever feeble resistance his none too robust scruples had attempted to offer. He did more than expect to retain all of the money in his possession. As he expressed it somewhat grimly to himself, he damn well intended to retain all of the money down to the last centime. He even considered for a moment his chances of success in walking out on his two henchwomen but reluctantly abandoned the idea. He knew Mrs. Hart's character well enough to realize that she would gracefully follow him through the most tortuous corridors of hell for the sake of five francs. And as for Marion Kerby, he had not the slightest doubt that that young lady would turn the earth and the air itself into a living inferno for him if he attempted to play her false in an enterprise involving money. Even while regretting the sordid characters of these two women he could not altogether detach from his regret a sort of unholy feeling of admiration. Moreover, Mrs. Hart and Marion might prove useful in future ventures. He would have to satisfy himself by holding out on them as much as possible—by taking advantage of their inability to deal rapidly and accurately with the intricacies of foreign money. He earnestly hoped that Mr. Topper, in the capacity of an ex-banker, would not step in as an unofficial observer at the division of the spoils.

As soon as the last race had dragged itself to its final collapse the Colonel became exceedingly busy in collecting his side bets, an enterprise in which he succeeded by the exercise of the most brutal methods. The professional gamblers with whom he had dealt, believing him thoroughly mad, had put him down as easy picking. They now discovered to their sorrow how terribly mistaken they had been. In spite of the arguments they properly advanced regarding the honesty of the races the outraged Colonel insisted on extracting his pound of flesh.

It was while dealing with the most stubborn of these dishonest gentlemen that several disconcerting incidents occurred—incidents which led to a scene that will long be remembered by the frequenters of that race track.

Profoundly moved by the pusillanimous and obviously unfair attitude of this reluctant gambler, the Colonel was calling loudly on God to take prompt and effective action when the avaricious shouts of his own clients were borne unpleasantly in on his ears. Among these shouts he distinguished one of outstanding ferocity. Turning with elaborate indignation, the excellent Colonel encountered the envenomed gaze of a gentleman clad unbecomingly in a blue undershirt and a pair of gaudily striped drawers which struck a faint spark in the Colonel's memory. Where had he seen those drawers before? Ah, yes. They were none other than the incredibly ill-chosen garments of the betrayed and assaulted bookmaker. This was serious. It grew even more serious when the Colonel remarked the presence of two evil-faced gendarmes standing on either side of the repellent looking bookmaker. The Colonel was not amused. He found nothing funny in the quaint appearance of the passionately vociferating bookmaker as so many disinterested spectators appeared to be doing. He realized with alarm that if caught in his present condition of solidity by this emotional French mob he would be torn franc from franc. Scenes from the French Revolution swept through his mind. The Colonel could take care of his body, but that was not enough. He wanted also to take care of the francs. Without the purchasing power of those francs the activities of his body would be seriously curtailed. Furthermore, there was the matter of the last uncollected bet. As critical as the situation was he had no intention of abandoning all that money in favor of a welshing Frenchman. To do so would be to establish a bad precedent for the noble institution of racing. He, the Colonel, would be actually encouraging dishonesty.

Accordingly, he felt that he was conferring a favor on France when he turned suddenly and, smiting the gambler to the ground, conscientiously rifled his pockets. A cry broke from the mob, and the gendarmes made hostile advances. Having impoverished his fallen enemy the Colonel quickly extracted several huge wads of francs from his own pockets and proceeded leisurely to dematerialize before the eyes of the incredulous spectators.

The borrowed garments of the accusing bookmaker fell from the Colonel's body, disclosing some rather flamboyant shorts in which the wearer could be only faintly discerned. An aggressive military mustache, two huge bundles of francs, and the drawers themselves, the whole being loosely held together by a filmy structure in the semblance of a man, were all that remained of the Colonel. Slowly and impressively he rose from the ground and remained poised in benign contemplation above the heads of the multitude as a light breeze gently swayed him to and fro.

"Regard that!" cried one of the Colonel's erstwhile clients, forgetting in his admiration that he was witnessing the irrevocable disappearance of his own winnings. "Monsieur the bookmaker has dissipated himself. It is that he has become as a god. A thing marvelous, this. Is it not?"

"But yes," replied another bilked client, not so easily carried away by the excitement of the moment. "It is of a marvelousness in full truth, but—*hein!* It is also an affair of the most lamentable nature, for is it not that there go an illimitable number of francs that should be rightfully ours?"

"Of a verity," responded the first Frenchman, his expression of admiration promptly changing to one of poignant despair. "It is but now being borne in on me that I am applauding a theft instead of a miracle. That one on high, semi-seen only and aloof, is far from what he seems."

"M'sieu, he is even less," said the other politely. "Bear witness, nevertheless, that the small little that remains still possesses sufficient astuteness to cling with a greed of the utmost tenacity to our francs."

"Indubitably, m'sieu, and one regrets that much," the first victim agreed. "It would be no less than a step of justice and wisdom if our brave gendarmes encumbered the drawers of the wicked one with lead."

"But, no!" cried the other thriftily. "It is that they might miss and so destroy a number of francs enormous."

"So far as we ourselves are concerned," observed the first Frenchman, whose intellect was not sufficient to follow the economic abstractions of his friend, "those francs of innumerable number are, if not destroyed, at least departed, and forever, alas."

It was of a truth. The francs were departing. Higher and higher ascended the Colonel above the heads of the gesticulating crowd. The military mustache became confused with the branches of trees on a distant hill. The drawers blended harmoniously with the sky now, shot with pastel shades from the lowering sun. Only the two huge bundles of francs remained visible to the tormented eyes of the mob, then they, too, slowly faded from mere specks to an aching void.

The Colonel had made good his escape. His highly questionable conduct had been most impressively dramatized. To his way of thinking he had given his baffled clients more than enough for their money. He was well pleased with the results of the day. Now for the automobile and Mr. Topper—perhaps a bit of an orgy.

———

If brevity is the soul of wit Marion's briefs were brilliant. They were short to the point of brusqueness—neat, concise little garments. The young lady, now back in the private room in the clubhouse with Mrs. Hart and Oscar, was holding these briefs in her hands preparatory to materializing in them when Mrs. Hart first noticed the absence of the bookmaker.

"He is gone, my dear," she announced.

"That's good," Marion replied abstractedly. "I'm glad he took those drawers away, or I'd never be able to get into my own."

"Weren't they fearful?" said Mrs. Hart, now busy about her own materialization. "Wonder who thought them up?"

In answer to this came a low growl from Oscar.

"My dear," called Marion, "I have the most uncanny sensation that someone is looking at my scanties askance. So, seemingly, has Oscar."

"So have I," replied Mrs. Hart. "Something tells me we're not alone."

"Evidently," said Marion calmly, turning towards the door. "Looks as if the whole damn Riviera has wedged itself into the room."

"What's the big idea?" demanded Mrs. Hart, following Marion's example and turning to confront a breathlessly interested group of club members, servants, and gendarmes.

"In place of the absent drawers," commented Marion, "we seem to have much of France."

"More of it than I need or want," gasped Mrs. Hart. "This is a terribly embarrassing situation. Do something about those briefs, my dear. You're in an awful state."

"I'll do what I can," said Marion. "You're not swathed in garments yourself, you know."

"Yes," chattered Mrs. Hart. "I know only too well, but I can't seem to manage my ectoplasm."

Marion, too, was experiencing difficulty in that direction. Their ectoplasm—at all times of a sensitive disposition—had received such a severe shock that its action had become atrophied. Consequently the ladies were left in a state of suspended materialization in which they appeared to be made of delicately tinted gelatine. They could neither return to nothing nor advance to more. Oscar had completely disappeared. There was not even a rump to be seen. As tired as she had become of seeing that part of the dog bunching itself about the landscape, Marion now decided it would at least be a comfort to have had even that unprepossessing object with them in this moment of crisis.

"The ladies," one of the gendarmes observed superfluously, "they are without costumes." He hesitated, then added as the ladies in question shrank into their briefs, "Or nearly so."

"They should be arrested and put into jail," remarked an American guest of the club. "If my husband were here I wouldn't know what to do."

"Is that so?" said Marion in a hard voice. "Well, lady, neither would he, or else he wouldn't have married you."

"They are the same as the ones who misled monsieur the bookmaker," put in another gendarme.

"He was certainly wearing a misleading pair of drawers," retorted Marion.

"But, my old," objected still another representative of French law and order, "that one assured us they undressed him and not themselves. He had hoped otherwise, he told us."

"He was a gentleman at least," replied Mrs. Hart. "He didn't want to brag."

"I'm getting sick of this back talk," said Marion. "Let's make a break."

"How?" asked Mrs. Hart.

"We'll scream our way out," Marion replied. "Grab up your clothes and follow me and yell like hell. Maybe Oscar will show some signs of life and limb."

Suddenly the room was filled with a volley of ear-splitting screams, shrieks, and imprecations. Two translucent ladies, clad only in the curtest of panties and clinging onto their outer raiment, danced weirdly about the room. From beneath a table arose the howling of a dog that increased in ferocity with the tempo of the dance. Presently the head of a mad dog appeared at the seat of the howls. Guests, servants, and club members vied with each other to give the gendarmes ample room in which to make their arrests.

"My God in heaven!" muttered an old *débauché*, mopping his forehead with a scented handkerchief. "I thought I had slept, in my time, with every manner of woman extant, but I must have completely overlooked that type. What are they?"

"Why, they're hardly anything at all, old chap," an English visitor explained. "Merely a pair of scandalously animated ladies' garments, so far as I could tell."

"Well, I recognized more than that," said the old gentleman. "And listen to them. Do you mean to tell me that a couple of pairs of jigging drawers can let out whoops like that?"

The Englishman, a trifle offended at the other's coarse way of putting things, stalked off. Anyway, this was France. He was not responsible for its morals. Joining a French show girl out of work whom he was maintaining at a favorable rate of exchange while on the Continent, he drove impeccably away from the clubhouse and later telegraphed his wife to be careful of Junior's cold.

The game old *débauché*, as if still fascinated by the riddle of the sexes, struggled back to the door of the private room and peered in between two gendarmes. He was just in time to witness the charge of the embattled panties foamingly led by the snapping fangs of Oscar.

"Strange women," mused the old gentleman as he got himself out of the way. "And an even stranger dog."

As Marion dashed through the door one of the gendarmes made a shrinking grab at her. There was the sound of ripping silk.

"There go the briefs!" cried Marion. "Hold onto yours, Clara. The godarme gendam—I mean, the goddam gendarme got 'em."

"Hope he keeps his beastly hands off mine," yelled Clara Hart as she dashed through the door, then triumphantly added, "Made it! Only an impertinent pinch."

"Mine weren't much, but they meant a lot to me," Marion called back over her shoulder.

"Easy come, easy go," Mrs. Hart panted as philosophically as one can pant.

"You mean, easy on, easy off," replied Marion. "That's why I liked 'em."

"Drape your dress around you and run like hell," Mrs. Hart urged. "The godarmes are following."

"I can't run like hell with this dress draped around me," Marion complained.

"Then just run like hell," said Mrs. Hart.

Down the main thoroughfare of the French resort the fascinating figures sped, a path being cleared before them by the anything but fascinating head of the baying Oscar. Shopkeepers, chauffeurs, and tourists saw them and blinked their eyes. Even the Colonel saw them, and joined the merry chase as it debouched into a palm-lined avenue that led to the Casino.

"Sic 'em, Oscar," called the Colonel, and the dog, at the sound of his master's voice, turned back and threw consternation into the ranks of the pursuing gendarmes.

"Oh, look at all the francs," cried Mrs. Hart in a delighted voice.

"You'd run naked through the streets of Paris for half that amount," Marion Kerby told her.

"Wouldn't I!" shouted Mrs. Hart. "I'd even loiter *sans costume* through the streets of New York itself for less than a third."

"Come! Come!" cried the Colonel. "This is no time for vulgar niceties. Run, girls, run."

"Well, we're not exactly crawling," said Clara Hart in an injured voice.

"I was under the impression we were literally killing the kilometers," put in Marion bitterly.

"What's wrong with your ectoplasm?" the flying Colonel inquired. "Why are you that way?"

"What's wrong with your own ectoplasm?" exploded Mrs. Hart. "You seem to be all francs and drawers. Ours is stuck, that's all."

Mr. Topper, seated at the wheel of his chartered machine, heard the tumult of their approach. To his startled eyes it seemed that the entire populace of the town proposed to take a ride in his machine. Preparing for the worst, he started up the engine. The Colonel, or rather, two wads of francs were the first to arrive.

"I must look queer to you," he laughed apologetically, "but everything is all right. Mrs. Hart has most of my clothes."

"Pardon my informal appearance," gasped that lady as she fell in beside the Colonel. "My ectoplasm will soon be in circulation."

Marion, in the front seat, was practically choking Topper with a pair of tapering diaphanous arms. Even the French witnesses to this intimate little scene were shocked into forgetting its romantic flavor. Some of them even remembered to take the number of the car. The French can be very much like that on occasions. Especially when it's at the expense of an apparently wealthy American.

"Journeys end in lovers meeting," Marion sang out.

"I think I can stand almost everything except the way Oscar is," remarked Mr. Topper judiciously. "I refuse to be responsible for the quality of my driving with that head in my lap."

Oscar, with a gendarme's cap gripped firmly in his teeth, was busily worming himself into the front seat beside Topper. Oscar liked this man. He was so solid. A good lap for a weary head. The poor beast had forgotten how unpalatable he looked.

"We'll deal with Oscar later," said the Colonel. "Now, if you love your liberty, for God's sake, look alive, even if we can't."

"Where away?" demanded Topper.

"Anywhere," replied the Colonel. "Anywhere but home. They'd trace you there as quick as a wink. Got to give 'em the slip. Head for Monte Carlo."

"Splendid!" cried Mrs. Hart.

"Shove off," commanded Marion. "If we must wash our soiled linen, let's do it in someone else's public."

"You don't seem to be wearing any linen at all," Mr. Topper observed.

"I didn't think you'd notice," Marion replied, making another dive for him.

"If you'll restrain this woman," said Mr. Topper with fastidious calm, "and drop a handkerchief over this dog's face, I'll try to budge along."

As the gendarmes arrived, the car sped on its way.

"Here's your cap, dearie," Marion called back. "Wish it had been your pants."

"Trousers," corrected Topper. "Are all women alike?"

"I don't know," replied Marion innocently, "but now's a good time to find out."

"Low. Always low," Mr. Topper murmured regretfully, as if to himself.

XVII

FROM TREE TO TREE

"The surveyor who laid out this bit of road must have been as cock-eyed as hell," the Colonel complained some minutes later.

"You're so crooked, Colonel," Marion observed dispassionately, "that all roads look cockeyed to you."

Nor was the Colonel cast down by this remark. His mood was benign and expansive. A hard wench, but a clever one, he mused, smiling at Marion.

The road to which he had been referring was the Corniche d'Or, one of the most picturesquely petrifying highways in the world—France's gift to back-seat drivers, nervous wrecks, and individuals desirous of ending it all. As the car hurtled round a corner Mrs. Hart, looking over its side, gazed down into the grinning jaws of a mouthful of fanglike rocks some hundred feet below. In spite of her indifference to natural laws, including that of gravity, the good lady shuddered.

"This isn't a road," she gasped. "It's a maze—that's what it is, and it has either driven Mr. Topper mad or he is driving us mad. I don't care which, because it comes to the same thing."

"The only way to travel comfortably on this web," said Marion, "is to get so blind drunk you either can't see it or else you see so crooked you begin to think it's straight."

"In that remark, though involved, there is a world of wisdom," quoth the Colonel. "It's been a hard day and a dry one. In spite of the pressure of the moment, I feel as if all of us would work better with a drink or so inside."

"You'll have to get dressed first," said Mr. Topper.

"We'll have to do more than that," Marion replied. "We'll have to finish up with our bodies. I feel like an unmade bed."

"Well, I can't make a scrap more body than I have already," Mrs. Hart declared, "unless we stop in some quiet spot and I'm allowed to concentrate on my various parts. This drive has shattered my nerves."

"And the Colonel isn't any body at all," observed Marion. "Merely drawers and francs."

"I like him better that way," said Mrs. Hart.

"I worked like the deuce for all this money," replied the Colonel.

"You mean, *we* did, dearie," put in Mrs. Hart.

"We won't begin that discussion now," said Mr. Topper, foreseeing trouble of the worst sort. "I want to be miles away when those francs are divided."

"Suits me," remarked the Colonel laconically.

"But not me," announced Marion. "We'll need an honest referee instead of a quick-change artist like his nibs there."

Marion glanced knowingly at the Colonel, who tried to look terribly hurt.

"How well you know the man," said Mrs. Hart. "But how can we be sure of Topper? Every man has his price, and he looks like a bargain to me."

"Damaged goods," agreed Marion sadly.

"Ruined," went on Mrs. Hart. "The two of them are like this." She held up two fingers. "In cahoots."

"I hate that word," exclaimed Marion. "It would break my heart if Topper were in cahoots. Of all the despicable characters a cahooter is the worst. They're so darned loud mouthed."

"You seem to be under the impression that a cahooter is much like a hog caller," remarked Mr. Topper.

"Not at all," retorted Marion. "He's more like an Alpine horn blower, only worse. If I ever catch you cahooting, may heaven help your soul, because that will be all that's left. Let's get out here."

Topper drove the car off the road near the edge of a pine forest. Its occupants, including Oscar, alighted, and the three most interested parties, bearing their attire, distributed themselves behind trees, there to dress and materialize at leisure. Oscar, like a perfect gentleman, sought the privacy of some bushes. Topper sat down on a matting of pine needles and wondered idly if it would not have been more comfortable had he continued on at home being a banker and chasing trains.

When presently he looked up from his musing, Mr. Topper was panic stricken to discover that there was now not only a fourth, but also a fifth interested party, the two added parties being so exceedingly interested that they were quivering with suppressed excitement. But for the moment, Topper was relieved to discover, they were not so much interested in him as in what was going on in the forest in general, and in particular, what was occurring behind those three pine trees.

Following the direction of the gendarme's absorbed gaze, Mr. Topper saw an assortment of heads, arms, legs and various other anatomical necessities busily popping back and forth from behind the pines. Viewing these unarboraceous actions through the eyes of the gendarmes, Topper realized that to them it must seem all very odd and irregular. Was it that something of a nature the most reprehensible was occurring behind those trees? And in a proximity so close to a public highway? The gendarmes could not conceive of any other explanation. But what daring! What ardor! What lack of restraint! With all the forest before them, why conduct themselves thus so close to the road? No. This must be brought to a finish. The gendarmes could condone much, but not this. It was a reflection on the fair name of France. These naked and impatient miscreants must be haled into the presence of *Monsieur le commissaire* himself.

Fascinated, Mr. Topper watched the two officers of the law concentrate on one of the trees. Stealthily they advanced over the soft pine needles, poised themselves, then sprang round the trunk.

"Whoops!" came the startled voice of Mrs. Hart. "The gendarmes! They are with us."

Promptly she faded out, dragging her clothing with her.

"There is nothing of all that was there," said one of the gendarmes.

"A voice, perhaps?" suggested the other.

"One cannot clip the bracelets on a voice," came the logical reply. "Rush the second tree with speed terrific."

And with speed that they hoped was terrific the gendarmes dashed for the pine behind which the Colonel had established his headquarters.

"Literally caught with my drawers down," that imperturbable gentleman shouted as two wads of francs and a bundle of clothes went leaping through the trees.

"Didn't see a thing," cried Marion as the thwarted gendarmes furiously attacked her tree. "Is my life going to be just one goddam after another? I loathe the very sight of them."

The gendarmes, thrice disappointed, now turned their attention to Topper. He, at least, seemed solid enough to arrest. But why was he, too, not naked? Perhaps he had been. Of a verity. They rushed upon the astounded Topper, and Topper lost his presence of mind. Instead of retreating to the automobile, as he should have, he scaled the side of a tree with an agility made possible only by fear of immediate seizure and long incarceration. Cries of encouragement rang through the woods. Topper had never before realized what a spirited tree climber he was. Neither had the gendarmes, apparently. They regarded his apelike progress with frankly astonished eyes. Perhaps he was not a man after all, but an overdressed monkey. One encountered almost everything along the Riviera.

"Arrest you there!" cried one of them. "Comprehend you, m'sieu? One demands that you descend."

Topper, having exhausted the resources of the tree, had little choice. He was forced to arrest himself. There was no place left to go. Descend, however, he refused to do. He doubted if he could descend even had he so desired. He would probably have to live in that tree all the days of his life. He remembered that Scollops had once got herself into a similar situation, and everyone had had an uncomfortable time of it, but none quite so uncomfortable as Scollops. He could readily understand that. The services of the Fire Company had been required to extricate the cat. Would he, too, be carried down ingloriously on the shoulder of a perfect stranger, some fire-fighting Frenchman, while the inevitable French mob ironically cheered and offered humiliating scraps of advice? How the hell had this all come about, anyway? The Colonel and Marion and Mrs. Hart, they were responsible for this seemingly endless series of contretemps—this uninterrupted rushing about. High aloft in his tree Topper decided that a man could pay too dear a price for the friendship of such persons. He felt more convinced of this than ever when the gendarme next addressed him.

"If you do not descend all at once," called the man, "it is that I will fire."

Even from his great height Topper decided that the revolver in the gendarme's hand looked vulgarly large and ostentatious.

"But, m'sieu, I cannot descend," Mr. Topper replied in a firm but reasonable voice.

The gendarme shrugged his shoulders with magnificent indifference.

"Perhaps, m'sieu, this will be of help," he answered.

A bullet ripped and snorted through the branches of the pine. To Mr. Topper it sounded like the scream of a wild stallion.

"Monsieur le gendarme," he sang out promptly, "I descend with a speed never before attempted."

"Don't you do it," warned a voice in his ear. "Are you ready, ladies? Then pull."

Topper, feeling strangely like a tattered rag doll, was snatched unceremoniously from his insecure perch, whisked through space, and deposited in another tree.

"God, Colonel," he protested, "give me a moment's warning the next time you do that. What do you think I am, a sort of flying squirrel? I feel so damn helpless I could gnash this tree to splinters. This is worse than dashing from pillar to post."

"We're saving your life for future taking," said Marion, invisible on a neighboring limb; then, cupping her lips in her hand, she shouted, "Hey, you little dressed up runt! I'll come down there and tweak your prying nose."

"M'sieu," called the gendarme, and even his distance from the treed Mr. Topper could not blunt the strained incredulity of his voice, "how did you achieve that impossible?"

"None of your business," shouted Marion Kerby. "Your mother was the keeper of a house of ill fame, and that other little pig's was an inmate. Shrug that off, you frog."

Assured that they were not only being mocked by the effeminate voice of the man in the tree, but also grossly insulted, both gendarmes now discharged their revolvers in his direction. Topper was promptly and breathlessly transferred to another tree. Like a huge, overstuffed bat, the man floated helplessly through the forest.

"Listen," gasped Mr. Topper, clinging desperately to a swaying limb, "you all toss me about from tree to tree altogether too carelessly. You seem to forget that I weigh in the neighborhood of one hundred and seventy-five pounds—that is, I did before I climbed up that damned pine. Since I've taken up tree-jumping I've lost considerable weight."

"Nonsense," replied Marion. "It's good for you. Best thing in the world."

"But not for my nerves," retorted Topper. "If you'll only put me down on solid earth I'll take a chance with those two gendarmes."

"Let's all go down and beat them up," suggested Marion. "I'm getting sick of them and their damn guns."

"I'm terribly tired of it all myself," said Topper, with marked sincerity. "I don't like all this monkey business. If anyone had told me this morning that before night I was going to be flying madly from tree to tree, I'd have laughed scoffingly in his face."

The implacable gendarmes had now taken up their stand beneath Topper's third tree.

"M'sieu," began the spokesman, "it is not seemly for a man to conduct himself in public as you are now doing."

"Well, if you'd only go away," called Topper, "I could continue to jump about these trees all by myself. Is there a law against tree-jumping in France?"

The gendarmes discussed this question for several minutes between themselves.

"M'sieu," said one of them at last, "is it that you would be willing to descend and allow us to examine your person?"

"For what?" asked the startled Topper.

"For wings, perhaps," suggested Marion.

"We wish only to observe you, m'sieu," said the second gendarme. "One is of a desire to see how you do it."

"In the customary manner," shouted Marion.

"What do you think?" asked Mr. Topper of his unseen friends. "Should I trust those damn godarmes?"

"We'll take you down," replied the Colonel, "then stand by for trouble."

Accordingly, Mr. Topper was taken down. That is, he was taken part of the way down. About fifteen feet from the ground the others seemed either to lose interest in what they were doing or to forget all about Mr. Topper—whatever it was, the results came to the same thing. Topper felt himself suddenly released. With a wild cry he descended heavily upon the upturned faces of the two gendarmes. When the three of them arose from the pine needles, Mr. Topper's arms were firmly held by each of the officers he had unwittingly assaulted.

"Monsieur," announced one gendarme, "it is that we must escort you to *Monsieur le commissaire.*"

"But no," wheezed the half-stunned Topper. "It is that you will play no such dirty trick on me. The words of your mouth herself were that it was you who would effect the inspection."

"That same thing has been effected," replied the gendarme, "and we believe you to be mad without hope."

"On what do you base such an opinion ridiculous?" asked Topper. "I'm without hope, I admit, but I'm not mad—not yet."

"No man, m'sieu, in his sanity complete would flit from tree to tree only to hurl himself through space regardless of the consequences either to himself or to the gendarmerie of France. M'sieu, if you are not mad, you are possessed of a thousand devils."

As the gendarme delivered himself of this belief the voice of an infuriated dog made itself heard in the forest. Topper took heart.

"Here comes one of those devils now," he said, as the foaming head of Oscar burst through the undergrowth and flung itself into action. Positions were speedily reversed. From the tree Mr. Topper had so recently quitted, the two gendarmes looked down moodily on an animal that could be none other than the most pervertedly conceived of all the demons in hell.

"To the car!" commanded the Colonel in his best parade-ground voice. "Those birds will remember their guns in a moment and start in plugging at Topper."

"Easy on that name, Colonel," cried Topper as he dashed through the woods in the direction of the car.

Bullets followed his retreat, but they had been fired without much hope. The gendarmes were disconcerted because Topper had escaped like an ordinary human being instead of flapping batlike through the trees. The name had been, Toppaire. They would remember.

When the active little party was once more under way Mr. Topper asked a question.

"Are things," he asked, "to be like this forever? What I mean is, are our nights to be devoted to orgies and our days given over to flight?"

"Give me my nightly orgy," said Marion Kerby calmly, "and you can do what you want with your days."

"I'd like to know how you spent your time when you were on a higher plane," remarked Mr. Topper.

"Oh, I just went about trying to drum up sex among a lot of people who didn't even know the meaning of the word," Marion replied.

"Any luck?" asked Mrs. Hart.

"Not a chance," said Marion. "I met one old duck who seemed to have some ideas. 'Sex,' he mused with a puzzled expression when I took up the matter with him. 'Now, I wonder what's familiar about that word.' He paused for a moment, then broke into horrid, derisive laughter. 'Oh, yes,' he chuckled, 'I remember now. Weren't we the silliest things? Tell me, does that puerile practice still maintain?' Well, you know, I felt quite silly myself for a while, then I got peeved. I told him that sex was making rapid progress, that it was even being glorified, and that without it there would be hardly any books and no moving pictures. 'Wouldn't that be nice,' said he quite happily, the old dog. 'Well,' said I, just to show my independence, 'a few chunks of sex round here would wake things up a bit. I'm going back where it comes from.' The old guy was quite disturbed. 'Don't try to go bootlegging any of it on this plane,' he said, 'because you won't find any customers unless you catch them when they first arrive. Don't know how you ever came up in the first place. You're a spiritual moron.' "

"Disgusting old thing," said Clara Hart sympathetically. "In life, I'll bet, he was a nasty man."

"Hell," remarked the Colonel. "Without sex there wouldn't be any planes at all."

"And I would be just as well pleased," commented Topper. "If I'm ever arrested now I'll spend the rest of my life in a dungeon."

"We'll come and visit you," said Marion.

"If you want that drink," he told her, "you'd better pull yourself and your friends together. I'm going to stop at the next place we come to, and I don't care a damn if I am arrested. There won't be any trees in jail."

When Topper drove up before a roadside café his friends, stimulated by the prospect of a drink, had made decided improvements in their appearances. Here, restfully on a broad, pleasant veranda perilously poised above a chasm of rocks against which the waves tore themselves to tatters, they sat and sipped champagne, then settled down to drink in earnest. Gradually the nervous tension slipped from Mr. Topper. He felt at peace with the world. Why not?

He had everything he wanted—Marion, the Mediterranean, lots of champagne, and no Mrs. Topper.

"Drink up," urged the Colonel expansively. "This wine is on me."

"Don't worry," Mrs. Hart tossed in, as women will inevitably at the wrong time. "The wine is on the three of us. Mr. Topper is our guest, of course, but the Colonel, there, he'll take it out of our winnings. He's the original pro-rater—the guy who invented that discouraging custom known as Dutch treating."

Once more the Colonel attempted to look grieved, which was almost impossible for him in the presence of champagne.

"Would you ladies like a salad?" Mr. Topper inquired. "I don't feel quite natural unless I'm paying for a little something."

"I could nibble a bush of romaine," replied Marion.

"Prefer that to endive?" he asked, thoughtfully studying the card.

"Too strong for me," said Mrs. Hart. "I never could bear ducks' eggs."

"Who asked you to bear ducks' eggs?" demanded the Colonel. "Leave that to the ducks. It's their business."

"How did we get on the subject of eggs and ducks?" asked Mr. Topper, a trifle confused. "Why not stick to salad? I wasn't inviting you all to breakfast or dinner, although I'm perfectly willing. I'll invite you to both if you feel like it."

"I merely brought up ducks in connection with romaine salad," Mrs. Hart explained.

"Romaine salad to a duck's egg is like a red flag to a bull," observed the Colonel profoundly.

"Bulls?" asked Mr. Topper. "Now, how on earth did bulls creep in?"

"Bulls don't creep in," said Marion. "Bulls bash in. Didn't you ever hear of the well known bulls of Bashan?"

"I've heard a little about those bulls," replied Mr. Topper, "but not much. Did they happen to like salad? Because if they didn't I see no reason to take them up either."

"Oh, hell," said Mrs. Hart. "Let's order ices. That will solve the whole problem. Things are getting too involved."

"All right," agreed the Colonel affably. "We'll make it champagne."

"Just the same," pursued Topper, "I'd like to know more about those bulls of Bashan. Who did they ever pinch?"

"They didn't," replied Marion. "They just horned in."

"That's different," said Mr. Topper in a pleased voice. "It makes everything even farther from satisfactory."

XVIII

THE DISAPPEARING SUICIDE

When Mr. Topper awoke the next morning he found himself in bed with a headless woman. Feeling already as if death would be a welcome release, the sight of his decapitated companion made him feel even worse. The fact that there was a definite declivity in the center of the neighboring pillow served only to heighten a situation that was already sufficiently unpleasant. Regular breathing and an occasional low moan issuing from the rim of this declivity added mental to the physical anguish the miserable man was already experiencing. Even the bare arms and shoulders so close to him lost something of their fascination as he reached out and roughly shook the unfinished body.

"Marion!" he said. "Wake up! And please do something about your head. Either add it to your body or add your body to it. My stomach is all upset."

"I'll claw your stomach to ribbons if you don't quit that shaking," were Marion's waking words.

"Wish you would," muttered Topper. "I could do without a lot of my stomach this morning. Don't know where we are or how we got here. Last thing I remember was sitting on the veranda of some damn café discussing ducks and bulls."

"You were very dull about those bulls," remarked the pillow. "Guess you don't even know where Bashan is."

"Don't even know where we are, I tell you," said Mr. Topper irritably, "let alone where those bulls came from. Must be some queer place in New York like Goshen."

"Both Bashan and Goshen are in Palestine," Marion told him, "and that's where the bulls came from."

"Which, Bashan or Goshen?" asked Topper.

"Bashan," replied Marion. "The bulls came from Bashan, but it's quite possible that some of them settled in Goshen. They were wild, you know, those bulls that came from Bashan."

"All bulls are wild to me," said Mr. Topper. "Why did they ever come from Bashan in the first place? Didn't they make out well there?"

"No mention is made of cows," observed Marion.

"But where there's a lot of bulls there should be a little cows," concluded Topper.

"Perhaps that's what made 'em wild," observed Marion.

"What?" inquired Topper.

"No cows," replied Marion.

"Then there must have been some cows, or at least a cow, in Goshen if——"

"Will you shut up?" Marion interrupted. "You're as drunk as a lord right now, or else you wouldn't be giving one damn whether there were bulls in Bashan and cows in Goshen or whether the twain shall meet. Let's go back to sleep."

"Will you make a head, then?" asked Topper.

"No, I won't," snapped Marion. "I've got one hell of a headache from all that champagne."

"Is that what you do when you have a hangover?" Topper inquired enviously.

"Yes," answered Marion. "I get rid of my head and that leaves the ache high and dry."

"You mean there's nothing there to ache in?" asked Topper.

"God, how dull you are this morning! If you ask me another question I'll do something desperate."

"It's desperate enough as it is, lying here looking at you," replied Topper moodily.

"I've got everything else but a head," retorted Marion with growing irritation. "Look at some other part."

"That's all right," complained Topper, "but how would you like to have me lying here without any head?"

"I wouldn't mind," she answered. "Do you imagine I'm deriving any pleasure in looking into that besotted face of yours? If your fortune had depended on that mask you'd have been a little match girl years ago."

"So you won't make a head?" persisted Topper.

"No, I won't make a head, you nincompoop."

"Then will you pull the covers up over that pillow, and I'll try to pretend it's there?"

"That settles it!" exclaimed Marion furiously. "I told you to leave me alone. Now you'll wish you had."

Springing from the bed, she materialized her head, and clad as she was in a towering rage, she rushed to a French window through which, to Topper's horror, she hurled herself, loudly shouting his name. Instead of hearing the thud of a falling body the man in bed heard the crash of an overturned chair just outside the window.

"Holy mackerel," came the voice of Marion Kerby. "We're on the ground floor."

"Madam, you're on my chest," a gentleman replied indignantly. "I'm on the ground floor, or, rather, veranda."

"A meticulous devil," Mr. Topper observed to himself, in spite of his consternation.

"Sorry, mister," he heard Marion saying. "Thought I was higher up. Wanted to commit suicide. My mistake."

"Hope you succeed next time," gasped the man.

Topper sneaked to the window and applied one timid eye to a slit in the curtain. What he saw was not reassuring. To all intents and purposes an overlarge, middle-aged gentleman was attacking an underclad, small young lady. It could have been the other way round, but the man in such affairs usually gets the blame. Numerous guests of the hotel were watching developments in an interested semicircle. Hotel factotums and officials were protesting in voluble French. Newcomers were arriving from all directions.

"Leave that brazen creature alone this instant!" cried a stout lady bursting through the crowd. "So this is why you were so anxious to come to France, is it? You'll pay dear for your folly, believe me."

Apparently the unfortunate gentleman did. Untangling himself from his fair obstruction, he left her flat on the veranda and got to his feet.

"My dear," he began in a mollifying voice.

"Don't stand there looking at her," his wife cut in. "Why doesn't someone throw something over the shameless thing?"

This suggestion was reluctantly acted upon. A man stepped leisurely forward and tossed a light overcoat over Marion, who had curled herself up into a small white ball.

"Madame," said the manager of the establishment in perfect English, "will you be so kind as to withdraw now to your own room?"

No answer from the overcoat. The manager cleared his throat.

"Do you wish us to carry you there?" he assayed, at which question the overcoat appeared to shrink a trifle and shake a negative head.

Receiving no answer, the manager signaled to several servants, who stepped forward and laid eager hands on the garment. Their expectations were doomed to disappointment. The overcoat was empty. When they lifted it only the spot where the body had been was revealed. Gasps and ejaculations of amazement from the throng. The manager had turned quite pale. Nevertheless, he retained his presence of mind and command of English.

"Return the overcoat to the considerate gentleman," he said. "This affair demands further investigation. It shall be made."

Topper quietly closed the window and crawled unhappily into bed. Within a very few minutes a firm knock sounded on the door.

"*Entrez!*" called Mr. Topper.

The manager stepped into the room, quietly closing the door behind him.

"Good-morning, m'sieu," said the manager. "Were you, by any

chance, forced to eject a naked woman through that window a few moments ago?"

"Certainly not," replied Mr. Topper indignantly. "I wouldn't throw a naked woman out of my window. Waste not, want not, say I."

The manager coughed delicately behind his hand.

"I can understand that," he agreed, Mr. Topper thought a shade too readily. "Nevertheless, an unclad woman emerged but a moment ago with great speed through that window."

The manager with a nod indicated the window through which Marion had hoped to commit suicide.

"For all I know, Earl Carroll's Vanities could have been bounding in and out of that window all morning," Mr. Topper calmly assured the manager. "I've been sleeping. You're the first person I've seen today, and I'm not particularly glad to see you. Go away."

"Yes," came a woman's quiet voice. "Why don't you get the deuce out of here and give my husband a chance to get some sleep?"

Marion Kerby, in the stunning costume she had worn at the races, appeared gloriously in the bathroom door and stood looking coldly upon the manager.

"Madame," he replied apologetically, admiration sharpening his eyes, "I ask a thousand pardons——"

"Well, I don't hand you one," she cut in curtly. "What's all this about windows and naked women?"

"One of them went through that window, madame," the manager explained.

"Do you want a naked woman?" Marion demanded.

"But no, madame. That was not my intention," protested the man.

"Then why do you come barging in here, putting ideas in my husband's mind? You could have seen at a glance it isn't any too strong. Anyway, you shouldn't be looking for naked women at this time of day."

"A mere matter of routine," declared the manager. "You were not perhaps that woman, madame?"

"Do I look as if I'd just been thrown through a window?" Marion asked haughtily.

"On the contrary, madame," the manager answered gallantly. "I only asked because she had such a glorious figure."

Marion was looking seriously at Topper.

"Do you think we could have got ourselves into a bad house by mistake?" she asked him. "The things this man says."

"I assure you, madame, this is a most respectable hotel."

"And yet you make a practice of asking your guests for naked women—practically begging them for naked women. Call that respectable? Aren't you able to get your own naked women? Must my husband turn procurer for your sake, may I ask? If there is going to be a naked woman in this room I'll be that woman. Understand? And if I catch any of yours in here I'll chuck them through that window, all right, but they'll go out in pieces. Get me?"

Marion had backed the manager against the door, which he was vainly trying to open. At that moment a door opening into an adjoining room flew back and nobody stood on its threshold. A voice husky with wine and sleep was the very utmost the Colonel could achieve for the present.

"Ask him where we are and the name of his hotel," said the Colonel. "Also what day it is and the time of day if any."

It was then that the manager began to have grave doubts of his own sanity. Had constant association with so many tourists affected his mind? Several of his colleagues had gone that way. Was it now his turn? It seemed so. Had he not already seen this morning a naked woman who disappeared? And was he not now hearing voices?

"M'sieu," he got out falteringly, "where is the one who speaks? I hear but I do not see him."

Topper laughed falsely from his bed.

"That's my friend," he replied. "His voice has the most remarkable carrying quality. He should be a radio announcer. He's in the next room, but one would swear he was right here, wouldn't one?"

Swearing that one would, the manager, not forgetting to bow to Marion, hastily withdrew. Topper seized the telephone as soon as the man was gone.

"I want two pitchers full of whisky sours," he told the bored clerk, "and a waiter who knows not only what place this is, but also the name of the hotel, the day and the time of day. All those things. Yes. And——"

Marion snatched the telephone from his hand.

"And ask *Monsieur le propriétaire*, when you see him," she said, "if he has found himself a naked woman yet. You understand? You would."

She set the instrument down, then turned and considered Topper.

"My aged and fat," she breathed. "I almost killed myself for you."

"It very much looks," replied Topper hopelessly, "as if one of those days have started again."

"Isn't it just too glorious!" said Marion. "And tonight the orgy, as usual."

"Yes," agreed Topper. "It's just too damn rotten glorious for words. Can't we do something about it? I yearn for a nice dull normal day. Why not go to the Muséum d'Océanographie and take a look at some fish for a change—that is, if we really are at Monaco?"

"Good idea, Topper," the Colonel invisibly joined in. "Nothing like looking at fish to get one back to normal. They're so indefatigably prolific. Think I'll go now and do myself into a man."

"And while you're doing it," suggested Topper, "I wish you'd do yourself into a less active man for a change. Can't you make yourself into a little man, Colonel—a little old tired man with a tremendous respect for the law?"

"My self-esteem would not permit me," said the Colonel.

"What's Clara doing?" asked Marion.

"Last time I saw her," replied the Colonel, "the lady was endeavoring to materialize from both ends at once. A quaint fancy. In one direction she had advanced as far as her knees, and in the other she had covered some pretty delicate territory."

"Hope she makes an accurate joining," observed Marion.

"That is most devoutly to be desired," agreed the Colonel. "I shall hasten to apprise her of the unfortunate consequences resulting from any careless craftsmanship. We will join you upon the arrival of those pitchers of—er—sours."

"You didn't have to shout out my name when you flung yourself

through that window," said Mr. Topper to Marion as she lit a ciga-
rette and curled herself up beside him on the bed.

"I know," she answered, "but you see, I was not myself at the moment."

"Then why make me myself?" asked Topper.

"That was the point of the whole suicide. I wanted everyone to
know I had died because of you. Then you'd have been a marked
man along the Riviera. Wherever you went people would have said,
'Why women kill themselves over that American pig I can't understand.'"

Topper winced.

"I'm a marked man already," he replied. "In fact, I'm damn well
striped. Don't you think you all are behaving just a little bit like the
Rollo Boys gone bad? This constant rollicking about is a trifle too
varsity for me. If we must be depraved, why can't we be so like sophisticated adults?"

"There's too much sophistication in the world already," Marion
said quite seriously. "Too much cheap sophistication. It burns me up.
Every damn thing is sophisticated and patronizing. Even the shop
windows are arrogantly sophisticated—magazines, books, plays,
conversation, and even bathrooms, all trying to be sophisticated and
falling short of the mark. First thing you know girl babies will be
born pregnant and the males will be carrying lilies in their hands."

"You're quite convincing," admitted Topper, "but don't you
think your prejudices occasionally carry you a little too far in the
opposite direction? For example, bouncing my hat up and down on
my head, then bouncing me up and down on a chair, dragging me
up to a bar, and whisking me from one tree to another—doesn't it
ever occur to you that such conduct is a trifle childish?"

"We do what amuses us at the moment," replied Marion, "and
not what we think may amuse others."

"Especially me," said Topper.

"Don't pretend," she told him, piling herself on his chest. "Secretly you're amused all the time."

"I'm not now," he answered as a waiter knocked and entered with
the tray and information.

"But the waiter is," said Marion. "Those sours look swell."

Promptly the Colonel appeared with Oscar, Mrs. Hart, and a French newspaper which he had ordered from the desk.

"Oscar," he announced, "has already breakfasted from the trays of others momentarily and most carelessly left unguarded along the hall. He seems to have done quite nicely for himself." Selecting a drink, the Colonel tossed it off with military precision. "I have been spelling out this French paper," he resumed, "and as far as I can discover, everything seems to have been wrong with those races yesterday except the track itself. We could have torn up that, had we thought of it. Unfortunately, the paper gives quite an accurate description of your humble servant. 'A man very distinguished and agreeable,' it says, or words to that effect. It seems that I am wanted."

"Is there a price on your head?" asked Marion eagerly.

"Not yet," replied the Colonel, "but if there were I would not take either of you ladies into my confidence. The point is, it will now be necessary for me to assume a disguise whenever I appear in public. I have always wondered how I would go in a beard."

"I hope you'd go away," said Mrs. Hart. "That dust mop on your lip is bad enough to have swishing about the house."

The Colonel chose to disregard this remark as being unworthy of notice.

He put down the glass, reached for the telephone, and summoned the head barber to his presence. Presently this one fragrantly arrived.

"I wish to be arranged becomingly in a beard," the Colonel stated.

"Arranged?" repeated the barber, momentarily puzzled by the word, then his face cleared. "Do you mean, m'sieu, as if in death?"

"God, no, my man!" exploded the Colonel. "As if in life. Gallantly arranged like an officer and a gentleman."

"You're not looking for a disguise, Colonel," observed Marion. "What you need is a reincarnation—an entirely new layout. That man's merely a barber and not a magician."

"Please be quiet," said the Colonel.

After thoughtfully studying the Colonel's face from all sides, the barber nodded several times to some secret reflection of his own.

"It doesn't matter from what direction you look at it," put in Mrs. Hart, "that face remains just as bad."

"Clara, do be still," protested the Colonel. "You'll discourage the man."

"He's more than that already," replied Clara. "That face has actually frightened him."

Assuring the Colonel of the speedy fulfillment of his wishes, the barber hurried away and returned almost immediately.

"Didn't take him long to grow it," remarked Marion.

"M'sieu," cried the barber, extracting a blue-black object from somewhere beneath his white apron, "it is here!"

"An odd place to wear it," was Mrs. Hart's comment.

"Ladies!" objected the Colonel. "Must you?"

"Most emphatically yes," said Mrs. Hart. "If you appear in public with that thing on the end of your face, I'm going to blacken mine and wear a curtain ring on the tip of my nose."

When finally the Colonel was arranged in the beard it looked neither gallant nor becoming on him. However, it did make him look different.

"Well, I must say," pronounced Mrs. Hart, hastily reaching for another drink, "you're an extraordinary-looking officer and a weird-looking gentleman. Why, you're not even human!"

"Look at Oscar," put in Marion.

Topper had thought he had seen the dog at his maddest, but never had he seen him wear such a completely gone expression as the one now torturing his face. As accustomed as he had become to the Colonel's vagaries, Oscar was not prepared to meet his master's eyes peering questioningly at him over the rim of that blue-black beard. With a low gurgle intended to convey profound mental agitation, the dog faded from view, for which he was roundly cursed by the incensed Colonel. The barber had long since departed. One look at the dog had been quite enough to speed him on his way. Like Oscar and the manager of the hotel, he, too, was prey to the gravest suspicions concerning his own mental stability.

When it came to a division of the previous day's spoils, the Colonel insisted on wearing his newly acquired facial decoration, while both of the ladies, with equal vigor and many more words, insisted on the removal of this disconcerting object, Marion Kerby pointing out quite properly that the Colonel would be able to tuck God only knew how many francs behind such a bush. Pretending to be revolted by such a reflection not only on his integrity but also on his good taste, the Colonel was finally prevailed upon to permit Topper to distribute the money. When this had been done amid a breathless hush and in the presence of three pairs of burning eyes, Marion Kerby handed Topper her roll of bills.

"Keep 'em for me," she said. "I don't want any more bulges about my body than nature has already provided."

"And you, my dear?" the Colonel inquired politely of Mrs. Hart.

"I'll pad my legs twice their size," she replied, "before I let you get your hands on these francs."

"That would hardly be the way to go about it," said the Colonel as he watched with peculiar intentness Mr. Topper's hand slipping Marion's share of francs into his right side trouser pocket.

Had Topper been able to intercept this glittering scrutiny of the Colonel's he would have been able to spare himself and another gentleman several moments of acute embarrassment.

The unpleasant affair arose over a misunderstanding which was intensified by the unladylike conduct of Marion Kerby. It happened after luncheon. Topper and Marion were seated comfortably on the veranda when the latter's after-eating placidity was disturbed by a slight twitching of his right side trouser pocket. In spite of the lulling influence of food and wine, Topper's faculties were still sufficiently acute to reason out that under normal conditions his pockets did not twitch for the mere pleasure of twitching. No. His pocket was being twitched by some outside influence. He turned quickly and regarded his neighbor on the right, then turned away. He hated to believe the truth. Such a nice old gentleman with such an honest face. And to think that this old gentleman was no better than a thief. In fact, he was a thief, or would be soon if he had his way about it. Had Topper not seen a furtive movement of the old man's clawlike left hand? Topper had, but what Topper did not know was that the old gentleman, in spite of the privileges accorded to age, still preferred to scratch himself as privately as conditions permitted. Had Topper known this, being a little precious about such things himself, his opinion of the old gentleman would have undergone a favorable change. No man who preferred to scratch himself in private would deliberately pick a pocket in public. As it was Mr. Topper took no definite action until several repetitions of the twitching warned him that Marion Kerby's money was actually in peril. He then reached out and snatched at the old gentleman's frantically moving hand.

"Why did you want to do that?" Topper demanded reproachfully, in a low voice.

"I couldn't help it," replied the old gentleman. "Stood it as long as I could."

"You mean you're a kleptomaniac?" asked Mr. Topper.

"I had to scratch," whispered the other.

"You had to scratch my pocket?" inquired Topper, pointing to the money that was nearly falling out.

"Sir!" cried the old gentleman. "Are you trying to accuse me of stealing your money?"

"What!" shouted Marion. "My money?"

Then she hurled herself into action. With hands no less frantic than those of the old gentleman, she now proceeded to scratch him far more thoroughly than he had been able to scratch himself.

"Give me my money," she kept repeating, "or I'll claw the gold from your teeth."

"Your money is safe," Topper tried to assure her. "You'll kill the old fellow."

"Of course I'll kill the old fellow," replied Marion. "I'd kill a thousand old fellows and half that amount of young ones for the sake of those francs."

At this moment the francs, slipping from Mr. Topper's pocket, caused him to look down; then everything became clear. About three inches from the floor of the veranda dangled a blue-black beard. So absorbed had the Colonel become in his nefarious operations that he had forgotten the fact that he could not dematerialize his disguise. He must have been lying flat on his nebulous stomach endeavoring with all the craft and patience of his perverse nature to tease with the end of a knitting needle Marion's francs from Topper's pocket. Even as Topper looked, the end of this needle was coaxing the roll of money closer and closer to the sinister black beard.

Marion, releasing her hold on the old gentleman, followed the direction of Mr. Topper's gaze. Then with a wild cry she dived head foremost over the body of her late victim and landed on the veranda with the beard clutched firmly in her hand.

A gasp of dismay fell from the Colonel's unseen lips, after which the air became so shot with oaths, imprecations, and obscenities, it was impossible to decide whether Marion or the Colonel held the advantage. Fortunately Marion decided, but solely for tactical reasons, to dematerialize. Where a woman had once been, the numerous spectators now saw merely a beard and a heap of clothes busily engaged in calling each other the vilest of names. Presently the clothes arose, clutching a roll of francs, and followed the beard down the veranda.

"Get along there," the clothes were heard to remark to the apparently cowed beard. "I'll tell Clara Hart exactly what you tried to do, and if she lets you into her bed again I'll never speak another word to her."

It was difficult for the spectators to conceive of anybody letting that beard into bed even once, let alone again.

"But, Marion," they heard the beard protesting, "hang it all, I was merely having a bit of a joke with Topper."

"Ha! Ha!" laughed the clothes, so viciously that several persons present turned quite faint, especially when they saw the roll of francs being shaken in the air. "You'll know better next time than to play jokes with my money and my man."

Her man turned, and after mumbling an apology to the old gentleman, hurried away. The old gentleman followed his example, vowing to himself that in future, if he ever needed to scratch, he would make no effort to conceal his intentions. He would go even further than that. He would publicly announce them, so that there would be no possibility of mistake.

When Mr. Topper entered his room a few minutes later he was surprised and not especially delighted to be greeted by a burst of laughter. Marion, Mrs. Hart, and the Colonel, in the best of spirits, were seated round a bucket from which protruded the neck of a huge bottle. No longer content with quarts, they were now ordering magnums.

"What the hell," began Topper, "was the meaning of that shameful brawl? Haven't you any better sense——"

But Topper never finished his sentence. Guiltily his three friends faded out. Only the occasional movement of a glass gave witness to the fact that they were there at all.

"Oh, all right," he declared at last, getting no kick from scolding at space. "We'll say no more about it. If you all are so downright low that you can forgive and condone deliberate theft and double-crossing, I see no reason why I should complain. It would be useless."

Topper had spoken the truth. Marion Kerby's anger against the enterprising Colonel had quickly evaporated. He had offered her a bottle of wine, and when Mrs. Hart's back was turned, slipped her a thousand francs. As the wine was charged to Topper and the francs had been detached in the scuffle from Marion's own roll the Colonel felt he could well afford this amicable gesture. Furthermore, Marion was so lost to honesty herself that she appreciated rather than deplored the Colonel's efforts to provide as handsomely for himself as possible. That he had failed so lamentably only added piquancy to the situation.

At Topper's hopeless words the three of them agreeably appeared once more, the Colonel, with his unfailing courtesy, providing Mr. Topper with a glass of wine. Topper polished it off with an absent-minded flip, then sank wearily to the side of the bed.

"I feel as if I'd lived all of my life in Monaco," he remarked, "so many things have happened."

"Well, nothing more is going to happen now," Marion Kerby assured him comfortingly. "We're going to have a nice normal time.

First you're going to buy us a bottle of wine, and then we're all going out and peer at a lot of silly-looking fish."

"Can't I go alone?" asked Topper wistfully. "I really would like to get a good look at all those fish and things."

Cries of horror and incredulity escaped the lips of his companions.

"What!" exclaimed Marion. "We could never hear of such a thing. Who can tell what terrible things might happen to you alone?"

"I'd like to know what hasn't happened to me already?" asked Mr. Topper hopelessly.

"There's lots left unhappened," was Marion Kerby's reply.

XIX

Looking at a Lot of Fish

Mr. Topper never did get a good look at all those fish and things. However, he did manage to look at some fish, and that was more than enough.

On the way to look at these fish, the Colonel insisted on a momentary interlude at a pleasantly situated sidewalk café overlooking the harbor of Monaco. It was a stage setting valued at many millions of dollars, represented chiefly by yachts and the money expended on their upkeep. It was a heady sort of paradise in which the most expensive things seemed attainable in the smiling presence of the Goddess of Chance. Mr. Topper had a feeling that beneath it all something was being held in check—concealed from the eyes of the spectators. At first he had suspected something straining, desperate, and tragic, but as he sat there and looked about him he decided that the principal quality lying beneath the surface gaiety of Monaco was one of utter and abject boredom. He even went so far as to attribute the many suicides induced by the place simply and solely to that—insufferable ennui. People did not kill themselves because they had lost all their money, but merely because they were so tired of Monaco they did not have the strength to leave it any other way.

"I don't know why I ever yielded to your entreaties," declared Marion, squinting thoughtfully at him through the ice in her glass. "You're such an old frump, Aunt Cosmo. And I don't know why we ever came to this dump, either. If you took away those lovely mountains behind us and sank all those yachts out there, this town would be just a glorified Atlantic City, and the dear God knows, nothing could be worse than that."

"Merely the difference between an old hooker in cotton tights and one in silk," replied Mr. Topper. "And please, Marion, don't do those things to your face. The passers-by will think you're a half-wit or something. Furthermore, the only entreating I did was to entreat you to get out of my bed."

"I must have missed my direction," was Marion's calm retort, "or got the signals mixed. It doesn't matter one way or the other. Here we are."

"And Monaco always gives me a feeling of unrest," said Colonel Scott. "I was trying to explain it to Mrs. Hart, but the poor thing can't understand. She likes it here because there are so many things to buy—so many useless, expensive things. As for myself, I'd feel more at home either in an old-time brothel or the cloister of a monastery, if you can get what I'm driving at."

"I'm sure, Colonel, you'd do equally well in either setting," Mr. Topper replied politely.

"He'd be more at home not in the cloister," Mrs. Hart contributed in a bored voice.

"Monaco's glamour fails to glam," continued Marion. "It's like a reformed prostitute looking at a peepshow through smoked glasses. When the exploitation of vice becomes perfected—all smooth and polished and refined—I begin to lose interest in vice itself. Of course, that doesn't go where you are concerned, Topper, my stout fellow."

"Well, you might as well lose interest in that, too," said Mr. Topper. "I'm going to look at a lot of fish."

More drinks followed, and more time was wasted, if such a thing is possible as wasting time at a sidewalk café. One by one Mr. Topper's companions drifted away from the table. After that he either forgot all about them or they forgot all about him. It came to the same thing. Topper found himself alone. It was the psychological moment to look at a lot of fish. He did not give one snap of his fingers for his friends. To prove this he tried to snap his fingers. No sound came. That did not matter either. Probably very important persons were unable to snap their fingers. He called the waiter and endeavored to show him how he, Topper, could not snap his fingers. As luck would have it, this time they snapped smartly. Nodding his head moodily, he left the place and hailed a cruising Victoria.

"Fish," he muttered tersely but inclusively to the driver. *"Chez poisson."*

"M'sieu," inquired the driver, "is it that you would buy of fish, or do you refer to some particular fish, perhaps?"

Mr. Topper thought this over.

"I do not know any particular fish," he replied, somewhat sadly, "nor do I want to buy any fish. Just fish is all I ask. Let me see some of them."

The driver shrugged, as French drivers will. He gazed patiently over the harbor, and prepared himself to wait until this inebriated American had settled in his own mind just what he wanted to do about fish. Mr. Topper was seized with the fear that between them he and the driver might make a mess of this business and that in the end he would see no fish at all. In spite of his mental agitation all he could say when he stepped into the Victoria and next addressed the driver was merely, "Fish."

The driver shrugged again and drove Mr. Topper off to the fish market. Here he turned in his seat and looked inquiringly at Topper's face to see his reactions to these fish. Utter hopelessness was registered on Mr. Topper's face. He shook his head and wiggled his hands in a fashion which to him was eloquently fishlike.

"Not dead fish," he told the driver reproachfully. "I do not desire to look upon the remains of a lot of dead fish. Behold, man, I want fish that go *vite.*"

Mr. Topper's hands darted out at the driver, who ducked just in time. It looked very much as if the man in the Victoria were attempting to hypnotize the man on the box. The driver alighted and held an animated conversation with a group of prospective fish eaters. Much argument and even more scrutinizing. Tolerantly amused glances were directed at Mr. Topper. He hated all this exceedingly. Presently a gendarme approached and looked inside Topper's passport as if hoping to find some fish concealed between its pages. Then, after a few hurried words to the driver, he strolled away, leaving Topper wistfully gazing after him. Thereupon the driver returned to his place of duty and smiled reassuringly at Mr. Topper.

"M'sieu," he cried, "we march! It is that I know now. You want to see some fish. We go."

Topper smiled back feebly.

"I don't know whether I do or not," he replied. "I grow more than a little fatigued with fish."

He sighed and leaned back in the carriage. This was like everything else in a foreign land. One had to work so hard to get any place that one was too tired and upset to enjoy it when one got there. Sightseeing was a demeaning occupation. He would abandon fish.

On his way back to the hotel he stopped at a sidewalk café to refresh himself and brace his nerves. Here he sat looking at the harbor and wondering what all those tourists debarking from an ocean liner were going to do with their time, money, and expectations. He hoped they would never see a fish wearing a blue-black beard. For a while they were going to have a pretty confused and anxious time of it, he decided. Preoccupations with details would make them forget they were in Europe at all. Luggage would vanish, husbands get drunk, children lost, hotels be misunderstood, food suspected, and the customs of the country severely criticized, before they would settle down to the fact that they were not having a particularly good time, but that, after all, they really were abroad, which was more than their neighbors at home could say. There was a kick in that, at any rate. Then there would always be the solace of picture postcards. Nothing like those things to get one back to good solid ground. After one had sent a flock of these garish missives home one felt as if one were really beginning to get to know the country a bit. They were the lowest common denominator of foreign travel. So thought Mr. Topper over his several drinks. He began to feel sorry for fish and tourists alike. His sympathy even embraced his missing companions, including the rump of Oscar, or his head. They were so bad, the lot of them—such terrible companions. Marion probably needed a dress. He himself needed evening clothes. He would arise now and purchase things with a large hand. If he bought enough garments, some of them might fit somebody.

When Topper eventually returned to his hotel, several attendants followed his progress bearing packages in their arms. He had bought enough clothing to costume a small musical comedy. He bathed, shaved, drank a bottle of cool wine, then sent for a valet. When the man arrived Topper considered him in silence.

"Do you speak English?" he asked at last.

"But, yes, m'sieu," answered the man. "Of a perfection."

"That would be too good for me," replied Topper. "I wouldn't understand you. Just get some of these clothes on my body, and we'll call it square. Hand me that glass first. I'm mentally and physically exhausted. Are you ever that way?"

"After arranging some of my gentlemen for their evenings," replied the valet, "I am frequently unable to enjoy those of my own."

"I can well understand that," said Mr. Topper, "after looking at some of the nervous wrecks littering up this coastline."

"I do not understand why they come here," went on the valet, deftly flicking Topper's legs into a pair of trousers. "Each year I see them older and wearier and their women younger and fresher. Money can make much of life, m'sieu, but there comes a time when even the youngest of mistresses cannot renew youth itself."

"I dare say you're right," said Topper somewhat sadly, catching sight of his own face in the mirror. "There comes a time, doesn't there, my friend?"

"Like a thief in the night," replied the valet.

"Well, thank God, we have a few more nights left," was Mr. Topper's answer to this.

In a none too festive frame of mind, Mr. Topper dined alone that night. In spite of the simple dignity of the meal he had to confess he missed his friends. In their rooms were the various presents he had bought them. He wished they had been there to receive them. It would have been nice to see them open the packages. Topper's mind was essentially simple. Unexpectedly his thoughts were interrupted.

"Listen to me, you," came a voice, pitched in a low, furious key. "I'm not dining with you tonight. I doubt if I'll ever eat again. You've actually sickened me, you have. How much money did you spend for all those things upstairs? Don't lie, mind."

"Not much, Marion. Only several thousand francs. Why?"

"Not much," gasped the voice. "Several thousand francs. Oh, God, do You hear this man? All of that money wasted when we could have stolen these things without the loss of a franc. It's a crime before Heaven."

"But, my dear," protested Topper, "would not that have been stealing and isn't stealing a crime?"

"No, you ninny, that would not have been stealing and stealing isn't a crime when you steal from thieves."

"There's something in that," propitiated Topper.

"Bet your boots there is," said Marion. "And even if there wasn't, do you want to know what we're going to do?"

"I'd rather not," replied Mr. Topper. "Your voice doesn't sound any too agreeable."

"I've made a list of all those shops that robbed you," Marion went on. "The three of us are going right back and get ours, good and plenty."

"Don't do that," protested Topper. "I don't want the money."

"Then we'll keep it ourselves just as we had intended to do all the time."

"I thought you might like the things," he mumbled. "Some of them, at any rate. Aren't any of them any good?"

Suddenly he felt two lips brush lightly across his wrist. Topper was so startled, his fork clattered against his plate.

"Thanks for that flame-colored gown," a voice murmured in his

ear. "I'll try to pour myself into it, but with you around I can't tell
from one minute to the next how long I'll stay poured. See you
later."

Much to Mr. Topper's embarrassment, his head was jerked back
at an awkward angle and his mouth was resoundingly kissed.

"Oh! I could tear you to pieces," a woman's voice exclaimed.

"You almost have," he muttered.

When Marion had left, the man she could have torn to pieces
kept his eyes fixed on his plate. He strongly suspected that the
waiter, who was, in truth, looking at him with a puzzled expression,
was thinking him slightly daft. Topper wondered how he could explain to the man in French that occasionally he talked to himself in
English just to keep from forgetting his native tongue. Topper abandoned the idea. It was altogether too involved. As he made his way
through his solitary repast he thought about Marion Kerby. He
might just as well be married to her the way she went on about
things. And he was seldom comfortable with her, yet never quite
himself without her. Both ways, she was a lot of trouble. Affection
was the thief of freedom. Love lowered a man's morale.

His dinner finished, Topper took a cab to the Casino, where he
strolled from room to room, wondering how so many people could
lose so much money and still retain their reason. Perhaps they were
mad already. That was why they were there.

Finding a vacant place at a table, he sat down. For the next fifteen
minutes he made mildly inquiring bets, until his modest stack of
chips had been unemotionally collected by an apparently self-
refrigerating croupier.

It was at this moment that Mr. Topper noticed for the first time
that a gentleman on his right seemed to be consumed with a timid
desire to make him a little present. A stack of chips from the man's
pile was unobtrusively edging its way along the table. With increasing annoyance Mr. Topper watched the chips furtively slide in his
direction and take up a position in front of him.

"Thank you," said Mr. Topper, a trifle haughtily, "but I'm not as
desperate as you seem to imagine. I can still afford to pay for my
own chips."

With this he returned the chips to the gentleman and bought a new stack for himself. The gentleman considered the returned chips, a puzzled expression on his face, then looked long at Mr. Topper.

"My dear sir," he began, "ill-fortune must have addled your brain. I have not attempted to give you any of my chips. Furthermore, I have no intention of giving you any of my chips."

"Then why did you push them at me?" asked Mr. Topper.

"Me push my chips at you?" laughed the gentleman unpleasantly. "What sort of man do you think I am?"

"One moment," replied Mr. Topper.

He was too busy to continue the conversation, all his efforts being directed toward fighting off the chips of the lady at his left. Her whole pile was moving with determination in his direction. Extending his left hand, he tried to push the chips back. For this his hand was sharply rapped by the lady.

"Madame," he muttered, "don't do that. Your chips—do something about them."

"No fear," replied the woman. "I've sat by your kind before."

Between the hostile eyes of his two neighbors Mr. Topper sat uncomfortably and blindly resumed his betting. A few minutes later a man's hand came within the vision of his eye. It seemed to be struggling with a stack of chips.

"I warn you," came the gentleman's voice. "Stop trying to sneak my chips. You should be ashamed of yourself."

"Me sneak your chips?" gasped Topper, giving the man's chips a violent shove. "Don't be ridiculous. I——"

A flank attack from the chips on his left forced him to turn sharply. The lady's chips were once more on the march. Topper gave them an impatient shove, but the chips stubbornly resisted his efforts.

"What's this?" demanded the woman in a tired, metallic voice. "After my chips again. Is this some new racket? Trying to grab my chips, then pretending I gave them to you?"

Topper could not reply. A scraping of chips from the right attracted his attention. Both of his hands were now occupied in resisting the generous impulses of his neighbors. The onlookers gained the impression that Mr. Topper was endeavoring violently to extract chips from two players at once.

"This is most embarrassing," he managed to get out. "Are you both deliberately trying to frame me? Please keep your chips to yourselves."

"I don't know how you are doing this thing," gritted the man, "but doing it you are. Take your hand off my chips."

"I'm afraid to," replied Topper, breaking out in a gentle sweat. "Suppose you hold onto them for a change."

At this moment a stack of chips came swooping gracefully across the table from a sallow-faced individual seated directly opposite Topper. It looked as if the man had either lost all patience or else was endeavoring to outdo the others in generosity. Topper, releasing his hold on the stacks of chips to the left and right of him, endeavored to repel this frontal attack. Too late. The three piles of chips ducked under his guard and clashed noisily together in front of the mortified man.

"I'm sure I thank you all," began Mr. Topper with a sick smile.

"How did you do that?" interrupted the individual from across the table. "I'll give you those chips if you tell me how."

"I didn't," cried Mr. Topper. "You must have hurled them at me."

"If he can gather money as easily as all that," observed a gentleman sitting next to Sallow Face, "why does he trouble to come here?"

"He should be picked up," said a woman maliciously.

"And chucked in," added a man.

"I assure you," began Mr. Topper, then his voice trailed away.

Piles of chips were now advancing upon him from several different directions. Topper felt not unlike Alice being attacked by the pack of cards. He was afraid that at any moment the chips would begin to fight their way into his pockets. With cool, penetrating eyes the croupier sat and regarded the scene. He earnestly desired to discover how all this was being done. Around the table various players were struggling with their chips, which were leaping at Mr. Topper like frantic fish.

"For God's sake, cut it out," muttered Topper passionately to the air about him. "Don't you realize they'll pull me in?"

He rose from the table and looked about him at the bewildered faces of the players.

"Sorry," he said in a strained voice. "If you insist on giving your chips away, you'll have to give them to someone else."

As if in answer to this, the wheel suddenly started in to spin rapidly of its own accord. And with this the frigidity of the croupier melted as if seared by the flames of hell.

"Mille tonnerre!" the man exclaimed, striving to restrain his eyes. "The play is at an end."

He endeavored to arrest the speeding wheel. It hesitated momentarily, then hurried with renewed vigor on its way.

Topper turned from the table, leaving the chips of the players as well as their nerves in a sadly confused condition. The croupier removed his fascinated eyes from the wheel long enough to signal to an attendant. From that time on Mr. Topper's movements were followed by the unobtrusive eyes of several professional observers. Fearing the chips might begin to follow him about the place, Topper collected his hat and stick and left the Casino. On the steps there was a brief and intense struggle. Unseen hands were trying to hold him back. Topper resisted furiously. Witnesses of the scene were both amused and alarmed to see a middle-aged gentleman, faultlessly dressed, dodging this way and that, as if endeavoring to elude his own shadow.

"I won't go back!" they heard him mutter. "Damned if I will. You'll have to carry me in. I'll lie down right here in the street."

But what surprised the witnesses even more than this seemingly fruitless quarrel with himself was the inexplicable presence of a beard—just that, a beard, an agitated blue-black beard that looked for all the world as if it were trying to whisper in the ear of the gentleman in evening clothes. With frantic hands Topper kept trying to push the beard away.

"Don't!" they heard him mutter several times. "I can't stand that beard. If you've anything to say, speak out."

"All right," came the Colonel's voice from space. "If he won't go back he won't go back. That's all there is to it. We can't carry him in and dump him on one of the tables."

"Then drag him along," said a woman's voice.

The witnesses then saw the middle-aged gentleman depart through the night in a peculiar slanting fashion. His feet were swinging behind him and were barely touching the ground.

"Mad as a hatter," remarked a man to his momentary mistress. "No doubt his losses have unhinged his reason."

"Well, that's no reason why he should try to unhinge mine," the woman complained fretfully as momentary or age-old mistresses will. "Let's give this place a miss and confine ourselves to drinking. My feet hurt."

"Put me down," Mr. Topper was crying aloud to darkness. "Let me walk. It's these exasperating little things that get the best of me."

He was allowed to walk back to his hotel, from which the manager for various reasons too painful to mention asked him to remove his party in the morning.

"We'll wreck the damn place before then," a woman's voice was heard to remark as the manager turned away.

However, this never occurred. Half an hour later four beautifully uniformed gendarmes escorted Topper and his jeering companions over the border into France.

XX

SANCTUARY

"As for me," weightily pronounced Monsieur Dalmas, the small French *avocat* as he daintily replaced his empty glass among the domesticated flies on the evil-looking table top, "as for me, Monsieur Toppaire, I admire America greatly. In fact, I might even say that I am my country's most passionate friend of your country."

"M'sieu," replied Mr. Topper, regarding the little man with mild alarm, "I did not know matters had gone as far as that."

"They have," said Monsieur Dalmas moodily. "Matters have advanced to that stage—even beyond."

"You are amiable, m'sieu," Mr. Topper assured him. "Also your heart is huge. As for me, I am no less inarticulately enamored of your fair country."

The two gracious gentlemen were seated in a little combination café and *épicerie* situated on the fringe of a pine forest which overhung the sea. Here in this quiet country settlement Topper had at last found sanctuary. Already the owner of the grocery-store-café loved him well. Likewise did the owner's wife, her two sons, her one daughter, and their tiny but voluble grandmother. It was Sunday—a day reverenced by the French because enjoyed with a light heart—and the bare, unpicturesque room of the café contained a small cross section of France. There were country folk gathered from the neighboring farms and vineyards, fishermen and fishermen's wives absent a moment from their nets, friends and relations drawn from the resort towns along the coast to visit for the day. And there was a sprinkling of soldiers and sailors, in constant demand by the French maidens, who danced, drank, laughed, and sweated, fought and made love, with impartial enthusiasm. There were children and dogs and a number of incredibly aged yet animated men and women. Some sinister-looking characters were present, many attractive ones, and an equal number of dull ones. Much excitement but little actual inebriety. There was too much concentrated thrift as well as poverty present in the room to permit of that indulgence.

Marion Kerby was dancing meaningless twirls with a confusingly nimble sailor. Her expression was surprised, amused, and a trifle strained. Mr. Topper preferred not to look at them. He preferred, rather, to drink with *Monsieur l'avocat*, a delightful little gentleman who spent most of his sober hours in knitting intricate little nets for the retention of even littler fishes. Needless to say *Monsieur l'avocat* was not knitting now, nor had he been for some time past. For the moment the little fish were free from the peril of his nets.

"But, Monsieur Toppaire," the old man resumed, "I am much fonder of America than you can achieve for France. Is it not so?"

"No, it is not so," said Topper promptly. "And don't be silly, Monsieur Dalmas. You, sir, loathe America in comparison with the intensity of my emotion for France."

"What then should we do about it?" demanded the lawyer a little hopelessly. "Or should we do anything at all except order fresh drinks?"

"How about exchanging countries?" suggested Mr. Topper, for lack of anything better to say.

"An excellent idea," replied the little lawyer solemnly. "But what would our respective countries have to say to such a high-handed procedure?"

"Our respective countries would remain agreeably silent," Mr. Topper continued. "We will exchange them secretly, without their knowledge and only between ourselves."

"You mean," said the small Frenchman, "we will do nothing to the countries—make no attempt to move them like——?" He ended his sentence by vaguely waving his hands across each other.

Mr. Topper thought deeply.

"No," he said at last, "that would be too difficult. One can hardly move countries in secret."

"Then is it that I can now consider myself entirely American?" asked Monsieur Dalmas eagerly.

"It is," replied Mr. Topper, wondering how he had ever got himself so deeply involved in this profitless subject. "And as for me, I am French to my finger tips."

"And is it that you feel changed, m'sieu—different, perhaps?" asked the lawyer.

"Thirstier," reflected Topper briefly, as indeed he was.

"Then you are of a full truth French," declared Monsieur Dalmas. "And for the reason that I feel even thirstier than that, I must be typically American."

Fresh glasses were ordered and speedily dispatched. It was a hot day, and the room was growing increasingly more crowded. The automatic piano jangled viciously through its four-piece repertoire.

"I shall sail for America within the week," the little lawyer continued contentedly. "It will be nice to return home, although I love your France."

Mr. Topper was truly alarmed by this turn of affairs. If Monsieur Dalmas started in to proclaim how much he loved Mr. Topper's France, and Mr. Topper were in turn forced to declare how deeply he admired Monsieur Dalmas's America, the conversation might continue on forever. In spite of this possibility, Mr. Topper answered almost sadly.

"I don't think I'll venture abroad this year," he said. "My place is right here in France."

The lawyer nodded comprehendingly.

"Yes," he replied. "Your country needs you now."

"But you will write?" Mr. Topper inquired.

"Assuredly, m'sieu," said the other. "We shall both write constantly."

"What about?" asked Mr. Topper.

"About the ineffable beauties of our respective countries," replied Monsieur Dalmas.

"And the one who succeeds in making the other homesick wins," said Mr. Topper.

"And I dare say you consider yourselves no end humorous," broke in the voice of Marion Kerby. "I've been listening to a lot of this—too much of it, in fact."

"Does she go with the exchange?" inquired the little lawyer hopefully.

Marion looked at him pityingly.

"You, Monsieur Dalmas," she observed, "had better go back to your little fish and your tatting."

Topper laughed at Marion's disgusted expression.

"You're a fine pair of olds," she said. "I am going to take this one out for a walk."

"I would very much like to accompany you," put in Monsieur Dalmas earnestly. "Monsieur Toppaire can point out to me the unique charms of his country. It is so helpful to a foreigner."

"You've both driven each other cuckoo, if you ask me," replied Marion. "But come along, and just to make you feel at home I'll play I'm a Siamese twin."

After a few more rounds of drinks Marion led her two men from the café after having first shaken hands with the *patron*, who stood looking after them admiringly.

Taking a path through the pines, they wound downward towards the sea. They came upon it in a quiet place where rocks were, and the murmurous washing of waves—waves rising and receding and rustling among the rocks. A breeze dipped in spray moved about this place—this little pine-framed cove—and made it cool. It was pleasant here, and quiet. A good place to rest in and to recapture one's self after a little too much grog. The pocket edition of French jurisprudence lay down and promptly fell asleep. Topper, after a slight struggle, followed his example. Marion aired her slim legs and considered the Mediterranean. Then she looked at the two men and thought them little better than dogs—an old dog and a middle-aged dog, both pleased with their own conceits. Idly she wondered what other women thought of when they had both the chance and the inclination to think at all. Perhaps they were, like her, appalled by the scanty realization of the abundant promise of life. Even the fullest of lives was two thirds of the time empty, alone, and discontented. The technique of living itself had been neglected.

In a world so rich that every human being in it could lie on his back half the day and watch the clouds roll by, why was it that only a handful enjoyed the leisure to travel and to sample a little of the diversity of life? Here were two sleeping sots who had spent nine tenths of their lives at work, and yet only small chunks of happiness had been vouchsafed them. Not desperate characters, either of them, yet the necessity to work according to their lights had probably forced them to do more harm than good to their fellow men along the way. Not a pleasant thought, that—the evil unconsciously created through the operations of the economic system. Yet you could not laugh it off. The very facts of a man's success were some other man's skids to failure, discouragement, and warped thoughts. Marion decided that every man should have the right to fail in his own peculiar way. If failure were not penalized by economic and social oblivion, more men would attempt the impossible and attain it. Neither success, nor strength, nor power should be the standards by which life was measured, for in themselves they were meaningless units devoid of any inherent or lasting value. And all this business about vice and virtue took up altogether too much time. God kept silent, perhaps, merely because He was ashamed of the various things His side had said both for and about him. A person who tried hard to be good and one who worked hard to be bad were wasting a lot of effort to arrive at the same end—disillusionment. There was not enough silence in the world, and not enough honest laughter, laughter straight from the belly. Sex should be taken out and aired and given a clean bill of health. It should be put on a self-supporting basis. There should be public sex parks as well as athletic parks. "Fields for friendly frolics," she said half aloud.

"What?" exclaimed Mr. Topper, suddenly sitting up.

She looked near-sightedly at him and smiled.

"Nothing," she said. "You're too gross to understand. I was thinking of a lot of lonely, ingrown men and women made so through the absence of a little band of gold."

"I can think of a lot who are made so through its presence," replied Mr. Topper.

"Are you speaking to me as a Frenchman or as an American?" demanded Marion.

"As one who has suffered," answered Topper.

"Wonder what the Colonel and Mrs. Hart are doing?" she mused, suddenly changing the subject.

"Something cheerfully sinful, no doubt," he told her.

"They're nice people," said Marion. "The world at least gets a kick out of their wickedness as some call it."

"I get a great deal more than a kick," replied Mr. Topper.

The Colonel and Mrs. Hart had departed on one of their customary side tours. For a week they had remained with Marion and Mr. Topper in this isolated place, then life had begun to pall, and they had gone with warm assurance of their speedy return. Topper had seen no reason to doubt their word. They always had returned—most calamitously. Two weeks had now elapsed, and the pair were still away. During their absence Topper had spent one of the happiest periods of his life.

From Monaco, their paradise, well lost, they had reached this place late the following night, after a day of riotous feasting along the way. Finally, taking a winding road that twisted among the hills, they had come upon a small hotel that seemed to have gone to sleep after waiting in vain for guests. The party of four heaven-sent customers, and the dog whose original point of departure was a little less well considered, were received with gracious good-nature even at that late hour, and provided with the best of rooms, wine, and service. From the first Topper felt that he had come home. There was an atmosphere of rest, comfort, and cleanliness about the place. Monsieur Poccard, his son, and the little maid of all work seemed sincere in their desire to please. Even the cook went out of his way to divert and edify the guests. He displayed before them rare but inexpensive dishes and occasionally wet them with a hose he seemed to enjoy squirting when not clattering about in his kitchen. The four of them had the place entirely to themselves, with the exception of Monsieur Dalmas, the little lawyer who spoke English, and an elderly French widow who appeared perfectly satisfied with a phonograph for her sole companion. Occasionally Monsieur Poccard would play to them on the piano, and on these occasions the son, to show his own goodwill, would sing. There were times when the two Poccards would sing all at once, and these times were quite awful. Stout operatic pieces sang the Poccards, with occasional surprising bursts into capricious Italian street songs. When it was over one felt thoroughly beaten yet strangely lighter of heart. One could not help feeling affectionately disposed towards two persons who must have done so much injury to their interior organs for the sake of giving pleasure to others.

The first night Mr. Topper slept deeply in a room that breathed with pines. Far below was the sea, and he could feel its presence, while above, quite close to his head, were the stars and a kindly God who kept the human touch by walking at night through vineyards and forests of silent pines. There was a path that made a short cut to the sea and the rocks, and Topper came to know this path intimately every foot of the way. Not so Mrs. Hart or the Colonel. They tried it once, then found excuses for staying at home. Once they had discovered the possibilities of the little grocery-café, they found staying at home not difficult to bear. Topper and Marion could stand a lot of silence and both of them could gaze on leagues of sea. For those two reasons, if for none other, they could stand a lot of each other's company. They felt no need to be entertaining— no strain for words. They merely lived and allowed time to take a ride for itself. They existed like a couple of pleasantly domesticated beasts amid congenial surroundings. Topper sent for his mail to be forwarded and learned about Mrs. Topper from herself, than whom there could be no better authority. Also, he learned about himself from the same source but failed to consider it reliable. He was a happy man, and to prove it he gave Colette, the trifle of a maid, sufficient money to purchase the liberty of her sweetheart, who was in unproductive durance for having mangled a sailor person who just previously had attempted to mangle Colette, but with a much more friendly intent.

Yes, Topper was happy, and Topper was free from care. Deprived of the example of her two associates, Marion settled down to a normal humdrum existence not entirely devoid of its romantic flavor. They walked long miles and looked thoughtfully at the gloomy remains of the Roman occupation. Here, in the shadow cast by an abandoned stone quarry filled with a smooth, mysterious body of motionless water, they ate bread and cheese and drank wine from bottles cooled in the water of the quarry.

Occasionally they visited the open-air movies at night, at which Marion saw pictures that had been passé even before she and George had hit the fatal tree. The French translations of the American idiom were a source of endless wonder and delight, being the best part of the evening's entertainment.

They swam much, drank a little, and ate whatever they could, supplementing the meals served by the hotel with purchases of cheese and crackers from the little *épicerie*. Most of the time they were hungry, yet all of the time contented. Moments of unease would come to Topper, moments in which he looked into an empty future in which there was no Marion—no companionship in life. And there were times when he caught her looking at him with a peculiar glitter in her eyes that made him extremely uncomfortable. On one occasion he found her in bed with a long-bladed knife she had stolen from the kitchen, and on another he turned round just in time to prevent her from crashing a large rock down on his unprotected head. She laughed it off by saying that she had simply intended to startle him. Topper joined in her laughter, but his sounded a trifle strained. Frequently she tried to induce him to dive from high places into shallow, rock-speckled water, and several times she had playfully endeavored to push him through his window or to lure him girlishly across the path of a speeding motor truck. Once, while lunching amid the Roman ruins, he had actually been forced to cling to a tree with one hand while furtively snapping at sandwiches held in the other, to prevent himself being hurled into the black waters of the quarry many feet below. When he inquired the exact nature of her intentions she told him bitterly that if he was only partially a gentleman he would jump into the damn place himself.

"Not while eating luncheon," said Mr. Topper. "I'm not a gentleman when I'm hungry."

Marion pelted him with her sandwiches and drank up all the wine out of sheer spite. These little incidents occurred so casually and were so deftly explained away that Topper had not the temerity to question Marion seriously about them. Nevertheless, like Agag, he walked lightly by her side, watched his step carefully, and never allowed her to get behind him in dangerous places. One would think that this sort of watchful existence might have ruined Mr. Topper's nerves, not to mention marring his tranquillity. Such was not the case. Topper's nerves had already been ruined, and he derived a certain grim satisfaction in quietly observing Marion's vexation whenever he prevented her from murdering him. However, it must be admitted that the situation was somewhat unusual, although, when understood, rather piquant.

Women have killed men to keep other women from having them, but here was a woman attempting to murder her lover in order to keep him with her. It would have been hard to explain.

On the day following their arrival Mrs. Hart discovered a traveling merry-go-round and brought her companions to see it. The hour was still early, yet the owner of the contraption, with an eye to business and effective publicity, induced the four of them to mount solemnly upon the most insecure-looking horses. No sooner were they astride than the mendacious owner set his machine to march at a furious pace; then, collecting a crowd of amazed men, women, and children, he pointed to his customers painfully revolving through space and proceeded to make a speech. He assured the gaping multitude that these so rich Americans had been so struck by the nobility of his horses, the luxury of his machine, and the fairness of his prices, that they had virtually fought their way into the saddle and threatened him with bodily hurt did he not promptly set his supreme equipage in motion. Topper's panting implorations to stop the damn thing from marching were lost in the applause of the crowd.

"They think we're American cowboys," cried the Colonel above the din. "This thing is a misery-go-round."

"I'm an American tragedy," called Mr. Topper, clinging to his hateful mount and wondering about the damage that was being done him.

He caught a glimpse of Marion's wild eyes and flashing teeth peering back at him over her shoulder. The sight of her taut body jouncing busily on an apparently insane horse was nearly enough to make him lose his grip. He wondered if he too looked as utterly foolish as she did. Finally, Topper in desperation hurled the owner a handful of francs. This one pounced on the money and turned a radiant face to the crowd.

"Regard!" he cried. "They enjoy it. They even demand more. Will they never stop? What people!"

And with this he sprang at a handle and gave it a vicious tug. So fast did the horses speed with this encouragement that Topper virtually lost consciousness. All knowledge of time and space grew vague. He felt sure he was foaming at the mouth. To make matters worse, he had the bitterness to see his companions fading one after the other from the backs of their cavorting mounts. He was alone with his sorrow, his so great misery. Had Topper been able to lay hand on the owner of the fiendish machine he would have pulled the man's tongue out by the roots, or whatever it is tongues have at the end of them.

"They have gone!" he heard the owner cry, some hours, it seemed, after the departure of his friends. "This is strange. I must arrest its progress and search. Perhaps they are in the wheels. If so——" The man shrugged his sentence to its horribly unuttered conclusion.

The merry-go-round came to an end, but Topper, for some moments, was unable to part from his horse. When he did so it was weakly and with the step of an aged and crippled man. At the moment he was not strong enough to do anything to the owner. The tongue part would have to come later.

"Your friends," demanded the man, "what have you done with them? You alone have paid. Am I a dog?"

"Yes," said Topper in a thick voice. "You're a dog, a dirty dog, and your mother was one before you. Find my friends, or I'll call the gendarmes. Tear that infernal machine apart and look for their mangled bodies among the wheels."

The rest of the morning had not been pleasant for the owner. Nor was his trade in that vicinity ever good.

Topper, as he sat there on the rocks, was thinking of this experience and enjoying it from a distance. Slowly he rose and helped Marion to rise. The little lawyer they left sleeping, not knowing what other disposition to make of his body. Slowly they mounted the grade that led back through the pines.

"Take a last look at it," said Marion. "We leave this place tomorrow."

She laid an arm on his shoulder, and instinctively Topper braced himself.

"Why must we leave, Marion?" he asked in a low voice. "I never want to go. Can't we just give the rest of the world a miss? We're well off here, you know."

Marion silently shook her head and gazed into his eyes with a peculiar intentness. Then she made as if to slip her arms round his neck. Topper, troubled by her look, ducked slightly and stepped back. In spite of the seriousness of the moment, Marion laughed softly.

"Don't do that, you American pig," she murmured. "I'm not going to murder you—not now, at any rate."

Mistrustfully Topper allowed her to put her arms up to his shoulders. He looked about for a tree to grab in case of any little trouble, any little slip or push. It was no trifle trying to be fondled by a woman who might just as likely as not choke you black in the face.

"Didn't it ever occur to you that Scollops might become *enceinte*," she asked in a low voice, "or worse still, that George might return from the wars? It takes more than a South American widow to hold that gay desperate in thrall."

"Hell," muttered Topper, holding Marion's eternally youthful body to him. "Both of your suggested possibilities are most unpleasant. It would be just like Scollops to deflower my home while I am away. And as for George—he's just too awful to think about."

"He always is," said Marion.

"Had a good time?" asked Topper.

"Slick," answered Marion.

"It's been all right," went on the man. "More than that for me."

Marion nodded dumbly, and her eyes sought the sea.

"Like me?" asked Topper.

Once more Marion nodded.

"Say it," said Topper.

"Look," replied Marion, pointing to the small figure of the Frenchman sleeping on the rocks. "It hasn't moved."

Together they considered the body.

"That damn little French lawyer," was all Topper said.

XXI

THE BROKEN WINDOW

The little inn was left behind—Monsieur Poccard, Monsieur Poccard's son, petite Colette, Monsieur Dalmas, the brave cook—all
were left behind. Sun filled the arms of the little cove, and waves
washed therein, but Marion Kerby's slim form and Topper's rather
stout one sported there no more. The last drink at the café had gone
the way of all drinks, good and bad alike. The *patron's* hand had been
shaken. All hands had been reshaken. A final, final drink was suggested. And the whole thing began over again with even more elaborate flourishes and expressions of even deeper mutual admiration.
The American couple were gone. A fine couple, free with francs. No
airs. No harsh orders and superior criticism. An exemplary couple.
But mad. Mad as only Americans can be mad. Mad in an inexplicable, altogether mad manner. They arrive. They settle down. They
are here, they are there. One never knows. Then suddenly they depart. One begins to doubt if they had ever been there at all. And
why they had ever arrived or why they had ever departed remain
twin mysteries of equal magnitude. Some things are known about
God. Even more can be devised. About Americans—no. Never.
Nothing can be known about them—nothing even suspected. One
thing, perhaps, yes. They drank like the veritable *poissons,* and they

drank all wrong. *Hein!* How could it be otherwise when their own President himself had locked up all their cellars? What a man! What a perfect demon of a President! However, the Mayor of New York—or was he the Duke of New York—he was a gallant, a true brave, a *type,* that one. He alone would save the States United and bring fresh prosperity to French vineyards. *Alors!* One must return from the dusty white road down which the American couple had but since departed. Time to sell cheese and other provender and perhaps a few bocks. The American invasion was at an end. Francs now would be even more difficult to find.

Meanwhile Mr. Topper and Marion, in a hired car, were being driven back to their original point of departure, the little fishing village where, in Topper's villa, perhaps lurked a pregnant Scollops, a cat who had betrayed her trust. Topper had decided to drive there first to discover if Marion's fearful suggestion had proved a shameful reality. Perhaps both Scollops and the maid Félice herself were a little bit that way. He would not have been surprised. No. If both had escaped scot-free the coincidence would be even more surprising. Topper could but wait and hope that only one of them was pregnant. Idly he speculated as to which one he preferred to be that way. It was hard to decide. Both were of a *type.* With the playful Monsieur Louis hanging about his garden, his wicked old eyes following every woman within sight and divining the presence of those outside his range of vision, it was a wonder the whole neighborhood was not with child. No good there. A thoroughly bad old fellow, that Louis person. Was Louis his first or his last name? And if it was his last name, why was it his last name? Topper never found out.

It was a hot day. A dry day. The road was dusty. Topper was in one of his farewell moods—*triste,* the French called it. Not a bad word, that. Less silly than most French words. He was absent-minded, spiritless, drifting. Marion was a little difficult. There was much she disliked about everything. There were many things she threatened to do. One of these things she actually did. For a long time the dust had been bothering her. She coughed with unnecessary bitterness, thought Topper. Dust was drenching her hair, lungs,

and eyes, she complained. In fact, she was simply dust. A large, uncomfortable particle. She would retire her head from contact with
the dust. That, at least, she would save. In spite of her bitter, com-
plaining mood she was as close to Topper as she could well wedge
her small body. She was leaning as heavily against him as she
could—leaning aggressively, hoping to make him uncomfortable.
Topper paid little attention to the lady. His eyes were on the road
and the sea. Occasionally they studied the unpleasant back of the
chauffeur's neck. Occasionally they caught a glimpse of the chauffeur's casually lascivious eyes in the driving mirror. Gradually, one
might say cautiously, Marion's small comely head withdrew into
the void. The rest of her body remained leaning against Topper.
The effect was that of a gentleman nonchalantly cuddling the body
of a headless woman. Had Topper been aware of this effect he
would not have been quite so nonchalant. However, he was not
aware, and time continued to march. Also, the machine. The road,
now so familiar to Topper, twisted its mad way along beside the sea,
but for the most part high above it. Villas one would love to own and
to live in appeared in the distance, approached, momentarily held
one's attention, then dropped behind—a moment of quiet beauty
lived and left. Other motors passed in both directions making sure
not to sound their high French horns until their sound was quite
uncalled for—in fact, insulting. Time kept on marching, the road
winding, and the dust rising.

Suddenly Topper caught a fresh glimpse of the chauffeur's eyes
in the mirror, and as much as he shrank from these furtive yet
strangely intimate contacts with the man, his, Topper's attention
was thoroughly engaged this time. There was an expression in the
driver's eyes that aroused something more than interest. Just what
was that expression, Topper wondered. Was it horror? Was it repul-
sion? Was it dread? Certainly the soul that dwelt behind those eyes
was not at peace with his God. No, far from it. Had the man run
over a child or a stray cat? No. The owner of such a face would not
be moved by an incident so trivial. He had doubtless run laughingly
over scores of both. There was another reason. Topper's eyes

searched the road ahead in hope of finding the cause of the man's disquietude. Perhaps a flood was doing, or an earthquake. More likely a landslide. The road appeared to be no more terror-evoking than usual. No extra special danger seemed afoot. Yet the man was undoubtedly in the clutch of fear. Topper peered back into the mirror. This time Topper was sure the man was looking at him as one would look at a murderer immediately after an especially revolting piece of work. As if fascinated, the driver's eyes first rested on Mr. Topper's face, moved downward to his shoulder, momentarily fluttered there, then moved away and fixed themselves on the road. Perhaps it was only a vagrant indisposition, hoped Mr. Topper, a passing mood, some congenital eccentricity wished upon the unfortunate chap by his indubitably criminal parents. Topper decided to put the unpleasant incident from his mind. He tried but did not succeed.

"I feel quite ill," said Marion in a decidedly accusing voice. "Anyone would feel the same in my position."

The erratic driving of the man at the wheel prevented Mr. Topper from replying to Marion's lament. He fixed his eyes on the man, only to find the man's eyes fixed on him, but this time the gaze was direct instead of reflected from the mirror.

"Turn round and look where you're going," Mr. Topper commanded. "Do you want to kill the three of us?"

"There are only two left to kill," replied the man. "You, m'sieu, have seen to that."

Topper's nerves were not good, neither was his temper.

"If you don't turn your head to the road," he gritted, "I'll knock the damn thing off."

"As you did the other one," muttered the man. "*Morbleu!* I must get out of this."

And he did. Stopping the car by the roadside he got out of it and ran rapidly down the road. Mr. Topper, slightly dazed, looked stupidly after the man.

"Now why did he want to do that?" he asked.

"Perhaps he needed to," Marion replied lazily.

At this moment an automobile that had appeared from the direction in which the chauffeur had vanished drew up beside them. The serious faces of two respectable-looking American gentlemen peered out of the car in the rear of which were a couple of less respectable-looking American ladies.

"Any trouble here?" inquired one of the gentlemen of Mr. Topper. "We saw a chauffeur running———"

He stopped suddenly and looked incredulously at Mr. Topper. Then he blinked rapidly and nudged his companion.

"Do you see what I am seeing?" he asked in a low voice.

His companion leaned far out of the car and looked with increasing horror at Mr. Topper, who under the combined scrutiny of the two gentlemen was beginning to feel decidedly uncomfortable.

"No," he told the gentlemen with a certain show of dignity. "There's no trouble here. Why should there be?"

There was a short pause during which the two gentlemen endeavored to get a grip on the situation.

"Well," said one of them at last, "a man in your position should consider himself in a lot of trouble unless he is used to the thing."

"What do you mean?" demanded Topper. "And why, may I ask, are you acting so funny? Have you both lost your heads over something?"

At this last question the two gentlemen shrank back a little and looked away from Mr. Topper.

"No," answered the spokesman slowly. "We haven't lost our heads, but we know who has. Did the chauffeur do it?"

"What a question to ask," exploded Mr. Topper. "How do I know whether the chauffeur has done it or not? I'm not interested."

"He's a cool customer," observed the second American. "Wonder how he did it? With his bare hands, perhaps. Yet I see no signs of bl———"

At this moment one of the women shrieked, then became deathly still. The other woman started in to babble while pointing at Mr. Topper.

"What's wrong with her?" demanded Topper. "Is this a car full of lunatics? Or are you all drunk?"

"Murderer!" cried the woman, suddenly finding words. "Jack-the-Ripper—Strangler Lewis."

"Not Strangler Lewis," corrected one of the gentlemen. "He at least allowed his opponents to live."

"Are these people all nutty?" asked Mr. Topper, glancing down for the first time at his headless companion and grasping that fact with a start of horror himself. "What the hell——" he began, but the woman cut him short.

"You may well ask," she cried in a nasty, hysterical voice. "First you ruin the poor creature, then you twist her head clean off her neck, then you take a drive with her body. Of all the nerve! What did you do with the head? Tell us that."

"You're perfectly right, madam," came Marion's voice from nowhere. "He did all those things and worse, and then he loses my head. Make the brute find my head for me, or I'll never rest in peace. Fancy he chucked it somewhere. Murderers usually do that with heads."

The four occupants of the other car were speechless. So was Mr. Topper. Indignation robbed him of words.

"The voice from the grave," the woman murmured at last. "The poor headless soul."

"Hardly from the grave," one of the gentlemen again corrected.

"Make him find my head," urged the voice. "I'm in a hell of a fix without a head. Just fancy my position. To lose one's hon——"

"Shut up, you!" cried Mr. Topper, also getting hold of some words of his own. "If I could only get my hands on your head I'd damn well twist it off."

"My God!" breathed one of the men. "Did you hear that? What callousness! He actually wants to do it again."

"I know," replied the correcting gentleman. "They're like that. They enjoy it."

"Certainly I enjoy it," retorted Topper in a grim voice. "I'd like to twist all of your heads off—every damn head."

"Better look out," warned Marion. "He'll do it. He threatened me more than once, but I never believed a man could be so mean. Then suddenly he ups and does it." Here she made a horrid noise, then added, "Just like that—no head. Zingo!"

The people in the car did not know whether to be more appalled by Marion's description of her death than by the horror of the act itself. They swallowed hard and took counsel among themselves. Here they had an obvious murderer and a loquacious murderee on their hands, and they had no ideas as to what to do about it all. The entire situation seemed palpably impossible, yet the plain facts of the case spoke otherwise. Here was a headless woman describing with revolting noises her terrible loss, and here was her murderer not only glorying in his ghastly deed but also fervently wishing he could repeat it. The fellow was actually threatening them with like treatment. An end was put to their indecision by a sudden act on the part of Mr. Topper. He pushed Marion violently from him.

"What? At it again?" her voice came querulously as her body slumped over on the seat. "I should think you'd be tired. I know I am."

"This is all wrong," said one of the gentlemen. "It just can't be so. I say, let's shove off."

"Keep an eye out for my head," called Marion. "An eye for a head instead of tooth for a tooth. Ta, ta, my braves."

A shriek of chilling laughter followed the departing motorists down the road.

"God!" breathed one of the gentlemen. "I'm glad Mary there didn't hear any of that. It might have brought her out of that faint, and I need some time for thought."

"But aren't you going to do anything about it?" demanded the one who had not fainted. "Tell a policeman or something?"

"Something," replied the other. "I'm going to tell it to a couple of stiff drinks at the nearest bar. That would be a pretty little bedtime story to slip across in French to a gendarme. We'd be the ones to get locked up."

Meanwhile Mr. Topper, with more agility than grace, had

climbed over into the front seat and blasphemously sent the automobile on its way.

"That was a pretty thing to do," he shouted furiously over his shoulder. "A hell of a thing to do—a typical Marion Kerby trick."

No answer.

"I suppose you think you're funny," he flung back hopefully. "Make a murderer of me, will you—a Strangler Lewis, a Peep the Tommer?"

"Please, mister," said a small voice beside him. "There's nobody back there now, not even a head. And Strangler Lewis is, or was, a wrestling gentleman, and the other one's name is Tom the Peeper."

"What do I care?" snapped Topper. "I wish I were Strangler Lewis and I had you on the mat."

"Oh, Mr. Topper, what a thing to say. And in front of all those people. Madison Square Garden, no less."

"For God's sake, be still," muttered the defeated man. "You should be ashamed of yourself."

"But not all Toms are Peeping Toms," continued Marion, returning in person to herself. "Never make that mistake. Some are mere Thumbs while others are no more than Cooks. Then there was a Tom who was the son of a piper and another——"

"Childish drivel," snorted Mr. Topper. "Wonder where that damn chauffeur has got himself to? Can't blame him much for running, considering what he saw."

"Yes," replied Marion. "You sadly misjudged the poor man's intentions."

Topper smiled slowly, reluctantly, then shrugged away his gloom entirely. The atmosphere seemed to have been cleared. There was even less dust, as both were riding in the front seat now, and protected by the windshield.

"You didn't disabuse my mind any," he said. "Oh, well, it's just another one of those things. Another little joke at my expense."

"You were far less upset than the others," Marion reminded him. "In fact, you came off quite well. Too bad you didn't meet the Widow."

"What widow?" demanded Topper.

"The one that chops your head off and drops it in a basket," Marion replied serenely.

"I've had enough of heads for one day," Topper told her.

"You mean you've not had enough," said Marion brightly. "By one."

"I hate smart people," was Topper's reply to this. "You know—the ready retort."

A few miles farther on they came upon the chauffeur sitting dejectedly by the roadside. At the approach of the car he rose wearily and started to run, but the man must have been sadly out of training, for he soon abandoned the attempt. Probably he decided that if he had to lose his breath one way or another he might just as well get it over with here and now, thus sparing himself the exertion of running himself to death.

The spent man and the automobile stopped side by side, and the spent man turned to be murdered. Much to his surprise and gratification he was confronted by the alluringly smiling face of Marion. Carefully scrutinizing her tender neck to see that her head was conventionally joined to her shoulders, he was able to produce an exhausted sigh of relief.

"See," offered Marion reassuringly, pointing to her head. "I have it, my friend, *la tête complète.*"

"Madame," stammered the man, "from where did it come, that head there?"

"Had it all the time," said Marion. "I was merely hiding it. Monsieur had said something—oh, such a wicked thing. Didn't you ever hide your head, my brave?"

"Madame," replied the man earnestly, "I have wanted to with all my heart. But a moment since I would have hidden it in the jaws of a lion enraged."

"I can well understand that," said Marion. "But have no fear, my friend. Monsieur is a bad, bad man, but a woman's head is always safe in his hands. He can *see* that. You comprehend?"

"Perfectly, madame," replied the chauffeur, smiling for the first time as he gazed with admiration upon the annoyed face of

Mr. Topper. "I myself am not unlike Monsieur. *L'amour* is my one——"

"But I am not at all like that," broke in Mr. Topper. "Let me assure you——"

"You are like that," declared Marion. "And I love it. We are wasting time for no good end. Mount into the back, my old, and Monsieur himself will show you things—maneuvers you never thought possible except in an aëroplane."

The chauffeur mounted accordingly, and the car resumed marching. He decided that Mr. Topper, in spite of his agreeable qualities, would be safer by far with both hands engaged at the wheel. So Mr. Topper drove over bridges spanning the tracks of the P. L. M. until his sense of the fitness of things could bear it no longer.

"Why does this road cross these tracks so damn many times?" he inquired. "It seems such a waste of effort and material, not to mention time."

"M'sieu," said the chauffeur rather timidly, "it is not the road that crosses the tracks, but it is the tracks themselves that undermine the road."

Mr. Topper was still trying mentally to digest this one when they drove into Cannes and met life in one of its pleasantest aspects.

"Food," observed Marion.

"And drink," agreed Topper.

The chauffeur beamed. This Monsieur was supremely human after all.

They drove along the Croisette, shops and hotels on one side, the beach and sea on the other. Mr. Topper looked at the women on the beach, and Marion sat quietly observing Topper.

"You know," she said, "I can read you like a book, and every page is vile."

Topper was mildly offended. He dearly loved to look at women either beautifully clad or unclad. It was one of his amusements, a quiet, harmless pleasure on which he could depend. Inasmuch as thought transference was not among his accomplishments no lady's sense of propriety was outraged. Although, if the truth must be known, if only a small percentage of the ladies Topper admired had been able to read his thoughts he would have been an extremely busy man.

"I don't see you blushing," he observed.

"I seldom blush in the customary manner. Mentally, I am suffused."

They dined at the Palm Beach Casino, and also danced. Marion insisted on this slight recognition of her sex. Topper was at all hours of the day or night perfectly willing to recognize sex with the utmost cordiality, but dancing was hardly his idea of the proper way of expressing his recognition. However, he enjoyed dancing with Marion. Also, he enjoyed the knowledge that he, Topper, was actually dancing without being stoned by observers or booed off the floor. Generous applications of wine that also danced increased his dexterity and daring. Often, during the dull, comfortable monotony of his married life, Topper had wanted to dance. Often he had danced, but always in the seclusion of his own room and alone or, at best, with a chair for his partner. If little can be said in favor of Marion Kerby it must be acknowledged at least that she was woman enough to understand the man in Cosmo Topper, although she took unpardonable liberties with her knowledge. She was taking them now, as she circled round the floor. Marion was actually floating. Her feet never touched the floor. Topper, holding her in his arms, was unable to see that he was carrying about with him only the upper half of a woman. Marion to obviate interference and to allow free play for her partner's feet had thoughtfully withdrawn the lower half of her body from circulation. So strongly had the idea appealed to her that she had entirely overlooked its possible effect upon observers unacquainted with his intentions.

Topper, to some of the diners, gave the impression of a man dancing alone but with a surprising display of enjoyment. As a matter of fact, so realistic was this impression that one man remarked to the lady sitting opposite him: "That man must be either the greatest egoist in the world or its greatest mimic. Never did see a chap derive so much enjoyment from his own company."

From another point of vantage Topper looked for all the world as if he were carrying round in his arms the upper section of a smartly clad display figure abstracted from the window of some fashionable shop along the Croisette. Numerous spectators were of this belief until they discovered that the thing not only talked and smiled, but actually turned its head.

"My God," said an American visitor, breaking into a gentle sweat, "that must be Madame Tussaud herself!"

The girl with him was clinging to his arm.

"Oh, look," she kept saying. "Look at her now. No bottom part at all."

"Like a mermaid without a tail," another girl remarked.

"Or a woman similarly disqualified," said her escort.

This remark started an argument as to whether a woman with only the upper half of her body present were disqualified or not.

Meanwhile, a drunken gentleman rose from his chair and began to follow Mr. Topper about the floor. The drunken gentleman had no intention of being offensive, but he did want to find out about all this. He even went so far as to pass his hand thoughtfully through sections of air which rightfully should have been displaced by Marion's body. Then he maneuvered himself into a position in which he was able to peer closely into Marion's face. Mr. Topper took exception to this.

"Go away," he said quietly. "Far away."

Marion merely winked her left eye slowly.

The man stepped back and placed a steadying hand on Mr. Topper's shoulder. Mr. Topper was not offended. He did not belong to the type that when sober finds cause for either amusement or scorn in the actions of others drunk.

"What's the matter, old man?" he asked.

"Look," was all the man could say, making a floor-sweeping gesture. "Down there. Look. There's nothing at all down there, nothing at all. No feet, no ankles, no legs, no—no—just nothing," he concluded lamely.

Mr. Topper looked and turned red.

"Do something quickly," he whispered furiously. "This morning it was your head, and now——"

"Heads I win. Tails you lose," Marion replied smilingly.

"Well, for God's sake, produce the latter and the other parts that go with it," Mr. Topper pleaded.

"I'd hate like the deuce to argue like that with only half a lady," the drunken gentleman announced to the crowd of dancers and diners that had gathered round.

Mr. Topper had an inspiration. He would pretend he was a professional magician.

"Meet me in the car," he whispered in Marion's ear. "Now, get the devil out of here."

He made a few Svengalian passes in the air, and Marion, having enjoyed her moment, had the grace to vanish entirely. There was a burst of applause. Topper bowed several times, then with great dignity returned to his table, paid his bill, and left the Casino. Marion was waiting for him in the automobile. Luckily for her the chauffeur had returned from his regal repast. Topper was unable to give expression to his emotions. Favoring them both with a sick smile, he climbed into the back of the car and motioned to the chauffeur to drive. He was through for the day. Once he viciously pinched Marion, causing her to emit a plaintive little shriek which was pleasant to hear, but when he caught in the mirror the expression of leering tolerance on the face of the driver, and when Marion called him a naughty man, he desisted from further hostilities and contented himself with dark looks and even darker oaths. It was dark, too, when they drove through the quiet streets of the little fishing village and stopped on its outskirts in front of Mr. Topper's pallid villa. They sat in the car and looked up at the windows of the place. Topper experienced a feeling of the ending of things. The interlude was nearly over. At his left the night surf came driving in upon the sands of Monsieur Sylvestre's so-called tranquil beach. Clouds were scudding across a moon that had nearly reached the full. On one side of his villa the home of the reprehensible Monsieur Louis lay in darkness, its owner probably at play—up to his old tricks. On the other side the villa occupied by that beastly old woman who watched at her window was in a similar condition of quietude. But was it? Certainly not. A faint light shone in one of the rooms, outlining against the window curtain the figure of a woman—the woman, the woman who in Mr. Topper's eyes symbolized all the malignant prudery, the narrowness and prurient curiosity that next to actual warfare did more than anything else in life to destroy the happiness, self-respect, and freedom of action of humanity. She stood for the type that stolidly claimed the woman was always wrong. And like the type she represented, she callously closed her eyes on the evil conditions in her own home only to peer into the windows of her neighbors. She represented bigotry, oppression, and ignorance, that old woman behind the window. Topper had seen it at work in offices, homes, and communities.

"The horrid old bitch," he muttered under his breath. "God deliver all the bad women from the tender mercies of the alleged good ones. And that includes you," he added, taking Marion's small, firm hand in his.

"Listen," said Marion. "Of course, it's none of my business, but doesn't it strike you as a bit odd that your villa should be so well lighted during the absence of its lord and master?"

Topper looked at his villa and noticed with a start of alarm that both upstairs and down the lights were gayly gleaming. It had seemed so natural at first that its true significance had not penetrated his brooding mind.

"Good God, don't tell me my wife has returned?" he burst out.

"Not from the nature of the sounds I hear," said Marion. "That is, not unless she has changed very much for the better."

It was true indeed. The sounds of disorganized revelry were issuing from the villa. Snatches of indecent song, small shrieks and deep vulgar laughter mingled to make a symphony of life in full foam.

Topper turned a pair of puzzled eyes on his companion. She was smiling up at him maliciously.

"Dear, dear," he observed. "I was expecting to find a pregnant cat, but it seems that the house itself is pregnant."

Suddenly the French windows on the ground floor burst open, and a flock of men and women poured out into the night led by the Colonel, clad only in his drawers.

"He seems to affect that costume," Marion observed quietly.

"What goes on here?" Mr. Topper asked in a daze.

From the merry rout Mrs. Hart emerged, dragging a semiclad Félice with her. In the moonlight she confronted the Colonel.

"An unfortunate misunderstanding, my dear," the watchers in the car heard him say in his suavest accents.

"That's one of the few actions in life," replied Mrs. Hart, "that denies a double interpretation. Colonel, I hate to say it, but you're nothing better than an exceedingly lousy liar."

"My dear," began the Colonel, then spying the tense figure of the woman at the window he seized upon her as a Godsent diversion. "Look!" he cried, waving one bare arm dramatically towards the window. "Behold, old evil eye! A filthy hypocrite hiding behind her inability either to give pleasure or to attract it. See! I do this!"

And the Colonel did just that. He tossed a champagne bottle through the window with the accuracy of a man trained in warfare. The crash of glass was followed by another one. Soon the whole disorderly party was hurling bottles, stones, gravel, and even the personal attire of its members through the windows of the villa. Marion was greatly pleased. She looked questioningly at Topper. There was a strange expression on his face, a sort of pleasurable excitement inevitably produced by the sound of crashing glass.

"Shall we join the party?" she asked in a low voice.

"It looks like an open break with law and order," he replied thoughtfully, "and as much as I deplore this sort of thing, I would like for once in my life to register my violent objection to wormeaten but organized and well entrenched joy killing."

He paid the frightened chauffeur far more than enough for his mental anguish and professional services; then, with Marion's hand in his, he left the car.

"My old and rare," she whispered with unaffected admiration. "In moments of crisis you rise to true greatness."

They mingled with the seemingly maddened throng and began throwing whatever object came nearest to hand in the general direction of the besieged villa. Soon Mr. Topper and Marion were as disheveled, dirty, and demented as the rest of the strange people

milling about them. It was a scene of epic action, of large ruthlessness and vast enjoyment. It was one of those things that in idle moments one dreams of doing, but which one never does except at
seats of learning where such things come under the head of educa-
tion. Topper was suddenly entangled and tripped. He found himself on his own back on his own ground. There was no comfort in
this. A large, naked gentleman was tugging at his shoe.

"Pardon me," came the courtly voice of the Colonel, "but I have
no shoes of my own, and there is nothing left to throw."

"Hi, there, Colonel!" cried Mr. Topper. "Lay off my foot."

"My friend!" exclaimed the Colonel joyfully. "My crime mate.
Here, take your shoe. I wish I had more to offer you. Congratulate
us, Topper. We have been keeping your home intact for you during
your protracted dalliance. But first let me help you to rise."

The Colonel pulled Topper to his feet just in time to meet the
assault of the united gendarmes of the district. Oaths, blows, and
imprecations now became general, yet above them all, loud and
clear boomed the voice of the Colonel.

"*Cinquante-cinq!*" he shouted. "*Quatre-vingt-dix!*"

"You're not cursing, Colonel," cried Topper. "You're counting."

"What the hell do I care?" bellowed the Colonel. "It sounds good
and fulsome. *Cinquante-cinq!* Tear the beggars up!"

Topper was now assaulted from all sides. He wondered where
Marion was. Then he caught a momentary glimpse of her. What he
saw did not augur well for the future happiness of a certain gendarme.

"Marion!" shouted Topper.

"With you, boy!" called Marion. "As soon as I ruin this lad."

"We have no fight with the gendarmes, Colonel," said Topper,
seizing the man's arm just as it was about to polish off a member of
the force.

"Looks mighty damn like a fight to me," replied that man of
brawn. "Not that I haven't been in worse."

"Then call off your crowd," said Topper, pushing a gendarme in
the stomach.

"Shall we take you with us?" asked the Colonel.

"God, no!" cried Topper. "All the trees in France wouldn't hold me after insurrection."

The Colonel issued a command, and a great silence fell upon the scene. Topper stood alone—alone, that is, save for the presence of a great multitude of gendarmes. The gendarmes looked at Topper, and Topper looked back at the gendarmes. Then all of them looked around.

"M'sieu," said an officer, stepping forward and clipping a pair of handcuffs on Mr. Topper's wrists, "your friends, where are they?"

A voice from the air answered for Topper, and even as the voice boomed out Topper felt a small hand slipped into his imprisoned ones.

"We are gone," intoned the deep voice. "We are those good Americans who come to Paris when they die. See you later, Topper."

Evidently the Colonel and Mrs. Hart had collected a flock of low-plane spirits during Mr. Topper's absence and had been entertaining them at his expense. The magnitude of the Colonel's cool effrontery appealed to Mr. Topper.

"Better one bird," said the officer philosophically, "than no bird at all. This affair is strange passing all belief. Perhaps you, m'sieu, will elucidate it for us before *Monsieur le commissaire* himself, is it not so?"

"But yes," replied Mr. Topper. "It is not so."

And all the way to the place whereat *Monsieur le commissaire* held court, Mr. Topper felt an unseen presence marching by his side. The heart of the man was gay and devoid of alarm, although filled with a multitude of rapidly crystallizing lies for the special edification of *Monsieur le commissaire* himself.

"A break like this just had to happen," said Mr. Topper to himself. "A person can't live peacefully on one plane and associate with the denizens of another."

XXII

THE LAW TAKES ITS
CASUAL COURSE

Monsieur le commissaire Devaux sat with weary elegance behind his desk in the small room at the police station. With an expression of polite disgust he regarded those within his sight, including his own officers of the law.

"Who are all these annoying-looking persons?" he asked of an officer standing near by. "These offensive smelling citizens, even if bent on crime, should first wash. Are they all criminals, Henri?"

"That, *Monsieur le commissaire,* is for you to judge."

"Why cannot the law take its course?" continued the commissaire. "I grow weary of inferior sinning. Where is our American monsieur? He interests me."

"He will arrive in but a moment," assured Henri. "Meantime these two women have a grievance against each other. Also, they have disturbed the peace by fighting and the excessive use of vile language."

"I know those two women," said Monsieur Devaux sadly, "and it pains me to hear that they use vile language, that is, to excess. A little vile language is good for all—it clears one's spiritual alimentary tract." Monsieur Devaux paused to appreciate this. He was alone in

his appreciation. "I am afraid they are very bad women," he resumed, "but why are they here at this hour of the night?"

"You were present, *Monsieur le commissaire*," said Henri simply,
"so we brought them."

"I see," observed Devaux. "Every time I am here you feel that
you must bring me something. That is thoughtful but unnecessary.
I prefer to be alone. Bring them to me."

A small thin Frenchwoman and a large fat Frenchwoman were
pushed before *Monsieur le commissaire*. Both began to talk volubly at
once. Both attempted to resume hostilities. Both were forcibly separated and quieted.

"Marie," asked Devaux, utterly untouched by the display of feminine ferocity he had witnessed, "why do you call your smaller
neighbor bad names and attack her?"

"M'sieu," replied the larger woman, "that one steals my husband."

"Do you mean she steals him repeatedly?" inquired the commissaire. "From day to day?"

"No, m'sieu," replied Marie. "From night to night. From day to
day he remains at home—supine."

"Naturally, from night to night," murmured Devaux. "My mistake. One should have known better. And you, Jeanne, what is your
complaint? It seems you should be grateful instead of offensive."

"That sow of ill repute will not allow her husband to remain
stolen," announced the small woman in an injured voice. "I am
small, and I need a man."

"I don't quite see that," said Devaux. "Marie is large. Does she
need two men?"

"She has the fishing front complete to a man," retorted the small
one. "She is notorious, that one."

"She deserves to be," observed Commissaire Devaux. "This all
seems to be more of a problem for God to decide than man."

Marie could no longer restrain herself.

"And, *Monsieur le commissaire*," she exploded, "when I confront
her with her theft she does this to me for all the world to behold."

By an inelegant gesture Marie showed the commissaire exactly what Jeanne did to her. The commissaire was visibly moved. He attempted to avert his eyes but was unable to do so. They were held fascinated by the titanic proportions of the primitive spectacle. Yet, even as he observed, he thought, in a detached manner, of the numerous objectionably human acts a public official was forced to look upon in the dispatch of his professional duties.

"And, m'sieu, if you do not know what that means——" began Marie.

"I'm very much afraid I do," Devaux interrupted hastily, "and it seems to be painting the lily a little."

"It means——" continued Marie, desirous of making sure the full significance of her demonstration was understood.

"Marie," broke in the commissaire, "do not hold that unnerving posture any longer. I think I can read the writing on the wall, especially when so trenchantly expressed."

"It means——" began Marie.

"Please take them away," said the commissaire. "She refuses to believe I know what it means, and I refuse to be told. You see, we are at an impasse."

As the ladies were being led out, Mr. Topper was briskly led in by a considerable number of gendarmes. He was brought into the presence of the commissaire himself.

"Ah!" exclaimed that one with obvious relief. "So you have at last arrived."

"You are confusing arrived with arrested, I fear, m'sieu," Mr. Topper amended.

Now Commissaire Devaux spoke perfect English, made so by dealing for years with far less perfect Americans and Englishmen. He was slightly offended by Mr. Topper's correction.

"M'sieu, you see fit to jest at a serious moment in your life," he observed easily. "More serious than you realize. You are lionlike at present. Later you may more resemble his prey—one of his minor meals." *Monsieur le commissaire* paused and regarded in sudden horror the vast quantities of gendarmes cluttering up his quarters. "Am I to be favored with a review?" he inquired of one of the officers; then, noticing the battered condition of many of the men, he added in French, "Lionlike is not the word. The man must be a menagerie in himself to have inflicted such punishment."

"But there were at least forty others," replied the officer. "Forty wild ones, *Monsieur le commissaire.*"

"Splendid!" cried Devaux. "Remove several hundred of these crippled-looking creatures that once were men and bring in the remaining forty prisoners."

"M'sieu," replied the officer haltingly, "we were successful in apprehending but one—that one before you—the others vanished into thin air."

The commissaire received this piece of information with admirable sangfroid.

"The air could not have been so remarkably thin," he observed, "to have consumed forty wild bodies." He looked thoughtfully at the officer. "Have you, perhaps, been drinking," he asked, "or were you struck heavily upon the head?"

"The latter, m'sieu," replied the officer. "Repeatedly. And not on the head alone."

He pulled back his tunic.

"Stop!" cried the commissaire. "Is it your intention to strip yourself before us to show us the extent of your injuries?"

"One thought you might like to see, m'sieu."

"Were they of an assuredly fatal nature, perhaps I would," replied Devaux. "With less than that I would not be satisfied." He turned his eyes upon Mr. Topper. "Ah, well," he continued at last, "we will have to do as thoroughly as possible with the one prisoner we have at our immediate disposal. Monsieur Topper, I can see a long stretch of the most boring years spanning your slow progress to the grave."

"But why?" demanded Topper. "Must I be sentenced for forty prisoners whose very existence remains yet to be established?"

"For at least forty," replied the commissaire. "The *juge d'instruction* whom you will later have the misfortune to meet may suggest more in his report. He is a strong believer in vicarious atonement. I shall content myself with a conservative forty. Is all clear, m'sieu?"

"Crystalline," retorted Topper. "M'sieu, is there no justice in France?"

"Obviously not," the commissaire informed him in the most astonished of tones. "Your question confounds me, but why confine it to France? Is there justice in any country in the world, Monsieur Topper? There are laws—there are laws everywhere. We do the best that we can with them. Do you not realize that man is not ready to receive justice, much less to administer it? If justice were done to humanity, there wouldn't be any humanity left. It would be poisoned, and the last prisoner would in the end have to poison himself, a piece of Quixotic integrity which passes belief. So you see, m'sieu, justice is a mere word. There can be no such thing as justice so long as justice is needed. But pardon me. You touched on my favorite topic. One moment, if you please. Who is that woman there?" he called out sharply. "She is making most disturbing sounds."

A middle-aged American woman was brought forward. She was crimson with wrathful indignation. In atrocious French she attacked the commissaire and the nation he represented. He listened politely to her for a moment, then waved her to silence.

"Madame," he said in a mildly rebuking voice, "if you must say such horrid things, please say them in English. I don't want my subordinates contaminated with seditious utterances. I can understand English, and, quite unofficially, I agree with much you say. Has this lady done anything, or has anyone done anything to her? The latter contingency seems hardly possible from where I am sitting."

It was explained to Commissaire Devaux that the lady was the wife of one of a group of visiting American politicians. These politicians had come to make speeches in France because their constituents at home would no longer listen to them. Also they desired to break a few speech-cramping French precedents and to set up several new ones. The lady had hurled a brick through the window of a restaurant in which the wife of another American politician was drinking champagne with some friends. Not content with this act of violence, she had thereupon delivered a speech in which her husband's name was frequently mentioned in connection with his noble determination to uphold prohibition not only in America but also the wide world over. The lady resisted arrest and mentioned freedom and liberty and something about stars and stripes.

Throughout this recital *Monsieur le commissaire* became more and more dismayed. Plainly the affair bore an international aspect. He must proceed with the utmost diplomacy, although it went against the grain. Sardonically he smiled upon Mr. Topper.

"How would you deal with such a case?" Devaux asked him with a touch of malice.

"If you will ask the lady to leave the room," said Mr. Topper, "I'll be delighted to advise you."

"That's the way I feel about it," replied Commissaire Devaux.

At this moment an exceedingly young-looking policeman entered the room. He was carrying with a great lack of enjoyment a six-inch piece of pipe sealed at both ends.

"What's that?" demanded the commissaire.

"*Mon commissaire,*" replied the youth, "it is believed to be a bomb found in the home of an estate agent."

"I could think of no better place for a bomb to be," replied Devaux without turning a hair. "But why bring it here? We desire to live, if you do not. That is, all save yourself, Monsieur Topper, who are facing a living death."

"If that damn thing is a bomb," said Topper with conviction, "all of us are facing immediate death."

The commissaire's face brightened up.

"I have it!" he exclaimed. "Give the bomb to the dry lady and tell her she is at liberty to take it wherever she pleases so long as it is a long way off. Perhaps her husband might like it to present to the city of Chicago with a speech. You see, Monsieur Topper, I am not without knowledge of conditions in your home of the free and land of the brave."

Suddenly the bomb was snatched by some unseen hand from those of the young policeman who looked momentarily relieved.

"Release the prisoner Topper," cried the voice of the Colonel as the bomb leaped aloft, "or I'll blow this place to atoms."

"And Topper with it, you fool," came the voice of Marion Kerby. "Give me that bomb this minute."

A struggle seemed to be in progress for possession of the bomb.

The commissaire looked at Topper with an expression of resigned horror.

"M'sieu," he said in a low voice, "this is the tensest moment of my life beside which the horrors of war were as slumber. If we live through this remind me to take up the matter of voices and bodies and other manifestations."

"If I still have control of my faculties," replied Mr. Topper.

The Colonel was laughing madly, while Marion stuck steadily to swearing. Suddenly the bomb began to fizz.

"Monsieur Topper," remarked Devaux, "it was a pleasure to have known you. Already I am trying to get used to the past tense. So that you won't be forced to accompany me to God as a suspect I hereby acquit you of all charges."

No sooner were the words spoken than the bomb went flying through the door to the center of a little square where stood the statue of a particularly stuffy-looking angel. There was a small explosion, and when the dust cleared away little of the angel remained.

"Good," remarked the commissaire, peering through the door at the scene of small ruin. "For some reason I never did like that angel. Some of you, *mes braves*, go out and effect a few tactfully selected arrests. I cannot hold the American Monsieur for this. I've already acquitted him." With a smile he turned back to Topper. "Well, m'sieu," he observed, "we have succeeded in eliminating the bomb and the angel, too."

"Also, we are still alive," replied Mr. Topper.

"And for that reason you should be in jail," the commissaire assured him, "but I see you are determined to take advantage of a hasty remark made under the stress of an abnormal situation."

"*Regardez là, mon commissaire!*" cried a gendarme, pointing excitedly to the square. "A veritable miracle is in progress."

On the splintered pedestal where the stuffy angel had once stood now appeared the figure of a flesh-and-blood woman, Marion Kerby, clad only in the briefest of scanties.

"A decided improvement," murmured Monsieur Devaux, "although a far greater distraction."

It was only a momentary manifestation, but that slim, debonair figure poised so impudently in the footsteps abandoned by the joyless symbol of piety enforced—sweet religious melancholy—stood out clear and distinct, like the provocative forerunner of a pleasanter day and age. It was like a high wind blowing away the stale perfume of ancient sin, ripping the gloomy masks from the images of long-libeled saints, and leaving in their places a row of cheerfully ironical grins. To Topper and the commissaire, standing in the door of the police station, that gleaming figure of a woman brought many irrelevant thoughts to mind, some comforting and some a little edged with regret. The air was filled with catcalls and shouts of unholy jubilation, tipsy laughter and scraps of song sung just a little off the key. And above all the disorderly noises boomed the brazen voice of the Colonel.

"We are those good Americans," he chanted, "who go to Paris when they die." This was followed by jeers and laughter, then: "Compliments of the season, Mr. Topper."

And just before the figure melted from the pedestal it turned towards the men standing in the doorway and mockingly thumbed its nose, or rather, her nose, for no one gazing at that slim, vital figure could think of Marion Kerby in terms of the neuter gender.

XXIII

An Invitation to Be
Murdered

"My friend," remarked the commissaire as the tumultuous sounds faded with the figure, "you seem to be known in some rather esoteric circles."

Before Topper could reply, a harsh voice was heard behind the two men.

"Am I at liberty to leave this awful place?" demanded the wife of the American visiting politician.

Devaux's face froze with pain at the sound of the woman's voice. He closed his eyes as if to retain the memory of the vision they had so recently seen. It was apparent that the good commissaire was exercising the utmost self-control to keep from performing some criminal act himself. France's reputation for politeness was in the balance.

"But certainly, madame," he managed to produce at last, together with a smile that must have cost him dear. "And with the utmost expedition. Please be so gracious as to consider the damages entailed by your ladylike conduct in hurling a brick through a hard-working *patron's* windows entirely on this municipality and the Republic of France itself."

"My husband will hear of this," was the gracious manner in which the lady accepted courtesy of the French Republic.

The commissaire beamed.

"I hope so, madame," he exclaimed. "Perhaps he would honor us with a speech when the new window is installed."

"I don't know about that," said the woman doubtfully, her grim features relaxing a little. "Perhaps he would. He's become a bit choosy about his speeches lately. Nevertheless, it would be an opportunity. The folks back home would get printed copies of it—my name would be mentioned—Betty Sanders would turn green with jealousy and . . ."

Thus musing the lady departed out of the lives of Monsieur Devaux and Mr. Topper. When she had gone the commissaire turned to his former prisoner.

"This night, my friend, I have seen and heard more than is good for a mere police official," he said. "Tell me—unofficially, of course—do you know the lady of the pedestal?"

"I know one who looks surprisingly like her," replied Topper.

"And is it true," continued the commissaire, "that sometimes she accompanies you merely as a head and sometimes with even more attractive portions displayed?"

"And frequently none at all," replied Mr. Topper, avoiding a direct admission.

As Topper walked down the street the eyes of Commissaire Devaux followed him enviously.

"Some men have all the luck," he reflected. "Could anything be more convenient on occasion than a disappearing mistress?"

Topper did not return to his villa that night. He felt hardly strong enough to look on the shambles the Colonel and his crew must have inevitably made of the place. He took his way to the Splendide, where his reception by the manager was marked by a demeanor of nervous suspicion almost amounting to awe.

As he passed down the hall leading to his quarters a lion's skin got up from the floor and followed him. And as if this were not sufficiently surprising, the lion's skin staggered a little in its gait. A peripatetic lion's skin *sans* lion is even more demoralizing to one's nervous system than one well filled with lion, although there is scant cause for self-congratulation in the presence of either. Topper's attendant seemed to take that view. So did all the other guests who were privileged to witness the strange procession—Topper being followed by a slightly drunken lion's skin trying to walk stealthily.

Topper looked back once to see what it was all about. Once was more than enough. He did not look again. He merely contented himself with wondering if there was anything under the face of the sun that could not happen to him. When he opened the door for himself—the attendant having been good enough to drop the key in his flight—the lion's skin crowded into the room behind him. Topper closed the door and turned to face his unusual visitor. The lion's skin had squared off and was making hostile passes at the air. Topper was more interested than alarmed. He realized that this was a thing he might never see again in his life—not that he was especially anxious.

"Put 'em up," came the thick voice of George Kerby. "Put 'em up, you bed presser. I'm going to give you the beating of your life, Topper, but I'm not going to kill you—not quite."

"How about a drink first, George?" suggested Topper. "I can give you more action with a little drink in me, although God knows what good you expect me to accomplish by cuffing that damn skin about."

"Don't swear at this skin," retorted the gesticulating shell of a lion. "I killed this lion myself with my own bare hands—strangled him to death—then I skinned the bum, and I'm going to show you just how I did it."

"Don't pull a tall one on me like that," said Topper. "You either bought or stole that skin, George. You know you did."

"But you don't know which," replied George with the innocence of a drunkard.

"No, I don't know that," admitted Topper. "Stop prancing about so much and tell me."

"All right," George conceded. "You order the drinks, and I'll tell you all about it. Then we'll have a fight—a good long one."

Topper was treated to the spectacle of seeing the lion's skin throw itself into a chair and carelessly cross its legs.

"Why do you wear it at all?" he ventured. "Don't you find it rather stuffy?"

"I stuff it," said George complacently. "I'm the stuffing."

"Well," observed Topper skeptically, "if you find any pleasure in playing stuffing for a lion's skin I see no reason why anyone should object."

"That's what I say," said George. "Topper, you're a man after my own heart. No. I forgot. I'm mad at you. I'm after your heart—your jet-black heart."

When the unsuspecting waiter arrived with the drinks he was so upset to find Mr. Topper listening attentively to a gesticulating lion's skin that he dropped the drinks and fled. The skin and Topper looked at the broken glass, then looked at each other.

"Too bad," said the skin.

"A pity," commented Topper. "I'm afraid the only way we'll be able to get a drink is for you to abandon your skin."

"Very well, then," said George. "To hell with the skin. I stole it from a dealer. Beat him at his own skin game. Not bad, eh, Topper?"

"Cleverly put," allowed Topper. "Very cleverly put. You're there, George, although I can't see you."

The skin was flung through the air and landed at Topper's feet.

"You can have the skin," declared George without heat. "You'll need one when I'm finished with you."

"You're getting better," said Topper. "Pulling them fast and funny."

"Am I, Topper?" asked George, greatly pleased. "Do you think I'm really funny?"

"You know I do, George."

"I'm glad you do, Cosmo. It's not going to last long."

"Nonsense! Keep it up."

"I'd like to," replied George. "I'd like to keep on being funnier and funnier, but I'm always afraid my tremendous temper will over-master me."

"A drink will help a lot," Mr. Topper assured him.

They arrived, the drinks, but this time three waiters arrived with them. They edged into the room, shrinkingly skirted the abandoned lion's skin, and placed the drinks on a table. And this was one of the rare occasions when Topper did not have an ample opportunity to offer a tip in France. He had no opportunity at all, for after depositing the tray on the table the nerves of the waiters snapped, to a man, and the three of them fought their way from the room, while George laughed heartily if invisibly.

"Did you bring back any more trophies, George?" Mr. Topper asked innocently after the drinks had been taken. "I'll bet you did, you old dog."

"Got some," admitted George. "Left 'em in an empty room on the next floor up. Couldn't stand another night with that South American woman—lots of spice but no bite. Want to see 'em? I've a bit of an elephant's tusk with a dirty picture carved on it. You'll like it."

"I'd love it," lied Topper, thinking of the depravity of the man. "Tell you what, George, you go get your stuff, and I'll order a lot of drinks."

"Might just as well make a night of it before we have that fight," agreed George, preparing to leave the room. "Of course you know where Marion is, but you won't let on."

"All I know is that she and her gang got me arrested," said Topper with feigned bitterness. "They play too fast for an old chap like myself. I dare say the lot of them are enjoying themselves somewhere."

When George left the room by the door, Marion Kerby came in through the window, and when George returned in the same manner he did not find Mr. Topper, but he did find a lot of drinks. Sobered a little, he considered things, tossed off a few drinks, then set off with the determination to find Topper, come what may.

In the meantime Topper and Marion were sitting on the rocks by the hidden beach. They were drinking wine and looking at a revolver, both of which objects Marion had brought along untidily wrapped in a towel.

"What do you want with that thing?" Topper asked a little nervously.

"I have a small plan," replied Marion, a peculiar expression in her eyes.

"I never like your small plans," said Mr. Topper. "I never seem to win."

"I'm afraid you won't like this one," replied Marion. "You see, I'd like to shoot you."

"What!"

"Yes," admitted Marion. "I want to murder you in cold blood."

"Good God!" Topper edged away.

Then Marion began to talk. She talked earnestly and convincingly. The burden of her talk was that she wanted Topper always with her. She could never tell what might happen. And she wanted Topper. Not Topper at a disadvantage, but a Topper as free and flexible as herself. Together they might rise to the highest plane or sink to the lowest. Who could tell? Topper's withdrawal from life would not make a great deal of difference. If he insisted on it she would murder Scollops, too. Mrs. Topper would be well provided for—happy with her sorrow and dyspepsia.

"After all," she concluded, "you have only two things to look forward to—old age and the unspeakable things George is sure to do to you some time in the near future."

As Topper sat there discussing his own murder he was not sure whether he was drunk or dreaming. He never knew. Neither of them knew that, acting on a tip from Clara Hart, George was already making his way towards the beach. It was a race of death against life.

"I know, Marion," said Topper, "but, hang it all, isn't that gun too large? It's a painful-looking weapon."

"No," said Marion, looking consideringly at the gun. "I think it will do the trick."

"Please," protested Mr. Topper. "Don't talk so snappily about my murder."

"This is the way I figure it," continued Marion in a businesslike voice. "If I can hit you in some vital spot with this thing your chances of life would be nil."

"What vital spot?" asked Topper with morbid curiosity.

"We won't go into that," said Marion.

"No, but a great big ugly bullet will," replied Topper, "and inasmuch as it's my spot, I feel that I ought to know."

"How about blowing your brains out?" suggested Marion easily.

Topper stifled a scream.

"Oh, no," he got out. "Oh, no, no, no. Don't, Marion. What a thing to say."

"Well, they say," went on Marion placidly, "that if you plug a guy in the stomach he's sure to be wiped out. Gangsters think highly of the stomach."

Topper let out a long breath that ended in "o-o-o-o."

"I'm not going to be murdered," he declared at last, "unless you can think of some better place and unless you speak a little more becomingly."

"How would you like to be shot in the heart?" asked Marion.

"Simply love it," replied Topper, "but suppose you missed?"

"I'd just keep on banging away at you until you were shot to pieces," said Marion coolly.

Topper nearly curled up at this.

"Literally full of holes," he muttered. "A sieve."

"Oh, a couple of shots will do," declared Marion. "You're sure to be murdered."

"But *how* is what burns me up," was Mr. Topper's reply.

He rose wearily to his feet.

"Would you be more comfortable lying down?" asked Marion in a professional voice.

He looked at her reproachfully.

"How can you speak of comfort at a time like this?" he asked her. "By gad, the way you talk, one would think I was getting my picture taken instead of my life."

"Why, there won't be enough left of you, my boy, to make a speck on a time exposure," Marion assured him.

"Ah-a-a-a!" was all the reply Topper was able to make to this.

After that things happened quickly. Marion kissed him lightly upon the lips. She had no idea of weakening her man. Then she moved back several yards and raised the gun.

"Half a minute," called Mr. Topper. "Have you been drinking, Marion?"

"Yes," admitted Marion, and this time it was her voice that shook.

"But you're all right, aren't you? I mean your hand doesn't wobble?"

"No, old dear," said Marion in a small voice. "Are you all right yourself?"

"Yes, kid, don't worry. I love——"

A fraction of a second before the sound of the gun shattered Topper's last words, George Kerby sprang forward and whirled him about. Then came the bang, and his body seemed filled with fire. He swayed, buckled to the ground, and, crumpling over on his back, lay still. Marion, opening her eyes, saw George kneeling down by the body.

"Where did I hit him?" she asked, running forward. "Is he dead yet?"

"Can't answer either question," said George briefly. "All I can say is that you must have been nuts, the pair of you."

Both of them were now kneeling by the fallen man, both frantically examining him.

"It's not here," said George, searching Topper's chest diligently for a wound.

"His stomach's okay," called Marion. "Take a look at his head."

"No hole here," said Kerby, "except the usual ones."

"Well, I give it up," remarked Marion. "He must be struck somewhere. I'll take a look here."

"Oh, no you won't," said Topper weakly, suddenly snapping out of his daze. "You damn fools, turn me over."

"Never thought of that," muttered George, rolling Topper over. "By jove! here it is. Now, how would the newspapers put it? 'Wealthy American Found Strangely Wounded in the——' Just how would one designate the spot?"

He began to laugh softly. Marion was almost crying. What an inglorious end to an enterprise so heroically conceived and executed! "I don't know what they'd call it," she said, sinking to the ground. "I'd call it a damn bad break. Why did you have to butt in?"

And the potential murderess broke into a series of low and painfully human sobs. Topper, with his nose on a clam shell, reached back and patted her hand. George stood over her and helplessly patted her back. Everything else was forgotten for the moment save Marion and her tears.

"There—there," said George soothingly. "The Colonel will fix him up as good as new."

"That's just the trouble," sobbed the girl. "I don't want him as good as new. I want him all dead."

Although the idea of the Colonel laying ruthless hands on his person did not appeal to Topper, he said nothing about it.

"Sure," he replied cheerfully. "Why go on like that over a mere shot in the pants—I mean, trousers?"

That night, after a somewhat drunken extraction performed braggingly by the enthusiastic Colonel to the accompaniment of a string of obscene and ill-timed jests, Topper became a little feverish. And all night long Marion, a little huddled, sat by his bed. When dawn broke she bent over and kissed him. Moving quietly about the room, she touched a few of his things here and there. But she never looked back at the bed as she went away.

XXIV

Night Thoughts on a Vanished Mistress

Topper is once more on his balcony. This time we have him seated somewhat tenderly on a pneumatic arrangement which he hopes to be able to give soon to some out of luck urchin on the beach. It is night now, and the path of the full moon goes glimmering on to Africa. Topper is alone save for Scollops. The cat sits by his chair. Topper is alone, and he fears very much he will always be alone. Marion is gone. George is gone—all of them all gone. Somewhere through the night Mrs. Topper is speeding towards her husband. And out there along that moonpath the small figure of Marion Kerby is speeding farther and farther away from him, Topper very much fears.

"Listen, Scollops," Topper mutters. "Did it ever get you anything to cry over spilled milk?"

Scollops was not helpful. Cats are not helpful. Their attraction lies in their monumental egotism. This cat yawned and thought prettily about her own affairs—if she thought at all.

"Because if it did," continued Topper aimlessly, "I'd flood the sea with tears."

Félice, looking her prettiest, appeared upon the *balcon*.

"*Bonsoir, m'sieu,*" she said in her rich, rather husky voice. "How goes the little wound tonight?"

"Not so damn *bien,* Félice," replied Topper.

"And yourself, m'sieu?" continued Félice.

"About as low as your morals, my girl," said the man. "You can judge for yourself how badly I feel."

At this sally Félice smiled contentedly. Look where she had advanced herself to without the exercise of morals.

"How fortunate," she murmured, "m'sieu was inconvenienced from behind."

Topper looked upon her with mildly disapproving eyes. Félice flexed her torso and withdrew into the room. Topper remained alone, his eyes fixed on the moonpath. Time passed, and the path shifted. Topper remained fixed. Presently he rose and moved over to the railing of the balcony, up to which a few small roses were still struggling. Softly he pounded his fist upon the railing. That nail needed hammering. He noticed that. Topper did not philosophize over the absence of Marion. He was hurt as an animal is hurt, and like an animal he remained dumb. He did not tell himself in so many words that with the vanishing of Marion also vanished much of himself—that she had carried away with her the glamour and buoyancy of life, its mirthfulness and its romance. Inside him this knowledge was making itself poignantly felt. Topper did not try to analyze it. Topper was not that way.

There he stood, not a large man, but certainly not a small—by no means a small. A little stout, if anything. Commonplace enough, but comfortable looking. He would never set the world afire. A man alone with his thoughts, and he hardly knew what they were. Would Marion ever come back? he wondered. She had not committed herself. That was something. She had backslid once. Why not again? Life was like that, always on the skids, always sliding back. Well, he had slid back, God knows, back into life with a bang. Back with a shot in his trousers.

A low moon now, dropping down and looking wan. Topper's eyes are in shadows. No one will ever know what manner of man looked out of them, what loneliness they held. Slowly his fist beat upon the railing as his darkened eyes followed the path of the moon. Was a small, debonair figure outlined against it? Topper's fist continued to beat, slowly, monotonously pounding. The clenched fingers tightened a little.

A song measured to the cadence of Taps came floating through the night. It was not much of a song, but it got inside Topper. A violin throbbed in the heart of its melody.

"Good-night, dear, good-night," came the voice. "For the last time tonight hold me tight."

"A cheap thing," thought Topper. "Just like all of them."

But, after all, weren't a lot of real things seemingly cheap, seemingly commonplace, yet real enough? Making love was cheap if considered in a certain light. Everybody did it more or less. And everybody got over it more or less—or did they? Hell, that damn tune with Taps beating through it was getting him. That was it. Taps always did. There was something so final about it. An ending. Lights out. Pipe down. You're through. Stand by for a new day. He smiled grimly as he thought of the new day. He would most assuredly have to keep his face with his wife, especially at unguarded moments. He could never explain away the scar of Marion's bullet.

"A sweet sort of souvenir," he mused. "A romantic keepsake. A little reminder of a moment of glorious folly." Trouble was he almost had to break his neck to see it.

His hand was tired from pounding, and his eyes heavy from watching. Had he been hoping for something? He guessed so. He damn well knew so. Some little sign. A hint, perhaps.

Topper relaxed his fingers and closed his eyes. A little breeze ran through the ramblers. Lips brushed against his. He stood very still, trembling only inside. The throbbing of Taps seemed to mill and flood about him. Words were being sounded upon his consciousness:

"If I ever backslide, old thing, I'll damn well slide back to you."

A little dog-eared rose all hot and crushed had found its way into his hand. He looked at the ragged petals, and a glint from the dropping moon struck a warm spark in his eyes.

"If I ever backslide, old thing," he repeated to himself, "I'll damn well slide back to you."

Topper smiled. It seemed fairly safe, knowing her as he did.

With this ray of hope in his heart and a small rose in his hand, not to mention a healing wound in the seat of his trousers, Topper turned to the French windows behind which Félice was waiting. She was not. Félice was sound asleep. However...

A NOTE ON THE TYPE

The principal text of this Modern Library edition
was set in a digitized version of Janson,
a typeface that dates from about 1690 and was cut by Nicholas Kis,
a Hungarian working in Amsterdam. The original matrices have
survived and are held by the Stempel foundry in Germany.
Hermann Zapf redesigned some of the weights and sizes for Stempel,
basing his revisions on the original design.

Printed in the United States
by Baker & Taylor Publisher Services